RACE
FOR GLORY

Steve Cahill, in the heat of the race, fought the steering wheel of the powerful boat as it pounded forward, skipping over the water. Somewhere behind him another boat went wildly out of control and flipped onto its side. Cahill looked to starboard and saw the *First Blood*. It had pulled up even with the *Sonic Boom*.

"Keep it flat-out now!" Cahill ordered. "Keep it going!"

"We're in the air too much!" his navigator yelled back. "We haven't got wings, Steve!"

The spray flew in his face and his gut was in knots. He wanted this race. "We have to stay in front when we make the last turn," Cahill responded. "Move this goddam thing!"

D1336284

THE
SEA RUNNERS

Ralph Hayes

TOWER BOOKS NEW YORK CITY

To Big John Carbonell,
who has been there—
and has the trophies to prove it.

A TOWER BOOK

Published by

Tower Publications, Inc.
Two Park Avenue
New York, N.Y. 10016

Copyright © 1981 by Tower Publications, Inc.

Chapter One

The scene unfolded with endless shades of green, dappled by hot sunlight shafting through fronds and lianas on oblique angles, spearing the dank dimness of the tropical foliage with goldleafing rays of filtered brilliance. Silence lay like eternity on the jungle floor, a quiet so absolute that it make the breath short and pebbled the flesh. No bird, no insect sound. Sweat beading off fevered brows, gunmetal slippery in tight fists.

"They're still here."

"I know." Hoarsely, subdued. Fearful.

In their skulls lingered reverberations of exploding guns, raping the tranquillity with cacophonous noise, splitting live wood, mauling and tearing.

A drop of crimson on a bright green frond.

"We've got to—get out of here."

"Don't talk!" Urgently.

The voices gone then, and breathless waiting. Broken trees, chewed bamboo, the acrid odor of gunsmoke cloyed by a sweeter smell. The droplet on the frond, but much more. In the grass, sprawled bodies. A twisted figure face-down in a sticky, dark puddle. A severed arm thrown up against a palm bole. A destroyed head, partially blown away, revealing unwanted secrets.

"There. I saw something. I think—they're moving off."

"Keep down, goddam it."

"We ought to check the others out."

"Be patient."

"I—can't move my leg, Steve. I can't move it."

Behind Steve Cahill's closed eyelids the death scene dissolved into nothingness. He opened his eyes and squinted into hard sunlight. The green of the Asian jungle was gone, replaced by the dark blue water of the New Jersey harbor, and the racing boat he was situated in. He stood in the driving bolster or cockpit of a sleek, long-keeled craft with two other men. Beside him on his right was his throttleman Boyd Lucas, and at the far gunwale was the navigator Ed Harris. Lucas was studying Cahill's face closely now, his own features somber behind his plastic face mask. "You okay, Steve?" His deep voice came through Cahill's earphones in the helmet he and the others wore, cutting through the extraneous noise from the other boats, and their own idling engines.

Cahill glanced toward Lucas, the dark vision now erased from his head. "Sure, Boyd. I'm fine." But a cold sweat was steadily forming on his upper lip and brow.

Ed Harris leaned past Lucas. "You ought to try the harness this time, Steve. You look under the weather." He was an older man, in his early fifties, but he was lean and trim. Lucas was big and chunky-looking, and had sandy hair under the helmet.

Cahill sighed slightly. He hated to be wet-nursed. But they had both noticed his anxiety in the last race, at Detroit. He did not like it that they had noticed, or that the tension mounted higher in him now, it seemed, with each race of the season. It was not fear of the danger, he was sure, although there was plenty of that. He had been through a lot more in the war, on many occasions. But it was brought on by race day, he had to acknowledge that now. In the first couple of races, out in California in the spring and summer, it had been all right. When Charlie Rossman had asked him to race the

Now It Ain't that season, in addition to his boat-show tour duties, Cahill had readily agreed, and he had raced out there without difficulty. Then, at New Orleans he had the nightmare the night before the race, about the war. About him and Josh Owens out there in Nam, trying to keep from getting killed. And Josh not succeeding. At Detroit it had caught hold of him right in the middle of the race, and had made him pale and short of breath. Yes, it was the racing, and the high-speed power boats that brought on the war nightmares, and he had absolutely no explanation for it.

He glanced toward Harris. Harris was strapped into the bolster with a heavy harness, as was Lucas, and as was customary for crew members on the racing craft. But Cahill, since California, had always found some reason to avoid the use of his harness. "You know I like to move around, Ed," he replied to Harris. His stomach felt all knotted up inside, suddenly. "I don't need that damned straightjacket."

Harris muttered something to himself, and turned to look along the long line of starters that now sat motionless, engines idling, behind a broader-beamed pace. An official on the pace boat now raised a yellow flag. "Here we go," Lucas said quietly into the intercom system.

Their boat began moving forward slowly as Lucas throttled it up slightly and into gear. The other boats moved up behind the pace boat in a long line, fifteen in all, looking long, slim, powerful. All crew members—three in each racing craft—wore the same orange-colored helmets, suits, life jackets, looking bulky and alien in their supercharged vehicles. The boats were all custom-made racers, up to over forty feet in length, with names on their sides like *High Velocity, Numero Uno,* and *Coyote.* Down the line a short distance was the *First Blood,* the most souped-up craft there, owned by millionaire Gus Beckering and driven by colorful Tony Falco, current Class One national champion in the spectacular and often dangerous offshore power boat races. Falco was also the hands-down favorite to repeat as champion in this grand prix-style season.

Cahill turned and glanced toward Falco's boat, knowing that once again Falco was the driver to beat. The three helmeted heads in the *First Blood* looked straight ahead, seeming very intense. Engines now were gunned loudly as all eyes were affixed to the starting flag. Coast Guard boats and other official craft swarmed about the racers, and a helicopter fluttered overhead, and Cahill momentarily got a mental flash of a big Huey, settling down near a rice paddy, doors open, machine guns mounted in its dark orifices.

"There it goes!"

Lucas's voice boomed through the intercom, and at that same split-instant he gave the boat full throttle. There was an ear-splitting roar along the line of racers then, as the bows were thrown high out of the blue water at the starting line and a great wake of white foam was kicked up behind them, the boats lurching toward the open sea.

"Keep it wide open until we break clear!" Cahill's voice came over the din of engines.

Lucas pressed the throttle all the way open, hunched grimly over the controls. Cahill gripped the steering wheel with leather-gloved hands, and Harris checked the gauges on the long dashboard.

"Watch P12 on your starboard!" Harris's voice came.

A lunging racer had crept too close to them in its initial charge for open water. Cahill swerved left slightly and saw that they were pulling ahead of most other craft. Only Tony Falco and another driver were keeping pace with Cahill, and that surprised Cahill and his crew. The *Now It Ain't* was not expected to be a money boat by Charlie Rossman. In San Francisco Cahill had come in a mediocre sixth—there had been a non-sanctioned race at Long Beach in which he had finished better, but

8

which did not count in the standings—and in New Orleans he had not done much better. But then, making some engine modifications on his own, with Lucas's help, he had come in second to Falco at Detroit, and now—well, now he was breaking into open sea neck-and-neck with Falco, the field falling quickly behind.

"Checkpoint one dead ahead at a half-mile," Harris now advised Cahill. "You're on course, Steve."

"Throttle up!" Cahill ordered Lucas.

Lucas glanced toward him. "We're flat out now, in four-foot seas!"

Now it was Cahill, Falco and a third boat about fifty yards behind them. Falco beat Cahill to the first turn, but Cahill rounded it just behind him, in his foaming wake. Waves smashed over the windshield and gunwales, hitting the crew in their faces, and face masks streamed sea water. The *Now It Ain't* plunged and bucked like a mustang, pounding Cahill and the others against the bolster and controls. Lucas eased back on the throttle, afraid of "stuffing" the craft into a thick wave, which would be like hitting a brick wall at high speed.

Cahill saw Falco pulling ahead as they raced for the second turn, where a red buoy marked the turn, and a check boat sat beside it. Sweep boats also sat in the water at specified points, to watch for accidents and assist in case of trouble. They raced on, and Cahill saw their second place weakening.

"Throttle up, damn it!" he yelled at Lucas. "We're falling back!"

Lucas glanced soberly toward Cahill as the boat thumped the sea, banging them around in it. "We're doing all this boat will take! We'll stuff it, or spin out!"

"To hell with that!" Cahill yelled back. "Look, we've got a chance! Let's win one for a change!"

Cahill pointed to the wheel, and Lucas took it for a moment, throttling the boat to full speed again, his face grim. Cahill climbed from the bolster, and Lucas eyed him incredulously.

"Where the hell are you going?"

Harris looked, too, dark-visaged.

"The engine canopy. It's come loose!" Cahill said in the intercom. He was than crawling back to the engine cover, which had popped open a couple of inches and was attached only by a latch at its bow end. Cahill bounced a couple of times as the boat broke over the sea, and then he had the cover and had closed it. He turned and came back, sliding once toward the gunwale. He climbed back into the bolster and took the wheel.

"Are you trying to kill yourself?" Harris yelled.

"If the cover had popped wide, we'd have had it," Cahill said. He was soaking wet; the sea had even gotten under his face mask. He grabbed the wheel back from Lucas, who was staring hard at him.

"Full throttle, Boyd!" he said loudly.

They rounded the second checkpoint, and they were catching Falco again, for some reason. Harris called off the compass points through the turn, and switched to a second gas tank. "Watch for that pleasure craft—at ten degrees!"

A spectator's boat had wandered into the race course by error. Cahill wheeled the sleek racer to port, and it caromed around the smaller boat.

"We lost a second or two," he said tightly. Lucas glanced toward him, and through the plastic face mask he could see the taut, drawn features of Cahill, the same as he had seen at Detroit, only more so. "But look!" Cahill added. "The *First Blood* is coughing, they're having trouble with the engines. Keep us moving, Boyd!"

Cahill's voice was hoarse with emotion. The boat slowly drew up beside the Falco racer, with its red hull and deck and white trim, and Cahill saw Falco turn and see them. But then Cahill did not see the ocean for a few moments. His field of vision crowded in on him, and he smelled the jungle, and the two men beside him were wearing a very different kind of helmet suddenly, a camouflaged military kind. Cahill's grip tightened on the wheel, and there was a sudden urgency to cover the distance ahead that was almost unbearable inside him.

"Faster, damn it, faster! We've got to make it through!"

Lucas and Harris both glanced toward him. Lucas turned and exchanged a dark look with Harris.

"Full-out, full-out!" They had passed Falco now, and were roaring around a third checkpoint, coming very close to the check boat, going too fast, almost out of control. There was only one checkpoint left, and then they headed back toward the finish line. White, salty spray broke over them, and the boat pummeled their bodies. They banged into a big wave, almost stuffing the craft into its depths, and Cahill was slammed against the windshield, cutting an arm through his suit. Lucas and Harris felt their harnesses cut into them. Lucas wanted to cut back on the throttle, but knew Cahill would resist their dropping speed. And Cahill was their captain.

Now Falco had dropped back thirty yards, but the *First Blood* had recovered from its temporary fit of coughing and was now flat-out again. Cahill steered around the last checkpoint at high speed, almost capsizing the check boat. Now they were on the last leg, and going strong. Falco, though, was closing the distance to twenty-five yards, and then twenty.

Harris looked ahead to the far-off harbor and finish line, and glanced at Falco, coming up on them. "By God, we've got an outside chance!" he said in a hushed, excited voice.

Cahill, though, was not with the race now. Cold sweat beaded up on his tanned face under the helmet and mask, and he felt a tight constriction in his guts that threatened to make him sick.

"Keep it going! Get down, damn it, Josh! You trying to get hit, for Christ's sake?" He was staring wild-eyed

11

now at Harris, past Lucas. *"They mean business out there!"*

Lucas and Harris cast dark looks toward Cahill, and kept at their work. "Ten degrees right, Steve!" Harris warned. "Then straight in!"

Cahill made the correction. *"Keep it going! Keep it going!"*

Lucas, getting into calmer water, kept the throttle full-out, and saw Falco's boat closing, on their starboard. But now it was only a hundred yards to the finish. Along the marina area there were wildly shouting spectators, and on the docks where they would finish, in the harbor. Lucas set his jaw and kept the throttle full, and he could see Falco's boat in the corner of his eye now, pulling up. Fifty yards. Thirty. Falco came up alongside, but Cahill's bow was still out front. Fifteen yards. Ten. Falco was almost even. Five, and a roar past the finish. The *Now it Ain't* thrusting its bow out front by three or four feet.

In the harbor past the finish, they throttled back and made a wide turn to the shouting crowd on the docks. The *First Blood* drifted in a big turn around behind them, and Lucas turned and saw Tony Falco raise his face mask, disgust written on his handsome Italian face.

Harris, unbelieving, raised his fist in a victory salute. "We did it, by God! We did it, Steve!"

They were drifting up toward the dock now, and Cahill turned blankly to Harris and Lucas. He was breathing hard, and looked very sick. He was coming back from some place where he would rather not have been.

"Uh. Yeah, right, Ed. I guess we did."

With Harris and Lucas watching him carefully, he leaned heavily onto the windshield as they came drifting now up to dock.

A few minutes later, they had tied up and disembarked, and officials, the press, and the public crowded around them. They removed the hard helmets and an official was pulling them to a bunting-decorated grandstand. Up there flashbulbs went off and Cahill was asked a hundred questions before the race committee chairman could get to him. He and the crew were then congratulated, and Cahill was handed a small gold trophy.

"Ladies and gentlemen," the mayor was then saying into a public address system, "it seems we suddenly have a challenger to Tony Falco in the run for the national championship. Your points are quickly adding up now, aren't they, Steve? With this win?"

Cahill, tanned with blond-streaked hair and standing at six feet even, looked very much like a potential champion at the microphone there. But he was still coming around from his ordeal on the water.

"Uh, well. We've got a few points now, yeah. But we're not setting our sights too high, Mayor." He was a good-looking young man still just under thirty, with an athletic build, serious, dark blue eyes, and a strong, aggressive chin. Before the war he had quit college and a sports program to join the merchant service, and had owned a small ketch for a while, until losing it on default of payments. Upon discharge from the U.S. Marines, just before the close of the war, he had gone to work in a shipyard, and then had left that to become a sales representative for Charlie Rossman, who built pleasure and racing boats. Now, in this third season of racing since his joining the firm, Rossman had talked him into driving the *Now It Ain't* in conjunction with his other company duties, because Rossman saw Cahill as a potentially top-notch racing driver.

"You want to add anything to that, Boyd?" the mayor was now asking Lucas.

Boyd Lucas was a very sizeable fellow, a couple of inches taller than Cahill, and a hefty, muscular man. Just a couple of years over thirty, he had sandy hair that now moved in the breeze off the water, brown eyes, and a small scar across his chin. He owned a small mechanic's garage in Baltimore and worked on racing cars when he was not involved in a power boat race. He had been in individual races in three past years, and knew Tony Falco and other racing men well.

"I think we were very lucky today," Lucas said seriously. "As for the championship, I guess we've never thought much about it."

The mayor grinned widely, and shoved the microphone over to Harris. Harris was the old-timer of the crew, over fifty and a seasoned race navigator. Slim and wiry-looking, with some gray in his hair, he looked very tired at that moment, but very happy.

"And here's Ed Harris, the old pro. Will this crew stick with it all the way now, Ed? To Freeport, Miami, and Key West?"

Harris squinted at him in the July sun. "I suppose that's up to Charlie Rossman," he said.

"To what do you attribute this big win? Is the Rossman boat really that good? Or was it Steve Cahill here?"

Harris eyed Cahill, who seemed not to be listening. Lucas and Harris exchanged sober looks. "I'd say it was Steve, not the boat," Harris opined.

There was applause from the spectators. A race official was now leading Tony Falco up onto the platform at the grandstand, too, and Cahill looked up just as Falco arrived. The thick-set mayor, sport shirt fluttering in an ocean breeze, brightened his grin.

"And here's our national champ, up here to tell us how it feels to come in second once in a great while. What do you say, Tony Falco? You seemed to be having trouble back there outside the harbor. Is that what allowed Steve Cahill here to pass you up and hold on for first?"

Falco came up to the microphone, and he and Cahill eyed each other for an instant. Falco was about Cahill's height, but slimmer, with dark hair and eyes and an Italian-film-star look. He was in his mid-thirties, married to a wealthy, good-looking woman, and he did little but race for a living. He hailed from Chicago, and had been an auto racer before getting into power boats. He had been good at both, and had been rated second nationally the year before winning the big title. He was ranked third in world ratings, and when he raced, he almost always won. He had come home first at San Francisco and Detroit, but had missed the New Orleans race because of a hangover. Falco was a drinker and, despite his marriage to Eva Falco, a sometime womanizer. He was an arrogant, often overbearing man privately, who knew exactly how good he was and worried little about the competition. But, with this New Jersey race, Steve Cahill the unknown had somehow sneaked up on him in the point totals, and that nettled Falco.

"We took some sea water into the engine," Falco was saying into the microphone. "That slowed us down for a while. But Steve here drove a great race and deserved to win. Congratulations, Steve."

Falco stuck his hand out to Cahill, with a big, flash grin. Cahill took it, and cameras clicked. "Thanks, Tony."

"There, did you hear that, ladies and gentlemen? Is that a real champ? Is that sportsmanship? You heard it, from Tony himself!"

There was a ringing of applause. Down in the crowd, blond Eva Falco stood and clapped mechanically, a sour look on her pretty face. There were a few extra words by the mayor, and a few more by the race committee chairman, and then Cahill and Falco and the others were able to climb back down to dock level, and head toward a parking lot nearby. A couple of young boys asked Cahill for his autograph, and he obliged. When he turned then to leave, Lucas was waiting for him at the gate to the parking lot, and Falco's throttleman, a tough-looking fellow as big as Lucas and long-armed and hairy, was having a few words with Lucas. His name was Art Kralich. He had been disciplined once by the American Power Boat Association for unsportsmanlike conduct, and Lucas had always disliked him. As for Kralich, he was a brawler and troublemaker who disliked almost everybody.

"That trophy was a goddam gift, Lucas," Kralich was saying to him as Cahill came up to them. "You couldn't win a kewpee doll with that rusty Rossman tub, if you had any competition."

"What's the matter, Kralich?" Lucas growled back at him. "You mad because you don't get to share in the prize money? I thought you were independently wealthy from betting on your own crew. Or did somebody tell you that was illegal?"

"Go to hell, Lucas," Kralich told him. They stood nose to nose in their orange suits, looking like colorfully clad spacemen.

"Come on, Boyd, you can do this some other time," Cahill said easily, relaxing now for the first time in twenty-four hours. "Let's go get us a beer at the marina." He started on past them, but Kralich stood in his way for a moment.

"You're a very lucky bastard, Cahill," Kralich said in a low, hard voice.

Cahill shrugged. "If that's what it takes," he said.

But at that moment, Tony Falco and Eva came up to the gate, too, and Falco had heard the exchange. He was not the grinning sportsman who had shaken hands with Cahill at the grandstand, but sour-looking now, and scowling.

"Art's right, Cahill," he said in a smooth, well-modulated voice. "That was a fluke today. If you're getting big ideas about the trophy—I mean *the* trophy —forget it. On my worst day I can run the *First Blood* right up your frigging ass. You ought to think that over before you make any plans for a celebrity tour."

Before Cahill could respond, Falco walked off to his car. Grinning harshly, Art Kralich followed. Eva Falco, shaking her blond head, stopped beside Cahill and met his gaze with a somber one. "Welcome to big-time racing," she said caustically.

Then she followed after her husband where he was already climbing into his metallic gray Porsche sports sedan.

That evening there was a celebration banquet, where Cahill was honored for his win. Cahill hated such events, but Rossman expected him to be there, he knew. Lucas and Harris were feted, too, but Cahill was the big hero of the moment. Tony Falco and Eva were noticeably absent, which was considered bad form by the local race committee. But Falco was already on his way to New York, to explain to Gus Beckering why he had taken only second place in this important race.

Falco's navigator Hank Wyatt was gone already, too, but for some reason Art Kralich showed up, sitting at a corner table and sulking moodily as he drank scotch by himself.

There were a couple of boring speeches by racing people, and Cahill had to say a few words about how the race went. He fumbled for words a couple of times and despised being there. Afterwards, Kralich insulted Boyd Lucas outside, and they brawled for a moment, both of them getting knocked down. Cahill and a couple of other drivers broke it up, and Kralich bellowed like a bull out in the blackness of the small Point Pleasant street.

Cahill then returned to the small hotel alone. Tomorrow they would all go their separate ways, parting company until the August race at Freeport. Lucas would return to Baltimore to repair cars, where he lived with a sister named Paige. Harris, who was early-retired from a job he had despised, would visit a daughter in Philadelphia until the next race. Cahill would haul the *Now It Ain't* to Manhattan, on its flatbed truck, and show it in a boat show there, together with a couple other products of Rossman Marine Corporation.

Cahill was tired when he got back to his room, but he did not go right to bed. He turned on a small color television and got the news, and there was a quick piece about the race, and a shot of his face as he received the trophy. Sitting there in the dim light of the TV in that small room, with its crookedly hanging and faded Paris prints and its wax-paper-covered plastic cups on a small bureau, Cahill remembered the emotional trauma he had sustained in the middle of the race, but did not recall shouting Josh Owens's name. He felt as if something were boiling up inside him, wanting release, and it seemed to have to do with the war. But why it all came rushing into his head at race time—and today in the very midst of the race itself—was something inexplicable to him. He was still mulling that, with the local news unwatched before him, when there was a knock on his door. When he went to answer it, he found Ed Harris there. He was wearing a rather loud sport shirt now, out at the waist, and his thin hair was slicked back. But somehow age showed more clearly on him at that moment than it had with his tired, wind-tanned face sticking out of that orange racing suit, on the grandstand.

"You got a minute, Steve?"

"Hell, yes, Ed. Come on in."

They sat on the edge of the bed together. Cahill had turned the sound down on the local news.

"Can I give you a beer? It's packed on ice."

Harris shook his head. "Not tonight, Steve. Say, Boyd told me to offer his apologies for getting you involved with Kralich."

Cahill grinned. He was in a short-sleeved shirt, with a tie pulled down at the collar. "Hell, Ed, you know I didn't mind that. That Kralich is a troublemaker, no doubt of that."

"Boyd wants you to know he wouldn't get into anything like that before a race."

"Christ, tell him to forget it. Really."

There was a brief silence between them, its weight in the room increasing with each moment that passed under it. "Steve, what was happening out there today?" Harris finally asked.

Cahill turned the serious blue eyes on him, and Harris could see something troubled behind them. But then Cahill grinned wryly and the moment was gone. "Happening?" Cahill said lightly.

"You know what I mean," Harris told him. "Boyd and I are concerned. You can't drive a race and have your mind somewhere else, Steve. Is something bothering you? You looked almost—sick out there for a while. You yelled some guy's name out. Do you remember that?"

Cahill frowned. "What name was that?" he said, his stomach lurching.

"I couldn't hear it clearly. And then that stunt of going to the engine hatch without a line on you. You're beginning to take chances, Steve. Unnecessary ones."

"If I'd waited to put a line and harness on, we'd have lost the race, probably," Cahill told him.

Harris eyed him narrowly. "You pushed Boyd too far. That sea wasn't made for flat out, today. I've run a lot of courses, Steve. I've learned that it's better to lose than to force an accident. I know a driver who pushed too hard, three years ago. The boat spun out on a crest and turned over. Like you, this driver and his crew had shunned safety harnesses. The driver sustained a fractured spine and a completely severed aorta, and did not live. His throttleman had four breaks in his right arm, one of them compound. The navigator, who was a good friend of mine, only had his left leg crushed."

Cahill glanced at Harris darkly. "I know what an accident can do, Ed." He resented the criticism, and that was not like him, either.

"I hope you do," Harris told him. He started to go on, but a telephone rang beside the bed.

Cahill excused himself, and answered the phone. "Cahill here," he said soberly.

The voice on the other end was at long distance, and it was Charlie Rossman, from Miami. "Steve, my boy! Charlie here, congrats on your big win today!"

"Oh, hi, Charlie," Cahill said. He cupped the receiver. "It's the boss, but stay, please."

Harris nodded.

"I wish to hell I could have been there," Rossman was saying. Cahill could imagine Rossman on the other end; heavy, round-faced, with serious, lined eyes. He had been fair with Cahill, but Cahill did not like selling boats very much. He wanted to get into the design and engineering end of the business. "How'd you do it, Steve? I didn't think that boat had it in it!"

"We made some modifications, Lucas and me," Cahill said. "And Falco had some trouble. If there had been another top-ranked driver in the race, like Rocky Aoki or Howard Quam, neither of us would have been in the running. We got lucky."

Harris, who had risen and was standing a few feet away, glowered toward Cahill. There had been luck, yes. But it was Cahill's crazy, suicidal driving that had won the race for them.

"Well, listen, Steve." It was Rossman again. "I just added up the point totals, and suddenly you're a contender, kid. You're only sixty-one points behind Falco. With only three races left, it's just you and him, by Jesus!"

Cahill sat there, a sober look on his face. He had been going to tell Rossman that he ought to get another driver, if he intended to run the last races of the season. "We probably won't beat Falco again, Charlie," he said. "Not with this boat."

Rossman laughed in his throat. "That's just it, kid! That new model I was talking to you about. We've got one off the production line, Steve, a Rossman Special. Thirty-eight feet of dynamite, but God! Kevlar hull, streamlined beam, modified trim tabs. With two souped-up Mercruiser engines, seven hundred horses apiece, and you can modify there, if you see the necessity."

"Here?" Cahill said.

"In New York. I've named the new boat the *Sonic Boom*, and I'm shipping it up there to you tomorrow morning. You'll show it with the other boats in New York. Then, my friend, you'll race it. In the last three races."

Cahill found himself suddenly interested. The boat Rossman had just described sounded like something extraordinary. "I'll be damned, Charlie. You're going to invest some real money in the races."

"I'm going for the big trophy," Rossman's voice came to him. "The national title. You and me are going to beat Gus Beckering's ass."

Cahill sat there, mulling that. The trauma of that race day came back to him, and he hesitated in replying to Rossman.

"Steve? What do you think? You want to be the big champ? The hottest race driver in America?"

Cahill made a face that Rossman could not see. "Why not give it a try, Charlie?" he said.

When he had hung up, he related to Ed Harris what Rossman had told him, and Harris, too, was surprised. "I never knew that Charlie wanted the national championship."

"I didn't either," Cahill said. He rose, too, from the bed, and walked over and stared at the silently running TV. A newscaster was mouthing unheard words with a serious face. "Could we really do it, Ed? Could we beat Tony Falco with a top-notch boat?" He turned to see Harris's face when he spoke.

Harris shrugged. "It's possible. Anything is possible, I guess. With Aoki and a couple of other drivers out for

21

the season, there's only Falco to best. The trouble is, there isn't anybody better than Falco. Unless it's you."

Cahill narrowed his dark blue eyes on his navigator.

"And you're very much an unknown factor, at this point," Harris added meaningfully.

"I'll be all right, Ed," Cahill said. "I promise you."

Harris nodded. "Frankly, I'd just as soon leave the hard racing to younger men. I don't look forward to a run for the title, even in a great boat. And then there's Gus Beckering."

"Yes?" Cahill said.

"You don't know him yet, Steve. If he senses you're a threat to his placing that national trophy on his shelf, he'll play rough. Last season he got a driver disqualified over a technicality, because he seemed a threat to Tony Falco. He has friends in the race committees all over the circuit."

Cahill grunted. "We'll let Charlie Rossman handle Gus Beckering. We're just here to race his boat."

"Some days that seems more than enough," Harris commented without smiling.

Chapter Two

The Two Friends Lounge had seen better days. Located on Fifty-fourth Street not far from the Museum of Modern Art, it got a rather intellectual trade in the evenings, a select clientele few in numbers and restricted in pocket money.

Gone were the beautiful people, the celebrities and Fifth Avenue ad executives who used to relax there. Now, the neon sign out on the walk had a letter out, and it was unfortunately the "r" in Friends," altering the place's name to the "Two Fiends" and giving Manhattanites a basis for several kinds of jokes about the lounge and its owners. Inside, there was a bar, tables, a wine rack, and usually a piano player. Two cocktail waitresses served the drinks, in very brief costumes, but few of the serious-talking young men noticed them. Dulcie Padgett was one of the two waitresses.

Dulcie had come to New York for modeling—her facial structure had been described as exquisite by a Milwaukee photographer—but she had found that field so fiercely competitive that it quickly lost its appeal for her. To pay the rent for her East Side room, she had taken the cocktail waitress job.

Back in Milwaukee, Dulcie had dropped out of college after her freshman year because of pregnancy, and the responsible boy had taken off for New England, on the pretense of transferring to a better dental school. That abandonment, and the ugly experience of abortion shortly thereafter, had done something to Dulcie inside that she had not yet recovered from. Her father had died young, and her mother had shown no understanding through Dulcie's trouble. It was more to get away from relatives and others that she had come to New York, rather than to make a big career in modeling.

Unluckily, not long after her arrival in Manhattan, Dulcie had a similar experience with an agency fellow. There had been several long nights together, and pledges of love, and then he had left for Chicago without saying goodbye. He called her from there later, saying he had taken over a branch office in the Windy City, and that he was sorry it had not worked out for them. It seemed he had also been seeing a young socialite from Chicago, and they had already had a wedding there, when he called.

Dulcie had shouted obscenities at him over the phone, and he had hung up on her. But after the shouting was over, she felt even more worthless, somewhere deep inside her, than she had in Wisconsin. Dulcie had gotten the notion that her good looks classified her as the kind of woman men want only for pleasure. Not in the top of her head, where she thought about it on a conscious level. It was deep inside her somewhere, this new notion that her only value in the world was to rouse men's appetites, give them something pretty to look at—and to use.

Her new job at the Two Friends did nothing to dispel this ulterior notion, either. Dressed in a scanty costume that showed much of her svelte bosom, all of her long, slim thighs, and some of her ripe buttocks, Dulcie was the object of many stares, jokes, and familiar touches by patrons. The other girl who worked there, whom Dulcie had befriended closely in recent weeks, was Mary Ann Spencer from Oklahoma. Mary Ann had more dramatic curves than Dulcie even, was pretty in a backwoods way, and had gotten Dulcie the job. Mary Ann, a simple, bucolic girl, did not mind the stares or the backpatting of the customers. In fact, she often went out with them, and spent the night with some. She saw nothing wrong with promiscuous sex or using her body to get what she wanted in life. Her goal was to find and marry a man who would "take care" of her in a fancy way. But she also required him to be someone who would offer her excitement and glamour. She was interested in TV actors, professional boxers, and race drivers.

Dulcie had moved in with Mary Ann in recent weeks, and her close association with the other girl subconsciously strengthened her own lack of respect for herself. It was not that Mary Ann was able to influence Dulcie's thinking. Dulcie was by far the stronger of the two personalities, guiding Mary Ann into reading and music, advising her on the men Mary Ann went out with, and generally taking care of her. But living with Mary Ann, with her breezy, almost innocent approach to life and her own behavior, allowed Dulcie to lower her standards for her own expectations of the world, and of herself. She dated some men just because Mary Ann saw nothing wrong with them, in that period of trying to find herself in Manhattan, and she went to bed with several of them, without really liking them. She had never done that in Wisconsin.

Now, though, after several months at the lounge and living with Mary Ann, Dulcie was becoming morose and restless, without really understanding why. She did not yet understand that she had accepted a life without life, and that that condition stretched endlessly before her, without change. Her friendship with Mary Ann was a shallow one, a stop-gap kind of thing that could never go anywhere because of the basic difference between Mary Ann and herself, so even that relationship gave her little comfort.

Dulcie was at a critical point in her life, without really recognizing it.

Consequently, one night after the customers were gone at the Two Friends, and the two of them were dressing to go home, in a tiny dressing room at the rear

25

of the place, and Mary Ann mentioned the upcoming Freeport Offshore Power Boat Regatta, Dulcie listened with more than usual interest.

Mary Ann stood nude before Dulcie, except for a tiny piece of cloth on her hips and a pair of high-heeled shoes. She had just removed her costume and was getting into her street clothes. She pulled a skirt up onto her hips, and buttoned it there, her large breasts moving heavily as she did so. She was shorter than Dulcie, with voluptuous curves, a rather round face, and short, dyed-red hair. Her eyes needed dark make-up to make them appear pretty, and her mouth was a bit crooked. But Mary Ann had what the men called equipment, so she did not have to be beautiful. She also was very aware of her sexiness, and flaunted it in a way that made men's groins ache.

"I'm telling you, it's going to be the most exciting thing to happen in this area for months," she was saying to Dulcie as she adjusted the skirt. "You just have to go with me. These men that race speed boats are just like the guys that race cars, only more so. They're macho, honey."

Dulcie was pulling off her own costume, and stepping out of it. Like Mary Ann, she was left only with bikini panties and a lot of flesh. But unlike Mary Ann, she was beautifully sculpted, in both face and form. Her breasts and hips were not so overblown, and her legs weren't dancer's legs. She grabbed a T-shirt and pulled it on over her torso, and her dark nipples showed through it.

"I don't know, Mary Ann. I think I've had it with men for a while." She walked across the small room in just the thin shirt and the panties, wearing sling-back open shoes with a high heel. She took a pair of slacks off a straight chair. "What does it get us, really?"

Mary Ann grinned. "How graphic do you want me to be?"

Dulcie pulled the slacks on, and tucked the T-shirt into them, making the thin cloth grab at her breasts in a way that would have been considered spectacular by the male patrons of the lounge. "I don't mean that. I mean, in the long run. There has to be more to life than hopping from one man's bed to another." She was still in her early twenties, like Mary Ann, but the make-up they had to wear on their jobs made them look older, especially Mary Ann. Dulcie had big, dark eyes and long, dark brown hair, and her background was mostly Irish. Her high-cheekboned features were very photogenic, with her full lips, aquiline nose, and the beauty-mark on her right cheek. When she did her hair in certain ways she was strikingly beautiful. Down, as it was now, it merely made her enticingly earthy to the kind of men who liked their sex objects sultry, and encouraged them to make breathless propositions to her.

Mary Ann had pulled a sweater on, and was now combing her red hair out briskly. "There is more, Dulcie. Some day one of these hero-types may just plant a big diamond on our fingers and pop the biggie. Then it will be fur coats for the Broadway shows, Paris in the summers, and sweet hard stuff every night. What else is there?"

Dulcie had donned a small vest over the shirt and looked terrific even with her clothes on. She made a face, and then smiled. "Okay, hold onto your big dream, kid. I'll go to the races with you. but are you sure that's our kind of thing? I've seen motorboat races, in Wisconsin. I got splashed with water when they came past the dock, and ruined a new dress."

Mary Ann frowned. "Honey, these aren't just *motor*boat races. These boats are monsters a block long with engines right out of a Boeing 747! They go so fast, they actually leave the water and fly! Honest to God, I went to two races last year. The guys that drive them are all suited up like astronauts, for God's sake. You have to see it to know what I'm talking about. You got water splashed on you, huh? If one of these babies came past the dock, you'd be under water for three days!"

27

Dulcie laughed at Mary Ann's typical exaggerations. "All right, all right, you've sold me. What does it cost to go watch these spectacular monsters race?"

Mary Ann smiled brightly. "Not a thing! You just drive to Freeport, go down to the marine dock, and set up your folding chair and watch."

Dulcie nodded. "Well, at least the price is right."

Fortunately for Tony Falco, Gus Beckering had been out of town when Falco arrived in Manhattan right after the New Jersey race. Beckering was on business in Boston, and did not return to his Manhattan penthouse until several days later. By that time, he had cooled off some about Falco's losing to Cahill at Point Pleasant. But he was still out of sorts.

"You shipped water! Shipped water, for Christ's sake! Do you know how goddam crazy that sounds? You lost a goddam race because you sprang a hull leak that hurt the engine! That's just great, Tony! Just great. What'll it be next time? That you misplaced the frigging boat?"

Beckering and Falco were sitting alone in Beckering's living room of his penthouse, Beckering slouched on a long sofa and Falco sitting ramrod-straight on a hard chair. Falco finally threw an arm over the back of the chair. "Take it easy, Gus. The *First Blood* has been fixed and is ready to go all the way. There's nothing that can beat it."

"I'm not talking about the goddam boat! I'm talking about you! You miss the frigging race at New Orleans because you overslept. And now this. That hull should have been inspected before race time. By you."

Falco cast a sour gaze on Beckering. Beckering was a big, obese man in his sixties, with reddish-brown hair speckled with white, a red-mottled face overgrown with wrinkles and fat, and light blue, piercing eyes. He owned three manufacturing companies, two hotels, and a fleet of freighters. He was worth millions, he loved racing, and he despised losing. "I've stopped the heavy boozing, Gus, I told you that. There won't be any more incidents like New Orleans, from here to the finish at Key West. I'll be in there every race, and I'll win." Falco's tanned, slightly hard face was somber with seriousness.

"I counted on Eva to keep you away from booze and women," Beckering grumbled. He looked across the wide room, with its two floor levels, wall tapestries, and glass window overlooking Manhattan and the river. Sunlight slanted in through the glass and lay on a thick carpet like a veneer of pale talcum. "But you obviously don't care a hell of a lot about her, or yourself. Well, I'll tell you now, Tony. You'd better care about that trophy." He was glaring at Falco again.

"The only driver close to my point total is that Cahill," Falco said evenly. "And he's a punk beginner, Gus. He won by default at Point Pleasant. I'll bury him in my wake at Freeport, you can count on it."

Beckering eyed him narrowly. "Did you know that Charlie Rossman is giving Cahill a new, improved racer for the rest of the season?" he said deliberately. "A slim, souped-up boat called the *Sonic Boom?*"

Falco frowned. "I hadn't heard."

"Well, now you have," Beckering grumbled. "And as you can see, that puts a whole new light on the run for the trophy. The *Sonic Boom* just might turn out to be as fast as the *First Blood*."

Falco shrugged. "Nothing Rossman has ever put together has matched your boats, Gus. But even if Cahill does have a better boat, he still has to outdrive me. And he can't."

Beckering half-lay on the sofa, glaring at Falco. "I haven't told you this, Tony, but I'm sick. Very sick. I won't see the outcome of a race season after this one."

Falco frowned more deeply. "Oh, hell, Gus. I don't believe that."

"Believe it. It's this abdominal thing, it's getting worse, and surgery is out. Last year, I grabbed onto you after the season started, and you won a couple with that Texas rancher's boat. That put a damper on my glory, Tony. This year I want that sponsor's trophy clean and unadulterated, and I want it with the *First Blood*. It will be my last big trophy, and I don't intend to miss it."

"Christ, Gus. You'll be okay."

Beckering heaved himself forward, toward the edge of the sofa, glowering at Falco from his mottled, heavy face. "Don't play around with my last big dream, Tony. Find out about this Cahill, who he is, what his weaknesses are. Learn how to beat him, in these last three races to the championship."

Falco's handsome face was sober. "Sure, Gus."

Beckering held his gaze with a hard one. "Let me down, Tony, and I'll see to it that you'll never race in a national again."

Falco just sat there, studying Beckering's suddenly sickly looking face. He had not understood the desperation inside Beckering, until that moment. He did not like the threat, but he let it pass.

"I'll keep that in mind, Gus," he said acidly.

Falco spent the next week refurbishing the *First Blood*, checking the hull again, replacing the port engine with a new, finely tuned Aeromarine, fitting it with modified trim tabs that stuck out in back of the boat like aircraft appendages and helped the craft keep an even keel.

Tony and Eva Falco had been married for over two years, and they had gotten along well at first, when Falco was still enamored of her physically. But then he had begun paying more and more attention to the young women and girls who clustered around race sites and racers, and occasionally he would take one to bed. Eva, who was a good-looking woman herself, found out about this in the spring of that year, and there had been a shouting argument, with Eva warning Falco to desist.

He had, too, for a while, but then in New Jersey he had taken an eighteen-year-old to a motel in mid-afternoon and stayed there with her throughout the rest of the day and evening. Caressing hot flesh, plumbing hot depths, making her cry out with painful pleasure. Falco could not seem to help himself. He had a continuing heat on for women in general. The more who pressed themselves on him, the greater the heat, and something had to give. Falco was not a really bad fellow at heart, but he had been brought up in a family that maintained double standards for men and women in marriage, and he could not take his fidelity toward Eva seriously. Also, being a self-assured, arrogant individual, Falco did not like having to answer to so many people: Gus Beckering, Eva, race officials. He despised having people look over his shoulder, or telling him what he could or could not do.

Within a week of the Freeport race, with Eva off on a two-day return to their home in Chicago—Tony were childless, but Eva's parents lived in Chciago—Tony Falco met Mary Ann Spencer and Dulcie Padgett at the Freeport marina bar. Mary Ann had talked Dulcie into taking owed vacation time early and spending it at the shore. Mary Ann wanted to be at the races ahead of time, to meet some drivers and owners, insisting that this was a great opportunity to meet some "real" men. Mary Ann flirted with Falco at the bar, and Falco, seeing Mary Ann's obvious attributes in the sweater she was wearing, introduced himself to her, and later, to Dulcie. Falco was even more interested in Dulcie than Mary Ann, but it was apparent that Mary Ann was the one he could get into bed the most readily. The very next day after their meeting, Falco took Mary Ann out on a rented ketch, and she tantalized him in a tiny swim suit. The same afternoon he invited both Mary Ann and Dulcie to the Manhattan boat show, and Dulcie accepted, and the three of them went together.

The show was at a new convention center at one of

the big hotels, and it was a spectacular one, with everything from sailing yawls to dinghies for cabin cruisers. Dulcie had never attended a boat show, and was wide-eyed at all the sights. There was a big crowd milling on the floor, and they had to go slowly. Mary Ann began hanging on Falco's arm, to get through the crowd, and Falco liked the proximity. He took Dulcie onto his other arm, and they braved the crowd as a trio, laughing and joking. Mary Ann was exuberant, with the national champion of offshore racing on her arm. She had confided to Dulcie that maybe Falco was her big find. Dulcie reminded her that Falco was married.

"This is a small racer," Falco was explaining to them as they came to a display. "A Carrera SS 9 M. Nice little boat for its class."

A middle-aged man came up to them. "Can I interest you in a racing boat?" His eyes narrowed. "Hey, aren't you Tony Falco?"

Falco was gratified. "That's right. And I've already got a boat that will run right over the top of your Carrera."

The fellow did not take offense. "You ought to know, Tony. Good luck at Freeport next week."

Falco nodded. "I don't need luck," he said lightly.

Mary Ann, wearing a low-cut dress and leather boots, glanced past Falco to Dulcie, and smiled knowingly. Dulcie returned it. She was dressed plainly, in a simple skirt and blouse, with her hair pulled back into a French twist behind her head. She did not want to steal Mary Ann's thunder. She was just along for the boat show excitement.

They moved past the Carrera display, and Mary Ann focused on the next one. There was a sign that advertised Rossman Marine products, and three boats on display, and one of them was a long, sleek racer.

"Hey, isn't that the kind of boat you drive?" Mary Ann said to Falco as they approached the display.

Falco focused on the boat, and saw the lettering on its

32

side: *Now It Ain't*, and then he spotted Steve Cahill talking to a potential customer. His face went somber for a moment. "Yes, that's a Class One racer," he told Mary Ann. "An inboard power racer with modified engines. It was in the New Jersey race." He took Mary Ann and Dulcie up to Cahill, one girl still on each arm.

Cahill, in a short-sleeved shirt and dark tie, was just saying a few last words to the spectator as he left. "Well, if you decide to order a small cruiser, Mr. Browne, just give us a call. We'll make a right price for you."

The fellow nodded, and left. When Cahill turned from him, Tony Falco and the girls were almost at his elbow. Cahill focused on Falco, and then Mary Ann, and lastly, Dulcie. His gaze lingered on her, and hers on him. "Well, I didn't expect to see you here, Falco." His gaze drifted reluctantly from Dulcie as he greeted Falco. "Are you in the market for a good boat?"

Falco held his gaze with a momentarily brittle one. "I think I'll go with what I have, Cahill. Girls, this is another race driver, Steve Cahill. A beginner whose real job is selling cabin cruisers and sloops to wealthy businessmen." Falco grinned at the assessment, and Cahill kept a straight face. "Cahill, this is Mary Ann Spencer and Dulcie Padgett. A couple of race fans." He was obviously displaying the girls proudly, with a certain smugness.

Cahill nodded. "Glad to meet you, Mary Ann. Dulcie." Dulcie met his even gaze again, and felt little ripples of excitement pass unexpectedly through her.

"Gosh, another driver!" Mary Ann was saying. "Will you be in the Freeport race, Steve?"

Cahill nodded. "I expect to, Mary Ann."

"That's if he can get away from shilling boats to the rich customers," Falco grinned. "Isn't that right, Cahill?"

Cahill cast an impassive look at Falco. "Oh, I think I'll find the time somehow, Falco."

"What happened to that new boat you were getting up from Rossman? Didn't he get it off the assembly line in time?"

"It'll be here tomorrow," Cahill replied evenly. Dulcie noted the mild hostility between them, and wondered what it was about. "Come back to the show and get a look at the best."

Falco did not like that comeback. He scowled now at Cahill. "I've seen the best," he retorted. "It's sitting at my marine space at Freeport. Just don't let that Rossman boat get behind it, or I'll give it a funeral at sea."

Cahill's blue eyes were somber. "Don't count your wreaths before last sacraments," he offered.

Mary Ann was enjoying the exchange immensely. Falco grabbed her arm more tightly. "Come on, girls. Let's get out of here before some salesman sticks us with a boat we don't want." He had accented the word "salesman" and now gave Cahill a hard grin as he moved off with Mary Ann and Dulcie.

"Glad to have met you, Steve," Mary Ann said pleasantly.

Cahill nodded, and met Dulcie's gaze for the last time. "Same to both of you," he said.

"The pleasure was ours, Steve," Dulcie said quietly.

Falco treated Mary Ann and Dulcie to dinner at a small Italian restaurant near Central Park, and then invited both of them to the small hotel suite that Beckering rented for him and Eva in lower Manhattan. There was nothing he would have enjoyed more than to have gotten both girls into bed with him at the same time. But Dulcie quickly declined, and returned to her and Mary Ann's small Manhattan flat by cab. It was mid-evening when Falco and Mary Ann arrived at the suite, and Mary Ann was impressed with it.

"Hey, this is nice. Do all racers have a place like this?"

Falco locked the outside door behind them, as Mary

Ann looked around the living room with its plush sofa, thick carpet, and expensive watercolor prints on its walls. "Not all, honey," he told her. He went to a low table and picked up a picture of him and Eva at a victory cricle, him still with his orange suit on, and turned it face down.

Mary Ann turned to him. "You say your wife is in Chicago?" she asked meaningfully.

"Yeah, she comes and goes, honey. We're not all that close nowadays. We each go our own way, get our own kind of kicks. You know what I mean?"

Mary Ann flirted with her eyes. "I think so," she smiled.

Falco poured them a drink, and turned on a Manhattan radio station with soft music. He went to a wall button and turned off an overhead light, leaving only a lamp lighted in a corner. He came and stood beside Mary Ann where she looked out over lower Manhattan through an open glass door. They sipped their drinks.

"Nice view, huh?" Falco said.

"Very nice," Mary Ann agreed. She saw him turn to appraise her profile, and she drew her shoulders back slightly.

"Beckering sets me up like this wherever I go," Falco said. "We get a place right in the French Quarter, in New Orleans." He laughed in his throat. "I got so damned drunk there that I missed the race."

Mary Ann turned and looked at him. "That sounds real glamorous, Tony. I'd love to follow the race circuit, and see them all."

He turned to her, and glanced at the deep cleavage where her dress showed it. "You ought to do it, then. There are a lot of drivers that would love to have you along, wherever they went."

She gave him a coy look. "Including you?"

Falco set his drink down on a nearby table, and then took hers and put it there, too. When he turned back to her, his dark eyes were sober. "I think you know you were driving me crazy in that bikini earlier. Don't you?"

She shrugged. "I hoped you'd like it."

"I wanted to strip that couple pieces of cloth off you, and jam it home right there on the deck," he said slowly, looking into her made-up eyes. Still looking into them, he reached forward and cupped her full breasts in his hands.

Mary Ann flinched just slightly, and averted her gaze, but made no move to remove his hands. He moved them firmly on her. "Nice. Very nice. You want to screw a little? Hmm?"

She looked at him. "You sure it's okay? I mean, with your wife and all." In a whispery voice.

"Forget my wife, honey. Just think of what nice things are going to happen to you now." Falco pushed her back against a glass door, grabbing her to him with one arm as he found her mouth hungrily. While they kissed, he raised her dress at her knees with his other hand, pulling it up until he found the warm place at the top of her thighs. Quickly, roughly, he was inside the piece of cloth that hugged her hips, and she felt him seek and find the warm, damp place. He caressed it roughly. She broke away from the kiss with a gasp.

"God!" she exclaimed.

"You're hot as a blowtorch," he grinned. "You're ready down there, and I've hardly touched you."

"That's—the way I am," she confessed hoarsely. "With someone that turns me on." She was slightly trembling inside with excitement.

"Good," he said in a throaty voice. "That's just the way I like them, baby." He had unfastened his trousers, and was fumbling with himself for release. With one strong hand, he firmly shoved down on Mary Ann's shoulders, and she found herself kneeling before him.

"Here, let's start off this way. As a kind of warm-up."

Mary Ann found herself confronting him at a very private place. She looked at what he offered her, and licked suddenly dry lips. "I don't usually do this," she said. "I thought we'd—"

"We will, honey. We'll do all of it," he said in a low voice. "Now don't talk anymore. Just get at it."

Mary Ann took one more long look, and then closed the small distance. Kissing, touching, caressing, taking him.

They never got to the bedroom. Mary Ann was so good with her mouth that Falco could not even wait to get his or her clothes off. The panties torn off her hips, the sheer dress pushed up around her waist, Falco joined with her recklessly, shoving and plunging on her then until she gasped loudly under him in an expectation that mixed pleasant anticipation with fear. Finally they climaxed with wild abandon, Mary Ann losing her anxiety and clasping her ample thighs around him to draw him into her innermost depths. A long wail issued from her throat through it, a cry of primeval satisfaction, and then Falco collapsed on her.

"Christ. I knew—you'd be good."

She looked up at him, with him still inside her. "I'm —glad you liked it. It was—great for me, too."

Falco let a relaxed grin inch onto his handsome face. "We'll have to do this again sometime."

"Why not?" she said, moving her hips on him.

"Maybe next time we'll get your girlfriend up here. What's her name—Dulcie?"

Mary Ann frowned slightly. "Yeah, Dulcie. Sure. I guess we could. If that's what you want, Tony."

"Not for this necessarily," he said quickly. "Have a couple of drinks, and a few laughs."

Mary Ann shrugged. "I can ask her."

"It's only a thought," he said.

Inside her, Mary Ann could still feel him there.

It was obvious the night was not over.

Chapter Three

Steve Cahill walked into the marina grounds from a parking area adjacent, and suddenly stopped and stared at the flatbed trailer with the glistening long hulk atop it.

"God*dam!*" he murmured. "You're beautiful!"

The *Sonic Boom* crouched aboard the trailer heavily, but with a feeling of speed that made it seem in motion. Dew sparkled on its white sides with their red racing trim, and on its snowy deck and cockpit. From its sleek bow to its formidable stern, it looked more like a space probe vehicle than a mere water craft. Twin Mercury inboard engines thrust their hindmost parts into the open behind the boat, showing off big prop blades and chromed tail pipes. Running, those Mercruisers would deafen the ears and make the ground tremble beneath the truck. But they were never run out of the water. Their brutal power was reserved for propelling the racer through the open sea at speeds of up to and over eighty knots.

Cahill climbed onto the trailer, and then by means of a small ladder, up to the gunwale of the boat. There was the driving bolster with its padded back rests and its polished mahogany dashboard and the big steering wheel, all uncovered from canvas just before Cahill's early morning arrival, at his request. Behind the bolster-cockpit was the big engine's cover, and forward of the angled windshield, on the long bow, were two hatch covers hiding the safety gear—life jackets, life raft, flares, safety lines, a survival kit. But Cahill knew that a driver or crew member was lucky if he had much of this with him when he went overboard. There was not much safety in power boat racing, and you could not make much.

Cahill ran a hand over the damp gunwale, and grinned slightly. If it raced as well as it looked, he would have a lot of boat under him. It would be up to him and the crew to show its potential.

The voice behind him surprised him, in his deep thoughts.

"She's a beauty, isn't she?"

Cahill turned and saw Ed Harris standing beside the flatbed, grinning up at him. Cahill returned the grin, nodding. "This is in a class with *First Blood*, I'd guess. And whatever else is out there. I'm in love with her already."

Cahill climbed down and leaned against the big rear wheel of the truck. "How long you been here?" His blond-streaked hair moved in a breeze off the harbor. Nearby was the big marina storage building, and the docks, with yacht club craft tied up there, and the blue water of the harbor.

"I got here just ahead of you. I had to see it, too. I just got back from Philly last night." Harris, lean and tanned, looked rested by his time off.

"How's your daughter and her family?"

"Just fine, Steve. They want me to quit racing, and come and live with them. The son-in-law has a small business I could help him in. I don't know, it sounded pretty good."

Cahill punched his arm lightly. "You've got a lot of races in you, Ed." He jerked a thumb upward toward the long boat that hung over his head. "What do you think? Do we have an outside chance with her?"

"For the trophy?" Harris said.

"For the big one. That's what Rossman has decided to go for."

Harris shrugged, and leaned against the boat with Cahill. "I guess it's a lot more boat than I've ever had under me. Maybe Boyd would say the same. In the old days, they weren't as long, or as well-designed, and they didn't have the power behind them. Now they're more like aircraft than boats. I feel a little uncomfortable in them sometimes, I'll admit. I don't feel in control, like I used to. Maybe it's the boats, maybe it's me. Most men stop this foolishness at a more tender age." He grinned.

Cahill returned the grin. "What got you into this, Ed? A smart guy like you?"

"What got you into it?" Harris countered.

Cahill's grin widened knowingly, but then it dissolved. "I know what you're talking about. But it's different with me, I was drafted, remember? This was all Rossman's idea. I never saw myself as a racer. Beating somebody else to a finish line never seemed like something I wanted to spend my life doing."

"Maybe not," Harris said, slowly, looking out over the other boats sitting around the marina yard: *Slingshot, Crazy Cuban, Spoiler*. They would all race at Freeport soon, in various classes. But the most prized trophies were in Class One, the class with the size, the power, the speed. "But when you think about it, it's bred into us. Especially on this side of the Atlantic."

"Hmm?" Cahill frowned.

"The motivation to run the race, to win. All of us are headed toward some kind of finish line or other, aren't we? Whether it's a six-figure bank account, or a vice-presidency with the company, or—maybe two men after the same woman. It could even be an imaginary line in the jungle, with black-shirted Asians standing between you and your race to the finish."

Harris was regarding Cahill closely, and Cahill turned and held his look for a dark moment. "Yes," he said. "I guess it could be that."

"I guess the important thing is to get into a race you enjoy running, don't out-class yourself, and keep the whole thing in perspective. Don't let it get control of you in the many ways it can.''

Cahill nodded. He could not explain, at that moment, that his way of driving had nothing to do with winning a trophy, or beating Tony Falco. Somehow it was that other race Cahill was still running, the one Harris had just mentioned, and Cahill had no idea why.

"I couldn't argue with that, Ed."

Harris looked up toward their new racing boat. "Why don't we take a look at those big engines?" he suggested. "They might give us a hint about how we'll fare here."

"I was just about to suggest that myself," Cahill smiled.

It was that same morning that Eva Falco arrived back from Chicago. Falco did not meet her at the airport, as he used to do, and was still in bed when Eva got to the hotel. He rose sleepily, with a hangover. He had had a second evening with Mary Ann Spencer the night before, and she had left in the early hours of morning. She had invited Dulcie to join her and Falco at the suite, and again Dulcie had declined, much to Falco's displeasure. Falco had bedded Mary Ann in late evening, after a long drinking bout, and he was still feeling the effects of it all. He sat at a window and sipped orange juice in his boxer shorts, his dark hair hanging onto his face, while Eva told him about her visit to her parents.

"Dad wanted to change his will, and leave me a bigger percentage of the estate. He's mad at my little brother. I told him I already had more money than I'd ever spend, because of the trust he settled on me." Eva was worth almost a million, through her smart investments before she met Falco, and she had wisely kept it all in her name.

Falco looked up moodily from the orange juice. "You did that without talking to me, for Christ's sake?"

Eva was picking up Falco's discarded clothing in the adjacent living room, and came upon a sheer scarf with a pretty flowered design on it. Her face sobered as she raised the cloth to her face, and smelled of it. It had a scent of cheap perfume. She went into the kitchenette where Falco sat looking nettled at the table there.

"I didn't think it concerned you," she said, with a new tone in her voice. She was a trim-looking, pretty blond with rather short hair, and her blue eyes were large and attractive. She wore an expensive tailored suit with a frilly blouse under it, and the suit hid plenty of feminine curves.

Falco frowned at her. "It didn't concern me? We're married, aren't we, goddam it? Of course your money concerns me! You know we can't live the way you want to on prize money! Get on the phone today and tell him you've reconsidered, Eva. Christ, you don't throw money away like that! You wouldn't know it, but it's pretty damned hard to come by."

She gave him a look. "Maybe you know all about it, Tony? Driving seven or eight races a year and boozing it up in between?" She held the scarf up where he could see it. "I found this in the living room."

Falco glanced at the scarf, and swore inside him. "Oh, yeah," he grumbled. He thought fast, sitting there. "Some kid dropped it in the elevator. I was going to turn it in at the desk."

Eva narrowed her pretty eyes on her husband. "Have you had somebody up here, damn it, Tony? I warned you, by God! You start that stuff again, I'll take all my nice money and leave you flat. I mean it!"

Falco glared at her for a moment, under her threat, but then his face softened. "I'm telling you, Eva. There was nobody here. Oh, one of the drivers stopped by yesterday, with a woman on his arm. We had a couple of drinks. You remember Buzz Langley. Damned nice kid. But the scarf doesn't belong to his broad. Some teenager came up in the elevator with me and an older woman. When the kid got off, I saw this scarf on the floor. I figured it was hers. I'll ask at the desk later today."

Falco lied freely when it was necessary to protect himself. The scarf belonged to Mary Ann, and it was her negligence that had caused her to leave it, and he cursed her inwardly for it.

"Just skip it," Eva was saying. "And I'm not calling Chicago, Tony. My kid brother deserves a fair share of the estate, and I'm going to see that he gets it."

Falco was doubly frustrated because the scarf incident had robbed him of his opportunity to argue the point about the will. "Your dad always liked you best," he grumbled. "You shouldn't kick that in the ass. You must have done something to deserve priority, or he wouldn't be offering it to you. Christ."

Eva removed the suit jacket, and then began unbuttoning the frilly blouse. "I'm going to clean up, Tony, and then go out and do some shopping." She took the blouse off, revealing a svelte bosom in a tiny bra. "Maybe you'd like to meet for lunch at Schraft's. If you can make the time."

He glanced up at her, and decided to drop the argument. He would bring it up at some other time. Maybe in bed, when she wanted him so badly that she would say anything to have that good, hot feeling inside her, have him fill her with the pulsing hardness.

"Sure," he said. "Why not?"

Eva softened with him. "There's a new Off-Broadway show opening tonight. *Bangles and Beads*, or some such thing. I know someone who can get us tickets. I thought we might go together."

Falco, though, had promised the driver Langley that he would have a few drinks with him at a riverside lounge that evening, and that was the kind of thing that Falco liked to do alone, without his wife.

"I'd sure as hell like to, Eva. But Beckering is after

me and Kralich to juice up the boat in these last few days. I'll have to drive out to the marina tonight.''

Eva eyed him sidewise. "The marina, Tony? It seems like you spend a lot of time at the marina lately, wherever we are. That boat can't require all that work you say you're giving it.''

"A minute ago you were complaining that I only race boats through the year," he reminded her. "Now you don't like it that I spend time in pre-race weeks working on the boat. It seems I can't win for losing with you, honey.''

Eva came over to him, looking very sexy in the small bra. "All I want from you is you, Tony. I've told you that over and over again.''

Falco got to his feet, and his shorts were sticking out in front. "It will always be me and you, baby. You know that." He brought her to him, and touched her mouth with his.

Eva responded mildly, and felt him pushing into her, down there. "Jesus, Tony. At this time of morning?''

He shoved the bra up, and grabbed at a bared breast. "You always did turn me on any hour of day or night," he told her.

Eva had forgotten the scarf. She wanted to believe him, wanted their marriage to last. She reached down and took him into her hand. "Maybe you'd like to share the shower with me?'' she offered.

Falco grinned. Even unshaven and tousle-haired, he looked good to her. That was her problem: he got to her physically too easily; he always had. "I was hoping you'd ask," he said.

That afternoon, after their lunch together, with Eva still out shopping, Falco got a call from Beckering, and Beckering wanted to see his crew within the hour. He sounded excited to Falco, but also he sounded scared.

Falco got Kralich and Hank Wyatt together without much of a problem—Kralich had arrived in town a couple of days previous, and Wyatt had shown up just the day before. They got up to Beckering's penthouse in late afternoon, and Beckering met them wearing a bathrobe and slippers. He had not been feeling well, and there was the odor of medicines lingering in the place. He took the three of them out onto a patio roof, where they were surrounded by potted palms and ivy, and seated them around a glass-topped table in lawn chairs.

"I've seen Rossman's boat," he began the conversation without preliminary. He was on a chaise lounge, puffing at a thin cigar. "Have any of you?"

Falco exchanged looks with Art Kralich. "I haven't been out to the marina in the past few days," he said.

"Why not?" Beckering growled. "You'd think you'd want to look over the competition. You too busy boozing and balling?"

Kralich laughed at that remark, but when he saw the scowl still on Beckering's face, he stifled the outburst. Kralich had played semi-professional football for a while, on the line, and he looked it. His face was hard, bony, mean. He and Wyatt were not treated to the royal patronage Falco received, and had to go their own way between races. Kralich had an interest in a bar in Atlantic City, and the older Wyatt had a small mail-order business out of his own house, in a suburb of Washington.

"Come on, Gus," Falco was complaining. "I'm there when you need me. I've been working on the *First Blood*, you know that. It's ready to go."

"So are a dozen other class one power boats at Freeport," Beckering said acidly. "And that so-called Rossman Special looks to be the best of the lot."

"I saw it this morning," Wyatt put in. He was also tough-looking, but much smaller than Kralich, with stringy brown hair, a pock-marked face, and hard, small eyes. But he had done a lot of racing before teaming with Falco, and he was known as a fair racer. He was a loner, and generally kept to himself before and after a race. "It'll set well in the water. Rossman has built it like a goddam javelin. It looks like it will fly."

Beckering nodded, grunting agreement through cigar smoke. "My thoughts exactly. I think Rossman has jammed a goddam torpedo up our asses."

"It won't beat the *First Blood*," Falco said. "Not with me driving it."

"That Cahill don't know his bunghole from a hatch vent," Kralich added. "He's green as frigging grass. He took some crazy chances at Point Pleasant, and got damned lucky."

"I don't know," Wyatt said slowly.

Everybody turned to stare at him.

"I got a look at him out there," Wyatt went on. "Crawling over the deck without a line. Pushing that other boat beyond its capacity. He acts a little crazy to me. And crazy people can be tough to beat."

There was a silence on the roof patio. A summer breeze moved around them, and Beckering puffed on the cigar.

"I asked you to get acquainted with Cahill," Beckering finally said to Falco. "Have you?"

Falco shrugged. "I talked to him at the boat show. What can I tell you? He seems pretty ordinary to me. Rossman has got him worrying more about selling boats than racing them. He's an ex-Marine with one foot still in Vietnam. They all have. His head isn't on straight, and never will be. He's a loser."

Beckering was frowning. "Vietnam? Are you sure?"

"That's what I hear," Falco replied with little interest.

Beckering turned back to Wyatt. "You think this guy pushes too hard in a race? Takes chances?"

"What I saw makes me think so," Wyatt told him.

"Then that's a weak spot, isn't it?" Beckering said, looking around at them, from one face to the other. "Isn't that a weakness on his part?"

Falco and Kralich traded looks again. "Hell, Gus," Falco said. "I'll beat his ass without trying to psychoanalyze the bastard. I just don't have the interest."

Beckering glared at Falco. "Goddam it, Tony! Will you get it straight in your head that this isn't some frigging game? *I want that trophy as much as I've ever wanted anything in my frigging life.* More than money, more than any woman. It's *important* to me, goddam it, and if it's important to me, it had damn well better be important to you. I don't care if you have to analyze him, threaten him, or kiss his ass! I only want you to beat him. Do you read me, for Christ's sake?"

Falco sighed heavily. "I read you, Gus."

Beckering looked over to Wyatt. He figured him for more brains than Kralich. "I say we work on this Cahill's apparent weakness. If he's a guy that takes chances, let's work that to our advantage. Goad him into making mistakes. Suggest he's afraid to race flat-out, or make the turns too fast, something like that. If he takes chances, maybe he's trying to prove something. Why do people join the Marines in the first place? You know what I'm talking about here?"

"Sure, Gus, I got it," Wyatt said quietly.

"The important thing now is to beat Cahill here. In New York. That will set him back on his ass, destroy his confidence. It's imperative to beat him *now*. Would you agree with that, Tony?"

Falco nodded. "Right, Gus. Beat him now. At Freeport. That's exactly what I intend to do."

"Get on his ass and push him," Beckering said. "Muscle him, crowd him. Make him do things he doesn't really want to do. Make him show off, take chances he shouldn't take. Make him push himself and his boat beyond their limits."

Kralich kneaded his big hands together. "That all might help. But there are things that are a hell of a lot more certain, by God."

Beckering eyed Kralich doubtfully. "Like what, Art?"

Kralich shrugged wide shoulders. "Like getting him

47

into a fight. He was quick enough to get in between me and Boyd Lucas at Point Pleasant. I think I could needle him into something. Catch him behind the marina some evening. When I got through with him, he wouldn't feel like racing at Freeport."

Wyatt glowered at Kralich. "For Christ's sake, Art. Is that your idea of competition?"

Kralich turned to Wyatt with a hard, stony look. "What's the matter, Hank, you afraid you'll get caught up in it and get your face busted?" He had never liked Wyatt the loner, because Wyatt had always acted superior to him.

Wyatt held his gaze with a tough one. "I can hold my own in a brawl as well as most," he said darkly. "But we're talking about racing, not brawling. What you're suggesting is stupid. It can get you thrown into jail, or earn you a goddam lawsuit. And besides that, it sucks!"

Kralich rose off the chair he sat on. "I don't like anybody calling me stupid, by God!"

Beckering said, "Sit down, Art."

Kralich glanced toward him, and then gave Wyatt another hard look. Finally, he took his seat again. "I don't like to be called stupid."

"Actually, it's an imaginative idea," Beckering said.

Kralich's face softened, and Wyatt hurled a dark glance at Beckering. "You make any plans like that, Gus, and you can get yourself another navigator."

There was a cool silence for a moment, then Beckering spoke again. "I said the idea was imaginative, Hank. Not feasible." He made a mental note, though, that he could count on Kralich to keep his eye on the trophy, and for loyalty to him. "Let's just remember that Cahill is an opponent. An adversary to be out-foxed, out-maneuvered, out-driven. Not in Key West. Now."

Falco nodded, remembering Beckering's private threat to him, on their previous meeting. That Falco would be out of racing if he did not win the national championship. "You can start writing your press release at any time, Gus," he said with assurance. "The Freeport race is as good as won."

Chapter Four

Boyd Lucas was packing to leave for New York. He had heard about the *Sonic Boom,* and Rossman's decision to make a run for the title, and had wondered if Steve Cahill would accept the challenge. He had half-expected Cahill to pull out of the racing, with this added pressure on him to win. He had been quite surprised to learn that Cahill would drive the last three races.

Lucas had bunked with Cahill a couple of times through the race season, and at Detroit he had been in the same room when Cahill had awakened from a sweating nightmare, yelling something unintelligible about the enemy, and gunfire. It was obvious that Cahill had a problem, that it got worse at race time, and that it was getting out of control.

Lucas was worried about Cahill. He considered Cahill as good a friend as he had, and he did not like to see him headed for trouble.

Lucas was mulling this over in his head as he got a couple of sport shirts from a bedroom closet and put them into a small suitcase on the bed. He would have packed half as much stuff, but his sister Paige always insisted he take more than he needed. At twenty-seven, Paige had never married. So when Lucas's young wife had died just a couple of years ago, taken by some rare disease, Paige had moved in with her brother to help him past his time of misery, and she was still there. Lucas also worried about Paige, because she had stopped having even infrequent dates after moving in with him, and seemed to accept a life as Lucas's house-keeper.

Lucas was still folding the shirts in the suitcase when Paige came in with a small pile of three fluffy towels. "Sometimes those motels don't keep you supplied, Boyd. Take these with you, just in case."

Lucas turned to her with a tired grin. "Paige, I can't cram all of that into this little suitcase. Aren't you over-doing it a little this time?"

She plunked the towels onto the bed deliberately. She was a rather tall, lanky girl, with plain brown hair, brown eyes and an unremarkable face. She wore rimless glasses that sat pertly on her nose, making her look like a librarian or schoolteacher. Actually, she was a job counselor who never took a vacation, never had any big weekends. She had never been attractive to men, or good with them. Now, she was using her brother to escape completely from the competition with the other girls with their creamy complexions and bouncy breasts. She did not want to compete anymore.

"I'm sorry if I'm mothering you too much, brother. But since we no longer have a mother, I guess it's not so bad. Take the towels. You may need them."

He grinned slightly. "All right, Paige. But that's it. I'm almost ready to leave."

"Don't worry, that's all I'm going to—"

She stopped short, when the doorbell rang, down-stairs.

"That might be Danny Del Rio," Lucas said. "He said he might stop by and wish me luck."

"I'll let him in," she told him.

Paige left, and in a couple of moments, a blocky young man appeared at the corridor doorway. He was of average height, with dark hair and a Latin look. He lived across town from Lucas in Baltimore, and he knew Steve Cahill slightly from the war, and from the racing circuit. He was a computer analyst who owned a cabin cruiser, knew navigation, and had subbed for race navi-

51

gators in a couple of production races, in smaller boats. His big ambition was to race in a Class One race as navigator.

"Hey, man. Where do you think you're going to, to China? I didn't take that much stuff to Nam!"

Lucas grinned, and shook Del Rio's hand. "It's the sis, Danny. You know how women are. They never feel they have enough clothes when they go somewhere. How's the computer business?"

Del Rio hunched thick shoulders. "Not bad, I guess. I'd rather be going to Freeport with you, though."

"Maybe some day I'll find a spot for you in class one," Lucas told him. "I know a couple of owners who change crew all the time."

"I'll be there waiting," Del Rio said. "I hear you've got a new boat this time. You got a chance at the title?"

"Hell, who knows, Danny? I guess it's pretty much up to Steve Cahill."

"Well, he beat Falco with a lesser boat than the new one," Del Rio said. "I'd say he's a hot new driver to watch, myself. I'd love to be racing with him."

Lucas narrowed his eyes on Del Rio. "Where was it you first met Steve over there in the war, Danny?"

"We were in the same battalion of the 25th Marine Regiment, in the Mekong Delta. I was at battalion headquarters for a while, and Steve used to come in there. A raw lieutenant trying to learn the ropes. I also saw him at Khe Sanh briefly, later. He had experience then, and was a real soldier. He'd lived with the napalm and mortar bursts and barbed wire for a while, then. I heard he almost got himself killed there, dragging his captain out of sniper fire. As they say in Texas, he'd do to ride the river with."

Lucas nodded, staring past Del Rio. "He never had any—problem with it, over there? I mean, like emotional trauma?"

Del Rio made a face. "Every damned leatherneck that spent his tour over there was traumatized, Boyd.

Unless he was some kind of animal to begin with. Why do you ask?''

Lucas shook his head. "I don't know. It's just that Steve is remembering the war now, and seemingly in a bad way.''

"We all do, sooner or later," Del Rio said. "Some guys go for years and think it's all crammed into the back of their heads somewhere. Then they start re-living it all again. Something triggers it, they rarely know what. It's tough."

Lucas held Del Rio's gaze for a moment. Then he said, "Well, it was nice of you to stop by, Danny. You've got some vacation time coming, haven't you? You ought to try to get to Miami for the race there. We'd show you around, Steve knows that whole area, that's his stomping ground now."

"I'll give that some thought, Boyd. I'd love to see a class one race this year."

Del Rio left a few minutes later, and Lucas was finally finished packing. Just as he closed the suitcase up, Paige came back into the bedroom.

"That's a nice boy," she said to Lucas.

"Boy? He's got a couple of years on you, Paige."

"But he seems so—young," she said. Her face was somber. "I heard him say he wanted to be a racer."

Lucas turned to his sister. "Is that so bad?" he said. Paige had never approved of racing. She considered it much too dangerous.

"While Danny was up here," she said quietly, "I was watching a newscast on the TV. A race driver was just killed in California. In a production race there."

A production race was not an open, Class One race, and generally there were lesser drivers involved in them. Lucas sighed heavily. "Did you catch the name?"

"It was somebody called Andrews, I think."

"I don't know him," he said gratefully.

"Boyd, I wish you'd beg off the last races, after this Freeport one. I have a bad feeling about all this, with

Rossman's new emphasis on winning, and—"

"And?" he said.

"And, well, you said that Steve Cahill is taking crazy chances. I don't like the way this season is developing, Boyd. You always paid attention to my feelings, before. I've been right a lot of times."

It was true. Paige often was able to sense danger or predict developments with uncanny accuracy. Lucas put a hand on her cheek. "Paige, I can't pull out of a run for the national title because of a feeling my sister has. I'm a member of a crew. People depend on me, including Steve. Besides, I kind of like the idea of being on a team that could take the big prize. It's a once-in-a-lifetime thing."

Paige looked away from him. "I guess we should talk about it later. Your plane is leaving soon."

"I'll be all right," he told her. "Honestly."

But, deep inside him, Lucas felt something of her anxiety, too.

And this was based on hard, cold fact.

It was only a couple of days before the Freeport race, now. Mary Ann Spencer had already seen Tony Falco once since Eva's arrival back, but nothing happened between them because Falco was called away from their brief meeting to work on the *First Blood* with Art Kralich. Mary Ann, though, had already met a boat owner who was also driving his own boat in the Freeport race. He was a well-to-do bachelor lawyer who laughed every time Mary Ann opened her mouth, because he thought she was "cute." Realizing that Falco's money was not his own, Mary Ann had a quick switch of affection and began seducing the young owner-lawyer. She had already been out with him once, and the only thing that kept her out of his motel bed was her monthly period.

"Tony's cuter, of course," she explained to Dulcie

that afternoon at their Manhattan room, a couple of hours before driving to work at the Two Friends. "But Bill is loaded, honey. And he's very macho, too, just like Tony." Mary Ann was standing before a full-length mirror at the end of the room, putting on lipstick. She was wearing a skirt and blouse, and was bra-less under the blouse, as both girls almost always were.

"I thought you liked Tony," Dulcie said. She was reclining on a short divan, in a sheer yellow dress, her knees up so that the dress came up around her hips, with her long legs bared. She was applying nail polish very carefully and expertly. "I thought you said he was a natural for you, because it was over between him and his wife."

"Oh, I do *like* him, honey. But there's more than balling, after all. I've got to think of my future, and Bill is a guy with a big one."

Dulcie had had to suppress a smile. Sometimes it seemed to her that all Mary Ann did think about was getting into bed with some virile man.

"Tony will probably be national champion," Dulcie reminded her.

Mary Ann nodded. "I know, I'll miss that. Being close to it. But when the season is over, and everybody goes back to his TV set, Bill will still be wealthy. And eligible. If I got serious with Tony, there'd be a sticky divorce thing. No, I'm better off."

Mary Ann had come over to the divan. She leaned on the back of it, and her breasts made arcing mounds in the thin blouse. "Tony is really interested in you, you know. I mean, really interested. Why don't you give him a tumble, Dulcie? God, is he good in bed! He's a real animal! And, I mean, he's got the hots for you. He as much as told me so."

Dulcie looked up at her. Her hair was up on her head, and small ringlets of it hung alongside her face. She looked regally beautiful. "You wouldn't mind?" she wondered. "I mean, if I made it with Tony?"

"Mind? Gosh, I'd love it!" Mary Ann smiled widely, showing slightly crooked teeth. "What's more fun than to compare notes with a best friend?"

Dulcie gave her a look. "I'm afraid I'm not much of a note-taker, Mary Ann."

"Look, I'm going out to Freeport after we get loose tonight. They'll still be drinking out there. Why don't you come along? Tony might be there."

"So might his wife," Dulcie said.

Mary Ann made a face. "Hell, she wouldn't care if he humped you on the bar. That's what Tony tells me, anyway."

"I was figuring on coming back here and reading a chapter of that new novel I bought." Dulcie sat up, waving her fingers to dry her nails.

"You want to read?" Mary Ann said in disgust. "When you can go meet some of the most exciting men in New York or anywhere?"

Dulcie did not take offense. "Tell you what, M.A. We have tomorrow night off if we want it. I'll ride out there with you then, and we'll make it an evening."

Mary Ann put on a mock scowl. "Is that a promise, college coed?"

Dulcie nodded. "I cross my heart, party girl."

In the water the next morning, the *Sonic Boom* looked even more impressive than it had on the flatbed trailer. Its gleaming hulk had been lowered into the harbor at dockside by an enormous, brontosaurus-like crane, that picked the racer up like a pterodactyl egg, delicately, and placed it without a tremor in its natural habitat.

The *Sonic Boom* was, as Rossman had promised, no ordinary boat. It seemed to float above the surface of the water, so light was its impact on the glittery facade. It gave the impression of straining to be off, to be moving, to be splitting the waves with the rapier bow.

Cahill had taken it out into the harbor on a couple of passes, and the engines sounded very good. Now Boyd Lucas had showed up, and Harris, and they were all climbing aboard for a maiden run outside the harbor, in the open sea. All kinds of tests had been made, of course, in Miami—in and out of the water. But it had yet to have a real racing crew aboard, and a real test by such a crew.

"I tell you, it's the most beautiful thing I've ever seen on water," Lucas was saying as they got aboard in their orange race suits. "I mean it, Steve, it's just gorgeous."

"I'm with you," Cahill grinned as he climbed into the bolster with Lucas. Ed Harris came in after him, looking tired. He had stayed up drinking the previous night, and he could not take that anymore.

"Well, the tanks are full," Harris said. "She's ready to show her stuff, I'd say. There's no need making her wait any longer."

An employee of the marina, a fellow who serviced only the race people, took a line off the dock and threw it onto the stern of the racer. Lucas turned and fastened it securely. On race day there would be no lines.

"Wind her up, Boyd," Cahill told him.

Lucas and Harris snapped their harnesses on, and Lucas watched Cahill shun his again. "Right, Steve."

Lucas started the port engine, and it roared to life, making the marina man squint from the noise. A second button was pushed, and the starboard engine joined in on the clamor. Cahill glanced to Lucas, and grinned, and nodded. He pulled the big Kevlar helmet onto his head and face, and Lucas and Harris did likewise. Cahill gestured to the marina man, and the second line was cast off. Harris secured it, and Cahill nodded again, and the *Sonic Boom* moved away from the dock effortlessly, making a big wave that washed up onto the dock and wet the marina employee's feet.

In moments the long boat was moving out of the harbor, past the pleasure boats and ketches and fishing craft, slicing the water like a knife, gliding with idled-down engines. At that beautiful moment, on that sunny summer morning with only blue water and blue sky around him, and the feel of the boat in his hands, Cahill felt a love for what he was out there doing. There had been no nightmare the night before, or recently, and he felt no anxiety at the wheel now. Maybe he had passed a crisis, he thought, as the *Sonic Boom* pulled away from the harbor and headed for open sea.

"Marker buoy thirty-six on your port bow at fifteen degrees," Harris was advising him through the intercom in the orange helmets. "Make a heading for one-fifty after passing the marker, Steve, and we'll be paralleling the north shore."

"Roger, old buddy," Cahill responded. "When we get turned, Boyd, start opening her up. And don't stop until you get her out flat."

"Right, Steve," Lucas replied.

The turn was made gracefully, and then the *Sonic Boom* began roaring in the summer morning, raising its bow out of the water and kicking up a turbulent wake behind. There was a three-foot sea, and the racer began pounding it as it accelerated, up to forty knots, fifty, sixty.

"It accelerates like a Swiss watch!" Lucas's voice came. "Not a jerk, not a vibration! Rossman really put one together!"

"It feels great, Boyd," Cahill agreed.

It was at seventy knots now, the outdrives of the engines blasting like jet engines. The boat was merely skimming the sea, skipping along over the crest of the waves like a spearhead, actually leaving the water and flying over the low gulleys. Harris checked the oil pressure on the gleaming dashboard gauge, and it was at over forty pounds per engine, and that was good. Lucas throttled back momentarily, in a flying leap over the water, and then the boat was at top throttle. Seventy-five knots, eighty, eighty-five. No hesitation, no faltering. The modified trim tabs at the rear kept the boat in perfect balance and kept the bouncing to a minimum. In higher seas, racing crews were pummeled by the boat mercilessly, through their backs and legs. Toe-nails were actually popped off feet, in the slamming the body had to absorb, and bones were occasionally broken. Now, at that moment in the *Sonic Boom*, Cahill, Lucas and Harris felt the trauma of the sea under them too, but it was a kind of beating they were accustomed to and had come to expect. The boat was roaring along at close to ninety knots now, and it was getting difficult to control the boat when it hit the white caps. Cahill gripped the wheel tightly, keeping the craft steady, trying to get the feel of it, hoping for an intimacy with it that might be needed badly in the coming races.

Then he felt the sweat breaking out on his lip, and the boiling begin again, in his guts.

What the hell, he thought. *Why, why?* He tried to ignore it, but his fists were now white over the wheel. His face had gone pale, and he hunched now over the wheel like a drugged man, seemingly unable to move, to think. The boat caromed off the sea, still at close to ninety knots, flying through the air half the time.

Lucas glanced over at Cahill. "Is that enough now, Steve? Shall I throttle down?"

Cahill hunched there, sweating, staring blindly ahead. Lucas squinted at him, seeing the look on Cahill's face. "Steve! Shall I throttle back?"

Harris, on the far side of Lucas, glanced toward Cahill, too, with a look of concern. Cahill finally looked over at Lucas, and stared at him for a moment. Then he nodded. "Yeah, right, Boyd. Throttle back."

The boat gunned down as Lucas eased down on the throttle. At the wheel, Cahill snapped his face mask off the Kevlar helmet, and let the salt spray bathe him, and the wind rush over his square features. *It's all right. Get control! You're supposed to be having a good time, for Christ's sake! What's wrong with you?"*

59

He ran a hand across his mouth. The racer had slowed to fifty knots, and was still slowing. Lucas gave Harris a look, then turned to Cahill. "You want to try some maneuvers now?"

Cahill held Lucas's gaze with an apologetic one for a very brief moment. "We'll make a one-eighty and then do a series of S turns," he said, his voice tight.

The rest of the test run was without incident. The long racer performed beautifully, and when it hove into the small harbor again, all three of them were pleased with it. It seemed to have the potential necessary to give them a competitive status with the likes of the *First Blood*.

When they arrived back at the dock, and had removed the big helmets, Harris climbed off the boat and onto the dock and helped secure it there. Lucas shut down the engines and checked the controls out, with Cahill assisting him. When Lucas was finished with that, he turned to Cahill.

"Are you sure this is something you want to do?" he said quietly.

Cahill held his sober gaze. "Why not?" he said.

"You know why not."

Cahill was suddenly and unreasonably angry. "I told you before, I'm going to be all right, Boyd. Now get off that and stay off it, damn it. Okay?"

Lucas held Cahill's dark look with his somber one. "Okay, Steve."

"Come on, for Christ's sake," Cahill added, in a softer voice. "Let me buy you a beer. We've got a real boat here."

Lucas nodded uncertainly. "I could use one too," he said.

That same evening, a lot of the drivers and crew members were at the local marina bar, getting together and talking boats before the race. Cahill and Lucas were there for a while, and just before they left for the evening, Mary Ann and Dulcie came into the place. Mary Ann met her new owner friend there, and the three of them had a couple of drinks together, but Dulcie felt like an intruder into their evening. Because of that, she went off to the bar by herself for a while, on the excuse that she wanted to have a drink re-mixed, and sat there by herself. While she was there, Cahill and Lucas came and sat down not far away, on barstools, and began talking racing with another driver. Dulcie recognized Cahill immediately from the boat show, and was even more impressed with him than before. He and the other driver were talking about Rolls-Royce engines and speed records and the longest offshore race, from Port Richborough near London to Monte Carlo on the Mediterranean. That went on for about twenty minutes, and then the other driver left, and Cahill and Lucas sat alone and drank. Dulcie, feeling lonely, decided to speak to Cahill on her way back to the table where Mary Ann and her friend were sitting.

"Hi, remember me?" she said as she went past. "Dulcie Padgett."

Cahill, though, was involved in a technical discussion about the *Sonic Boom* with Lucas, did not recognize Dulcie with the quick glance he gave her, and figured her for just one of the locals who hung around race drivers.

"Oh, yeah. Good to see you again." Then he turned back to his conversation with Lucas.

Dulcie, embarrassed and hurt, moved off to Mary Ann's table. She did not often press herself on a man. To do so and have him ignore her was a blow to her super-sensitive ego, and very deflating to her. The feeling of worthlessness welled up inside her again, strong, and she felt as if she could not sit with Mary Ann and Bill any longer that evening, and feel like an outsider with them. She looked back at the bar, and Cahill and Lucas had now left. She was just about to tell Mary Ann that she was going back into town, too, when Tony

Falco came in with Art Kralich. Falco came past their table, and said hello to Mary Ann.

"How you doing, sweetheart? Bill." He gave the rusty-haired owner-lawyer a knowing look. "I thought you two would be in bed by now."

Mary Ann gave him a look. "Oh, Tony!"

But Falco was already staring at Dulcie. "Hey, you've got the girlfriend out again. How's everything, Dulcie?"

Dulcie shrugged. "Not bad, Tony." She was still smarting from the brief encounter with Cahill.

"Hey, why don't you come and have a drink with me? Just you and me, at that corner table? I'll tell you all about how I'm going to win the Freeport race." He grinned widely, and showed the white teeth.

"Go on, honey," Mary Ann said. "We can muddle along without you for a while."

Dulcie hesitated. She needed for someone to want her, to think she was worth talking to. Even if it was Tony Falco. "All right," she finally said. She tried a smile. "I guess I can at least have a drink with the dangerous Tony Falco."

Falco liked that. He was grinning broadly when they moved off to a corner of the place, where the lights were dim and they were relatively alone. When they had ordered drinks and the waiter had brought them, Falco leaned forward and spoke to Dulcie quietly.

"You're nothing like her. Mary Ann, I mean. I could tell it the first time I met you two."

Dulcie held his frank gaze. She had her hair down long over her bare shoulders, wearing a thin-strap yellow dress with an open bodice that showed part of a svelte cleavage. She had worn eye make-up at Mary Ann's urging, even though she did not need it, and she looked very sultry and sensual to Falco.

"I don't like being compared with other girls," she said easily.

Falco swigged most of his drink. "That wasn't the intention," he said. "I just want you to know that I see you're special."

Dulcie sipped at her mixed drink, a vodka and Schweppes. "Where's your wife tonight?" she said pointedly.

"Oh, Eva? Hell, she's probably out with some of her theater friends. She likes actors," he lied. "I don't really keep track of her nowadays."

"She comes to the races with you," Dulcie said.

He made a sour face. "She knows people everywhere we go. Different people from my friends. She goes her way, I don't interfere. You know what I mean?"

Dulcie sipped her drink.

"I wanted to see you from the first," he said. "But you weren't as friendly as Mary Ann. That was just a diversion, with her. She knew it."

"Do you ever have anything other than diversions?" she suggested. "With women?"

Falco grinned easily. "I know what people say about me, behind my back. They run to Eva mostly, with those reports. Some guys around the circuit have the crazy idea I take a different girl to bed every night." He watched her face.

"And that's a wrong idea of the real Tony Falco?" she said to him.

Falco hunched his shoulders, and made his dark eyes somber. "I don't have much at home," he said. "Physical or otherwise. So I sometimes look for it elsewhere. I guess I keep looking for real affection, Dulcie, from someone special." He reached and touched her hand. "Maybe someone like you."

Dulcie had to hand it to him, he was smooth. She wanted to believe it, but it was ridiculous to consider it. "How many girls have you said that to, in the past week or so?" she wondered out loud.

Falco did not take offense. He could not afford to, in his continuing game of seduction. "No, I mean it, Dulcie. When you open your mouth, you say something. A man needs more than just to get into a girl's underclothes. You follow me?"

"Sure, Tony," she said impassively.

"Listen, it's stuffy in here. Why don't you let me show you that cabin cruiser Mary Ann was telling you about? It's in drydock getting a paint job, my friend is a nut about keeping it up. What do you say?"

Dulcie hesitated, then nodded. "Sure, why not."

They said a few words to Mary Ann and Bill on their way out. Kralich was getting drunk at the bar, sitting with a navigator. When they got outside, Falco led Dulcie across a parking area to the marina building where boats were kept and repaired. There were several racing boats there that evening, and Falco pointed them out to her. Then they went over to a wall where pleasure boats were stacked in bins, all the way up to a high ceiling. Falco pointed to one up on the third tier. "Up there. It's that one there. You want a closer look?"

Dulcie shrugged. "Sure," she said.

Falco got a ladder, and Dulcie preceded him up it, and Falco got a good look at her long thighs under the yellow dress, as she climbed. He came up after her, helping her onto the boat, where they had head room in the bin. They climbed into the cockpit behind the cabin, with Falco explaining things to her.

"This is the wheel, up here under the canopy," he was saying. "These babies don't go very fast, but they've got a lot of comfort aboard them. We can see the cabin, if you'd like."

"Oh, I'll just take a peek from here," Dulcie said. She bent and peered through the open hatchway, and saw the bunks inside.

"Sure you won't go inside?" Falco said from behind her.

Dulcie realized they were very alone in the building, and well out of sight up on the boat. All Falco needed for a seduction was a comfortable place. The overhead lights in the marina building were dim up there in the bin—just right for what she was beginning to believe was his purpose.

"Yes, I've seen enough," she said. She turned back

64

and straightened, and Falco was very close to her.

He reached and took her to him, and suddenly he was kissing her. Dulcie protested some, with her hands, but then let it happen. When it was finished, she was breathless.

"I didn't—encourage that," she told him.

"You don't have to do a thing, honey. You just have to be there. You make me hot all the way through, with your high cheekbones and pouty mouth and the way you talk in the cultured voice. You get to me, baby."

Dulcie stared at him. "I think you've gotten a wrong impression about me, Tony." She was slightly angry that he should try a seduction in such a place, not even having the courtesy of offering her a bed. Even Mary Lou he had taken to his hotel suite. "I'm not so impressed by race champions that I'll submit to coupling with one at the slightest suggestion."

He grinned. With his left hand he pushed her gently onto a bench at the gunwale of the boat, and sat down there beside her. "Don't play with me, honey. What do I have to do, beg you?" He kissed her again, and she felt his strong hand go up her dress underneath, and find her under there. She put a hand on his under the cloth, and tried to stop him, but he was very strong.

"Wait!" she protested, breaking free of the kiss. "Let's go back—Tony. Please."

The hand was moving on her now, and she was still trying to prevent it, but unsuccessfully. She was about to wrestle herself out of his grasp, when he spoke again.

"Go back, hell. You came up here to screw, didn't you? Why make a game of it, baby? We both know what we want. You can drop the hard-to-get routine with me, old Tony has seen it before." The hand was working the small piece of cloth down from her hips now, as he pressed her back on the bench. "Come on, honey, you know what's going to happen, you've been there before."

Dulcie stared hard at him for a moment, and something settled and hardened inside her. Yes, she was special, all right. So special that he was not going to even waste a motel bill on her. In that moment, she lost all feeling for objection, all sense of caring. When she spoke, her voice was hard and cold.

"Sure, why not?" she said. "I'm just like the rest of them you lay, Tony, all I want is a quick piece from the big racing champ." She helped him pull the panties down off her thighs. "Go ahead, do it! We don't want to waste any time! Your friends might be gone, at the bar!"

Falco noted the sarcasm, but it rolled off him almost without effect. Dulcie's yellow dress was up around her waist now, revealing the long thighs to him, and the dark place between them. He fumbled with himself and then mounted her eagerly, before she changed her mind. There was an awkward, hot union, and then he was moving on her, making her respond physically even though she did not want it. She heard his deep grunting in her ear, and felt his hard thighs against hers, and she was full of the heat of him for a few brief moments. Then there was a thrusting climax in which she did not share, and the eruption of him inside her, and finally a heavy collapse onto her hard-nippled breasts, with him groaning softly in deep satiation.

When he finally separated them, he looked at her curiously. "You—didn't participate much."

"I didn't think you'd notice," she said bitterly. She felt empty inside, and dirty.

"Hey. Don't act that way about it. It wasn't so bad, was it?"

"Hell, no, Tony. It wasn't so bad."

"The next time we'll really get it on."

Dulcie gave him a hard look. "Maybe we ought to get back to the bar."

"Sure," he said lightly. "We'll have time for a few more drinks before they close up. You're okay, aren't you?"

"I've never felt better," she said in the hard voice.

Chapter Five

When Falco and Dulcie returned to the bar after the marina interlude, Falco's wife Eva was there. She was sitting at the bar with a driver she and Falco knew well, wondering where Falco was, when he and Dulcie walked in. Eva saw them immediately, and Falco saw her. Eva gave him a hard, long look, and then turned back to the bar. Falco stopped and spoke to Dulcie.

"Christ, that's Eva. Out slumming, I guess, spying on me."

Dulcie glanced at the stiff-backed, blond woman at the bar and felt something in common with her.

"I'll have to go speak with her," Falco said. "Why don't you rejoin Mary Ann and Bill? I'll catch you later, okay?"

Dulcie gave him a look. "Sure, Tony. We got what we wanted, didn't we?"

He narrowed his eyes on her for a moment, hearing the acidity in her voice. "Right, babe." He patted her arm lightly, and moved away. Dulcie stared after him for a moment, as Falco approached his wife to explain that he was just showing boats to a friend of an owner. She saw him speak to her, and the dark reaction of Eva, and she suddenly felt very guilty. Just seeing that exchange, she knew it was not as Falco had said, between him and his wife. Eva did care what he did; she still felt for him, that was plain.

Feeling dirty and cast-off, Dulcie started for Mary Ann's table. But she halted again, seeing Mary Ann having a good time there, laughing and talking with Bill.

Dulcie would only spoil that, and she had no interest in talking with them. She would just leave, maybe call from home later and tell Mary Ann she had left. She turned and headed for the outside door. When she got there, she almost bumped into Steve Cahill coming in.

"Oh. Excuse me," he said to her. He had come back into the bar after a visit to the *Sonic Boom*, hoping to find Lucas there. His light-hued hair was slightly mussed, and he looked ruggedly handsome to her, even in her current state of mind. "Oh, you're the girl who spoke earlier. Didn't I meet you at the boat show?"

Dulcie's face relaxed some. "Yes, that's right," she said without smiling.

"You were with Tony Falco, weren't you?" He was really looking at her now, and remembering how beautiful she was.

"Yes, Tony," she said flatly.

He noted the change in her voice, and saw that she was upset. He glanced past her, and saw Falco at the bar, with Eva. They were discussing heatedly. "Maybe you'd like for me to buy you a drink?" Cahill suggested.

Dulcie, though, only wanted to get out of there and away from Falco and Eva, away from the laughing and drinking and inanity. But she did appreciate the offer. Somehow it made her feel less dehumanized, less violated.

"Thanks. Maybe some other time," she told him. Then she moved on past him in the yellow dress, and out into the night.

Cahill looked after her soberly, as she had looked after Falco. "My God, you're beautiful!" he muttered under his breath. He must have been very preoccupied, he mused, not to have recognized her earlier. He turned and went over to the bar, looking around.

Lucas had left for the second time that evening. Cahill ordered a scotch and water, and sat there sipping it alone. At Saigon, he and Josh Owens had taken R and

R together. They had sat drinking scotch at one bar after another, in those dark days. Nothing ever seemed real over there. It was like being in the middle of a long play, acting out a role without a script. You never knew what plot development was going to occur next, or how it was going to come out. It was like being part of the audience, yet onstage, with a part to play. But through it all, even the death and the ugliness, you had the idea that it could all be stopped with a wave of the hand, and set in motion differently. It had been that kind of war, with black marketeering, drugs, and limited offensives. It was a war that had been hard to believe in. Even now, it all seemed somehow like a book he had read, rather than a thing he had lived through. The one real thing that emerged from it all was that Josh had not come back from it. His body had not even been shipped home, it still lay in the jungle somewhere back there, in a shallow Mekong Delta strip of rain forest.

"Well, Cahill. Have you taken to drinking alone?"

Cahill was dragged up from the well of his thoughts still dripping with the remnants of them, still half-buried in the Asian war with the stink of death around him.

"Oh. Falco." He focused on the other driver slowly, resenting the interference with his privacy. "What's the matter? Get tired of your wife's company?"

Falco's face settled into harder lines. "Don't concern yourself about me and my wife, fellow. I can handle her. I always have." He sat on a stool next to Cahill, looking very Latin sitting there with a lock of dark hair hanging onto his forehead.

Cahill looked and saw that Eva had left, apparently alone. He figured something had happened between Dulcie and Falco, and found himself feeling sorry for Eva. "I saw Dulcie Padgett as she left. She seemed a little upset."

Falco grinned a hard grin. "She's a little mixed up in her pretty head. She wants it and she doesn't, you know what I'm saying? But she came across when the chips were down." Cahill glanced quickly toward him, feeling a heaviness in his insides. "Nice piece, but too high-strung for me. I like them earthy, you know what I mean."

Cahill had suspected an intimacy between them, but had hoped he was wrong. He had liked Dulcie, not just her extraordinary good looks, but the way she spoke and acted.

"Well, you can't win them all," Cahill said evenly.

Falco glanced toward him. "That depends on whether you're talking women or racing," he said.

"Is there a difference?"

"Oh, yes. I can control more aspects of racing." He said the next very deliberately. "I can always win a race if I put my mind to it."

Cahill smiled slightly. "You make it sound as if there's little point in the rest of us getting our boats into the water here."

Falco turned and held his gaze. "Now that you mention it, there isn't."

Cahill did not reply. He sipped at his drink, trying to ignore Falco in the hope that he would go away.

"I hear you ran that new boat today. And that you're pretty high on it."

"It's a good boat," Cahill said. He felt a little chill run through him as he said those words, and hoped Falco did not notice.

"You'd have to race it flat out to come close to the *First Blood* at the finish line," Falco told him. "You got the guts to push it that hard, Cahill?"

Cahill caught his hard look. "Why don't we wait and find out?" He was surprised by the remark, though, because nobody close to him doubted his willingness to push a boat to its limit.

"Somebody told me you get choked up out there. That you lose your balls."

Cahill turned and looked at Falco again, and when

Falco saw the look on Cahill's square face, he eased back on his stool, away from him.

"There was a guy in Nam that mouthed off to me like you just did, Falco. They were busy setting his bones for six months afterwards. It delayed his return home for almost a year."

Falco swallowed hard. He had never entertained the notion of physical combat with Cahill, even though Cahill was not a big man, because Cahill just looked like the kind of fellow who would be almost impossible to put down. But Falco had not seen into him until that very moment, behind the somber blue eyes that now looked like polar ice, and what he saw scared him badly. He saw a man who had done things and seen things that went far beyond the winning of a race and who could be a deadly opponent in anything you might set for him to do.

Falco laughed nervously. "Hey, don't take offense for Christ's sake. I'm just repeating what I heard. You don't have to prove anything to me, Cahill. All you have to do is beat me in the next three races, and nobody will care what happens to you out there on the water." The last was said sourly.

Cahill rose off his stool, and Falco eyed him apprehensively. "That's just what I've got in mind," Cahill told him. Then he turned and strode off without waiting for a further comment by Falco.

Cahill had moved to Freeport now, and he drove back to a motel there from the marina, after his discussion with Falco. Boiling inside from Falco's remarks, he wished he had hit him. But then you did not attack a champion race driver just before a race, if you were one of his competitors. A fan might knock Falco down without repercussion, but if another driver did so, he would be suspect, and maybe disqualified from the race. Falco was insulated to a certain extent, and had known so when he insulted Cahill.

Cahill had a private room at the motel, and Harris

and Lucas shared a room down the hall. They had already returned and gone to bed when Cahill arrived, so he did not bother them. He went directly to bed himself, but could not get to sleep. He turned and turned on the bed, and finally he fell into a fitful sleep. But then he began to dream.

They were crawling, the two of them. No, it was Cahill crawling, he saw, and dragging Josh Owens with him, on his back. Josh had been hit in the firefight, by an AK-47, and could not move his legs well. All the rest of the squad had been killed; there were no medics, no relief troops. Josh had lost his rifle. The Cong had gotten behind them and they could not return to command post now. There were no trenches to dig, no hootches. The mortars and rockets had ceased, and the gunfire had quieted, and the Cong had moved on. But they might as wll have been in Hanoi, for any help they could expect.

Cahill crawled along in the sticky heat, insects buzzing on his face, trying to lug Josh with him, trying to keep hold of his own rifle. Watching for signs of booby traps, or their own bouncing Betties, or kraits that were more deadly than gunfire. As he crawled, Josh moaned in pain on his shoulder, saying over and over again that they would never get out alive.

"You won't leave me here, will you, Steve? For God's sake, don't leave me here!"

"I'm not leaving you, goddam it, Josh! Now keep quiet, will you? They're everywhere in here!" In a hushed, sweaty whisper. *"Just hang onto me. Hang on!"*

The singing of insects in their ears, and the hot crawling. Yard by yard. Foot by foot. Cahill collapsing several times, under the strain, but going on. Trying to find the river. Knowing that if they found the river, there was hope. There were patrol boats that might find them.

"I can't go any farther. I'm blacking out."

"The hell you can't!" Cahill, angry with his friend. *"Just grab my neck. Close your eyes and hang on!"*

The insect sounds stopped, silent. Cahill peering through the thick, green foliage. *"Did you hear anything?"*

An explosion from a tree, a yellow flash of light, and the shock of impact in Cahill's side. He fell heavily, dropping Josh to the ground. Crimson seeping through his shirt. He rolled over once, and another shot came, spraying up dirt beside him. The shadow in the kapok tree, the blast from Cahill's rifle. The figure toppling to the ground. The head destroyed.

"Good Jesus, you're hit! Now there's—no hope."

"Oh, shit!"

"No hope now. No hope."

"Shut up, Josh! Just shut up, goddam it!"

Cahill was yelling the words into the darkness of the motel room, sitting upright on the bed, naked in the night. "Goddam it, Josh! Goddam it, shut up, will you?"

He sat there breathing hard, cool sweat running off his face and chest. His eyes focused, and he looked around the room. He could not believe what he saw, that it was all over, and he was not bleeding onto that jungle floor.

"Christ," he muttered, shaking all over.

He could not remember how it had happened. It was after they had gotten to the river. A sniper bullet, a booby trap, maybe. But Josh had not made it, that he knew. Josh had not survived.

Why can't I recall? Why don't I ever see that, in my head? I've seen all kinds of death. It can't be so bad.

After a while, he fell asleep again and slept soundly. The torment was over, for that night.

But just before he had fallen off to sleep, the thought occurred to him: maybe that John Wayne-movie-type war, that seemingly unreal segment of his life, was the only reality there was, and this was the figment of his

73

mind. Maybe he was still lying on that jungle grass, bleeding to death, and this was all something he had made up to make it horrible. Lying there in the darkness of that room, with the sweat still on him, he had almost been able to believe in that possibility, as some people are able to believe in the devil, or in hell.

For at that time of his life, the nightmares were a kind of special hell for Cahill, one that held a dark mystery that he was not at all certain he wanted unveiled.

Because he was morbidly afraid that when he saw what was at the bottom of that black hole he would learn something quite terrible about himself.

The next day, the day before the race, Cahill spent all day making last-minute tune-ups on the engines of the *Sonic Boom*, and in readying gear. Boyd Lucas helped out in the morning, and Harris came past for some last-minute advice about the navigation hazards they might encounter in the race. In the afternoon, Cahill revved the engines and checked gauges, and some race officials came past and asked some questions about the new boat. Cahill felt relaxed and hoped he could stay that way.

In early evening there was the usual cocktail party and mandatory drivers' meeting at the banquet room of the marina, and Tony Falco ignored Cahill, staying away from him. The drivers were advised of special race rules at Freeport, and information concerning the course was exchanged. A Coast Guard official was there, and a couple of members of the local race committee. There was some business done, but it was very informal. No press was allowed, and no outsiders.

When Cahill finished with that, he and Boyd Lucas returned to the motel together, a place on the water near the marina. Harris stayed around and talked to some other navigators. Cahill asked Lucas into his room for a drink, but Lucas declined. He had promised his sister

Paige that he would not drink the night before the race. Lucas also mentioned Danny Del Rio, and Cahill remembered him. There was some small talk about Lucas's trying to get Del Rio a place in racing, and then Cahill told Lucas goodnight.

When he went into his room, the place was ablaze with lights, and there was the odor of fried eggs coming from the tiny kitchenette of the room. Dulcie Padgett was in that cubby-hole, wearing a white apron over short shorts and a skimpy halter. She was carefully cooking a frying-pan full of eggs.

"What the hell!" Cahill said soberly.

"Hi, Steve," Dulcie smiled. "You do like them over once, don't you?" Her thick dark hair was in a braid down her back, and she had only sandals on her feet.

Cahill came over to her, at the kitchenette, and stared hard at her. His face softened, and he nodded. "How did you know that?"

"I spoke to Ed Harris earlier today. He said you often have a couple of eggs before bedtime on a race night, and a piece of toast. He said you called it an early breakfast. Said you can't eat in the morning."

"You must have had quite a chat," he said. He found himself staring at her long thighs, and the sensual way the halter showed off her curvaceous torso.

"I told the clerk at the desk you were a close friend, and he let me in. I should have been a burglar."

Cahill smiled, finally. Dulcie was now dishing the eggs up onto paper plates, three for him and one for her. "I didn't find a toaster. Do you mind?"

He shook his head. "No, not at all."

If Cahill had found Dulcie in his room before hearing about her and Falco, he would have been delighted. But now it was different, he could not help it. He had hoped she was more than just a race groupie, like her friend Mary Ann. But it appeared to him that she was not.

She was setting the eggs on a small counter now, and he came and began eating them, standing. She joined in.

75

They ate for several minutes without talking.

"Mmm," he finally said. "You can cook. You didn't burn them, or under-fry them."

"Just don't ask for anything fancy," she smiled, "and I can do it."

Cahill watched her finish up and turn away to dispose of the paper plate and plastic fork. There had been no utensils in the room. She bent to put the stuff in a wastebasket, and he found himself staring hungrily at the long thighs, and the beginning of curves at the top of them, where the shorts stopped. *What the hell, forget what could have been. Enjoy what is, take what she's offering you.*

He was finishing, too. He knew what would come next. She would subtly place herself before him, expect him to offer his bed for the night. She would protest lightly, but end in accepting. He knew the routine. He went and disposed of his things, too, and in doing so, brushed her hip. In a moment, he turned back to her.

"Why did you go to this trouble, Dulcie?"

Dulcie shrugged, and her breasts moved. "I don't know. You were nice to me."

Cahill met her open gaze, and was struck by the beauty of her hazel-hued eyes.

"I hope I'm not acting too silly," she added.

Cahill grinned slightly. "Hell, what's wrong with silly?" he said. They were quite close. He reached and took her by her narrow waist, and pulled her to him, and she felt his extra strength, in comparison with Falco. He touched his mouth to hers lightly, and she did not protest. Then he kissed her long and hungrily, surprising himself with his sudden appetite. He had not had a woman for quite some time. When they finally parted, Dulcie's eyes were big, and she was breathless.

She had known in advance it would be special, but she had not known how special. "Oh, wow," she murmured.

Cahill touched her cheek with his hand. He had had

only one woman in his life—one who mattered—and she had had high cheekbones, too. He had met her just after the war, and had been over-ready to be loved, to be comforted, to be told the world was still an all right place. He had fallen deeply in love, and then she had left him for a career in acting, in California.

"I suppose it's getting a little late for you to be driving all the way back to the city tonight?" Cahill suggested to her. "I mean, it would be better if you stayed here in Freeport. Wouldn't it?"

Dulcie shrugged again. "I hadn't thought much about it."

"You've already had breakfast with me," he said, "so you've lost your reputation, anyway. Why not stay the night, too?"

Dulcie nodded. "Oh, I see." She pushed gently away from him. "You think that's why I came here." She moved to the counter, took the apron off, and showed more of her lithe figure. She went on to the bedroom and picked up a small purse on a table there. "It's my fault, I gave you the wrong impression."

Cahill followed after her, perplexed. "You mean you won't stay? I thought we were getting along fine."

"We are," she said. "That's why I'm leaving, Steve." She walked to the corridor door, and opened it. Then she turned back to him with a dazzling, effortless smile that was disarming, and that reminded him how young she was. "I hope the eggs will prepare you to drive a great race tomorrow. See you at the marina."

Cahill managed to find his voice. "Sure, Dulcie. I'll see you there."

Then he was alone in the room.

Chapter Six

The Freeport marina buzzed with excitement. Crowds of fans surged onto the dock areas, watching the big boats lowered into the water, snapping photographs, milling around drivers. Newspaper and television reporters were there, and the TV people had a live camera. There were town officials, race officials, owners and crews, all busy preparing for the start of the race. It was a beautiful day, with a calm sea. Check boats and sweep boats were already on their way out to their assigned sites on the course, in contact with shore by radio. The Coast Guard was busy trying to keep masses of pleasure craft off the course and out of danger.

Cahill arrived at the marina at about nine with Lucas and Harris. Rossman had wanted to fly there for the race, but had phoned at the last moment, saying he would wait until they came to Miami to see the *Sonic Boom* in action. He had pressing business. Cahill heard that Gus Beckering was there, though, and he knew that would make Falco even tougher—if that was possible.

The *Sonic Boom* was already in the water, tied up to the marina dock, and it looked ready to beat the world. After a quick look at its engines, Cahill went into the marina to a special locker room set up for the crews, and he and Lucas and Harris suited up. Other crews were in there, too, and there was a lot of laughing and joking to relieve tension.

Cahill had had no nightmares the previous night, for which he was grateful. But, as he began shaving that morning, he felt a dampness in his palms that would not go away, and now, in the locker room, there was a queaziness in his stomach. He ignored it, suited up quickly, and got back out into the summer sun. When he arrived at the dock area, Falco was there, with his throttleman Kralich and Gus Beckering. Cahill paid no attention to them, but climbed aboard the *Sonic Boom*, where Harris was already checking the gauges on its dashboard. Harris saw the somber look on Cahill's face.

"Everything okay, Steve?"

Cahill glanced at him, then nodded. "Sure." In a tight voice.

Down the dock, a TV reporter had turned a live camera on Tony Falco, and was asking him questions. A race official came past and examined the *Sonic Boom* and made some notations on a clipboard. Cahill felt the upset stronger in his stomach.

"Well, well. So this is the new challenger!"

Cahill turned and saw Gus Beckering standing beside the boat on the dock, looking obese and sick, even in the morning sun. He wore a big flowered sport shirt that made him look even bigger and more sickly. He was grinning inanely at Cahill, in a way that made Cahill frown. "I'm Gus Beckering, Cahill. That's quite a new boat Charlie Rossman sent you."

Harris looked toward Beckering with a sober glance. He had heard a lot about Beckering, and not much of it was good. Cahill nodded to Beckering. "We like it, Beckering."

"I guess old Charlie is trying to put my *First Blood* to shame, heh?" Beckering went on, in the pseudo-jovial mood.

"I don't think you have to worry about that," Cahill replied. He was very tense now and not interested in small talk. He flipped a switch on the dashboard.

Beckering's smile faded imperceptibly, like a haze off the early morning sea. "It's not much like the Marines, is it?''

Cahill glanced toward him. "What?"

"Racing," Beckering said, quietly now. "It's not like having a whole battalion behind you, I'd guess. Out there, it's pretty much up to you, and the boat."

Cahill fixed him with a stony look. "I guess that's about it, Beckering."

"It would scare the hell out of me," Beckering said slowly. "But then I'm not a war hero."

Harris gave Beckering a hard look, and Cahill turned away from him. "You'll have to excuse me, I have work to do here."

"Surely," Beckering said. "I just want to wish you all the best today, Cahill." The hard smile again.

"Right," Cahill replied tightly.

Beckering was gone then, and Harris sighed heavily. "That sonofabitch," he growled.

"I got the feeling he wanted to hold my head underwater," Cahill said sourly, "for about ten minutes."

"The bastard is so obvious," Harris said.

Boyd Lucas came down the dock now, and greeted them with a comment about Falco as he climbed aboard. "Our national champ is feeding the press boys a line down there," he said, shaking his head. "My God, he can talk."

"He can race, too," Cahill said.

They both looked at him. There was a moment of tension among them, and then Lucas broke it. "Well, he'll have to today."

Harris pulled on his big helmet as other drivers began pulling away from the docks now, heading out toward the starting line. It was only fifteen minutes until they all lined up behind the pace boat and began following the yellow flag. Boyd Lucas donned his helmet, too, and Cahill was about to follow suit, when suddenly he saw Dulcie come up to the boat, along the dock. She had left Mary Ann down the way, talking to her owner-driver. Dulcie was dressed in low-heeled shoes, with a simple skirt and blouse, and had her hair in dark pigtails. She looked about sixteen.

"Hi, Steve."

Cahill nodded to her. "How's everything this morning, Dulcie?"

She smiled brightly. "Just fine. Just really fine."

Cahill smiled, and she noticed how tense he seemed. "I wanted to say I hope you beat that bastard," she said nicely.

Cahill was slightly surprised. "Falco?"

"That's right," she said, still smiling.

Harris grunted in his throat, and Lucas grinned. "We'll give it a try," Cahill told her.

"Good luck, Steve."

Cahill held her gaze for a moment, then pulled the big orange helmet on. Lucas started the big engines, one at a time, and the roar drowned out all other noise. "Take her out," Cahill told him.

Dulcie was still standing there, looking like Dorothy in *The Wizard of Oz*, when they moved the boat away from the dock with the assistance of a marina employee.

Now, as the engines of the racers revved all around them and the boats began forming a long line—almost twenty in all—behind a gray pace boat, Cahill began concentrating on the race. He steered the *Sonic Boom* into the line, and then cut its power as the yellow flag showed. Harris buckled in, and then Lucas. Lucas turned and saw that Cahill's harness was not affixed to the bolster.

"What happened to your harness?" he asked through the intercom.

Cahill turned to look. "Oh, I took it off to have a look at the bolster. I guess I forgot to put it back."

Lucas gave him a look, from behind the plastic face mask. "Right," he said soberly. *Next, he'll throw the goddam helmet away.* "Okay, here we go."

The pace boat had pulled out, and the racers were following. Two boats to their right was the *First Blood*,

81

with Falco, Kralich and Wyatt aboard, the team that expected to be national champions again. Cahill gripped the wheel tightly, feeling the winchwire tightness in his gut.

The green flag went up, and then came down in a rush, and the race was on with a deafening roar.

The *Sonic Boom* leapt ahead effortlessly, nosing out the other boats at first, and then as they came out of the harbor, pulling well ahead of the field. Only two other boats were anywhere near—a thirty-six foot Sutphen named the *Bad News* and the *First Blood*. Boyd Lucas held the throttle all the way out, and the *Sonic Boom* fairly flew over the water. The *Bad News* dropped back badly, and the *First Blood* held almost even, as the race took shape with its two leaders, the boats racing down the coastline to their turn-around, where they would head back past the Freeport harbor, go on north to a second turn-around, head out into the open sea for a fast dash, then roar right back to the harbor. The course was well over a hundred nautical miles, and was expected to take the rest of the morning to run.

About halfway to the first turn-around, on an almost glassy sea, the *First Blood* inched ahead of them, and they saw Art Kralich lift a big fist and shake it. Boyd Lucas, who despised Kralich, growled an obscenity under his breath.

Cahill, in the heat of the race, forgot his stomach and the way he felt inside, and fought the steering wheel of the powerful boat as it pounded along, skipping over the water like a tossed stone. The bolster slammed at his back, and the floor of the boat hammered at his shoes. At the turn, Tony Falco had a small lead. Cahill rounded the turn-around check boat recklessly, trying to make up the distance, telling Lucas to hold the throttle open. Harris turned at one point to study Cahill's face, but could not see it behind the plastic mask and the sprayed water. The sea came into the bolster from the port gunwale, and knocked them about for a moment, and Cahill without his harness was almost thrown away from the wheel. They gained on Falco along the long leg back past the Freeport docks, and when they passed there, seeing the waving crowds on the dock area, Cahill had come abreast of Falco and had nosed ahead of him.

It was then that the sweat began forming on his face and crawling down his side under his suit. His stomach tied itself into knots as they approached the second turn, roared around it, and headed out into the sea. Pleasure boats were everywhere, and sweep boats that stood by to watch for accidents. Somewhere behind them, a boat went wildly out of control and flipped onto its side, and two sweep boats went to its rescue. Cahill looked to its side, and saw the *First Blood*. It had pulled up to even again, and Falco had ripped his helmet off and was shouting something at them that was unintelligible, but that they all recognized as his last challenge to them.

"Keep it flat-out now!" Cahill was saying, his face white under the mask. *"Keep it going, goddam it!"*

"We're in the air too much!" Lucas argued back. *"We haven't got wings, Steve!"*

"When we head back in, we have to be out front! Don't you understand that? Move this goddam thing!"

In the heat of the moment, Cahill got a flash inside his head of an ashen face, blood-smeared. It was Josh, and he was staring up at Cahill uncomprehendingly, with death in his eyes.

Oh God, he groaned inside him. He began breathing shallowly, and the sea swam before him for a moment.

"Make your sixty-degree turn!" Harris's voice came to him. *"And don't crowd the check boat!"*

Cahill fought the wheel, wrestling the boat into its turn. Spray canopied them, making diamonds fly through the air over their heads. Cahill was gripping the wheel so tightly that his hands hurt in his gloves.

"Now the big one-twenty, and back!" Harris yelled.

"I'm switching to tank two."

"We beat Falco to the turn!" Lucas cried out. *"He's eating our wake!"*

But Cahill did not respond to that enthusiasm. He felt as if he would explode inside as he saw the white wake beside them and felt the spray on him. Josh Owens's face kept coming back to him—he could not seem to shake it—and then he seemed to go black for a few moments.

"Keep it going!" his shaky voice came to them. *"They're cutting us up bad! Get us out of here—keep going!"*

Harris had taken a quick glance toward him, and Lucas now turned to study Cahill somberly. With every race he seemed to get worse, and Lucas was sure it was related to the war, and whatever had happened to Cahill over there. He turned back to look ahead and saw the site of the accident that had occurred behind them on the way out. They were headed right for one of the sweep boats and had to get around it. But Cahill had not told him to throttle back, and he was making no steering correction. They were fairly flying toward the other craft.

"Steve, make a thirty-degree to starboard!" Harris was saying for the second time. *"Get around that sweep boat!"*

Lucas throttled back on his own, knowing it was necessary to make the maneuver. But Cahill glanced toward him fiercely. *"Keep it going, goddam it!"*

Lucas vacillated. He knew he should slow the boat even more, for safety, but Cahill was technically in charge. Cahill blinked his eyes, and the sweep boat became a black, primitive punt, with black-suited Cong aboard it. He headed right toward it, swearing under his breath.

"Steve, for Christ's sake!"

The vision was gone, and Cahill was suddenly wheeling the *Sonic Boom* desperately. It made a sharp turn, slicing up waves as it roared past the sweep boat, missing it narrowly. But then, in the middle of the turn, it began floating off the water, and turning onto its side, spinning out of control.

"Hold it!" Boyd Lucas was yelling. *"Hold it, Steve!"*

But when the *Sonic Boom* came down, it was on its side. In the next violent moments, Harris and Lucas were jarred almost out of their harnesses, banging against gunwale and windshield as the big boat skimmed along on its side. Cahill felt a lurching under him and was then in the air, going head over heels out of the boat. His helmet cracked the windshield. Then his thigh raked along the break, and he was sailing well out over the water, finally turning over and dropping toward the sea. But at the last moment the boat turned back onto its keel, and when Cahill came down he landed on the gunwale instead of in the sea. He felt a rib snap as he hit, and then he was hanging on desperately. Harris was grabbing at him, holding onto him so he would not be torn loose, and Lucas was steering the boat back into control, throttling down.

As Cahill climbed groggily over the gunwale, Harris straining to get him aboard, he saw the *First Blood* go roaring past on their starboard side. He climbed into the bolster, blood on his left thigh, and squeezed past Lucas.

"Throttle up, Boyd! I'm—all right!" He looked and saw two other boats coming up fast on them.

"Steve, for God's sake!" Lucas objected, glancing at Cahill.

"Please, Boyd. Don't quit." Cahill grabbed the wheel back, hunching over it urgently, his busted rib giving him a lot of pain.

Lucas gave him another look, and Harris nodded to him. He throttled the boat hard, and it lurched ahead. Falco was way out in front now, there was no chance of catching him. But slowly, the other contenders dropped back as Lucas kept the *Sonic Boom* at full throttle and Cahill fought the wheel despite his injured condition. The harbor loomed into view, and they were gaining on Falco. The *First Blood* was only a hundred yards in front. It entered the harbor and crossed the finish line, roaring past the wildly cheering fans on the docks. The *Sonic Boom* came right behind, kicking up a white wake. The third-place boat was over two hundred yards behind Cahill.

A few minutes later, the *Sonic Boom* coasted to a halt at the dock, and was quickly tied up there. Coast Guard officials, advised of the accident, had gathered there, and had brought an ambulance over. The people from the other boat had not been brought in yet, the one that had spun out. Another ambulance was being brought for them, even though ship-to-shore radio reported no serious injuries.

Aboard the *Sonic Boom,* Cahill leaned over the steering wheel, his helmeted head on the windshield. The crowds had been kept away from the dock with ropes, and only police and officials were there. Up on the other end of the dock where the fans were allowed, Falco was already taking bows as winner and signing autographs. But most fans were at the ropes where the *Sonic Boom* had come in, concerned about its crew.

When Harris and Lucas got their helmets off, they pulled Cahill off the steering wheel and helped him over to the gunwale. He had received a hit on the head through the helmet and was dazed. Two burly officials pulled him onto the dock, and he found he could not stand very well on the leg. They eased him onto a stretcher. Lucas and Harris were also being helped from the boat. Harris had a dislocated shoulder and was badly bruised in his rib cage and hip. Lucas had a bad cut across his lower leg, and he had almost severed a ring finger on the broken windshield. Harris, very shaken up, was put on a stretcher, and Lucas sat on a bench in the back of the ambulance after they had put Cahill and Harris in.

While the ambulance driver was getting instructions about which hospital to take them to, a local reporter got past the guards somehow, and stuck his head into the ambulance at the rear.

"Which one of you is Cahill?"

Lucas glared at him. "Over there. On the stretcher."

"Can he give a statement about the accident, what do you think?"

"Get to hell out of here," Lucas growled. His hand was bleeding through a makeshift bandage.

"Was the accident his fault? What happened out there?"

Just at that moment, though, an attendant came and jumped aboard and closed the doors on the reporter. He had examined them briefly as they were brought ashore, and he was shaking his head now. "Do you guys always look like this when you finish a race?"

Lucas grunted. "How's Steve?" Cahill lay there half-conscious, staring at the ceiling of the ambulance, as it moved forward and started out of the marina dock area.

The attendant shrugged. "From what I can see, he has two busted ribs, a possibly chipped vertebra in his back, a deep laceration in his left thigh, a severe concussion with possible skull fracture, and maybe internal injuries. That's not to mention the cuts and bruises he absorbed that are more ordinary."

"Jesus Christ," Lucas muttered.

Cahill, lying there trying to focus his vision, did not hear the exchange. As the ambulance made a turn out of a gate, he got a glimpse through the rear window of Tony Falco, surrounded by a crowd, grinning and giving out autographs.

"Sonofabitch," Cahill grunted.

He had let his crew down, and Rossman, and himself.

Out there on the sea, he had been violently traumatized by the past in a way he could not understand, and maybe never would.

And it was getting worse.

Chapter Seven

Dulcie Padgett had seen Cahill hauled off the *Sonic Boom* almost unconscious. She had asked to see him, but the guards would not let her through. Later, at the hospital, she was told that Cahill could not have any visitors that first night, and she became very angry with an admissions employee. But she had to leave without seeing him.

Mary Ann had not shown any interest in Cahill's condition, too busy with her sixth-place lawyer and Tony Falco to think much about Cahill's injuries. This hurt Dulcie, too, but she kept it to herself. Mary Ann might not be everything Dulcie hoped, at times, but she was the only friend she had, unless Dulcie counted Steve Cahill.

The morning after the race, Cahill was already feeling better. His vision had cleared, and his concussion was gone. X-rays had revealed no skull fracture, and his rib breaks were not bad ones. There was a small chip in a lumbar vertebra, but it was not expected to give him real trouble. His worst injury was the deep cut along his left thigh. He had lost a lot of blood, and had had to have surgery to sew the wound up. He would have to use a cane to walk, for a couple of weeks or more.

Lucas and Harris came to visit Cahill that morning after breakfast. Ed Harris had had a cast applied to his shoulder, but it was expected to heal well. Lucas's finger had been stitched, and he was expected to retain use of it. His lower leg had been bandaged and would be all right, too, although he limped on it.

When Cahill saw them come into the room, with their bandages and injuries, his face went straight-lined. "Good Jesus," he muttered.

They greeted him jovially. "Hell, I'll be as good as new in a day or two, and Ed here just has to rest that shoulder for a while," Lucas said, grinning.

"How are you doing today, Steve?" Harris asked, looking lined and older.

"They sewed up my leg and taped my ribs," he told them. "I wanted to leave this morning, but they want me to stick around for a couple of days. Seems I lost some blood."

"You should have had the harness on," Harris said soberly.

Cahill averted his eyes. "I know." He sighed heavily. "I deserved what I got. But you guys didn't."

"Power boat racing is a dangerous sport," Lucas said. "Ed and I know that. The only thing you did wrong was wait till the last minute to pull around that sweep boat. And frankly, I think we'd have spun out even if you'd swung out sooner."

"Any driver out there could have done the same thing," Harris added.

"Any driver didn't, though," Cahill said. "I did."

Lucas put his good hand on Cahill's arm. "It took a lot of guts to get behind that wheel again and go for second place. A hell of a lot more than I would have had."

Cahill sighed. He had a thick bandage around his head, too, because of a cut on the scalp.

"Falco should have slowed to see if he could help," Harris told Cahill. Harris's arm was in a sling, and he had a small bandage on his face. "The officials didn't say anything, though. He's the national champ, after all."

"What about me?" Cahill asked. "Did the sweep boat put in a complaint?"

Lucas shook his head. "None that we know of,

Steve."

Cahill was staring toward the foot of his bed. "I couldn't do it, Boyd. I couldn't turn the boat. Something happened to me, I was seeing things that weren't there."

"You were back in Vietnam," Harris suggested in a level voice.

Cahill glanced at him. "Yeah. I guess I was."

Harris stepped closer to the bed. "You're going to have to get a new navigator, Steve. They say this shoulder will heal fast, but that I shouldn't compete in the last two races."

Cahill stared at him, dully.

"I suggested Danny Del Rio, and Ed thought it was a good idea," Lucas said to him.

But Cahill was shaking his head. "It doesn't matter about Danny," he told them. "Not unless Rossman can find another driver. Because I'm not driving the Florida races."

Harris narrowed his eyes on Cahill, and Lucas's face registered immediate shock and disbelief. "Hell, come on, Steve. Don't even talk like that."

"No, I mean it," Cahill said firmly. "I don't belong out there, both of you know that. You tell me I take too many chances with my own neck, Boyd. But when I do that, I drag you and Ed along with me. And I can't seem to control it. We all know it could have been much worse out there today. If the *Sonic Boom* had flipped over. One of you could have been killed. Or both. No, I can't go on with that kind of responsibility hanging over me."

At the end of his short speech he had begun to tremble, and beads of glistening perspiration had popped out on his upper lip. Lucas frowned, and swallowed hard.

"But you saved the day with second place!" Lucas said weakly. "If you were to beat Falco at Miami—your hometown—you'd be right up there in points again. You could take everything at Key West!"

"And maybe get somebody killed," Cahill said bitterly. He was getting himself under control again. "No, thanks, Boyd. A trophy isn't that important to me."

"Well," Harris said. "It won't make much difference to me personally. As a matter of fact, I kind of think I'm ready for retirement from this kind of thing. I doubt I'll race next year. But you've got something special, Steve. I saw it the first time you drove. You could be champion, maybe, if you could control whatever's eating at your insides. If you can't—I think there's a good chance you're going to kill yourself."

After that summary, a silence hung in the whiteness of the room like a grim shadow over Cahill's future. But Harris had felt it had to be said.

Cahill was discharged three days later, with Harris and Lucas already gone. Harris had flown off to his family for recuperation, but Lucas was still in New York. He had not given up on Cahill yet, he still thought Steve should drive the final two races.

Rossman had spoken to Cahill on the phone, and Cahill advised him that there were minor repairs to be made to the *Sonic Boom*. When he told Rossman he would not be driving it again, Rossman was silent on the other end for a long moment. Sitting on the edge of the hospital bed, Cahill could imagine Rossman's heavy face, full of pensiveness.

"That's a big decision, Steve."

"I know. It wasn't made lightly."

"If I know you—you're thinking about Harris and Lucas."

"They deserve more than I can give them out there, Charlie," Cahill said. "Boyd already has a replacement for Ed Harris. A guy I knew in the war, Danny Del Rio. All you'll have to do is find a driver, if you still want to go all the way."

"You make it sound easy," Rossman said with a laugh.

"I'm sorry, Charlie. I'll sell your boats for you. But I

really don't think I should be driving them."

"Do you mind if we talk about it some more, when you get back here to Miami?"

Cahill sighed. "I can't keep you from talking, Charlie."

Cahill spent a few days in Manhattan with Boyd Lucas before leaving for Florida and home. He had to arrange for special shipment for the *Sonic Boom,* and answer some questions by race officials. Lucas probed Cahill once more about the last races, and Cahill was adamant. Rossman had asked Lucas to come on down to Miami and discuss the Miami race with him, in case they had to get a driver, so Lucas had decided to fly down with Cahill.

On the afternoon before they were to leave, Cahill got a phone call from Dulcie. Cahill was surprised to hear her voice, thinking he had probably seen the last of her.

"I tried to see you at Freeport, but they wouldn't let me," she told him. "How are you, Steve?"

Cahill shrugged, sitting on the bed in his hotel room. "Hell, I've felt worse with a hangover," he grinned.

"I heard you had broken some bones. I was really worried."

Cahill hesitated before replying, mulling that remark. "It was just a couple of ribs, Dulcie." It was odd, her voice sounded so different on the phone, when he could not see her. She sounded about twelve years old.

"That's bad enough," she said.

"I'll be turning cartwheels in a couple of weeks."

"I'm sorry about the race. I mean, that you didn't win. You would have, wouldn't you?"

"Nobody ever knows, Dulcie," he told her.

"Will you be ready for Miami?"

"I'm not racing at Miami," he said.

"Oh."

"It's not the injuries."

A brief silence. Then she said, "I'd like to see you before you leave. If you have the time."

Cahill thought for a moment. "I've got some things to do. Would you like to stop by here?"

"I'd like to very much. When?"

"How about now?" he suggested.

Dulcie arrived at the hotel on 48th Street in less than an hour. There was a light summer rain outside, and she had to run through it from her cab. When she got upstairs to Cahill's room, she still smelled of it. She looked very good to him, with her damp, dark hair streaming over her shoulders. They greeted each other quietly at the door, and then she took off a light raincoat. She was wearing a bra-less Jersey blouse under it and a cotton skirt, with heels.

"I hope you don't mind my taking up your time, just before you leave."

"Actually, I was feeling a little lonely, with Boyd gone for the afternoon," Cahill admitted. "I was glad to get your call. I always seem to get a small let-down after a race. I'm told it's a natural phenomenon."

Cahill poured them a brandy from a bottle he kept in the room, and they sat and sipped the drinks without talking much. Dulcie looked particularly lovely to Cahill, sitting there near him in an arm-chair, asking about his injuries. She had been surprised to see him on a cane. Cahill found that he wanted her very much, that he had wanted her ever since that first time he had seen her, at the boat show. It did not matter about her and Falco, or what her values were. Not at that rain-scented moment in Manhattan.

". . .And there was a big traffic jam at the park," she was telling him. "There's a light fog on the river, and I could hear the horns blowing on the Ambrose Channel." She was telling him why it was good that he had not tried to come to her on the cane.

"It sounds nice out there," he said. "Just the way I like New York."

She smiled. "It seems strange that all this is over. The Freeport race, I mean, and all that went with it. I'll miss the excitement, I think. And the people I've met." She said the last slowly, averting her lovely eyes.

"I want you, Dulcie," he said.

She looked up at him quickly, her pulse suddenly pummeling inside her head. Steve Cahill did something to her that nobody else ever had. Just sitting near him made little electric currents run up and down through her. She held his gaze for a moment, then looked down.

"I'm sorry to be so abrupt," he said. "But it seems I don't have much time."

Dulcie nodded. She rose from the chair, walked to the single window in the room, and pulled a yellow shade down, throwing the room into a semi-darkness. Facing away from him, she drew the jersey blouse off over her head, and threw it onto the chair she had just vacated. She reached and unfastened the skirt, and it slid to the floor. She kicked out of it, and then removed the shoes. When she turned back to face him, she wore only a tiny piece of sheer underclothing on her hips.

"Damn," he muttered. "You're even more gorgeous than I thought."

She came over to him, walking barefoot on the carpet, all of her moving nicely as she came. When she got there, he rose from the straight chair he had been occupying, without his cane, and pulled her to him. In the next moment they were kissing hotly, with Cahill's hands on her breasts, her hips, her slim waist. After a moment Dulcie broke away, so quickly aroused that it was a little frightening to her. She was breathing heavily, her breasts moving against him. No man had ever gotten to her quite so easily and so completely. She felt herself trembling slightly inside as she began unbuttoning his shirt. "Let's—hurry," she whispered.

Cahill somehow got to the bed and onto it, but he would never remember how, later. With Dulcie's help his clothing came off, and then he was pulling the last piece of cloth down over her hips and thighs. There was a lot of fiery touching, exploring, fumbling. Dulcie felt his strong hand caressing her between her thighs, and his hungry mouth on her breasts. He started to mount her, but fell to her side, groaning slightly. There was a heavy bandage on his left thigh, and tape on his rib cage.

"Never mind, I'll do it," she said softly, urgently.

Now Cahill was on his back, and Dulcie was kneeling over him, her breasts hanging in perfect arcs above him, her long thighs straddling him. Then she guided him to a tight, full union so perfect it made her gasp aloud.

"Mmm, God!" she breathed.

There was a moment of pleasant anticipation then, and after that it was all a mounting crescendo of unleashed passion, hot desire, and the desperate reaching and reaching for total possession. When climax came for them it was mutual, primitive, and rather violent, with Dulcie's small back arched like a bow, Cahill's torso corded with taut musculature, his strong arms locked against her hips, pulling her tight against him.

She knelt propped over him afterwards, mouth ajar, lips moist, sucking in lungfuls of air.

"Mmmmm!" she finally managed.

"It was—beautiful," he gasped out.

A few minutes later Dulcie separated them and nestled herself beside his still-hot flesh, as they lay snuggled close all along their lengths.

"And they say there's nothing to do on a rainy day," he said.

Dulcie smiled prettily. The smile dissolved slowly, though, as she touched his hairy chest with a finger. "It seemed like a nice way to say goodbye."

Cahill looked at her, mixed feelings crowding through him about her. She was beautiful, she was fantastic in bed, she was interesting. But she gave of herself too readily, it seemed to him. He wanted to like her, to allow himself to reach out, inwardly, to her. But he remembered that look on Falco's face, telling him how nice it had been with her, and it all became very complicated to Cahill. It was a needle in Cahill's side that Falco had had Dulcie, and that maybe others had.

"It was," he finally responded. "But maybe it isn't goodbye, Dulcie. Maybe you'll get to Miami one of these days." He wanted to invite her there, but he found he could not. He had enough problems inside him already. He did not want to begin acting foolish with women. You did not invite a Mary Ann to come visit you in Miami, without having your friends laugh at you. Maybe Dulcie was not all that different from her friend, despite her sensational good looks.

"Maybe I will," she told him, quietly. She rose off the bed, and went over to the chair where her clothes lay, and he thought he had never seen a woman move more beautifully. She began dressing slowly, and he watched her.

"Is everything all right?"

"Sure," she said, turning and giving him a formal smile.

She had expected more; that was obvious to him. "Hey, maybe we could go get a drink together before I start packing. I'm not an invalid, you know."

She pulled the blouse on over full breasts. "No, Steve. It's better I leave now and give you some time to yourself." He sat up on the bed, while she slipped her shoes on. "I've got some things to do, too. Really."

A few minutes later, with Cahill sitting nude on the edge of the bed, she was ready to leave.

"I suddenly wish I weren't leaving early tomorrow," he admitted as she stood at the door.

She smiled a more relaxed smile. She had gotten somewhat past the disappointment of his reaction to their intimacy. "Send me a card from Miami Beach. I've always wanted to swim in the surf there."

"If you ever get down there, we'll do it together," he said.

Dulcie nodded. "I'll remember that, Steve."

Late the following day Cahill and Lucas arrived in Miami. Cahill had insisted that Lucas stay with him while he was in town, and Lucas finally accepted the invitation. Cahill had a two-bedroom condominium in North Miami Beach, facing the water, and it was his home most of the year, when he was not on the road for Charlie Rossman. It was open and breezy, done in a Spanish style, with archways between the rooms, and dark-wood, Moorish doors, and Lucas liked it. There was a small balcony looking out to sea, and there were always boats of some kind to look at out there—mostly sail, some power cruisers, and occasionally a freighter.

Cahill and Lucas just rested for a couple of days— Cahill was not expected back to work just yet—reading, listening to the news, and keeping out of the sun. It was late August now, and Miami was boiling hot. Automobiles heated up and stalled on the Palmetto Expressway, shoppers kept to the shady side of the street, and most locals stayed inside during the Hades-like afternoons. Lucas finally spoke to Rossman on the phone, when Rossman called to make certain Cahill was ready to come back to work on a Monday, and Rossman told Lucas he definitely wanted him for the Miami race, if he could find a driver. In the meantime, Lucas could work on the *Sonic Boom*, supervising its repairs.

When Cahill went in to work at Rossman Marine, Inc., on a muggy, overcast Monday, Rossman called him into his private office at the Hialeah plant and set him down at his desk there. Cahill was still using the cane and limping. Otherwise, he showed no evidence of injury. He had hurt some inside for a couple of days, and his rib cage was still sore and taped, but the leg was his primary problem.

"I keep thinking you could have been killed up there at Freeport," Rossman told him when they were sitting across from each other at the desk.

Cahill regarded Rossman's round, lined face with a wry grin. Rossman had some gray in his sideburns and was overweight and had always wanted to race boats but never found the time. Cahill had been his excitement by proxy, his close tie to the thrill of racing.

"I wasn't paying attention," Cahill said. "It was all my fault, the boat was great. It deserves a better driver than I am."

Rossman lighted a thin cigar and puffed on it to get it going. He did not offer Cahill one, because he knew he would not take it. "I don't know a better driver than you, Steve."

Cahill eyed him soberly. "I hear you've talked to a couple of people."

Rossman nodded, puffing at the cigar. A couple of perfect smoke rings floated slowly upward toward the ceiling. "Yeah. Young punks, kids. Think they're world-beaters, both of them. They'd fold at the slightest trouble. Falco would eat them alive."

"Did Lucas contact Danny Del Rio yet?"

Rossman nodded. "Del Rio is coming on down next week. I told Lucas he could help work on the *Sonic Boom*. Frankly, I would have preferred he stay in Baltimore until I know for sure what's happening. I'm not entering the Miami race with just anybody driving, Steve. My boat ought to have a driver, if it's entered."

"Boyd Lucas has driven in a couple of races. You might try him and find another throttleman."

Rossman shook his head. "He's good, Steve, but he's not a driver. That would be like Shula taking a tight end and trying to make him a quarterback without giving him any experience at it. No, I need a top throttleman in the race, too, and Boyd is as good a one as I know of."

Cahill shrugged. "Well."

Rossman leaned forward on his desk. "You'll be in shape to run that race, Steve. Accidents happen to everybody for Christ's sake. Oh, I'm not going to tell you that you have to race here—I wouldn't want the responsibility. You can sit here at a desk and take boat purchase orders through September if you want to. But you'd make next month a hell of a lot more exciting for everybody, if you were out there trying to beat Falco."

Cahill sighed heavily and leaned back in his chair. His almost-blond hair was slicked back, and his square jaw was tanned from the New York summer sun. "I shouldn't have to tell you this, Charlie, since everybody has probably told you anyway. But I'm having trouble out there on the courses. I seem to—go to pieces out there. Sometimes I lose all contact with reality; I see things that aren't there and get all jumpy inside. It's like I'm scared of my own safety. It's about the war, somehow, and the race seems to bring it on. It's fear, and—guilt, maybe, I don't know. There's a period there in the war, of just part of a day and night, that I can't put together in my head."

Cahill paused, and Rossman noticed that his face wore a sheen of light perspiration that had not been there a moment before.

"Josh Owens and I were there in the delta, both injured. Me trying to lug him out of there. Then there's this blank period in my head, and the next thing I can recall is Josh lying dead in my arms, on the bank of a river. He had just been shot by a sniper, I guess. A Huey was landing with medics, to pick us up."

Cahill passed a hand over his mouth. When he had spoken the last two sentences, a sharp pain gripped his insides, like a pair of pliers in there. He decided not to mention it to Rossman.

"Josh was taken on the first copter, and I had to wait for the second. There were others there, too, dead and wounded. They had got caught by the same snipers, I guess, just after we found them. An army outfit, I think Special Forces. I never saw Josh again. That first Huey was shot down, and his body was lost in the jungle."

When Cahill finished talking about Josh Owens, the pain in his guts subsided slowly.

"I'm sorry, Steve," Rossman said.

"Maybe something awful happened in that interim I

can't remember," Cahill said aloud, but more to himself than to Rossman. He had never talked about it with a living soul, before. "Something I would feel damned bad about, if I could remember. I don't know." A cold chill passed through him.

Rossman was squinting through cigar smoke at him. "What do you mean, Steve? Something like a My Lai thing?"

"I don't know. I got to hating the Cong a lot, Charlie. When I was out there in the Freeport race, I remembered a skiff full of Cong, and it was like they were right there on the sea with us, us headed right for them. They were armed, Charlie, and ready to fire on us. I was going to ram them, and it took Boyd to remind me I was really heading for a sweep boat. I swerved just in time to avoid hitting it and damn near turned us over."

Rossman sat there, mulling all of that. "Were you on a boat at any time in the war?"

A split-instant flash of a gray launch on a jungle river. The roar of engines. "No," Cahill said quickly. "Hell, no, Charlie, whatever gave you an idea like that?" Sweat popping on his brow.

Rossman eyed him narrowly. "I just thought I'd ask, Steve. Maybe it was a crazy idea."

"I was never on any boat," Cahill murmured to himself, staring past Rossman. "Never anything like that."

Rossman studied Cahill's somber face for a long, serious moment. "This skiff you mentioned. You think you saw it from a river bank?"

Cahill focused on him. "Yeah, that must have been it. I just can't remember, Charlie. I just can't remember."

"Maybe you shouldn't try," Rossman said meaningfully.

Cahill caught Rossman's eye. "Maybe. Maybe now that I'm out of the races, I should try to forget it."

"Or maybe," Rossman said even more slowly, "you

should confront it. Get in the Miami and Key West races and let come what may. That may be the only way you'll ever get it all out of you and come to terms with it.''

Cahill grunted. "Yeah, it might be great therapy," he said acidly. "But I also might just kill somebody."

"I suspect most of the danger is to yourself," Rossman said. "But Lucas says he wants to race with you. He says he wants to race with a winner, and you're a winner."

"Oh, Christ, Charlie." He rose from the chair.

Rossman shrugged. "Oh, yeah. You got a note from the Owenses while you were gone. The parents of that friend of yours who died out there in Asia, the one you just mentioned. Some secretary here opened it by mistake, thought it was business."

Cahill scowled as he took the envelope and pulled the card out. It was an ordinary greeting card, a friendship card that told Cahill that Josh Owens's parents were thinking of Cahill on the anniversary of Josh's death.

Quite suddenly Cahill seemed to change character before Rossman's eyes. "Sonofa*bitch!*" he said savagely. He was tearing the card into pieces, fury written on his square face. "Why can't they leave me alone? *Why can't they just leave me to hell alone!*"

Then, before Rossman could react, Cahill turned and stormed from the office, more upset than Rossman had ever seen him.

Rossman sat there stunned, staring at the slammed door, wondering what had gone wrong.

Chapter Eight

Rachel McKenzie lounged on a long white sofa of her spacious Fort Lauderdale living room. She was reading the Sunday edition of the *Miami Herald* and, for some unaccountable reason, was paging through the sports section.

Just over forty, but with the looks of a thirty-year-old, Rachel had been a fashion model at one time. Her hair was raven black, her eyes dark, and her complexion Italian-marble pale. She was dressed in lounging pajamas and sandals, both peach-hued, her long legs up on the sofa. Under the wispy clothing, purchased in Paris only recently, Rachel had a very slim but very feminine body, a body that photographed well in almost anything she chose to wear, and which caused stares whenever she appeared in public at a Miami Beach nightclub, or a social function, or at the Lauderdale Yacht Club.

The plush living room was thickly carpeted, with one wall open to a garden and canal, and potted tropical plants were everywhere. Oil paintings by some of Europe's most talked-about artists hung on the walls, and there was one rather small Jackson Pollack. Across the room from Rachel, an elderly man slouched on a big chair, studying the financial section through a reading glass. He was dressed in a bathrobe made of the finest silk and wore a scarf at his neck despite the summer heat in the room. His hair was wispy-white, his skin sunken and lined. He had been a business tycoon at one time, and had made more money than he could ever spend. He was Milton "Mac" McKenzie, Rachel's rich, almost-forty-years-older husband, a man who had bought Rachel fifteen years ago in the same way he might purchase a Rolls-Royce or a penthouse condominium. He had gotten his money's worth, too, in those first ten years, with a young, desirable woman in his bed. But then McKenzie's fires had cooled, and later gone out altogether. Now Rachel, who still had the spark of sensuality in her, was obliged to find her physical love elsewhere when she wanted it, and she had done so with a fair degree of regularity in recent years. McKenzie had learned of a couple of her men and had thrown a tantrum on the first occasion, threatening to divorce her. But Rachel was too much a part of him now; he depended on her for too many things. He could not throw her out. So he tolerated her occasional affairs as a parent will tolerate delinquencies of a recalcitrant daughter.

Rachel, for her part, was discreet in her liaisons, and never demanded more of them than physical satisfaction. She could not afford to. She had money of her own, but not like McKenzie had money. She liked being rich, and she liked the prospect of being McKenzie's rich widow some day in the foreseeable future.

"Mac, did you see this? The offshore races are coming here again soon. Do you remember how much you used to like watching boats race?" Her voice was deep, smooth, well-modulated. Cultured.

McKenzie looked past the big reading glass, toward her. "Hmmph? Oh, yes." There was gravel in his voice, and he seemed to dredge it up laboriously to speak. He looked back into the magnifier. "By God, Apex Chemical rose again Friday. I told you I should have bought twice as much as that damned broker recommended. It just makes me sick to think of what I'm losing every day in that stock."

"You don't lose when the price rises, Mac," Rachel said languidly. "I know that much about the market."

McKenzie was already immersed in the rows of figures, though, and just grunted at her remark. Rachel went on reading—about the boats with their colorful names, the leading contenders for the national championship. She made a mental note of the names Tony Falco and Steve Cahill. There were some statistics given, and some talk about the Harmsworth Trophy on the international scene, and the Outstanding Performance Award given in the Miami race. The race was to be a long one, from Miami to Bimini and back, and there was hope that the weather would be good. There was talk of "spinning out" and "stuffing," and it all sounded exciting to Rachel. One of the men she had had a brief affair with in the past was a boat racing driver, but he had not been in the big league of Class One racing.

"Why don't you take me to the Miami races, Mac?" she persisted. "It's been so damned dull around here this summer. You promised to take me to Carolina and didn't."

"You went to Rome in May," McKenzie grated out, not looking up from the paper. "By yourself," he added meaningfully.

"I'm not talking about May," she argued. "I'm talking about now. You haven't gotten out of that chair all summer, Mac. It's bad for your back. Either take me to the races, or fly with me to New York for a play weekend."

McKenzie glanced toward her. "You want to see power boats roar around all day, get one of your friends to go with you. One of your female friends, that is," he said sourly.

Rachel made a face, and looked pouty. "God, Mac. You never go anywhere anymore. Your doctor told you that exercise would do you a lot of good."

"Let him take it then," McKenzie snorted. "He can handle it, he's only fifty. When I was his age, I was beating kids at tennis."

Rachel stopped listening as he went on grumbling. She was getting stir-crazy. It seemed to happen with regularity, living with McKenzie. If he was going to play dead, she wished he would go ahead and do it right. Some days she felt like things were passing her by, sitting and watching McKenzie read the financial page. His pleasure now was in counting his money, but she was still young and vital. She needed adventure in her life.

New friends, new faces.

Maybe a race driver.

In Manhattan, Mary Ann Spencer had just received a call from her racer-lawyer friend, from Philadelphia, the fellow named Bill who laughed at Mary Ann's jokes and loved to watch her take her clothes off. He had entered his boat in the Miami-Bimini Offshore Open Regatta, and wondered if Mary Ann could get time off to come down to Florida for the race weekend.

Mary Ann was thrilled to be asked, but she had a problem. She had already taken all her vacation time from the Two Friends Lounge, and the manager there had just advised both Mary Ann and Dulcie that they could have no more time off.

Mary Ann had just gotten the call before coming to work at the lounge one evening, and since Dulcie had come to work from shopping, she had not had a chance to mention it yet to Dulcie.

It was a slow evening at the lounge. There were three couples at tables, a middle-aged piano player plunking out old favorites, and, at the end of the bar, a TV going with the sound down.

Dulcie was missing Cahill. She had given more of herself to him than even she realized. She thought about him in bed a lot, and when she walked down to the river, and at other times. But mostly in bed. She ached for him inside her. But it was more than that, too. She liked his open, serious face, and the way he talked, and the occasional glimpses she got of his vulnerability to the world. She had the feeling that something had hurt him, in his past, and that the hurt was not healed. She wanted to be the one to help him get past that, whatever it was. He needed her, she had convinced herself, and that was a good feeling, to be needed. It gave her a taste of dignity that she needed very badly.

But Dulcie had not even considered the possibility of following Cahill to Miami. In the first place, he had not asked her. But in the second, she was reluctant to chase after a man, no matter what he meant to her. If he did not realize, on his own, how special they were together, it was wrong to press it.

Dulcie had spoken to Mary Ann briefly when they arrived and changed into their scanty costumes, but they had not had a chance to really talk yet. Dulcie left Mary Ann at the bar after they had been there about an hour, and served drinks to a couple at a corner table near the piano player. She flashed her smile at them, and the fellow watched her hips swing as she left.

"Now, *that's* a girl."

"Never mind, Howard."

Back at the bar, Dulcie put her tray down and gave Mary Ann a tired look. "God, there has to be something better than this."

The piano player was playing *As Time Goes By*, and a memory of Bogart and Bergman flashed into Dulcie's head. Did love affairs like that really happen? she wondered. Or were they just in movies and books?

Mary Ann had glanced toward Dulcie at Dulcie's remark. Mary Ann was voluptuously sexy in the costume, but a little hard-looking with her heavy eye make-up, red lipstick and dyed red hair.

"Bill called me today," she said. She had a small piece of chewing gum in her mouth, which she worked sensually as she spoke. "He wants me to come to Miami for the race there."

Dulcie smiled. "Oh, really?" The smile faded. "But you don't have any more time off."

"Tell me about it," Mary Ann said bitterly. She turned and stared toward the piano player. Down at the far end of the bar, the bartender arranged some liquor bottles on a shelf.

"What are you going to do?" Dulcie said, seeing the defiant look in Mary Ann's round face.

Mary Ann turned toward her. "You said it yourself. There has to be something better than this. Maybe it's in Miami."

Dulcie frowned slightly. "You'd quit your job here?" Dulcie had considered it a number of times, but figured Mary Ann was happy doing just what she did for a living.

"Why not? I'm not exactly running the place here, you know. I could quit tomorrow and find something just as good across town. But maybe my future isn't across town."

"Bill?" Dulcie said.

Mary Ann shrugged. "He likes me. We get along great in bed, honey. I told you how he is."

"Is that a good enough reason to meet him in Miami? At the expense of giving up your job here?"

Mary Ann looked around, to make sure they would not be overheard. "Miami is a terrific town, Dulcie. A customer just the other day was saying how there's lots of work there. In hotels, nightclubs, tourist places."

"That wouldn't get you next to Bill. He lives in Philadelphia."

"He's going down there early and is going to stay around a while, on some legal business," Mary Ann said. "I'd have plenty of time with him there. Maybe something would develop. If not, at least I'd be in sunny Miami, instead of here in this creepy smoke-filled hole."

Dulcie smiled. "There are probably some creepy, smoke-filled holes in Miami, too."

"Maybe. But you won't find me in them. I see myself behind the desk at some swanky hotel on the beach, telling guests in mink stoles where to find the coffee shop. Or maybe planning games for the old ladies to play on the patio. Something civilized."

Dulcie had to suppress a smile, thinking of Mary Ann as an entertainment director for the older set. "You're really serious about this, I see."

Mary Ann nodded. "I'm ready for a change." She looked into Dulcie's eyes. "So are you, aren't you, honey?"

Dulcie met her studied gaze.

"You said as much," Mary Ann added.

"Yes. I said as much."

"You may have a better reason for going to Miami than I do, anyway," Mary Ann suggested.

Dulcie frowned slightly. "Steve Cahill?"

"You're hung up on him even more than I am on Bill. I can tell. And he lives in Miami, doesn't he?"

Dulcie shook her pretty head. "I like Steve a lot, but I'm not hung up at all."

Mary Ann smiled. "Call it what you want, but I've seen the way you look at him." She lowered her voice to a whisper. "I don't want to go without you, honey. Let's do it together. Let's go lower the boom on the management tonight. We can be in Miami by the weekend. Bill would probably put us both up there for a while, until we get settled in."

Dulcie had to admit it sounded good to her. Particularly since Mary Ann seemed determined to quit. It would be grim there at the lounge without her, and in their apartment. The trouble was, Dulcie did not want to crowd Cahill by showing up uninvited on his own turf.

"Steve would think I'm after him."

"If you worry about that, don't call him. Let him find out on his own that you're there. I'll make sure he knows." Mary Ann wore her crafty grin.

Dulcie could not help returning it. Mary Ann saw things much more simply than she, which aggravated and worried Dulcie often. But she was basically a nice person to be with.

"All right," Dulcie said firmly. "I'll go."

Mary Ann smiled happily. "You will? God, that's great!"

"But none of that business about letting Steve know. I'm going to Miami for work. Not to chase Steve."

"You've got a deal," Mary Ann said brightly.

Two days later, Dulcie and Mary Ann arrived in Miami. Dulcie wanted to give a week's notice at the lounge, but the manager became upset with them and told them he did not want them around. Mary Ann called him a couple of names to his face and a lot more, later. When they left the place that night, Dulcie felt more free than she had in a long time.

It was hot in Miami in early September. Mary Ann's friend Bill had not arrived yet, but had wired money for a room at a fancy motel not far from the Beach Marina, where the races were going to take place. Dulcie agreed to stay there with Mary Ann until Bill's arrival, at which time she would find a room of her own. She had enough money to last her for several weeks without a job, and she resolved not to impose on Mary Ann and Bill. One of the first things Dulcie did was look up Cahill's address in North Miami Beach, in the phone book. But she made no move to call him or contact him in any way. Mary Ann could not understand this, but Dulcie was adamant about it.

Cahill was just relaxing and healing from his Freeport accident. Rossman had put no new pressure on him to race in the Miami-Bimini contest, but made the further report that he still had no driver for the *Sonic Boom*. Lucas had sent for Danny Del Rio, though, because Rossman had made it clear he intended to race the *Sonic*

Boom somehow. Del Rio was expected in a couple of days, and Cahill had already told Boyd Lucas that Del Rio might also stay at Cahill's place through the race, if he so wished.

Cahill and Lucas were together a lot of the time outside Cahill's working hours, and they often went down to the Beach Marina to see what boats were coming in. The marina was also a yacht club, which was affiliated with the local race committee, and Cahill had recently become a member there under Rossman's auspices, so he and Lucas spent some time at the club bar there, too, where they met other racing people. Lucas had thought that Cahill would want to avoid them, now that he had backed off racing at Miami, but Cahill surprised him. Cahill was still wrestling with the possibility of racing again, deep down inside him somewhere, where he did not really know what was going on. A part of him was very disturbed that he was not going to race at Miami, even though he did not admit that to himself on a conscious level. He would not have had an explanation for that repressed feeling.

It was a warm late-summer evening that Cahill and Lucas made one of their stops at the yacht club bar, just the night before Del Rio was to arrive. There were several other drivers there that evening, a couple of lesser Class One drivers and a few Class Two men. Rachel McKenzie had stopped by with a woman friend and the friend's husband, and had invited two drivers to have drinks at their table.

Rachel was having a good time when Cahill and Lucas arrived. She was interrogating the two young drivers about racing, and particularly Class One racing and was becoming educated about it. But she had hoped to find a race celebrity there and had been disappointed in that respect until Cahill arrived. She saw him as soon as he came in, was impressed by his rugged good looks, and asked who he was.

"Oh, that's Steve Cahill," a young driver told her.

"He was a contender for the title, until he pulled out of the Miami race. Had an accident in New York, in the race there. Got busted up pretty bad."

Cahill had finally discarded the cane but was still limping on his healing leg. Rachel had noticed the limp when he came in, and the injury made him seem even more glamorous to her. She asked if she might meet him, just after Boyd Lucas had left Cahill's table to go speak to a race official at the bar. A moment later, the driver was at Cahill's table.

"Hi, Steve, remember me? Doug Bremer, I came in at the back of the pack at Freeport. The port engine broke down on us."

Cahill nodded. "Nice to see you again, Doug."

The other driver jerked a thumb toward the table across the room. "There's a lady over there that would like to meet you. Name's Rachel McKenzie."

Cahill glanced past the other man and saw Rachel looking toward him. She looked pretty spectacular to him, in a red gown, with her black hair and pale, glowing skin. Also, at that distance, she looked about his age.

"She's very rich," the fellow named Bremer said with a grin. "She's married, but it don't count. Her husband is some old guy that's ready for a nursing home, I hear. Come on over, she's buying the drinks."

Cahill shook his head. "I guess I'll pass it up tonight, Bremer."

Bremer shrugged. "Whatever you say. But she's real class, Steve."

He returned to the other table, and Cahill saw him impart the refusal to Rachel. Rachel looked toward Cahill soberly, and Cahill returned the look. She leaned over to her friends, said something to them, picked up two full glasses of brandy, and rose and walked over to him.

She walked proudly, not moving from the hips up, her posture perfect. He had never seen so elegant-looking a woman up close. Now, as she came up, he saw the fine lines in her face that revealed her age as older than his. But she had lost no beauty with the years. She was quite stunning.

"You refused to join me at my table, so I thought you might not mind my offering you a brandy here. Mr. Bremer says he thinks you like brandy. Is he right?"

Cahill rose, and looked into her dark eyes. Her speech, even, was elegant. She smelled of money. Of Vassar and yachts and blue chip stocks. "Yes, he's right," he said quietly. "I didn't mean to be unfriendly, Mrs. McKenzie. But I have a friend returning to this table."

"Would you mind if I sat with you until he comes back?"

Cahill was flattered by such attention from such a woman. He shrugged. "No, of course not."

She sat down, and they drank from the glasses. She asked him a few questions about racing, and he replied to them, keeping his answers as non-technical as he could. She seemed pleased with them. She looked deeply into his blue eyes.

"The idea of power boat racing excites me, Steve. May we be on a first name basis?"

He nodded. "Sure."

"Do you think it has to do with the symbolism of the powerful, phallic-shaped boats," she suggested carefully, "thrusting their way through the sea?"

Cahill was surprised. "I'd never thought of it," he said. He smiled. "But it's an interesting notion."

Rachel returned the smile. "Forgive my staring. I'm trying to decide whether you're a Captain Ahab, or a Santiago," she said.

Cahill frowned. "What?"

"You've read Herman Melville, haven't you? And *The Old Man and the Sea?*"

"I don't do much reading," he told her.

"No, I guess you wouldn't," she said, giving him a

112

sexy look. "I was just trying to understand your motivation for racing across the open sea in a power boat with the obvious dangers involved."

Nobody had ever asked him that question before, and he was impressed that she would think to do so. "I don't think I understand it yet myself," he said.

She nodded. "You're a very interesting fellow, Steve Cahill."

"So are you, Rachel," he admitted.

"I understand you may not race here at Miami. Is it the injuries you received at Freeport?"

Cahill shook his head. "No, I'm healing well," he said. "It's personal."

"Mmm. I love a man with secrets," she said flirtatiously. "I'd like the chance to unveil some of them, sometime, when we can be alone."

Her meaning was unmistakable. Cahill held her arched, sultry gaze and found that Rachel was very appealing to him. He had never been the subject of such attention from a rich, beautiful, cultured woman, and it was very flattering to him. "I suppose that could be arranged."

"You seem unsure. Does it bother you that I'm a bit older than you?"

Cahill said the right thing. "I didn't know you were," he lied.

Rachel smiled shyly. "Then what?" she said.

"Well. You are married."

Rachel made a low sound in her long, white throat. "My dear, put that thought from your mind. I'm living with the shadow of a man, a man that used to be. Mac is almost eighty. Quite a few years ago, when his first wife died, he decided he wanted a sweet young thing on his second try. He bought me and paid for me, and our relationship has never risen far above the level of that business transaction. Mac knew a day like this would come. Don't waste any sympathy on him, he is completely undeserving."

113

Cahill nodded. "All right. I won't."

"Good. Can we get together some time soon, then?"

"Why not, Rachel?" Cahill said. "I hear Sinatra is coming to town next week, just before race weekend. We could catch his show together, if you'd like."

Rachel smiled nicely, showing perfect teeth. It was a cover-girl smile if Cahill had ever seen one. He could almost see the framed close-up on the cover of *Redbook*. "Yes, I'd like very much," she told him.

It was the next morning that Del Rio appeared at Cahill's condominium at the Beach. Cahill was at work, but Lucas was there to greet his Baltimore friend. Del Rio was excited about the prospect of racing in Miami, but very disappointed that Cahill had announced his withdrawal from it. He had always wanted to race in the Class One power boat races but recently he had also had the hope that it would be with Steve Cahill, when he got his chance.

Lucas got Del Rio moved in—his bags unpacked and the sleeping arrangement settled. By noon, when Cahill arrived to welcome him, Del Rio had discussed the race situation with Lucas and had been filled in about Rossman's unsuccessful hunt for another driver. Del Rio was sitting in front of open sliding glass doors, looking out toward the ocean, when Cahill entered the place, with Boyd Lucas in the kitchen fixing them all cold sandwiches. There was a moment of warm greeting before Lucas brought the sandwiches and they all sat on chairs before the big glass doors, talking as they ate.

Del Rio had met Cahill only twice since their return from the war: once in Miami, on Del Rio's way through, and once in Baltimore, when Cahill went to talk boats with Boyd Lucas. Del Rio and Cahill had briefly mentioned the war on those occasions but had not really gotten into any discussions about it. Now, as Del Rio ate his sandwich, washing it down with refrigerated beer, he was telling Lucas about his first meeting with Cahill in Vietnam.

"You should have seen Steve when he walked into battalion headquarters that muggy day," Del Rio was grinning. He swigged part of his can of beer. "He was a real rookie, a greenie. Was wearing a tie for Christ's sake. A tie." He laughed genially. "Asked me if we supplied condoms—remember, Steve?"

Cahill grinned. "Some sergeant of ours had the Vietnam girls sounding like sex queens." The smile evaporated. "In a few weeks, I'd forgotten all that. That was no longer part of the John Wayne movie."

Lucas glanced toward Del Rio quickly.

"Well. When I saw you again at Khe Sanh, it was sure different. I'd have been scared to meet you in a dark alley. You had learned fast, just as we all had. The first thing I heard about you was that you had led a search-and-destroy patrol into enemy territory and had run into heavy mortar fire. You apparently dragged your captain out of range after he was hit and saved his ass."

Cahill's face had gone somber. "That was a bunch of exaggerated bullshit, Danny." He spoke quietly, tightly.

There was a brief silence, then Del Rio interrupted it. "I guess the whole Khe Sanh thing was exaggerated, to us and to the public back home. That's the kind of war it was. Half-truths, lies. You lost a friend over there, didn't you, Steve?"

Without warning, Cahill's gut began hurting. "Yes, that's right."

"Somebody mentioned it to me in Saigon when I was leaving for home," Del Rio said.

"Josh and I got caught in a goddamn firestorm," Cahill said. "On patrol. We both got hit. We got to a river, but he died there before help came."

Del Rio frowned, listening to the summary. "That's funny, I heard that—"

But Cahill went on, quickly. "I wanted to go in the same copter with him, but they made me wait for the next one. That copter was shot down, the first one.

They never found Josh's body."

Cahill had begun to perspire lightly, and his whole manner had changed. He sat there staring out through the open doors, remembering, mashing his sandwich in his right hand.

"Well, that's all behind us now," Lucas finally said, brightly. His big frame was hunched awkwardly in a studio chair, and his dark eyes looked sober, despite his lightness of speech. "Best to let the past lie undisturbed, I say. What's gone is gone."

"Amen," Del Rio agreed.

Cahill had come back from that far-off place now. He turned to Del Rio with an uncertain grin. "I guess the past can't hurt you, if you won't let it."

Del Rio nodded. "None of that exists now, it's not a part of reality. To hell with it—it never happened. Just like that Freeport race, right, Steve?"

Cahill glanced at him. "That accident was my fault, Danny."

Del Rio, looking square-set and dark in the chair, nodded. "Maybe so. But so what? I made mistakes in Nam, but I didn't ask to be transferred out of the fighting."

Cahill got a small chill through him.

"Does a doctor or a president, even, let a mistake stop him?" Del Rio went on. "Not any I've ever heard about. And they're right. It's right to keep going, and learning."

Cahill smiled at Del Rio's simplistic logic. "These are races we're talking about, Danny. A kind of entertainment. Not heart surgery or political maneuvering. It isn't important to the scheme of things that I ever race again. And I haven't learned. I don't know why I made the mistake or what to do about it."

But now Boyd Lucas spoke up. "I'm not saying you owe Charlie Rossman anything. He can live without a national trophy. But what about racing as a sport and the fans who follow it, Steve? Is Tony Falco the kind of

116

champion to represent us to them? And what about Gus Beckering, the guy who always gets what he wants? Wouldn't it be satisfying to put the sponsor's trophy on Rossman's shelf this year, instead of letting Beckering grab it again?"

Cahill cast a dubious look at Lucas. "You make it sound as if I'm giving the trophy away by not racing here. If Falco wins either here or at Key West he takes the championship."

Lucas leaned forward seriously in his chair. "Forget Key West. If you were to race and win here at Miami, you'd have won a crack at the trophy, at least. Nobody else in the point standings can make that statement."

Now Del Rio leaned forward, too. "I want to race with *you,* Steve. Not some kid that Rossman pulls off the marina dock. I have this gut feeling. That the three of us together would make a great crew. That we can beat Falco."

"It would be a great year for racing," Lucas said, "if we could grab the title from Falco and Beckering. I'd give a year's earnings just to see the look on Art Kralich's face if you took the trophy."

Cahill held Lucas's serious look. "You know what happens to me out there, in the heat of the race. Does Danny?"

Lucas nodded. "I've discussed it with him. It doesn't worry him, and it doesn't worry me. Not for ourselves. It's you we're concerned about. But we think you can handle it, with us out there with you."

"You've got to pull all that Nam stuff out of your head, Steve," Del Rio said ingenuously but earnestly. "Then you'll be all right, we're sure of it."

Cahill turned to Danny Del Rio, and felt a sudden affection for this ex-Marine who had been there in Asia with him and who now wanted so desperately to race with him. He put a hand on Del Rio's shoulder. "You know, you could be right, Danny," he said with an easy smile.

Del Rio grinned. "Does that mean you'll race?"

Cahill turned and looked out through the doors to the sea. It was out there, on the water, in a speeding boat, that held the dark mystery locked inside his head. Maybe Rossman had been right. Maybe if he confronted it, he could beat it. He heard Ed Harris's voice, though, in his head. *You could be champion, maybe, if you could control whatever's eating at your insides. If you can't—I think there's a good chance you're going to kill yourself.*

"Yes," Cahill said solemnly. "I guess that means I'll race."

Lucas grinned, too. "Well, I'll be damned!"

Cahill rubbed at his leg. "I'll have to work at it, in the next week. I'll have to work this leg, and then work it some more. The ribs have pretty well healed, I think."

"I'll help," Del Rio told him. "I know some therapy exercises. We'll get you in shape pronto. We'll have the best damned crew in racing!"

Cahill nodded, grinning awkwardly. Deep inside, he was not sure whether he felt good or bad about his decision. "Okay, Danny," he said in a subdued voice. "We'll see."

Chapter Nine

Charlie Rossman was pleased to learn of Cahill's decision. The *Sonic Boom* was ready to race, and now Rossman had his team back, with a younger, more aggressive navigator than before.

Dulcie and Mary Ann were settled in now. Bill the lawyer had arrived with his boat, and Dulcie had moved out of the room at the motel, finding a cheaper one downtown, against Mary Ann and Bill's wishes. The three had had a few meals together, but Dulcie tried to avoid interfering with their evenings. In the daytime, she went job-hunting alone, because Mary Ann was too busy with Bill to take such an activity seriously, yet. The trouble was, there were no decent jobs to be had. Dulcie could have had two different jobs as a waitress at Miami Beach restaurants, or one as an office clerk at Jackson Memorial Hospital. The waitress jobs paid only tips and were hard manual labor. The hospital job paid just above minimum wage and would have driven Dulcie crazy with boredom. She took none of them.

On one evening, Dulcie did spend part of it with Mary Ann and Bill, because they went to the yacht club marina for drinks, and Mary Ann was certain that Dulcie would run into Cahill there. But Cahill was not there, and Dulcie left early to return downtown to her room alone. Mary Ann had told everybody in the racing fraternity that she met that Dulcie was in town, but none of it got back to Cahill. Mary Ann begged Dulcie to let her call Cahill, but Dulcie refused adamantly.

Then, just a few days before the race, Mary Ann had a bad break. Bill's boat developed serious engine trouble. He withdrew from the Class One race, and within twenty-four hours he was gone from Miami. He did not ask Mary Ann to join him in Philadelphia. They had spent three nights together, and his appetite for her was satiated.

Mary Ann, at Dulcie's insistence, moved in at the Biscayne Hotel where Dulcie had an efficiency room and could cook her meals there. Twin beds were moved in, and the girls were roommates again.

Mary Ann was, of course, forlorn. She had allowed herself to believe that something was developing between her and Bill. Dulcie soothed her and cooked her a nice Italian meal of tagliatella Bolognese, which Mary Ann dearly loved. Then, one night out at the yacht club alone, Mary Ann met Tony Falco who had just arrived in town with the *First Blood*.

Falco had had no extramarital fling since Dulcie and was getting very bored again by now. He was also feeling very much the race hero again, with his name in all the newspapers. A hero was entitled to certain privileges, Falco reasoned, so when he found Mary Ann at the yacht club, he invited her to a nearby motel—the same one she had just vacated with Bill—and Mary Ann, still hurting from Bill's rejection, accepted. In a small, bougainvillea-covered cottage, Falco undressed Mary Ann in what must have been record time, took her brutally and without amenity and then fell heavily asleep, leaving her to her own devices. When Falco awoke at two A.M., Mary Ann was gone, he had a bad taste of stale liquor in his mouth, and certain of his private parts had been painted with lipstick as Mary Ann's protest over his abandoning her before evening's end.

Falco was still muttering obscenities about the lipstick long after he had cleaned up and was on his way back to the hotel suite Beckering had obtained for him and Eva at the glamorous Eden Roc Hotel. But when he got there, he had something else to occupy his mind. Eva was waiting up for him.

He squinted at her in the light of a corner table lamp when he came into the sunken living room of the suite, with its thick carpeting and potted palms. Eva was in a sheer peignoir, her arms crossed across her breasts, and her face was stern-looking.

"Where the hell have you been?" were the first words out of her mouth.

Falco turned from her, and threw a light sport jacket onto a chair. "I told you where I was going. Kralich and I had a few drinks at the Beach Yacht Club. What do you want, an inventory?"

Eva glared hotly at him. "You left the yacht club at eleven, with a girl. Her name was Mary Ann, and she's one of those girls that follow the races."

Falco turned to her with a deep scowl. "What the hell you been doing, having a goddam private dick follow me around?"

"I don't have to, damn you, you do it right out in the open! I called the bartender there, and he gave me the whole story. I guess you hadn't thought of bribing him, yet, to keep his mouth shut about you!"

"I knew he was a goddam loudmouth when he served Kralich and me," Falco muttered.

"Where did you take her, Tony? To some cheap hot-pillow place on the beach? Or did you just bang her in the parking lot?"

Falco turned away from her, going over to a small bar at the nearby wall. He poured himself a scotch. "So I left with a girl. She wanted to have a look at the *First Blood*, and I showed her."

"I'll bet you showed her!" Eva said loudly. "And I'm sure she showed you, damn you!"

"I'm telling you. It was just some kid that wanted to see a real racing boat. I left her at the marina, stopped at another bar, and had a couple of drinks by myself."

"Bullshit," Eva said.

Falco turned and looked at her, and swigged the entire drink in one long gulp. "All right, Eva. I took her to the nearest motel I could find, and I screwed her." He was still inebriated, and was not as cautious as usual with her. "I fell asleep then, and when I came around, she was gone. That's a full confession. Now what are you going to do, arrest me?"

Eva glared hard at him for a long moment, then turned away. "Goddam you," she muttered. "I'm not putting up with this." She whirled back toward him. *"I'm not putting up with it!"*

"Just get off my back!" he growled at her. "Give me some goddam breathing room!"

"Oh, is that what you want, you sonofabitch! I'll give you all the breathing room you can take! You can have this whole damned town, this entire hemisphere!" She glared at him for another intense moment, then turned and ran into their bedroom, slamming and locking the door after her.

Falco was obliged to sleep on the sofa that night, in his clothes. A few hours later, he awoke, realized how stupid he had been with his admission, and tried to wake Eva and apologize to her. She was, after all, his real meal ticket in the harsh world around him, not Gus Beckering. But Eva would neither unlock the door nor speak with him. When he woke again in the morning, she had left the suite. He was relieved to find her clothing and things still there.

Eva had gone out by herself that morning to try to clear her head and assess what had gone wrong with her life. She had breakfast at the Bal Harbor Mall, where there were lush tropical plantings and birds flitting in the sunlit foliage and a black man hosing down the pavement. She had always liked Miami, but her whole feeling about it on this trip was colored by her husband. She had tried to make herself think she could control him, but she could not. It was the championship he had won and all the attendant publicity—that had made it all worse.

She got in her rental car after breakfast and drove the Buick out to the Beach Yacht Club and Marina. She did not plan to end up there, but she looked up at the end of her drive and there she was. She got out of the car and went down to the dock area and walked along looking at the parked trailers and flatbeds with the long racing boats squatting bulkily on them. There were no other race people about at the moment, so she was able to enjoy her privacy. It was these boats, and the races, that had changed her life for the worse. She moved along under their shadows, staring at their smooth hulls with hostility. Maybe if she could wave a magic wand and send them all to the bottom of Biscayne Bay her life would be tolerable again.

No, she thought. *Not a chance.*

She turned a corner around a flatbed and there was Boyd Lucas, only thirty feet away. He was standing under the flatbed that held the *Sonic Boom* and was examining its hull. He had not seen Eva, so she almost turned away. But then she walked on over to him. He had always been nice to her, and she suddenly felt the need for someone to be nice to her.

"Good morning, Boyd."

Lucas turned and narrowed his eyes on her. "Eva! My gosh, this is a pleasant surprise." He glanced past her, looking for Falco. "You out here alone?"

Eva nodded and leaned against a big wheel of the flatbed trailer. "Yes, alone. The way I usually am, lately." She was wearing her blond hair in loose curls all over her head, and a blue-patterned blouse brought out the color of her eyes. "Are you going to race the *Sonic Boom* here, Boyd?"

Lucas nodded. He towered over Eva and looked particularly big in the olive drab jump suit he was wearing. He had been looking at the engines earlier, and had a small smudge of grease on the side of his face. He leaned on the wheel beside Eva. "Yeah, we got lucky. Steve Cahill has changed his mind, he's driving this race after all."

Eva nodded, staring out to where blue water sparkled in the morning sun. "I hope he runs Tony right off the goddam course."

Lucas turned and studied her aquiline, pretty face. "Are you all right, Eva?"

Eva shrugged. Her eyes watered up quite unexpectedly, and she brushed at one of them. "Don't mind me, I'm feeling sorry for myself this morning, I guess."

"And it's because of Tony?" Lucas said.

Eva hesitated, then nodded again. "Who else?" she said bitterly.

"I'm—really sorry, Eva," Lucas told her.

"That bastard does exactly what he wants," she said, more to herself than to Lucas. "Girls, booze. I could talk to him before he won that damned trophy last year. Now reporters crowd around him, and all the giggly little groupies are hot to get him into bed, and he suddenly thinks he's above the rules."

Lucas stood there, now knowing what to say. "I can't imagine anyone treating a woman like you the way he does," he finally said. "You deserve better than that. I've always thought so."

Eva turned and stared at him and saw something she had missed before. Boyd Lucas liked her.

"I appreciate that, Boyd. I needed someone to say that."

"I mean it, Eva. I always thought Tony was a pretty lucky guy, married to you. I just don't understand him."

Eva smiled wanly. "That makes at least two of us."

Lucas returned the smile. "I think the coffee counter is open in the club. Can I get you a cup? I haven't had one yet."

Eva hesitated only momentarily. "I think I'd like that."

It was that same evening that Cahill finally learned Dulcie was in town. Mary Ann asked Dulcie to go out to the yacht club one last time with her before the races, which were only a few days off. There was another owner whom Bill had known and who had liked Mary Ann and, despite her unsatisfactory second fling with Falco, she was still interested in and enamored of men connected with the racing season. She was still convinced that this was where the action was, where her chances were greatest for finding somebody special. Dulcie agreed to go out there for just a brief time, and while she was there Cahill came in.

Dulcie was sitting with Mary Ann and the new friend, a man in his forties who owned a production class boat and was new to racing. When Cahill spotted Dulcie, he left Boyd Lucas and Danny Del Rio at the bar and came over and just stared openly at her for a moment without speaking.

"I thought I was seeing visions," he finally told her.

"Oh, hi, Steve," Mary Ann said, giving Dulcie a look.

Dulcie smiled at him. Just the sight of him made her all fluttery inside. Cahill nodded to Mary Ann and turned back to her. "What the hell are you doing in Miami?"

Dulcie shrugged. "Mary Ann thought there would be work for us down here. So far, there isn't."

"Steve, this is Phil Ramos," Mary Ann told him.

"We've met," Ramos said, rising and shaking Cahill's hand vigorously. He was a square-built, swarthy-looking fellow with balding dark hair and a belly.

"Good to see you again, Ramos," Cahill told him.

"I hear you're back in the Bimini race," Ramos said.

Cahill nodded. "I wasn't feeling so great for a while, but I'm better now." He was limping almost unnoticeably now on the healing leg. He appraised Dulcie as he spoke. As usual, she looked great. Her dark hair was in a French twist, and her eyes looked big and lovely. She wore a deep-cut lime-green dress that showed more of Dulcie than Cahill thought was proper. It bothered him to find her here, in Miami, showing herself off to everybody—making the circuit with Mary Ann. There was no reason why it should bother him, but it did. He wished he could just enjoy her for what she was; there were not many around with her beauty and willingness. But he kept finding himself wishing he had discovered her on a college campus, before she had found her way to New York. All pink cotton and innocence.

"I'm glad you're going to race again, Steve," Dulcie was saying to him.

Cahill nodded. "I see you're not drinking. I was going to drive over to the beach. You want to come along?"

Dulcie hesitated. She did not want to seem too interested. She was afraid she had already given him the wrong impressions about herself, that maybe she was a girl who was ready to hop into any man's bed at the slightest hint. But she did feel that way toward Cahill, and there seemed to be little she could do to hide it.

"Sure, why not?" she said lightly.

Dulcie and Cahill made excuses to Mary Ann and Ramos and left the bar. Outside, they got into Cahill's gray Jaguar sports coupe and drove along Collins Avenue for a while, sucking in lungfuls of sea breeze. Finally Cahill stopped at a small beach, secluded and private. He parked the car and they got out, walking down to the surf. It came rolling in blue-looking under a third-quarter moon. Cahill walked Dulcie down beyond some mangrove trees where it was even more private.

"I thought we might go for a quick swim," he suggested then.

They had made only small talk on the way, about the race and the Two Friends Lounge, avoiding anything personal. Dulcie looked up at him. His blond-streaked hair was moving in the breeze, and he looked very handsome to her.

126

"I don't have a suit," she said.

"Neither do I."

Dulcie smiled uncertainly.

"We can't let that stop us, can we?" he said.

She did not respond. She worried that it was all going too fast again, that he was getting a wrong impression about what she expected from him.

"Come on," he said, taking his print sport shirt off, revealing bronze muscles in his chest and arms. "It isn't as if we haven't seen each other with our clothes off." He grinned.

Dulcie watched him for a moment, then turned away and began undressing. Her clothing fell off piece by piece, lying at her feet in the sand. Then, without turning back to him, she ran down and immersed herself in the surf.

Cahill was right behind her. The waves broke over them, cool and refreshing, and Cahill was aroused by their caresses as he had known he would be. He splashed water at Dulcie, and she splashed some back, and then he was grabbing at her nude, wet body, wrestling with her. She felt his strong, muscled arms around her, on her curves, touching her most private places. The surf roared in their ears, and they were breathless in its surging.

"I'm glad you came," he said harshly into her ear. Then he was pushing himself hard against her, and she felt the hard probing of him against her thigh, and his hand was fumbling to unite them as they stood there in waist-high surf.

But before he could manage it, Dulcie pulled back and put a hand on his. "Please," she breathed unevenly. He was taking it all for granted, there was no affection, no respect for what she might want. It was too much like it had been with Tony Falco.

Cahill was frowning. "What is it?"

"I—don't want it to happen here," she said. "It's—not right for me, Steve."

Cahill still had his hands on her. He caressed her

breasts, her hips, with his hands. "To hell with it," he said thickly. "Anywhere is all right, honey." He was now pressing her hand away, trying again to join them.

But now Dulcie stumbled away from him, breaking free of him forcibly, falling momentarily in the surf. He did not try to help her up, but just watched as she struggled to her feet, her dark hair wet, her breasts dripping sea water. "Don't, Steve!"

Cahill had seldom been so frustrated, and the frustration quickly turned to anger. Breathlessly, he replied to her, "I don't get it! Are you going fancy on me, for Christ's sake? Didn't you come down here hoping we'd get together again? Or were you just looking for it from anybody that came along?"

Dulcie stood there staring hard at him suddenly. "Is that what you think about me?"

"I just don't understand the sudden virgin act," he said, still angry. "I mean, it's a little late, isn't it, for God's sake? After Tony Falco and all the others?"

Dulcie was stunned. She turned and stumbled out of the surf and up onto the soft sand, grabbing at her clothing and pulling it on. Cahill came up behind her and, without speaking, also began putting his things on. When she saw him there, she took her dress and began walking down the beach with it and her sandals, dressed just in panties and a half slip. Cahill drew his trousers on and headed after her.

"Dulcie! Wait!"

He caught her, and turned her to him. She glared at him.

"Look, I shouldn't have said that. I don't know what the hell got into me."

"Please leave me alone," she said gratingly. "I can find my way back by myself."

"No, it's too far."

"Just leave me alone!"

"I won't touch you, or even speak to you. Just let me drive you back into town."

Dulcie stood there trying not to cry. She pulled her dress on, and it hung crookedly on her. "There's a taxi stand not far from here. I'll be all right." She turned and began heading toward the street, up a small hill.

Cahill looked after her, still very disturbed. "Okay, goddam it! Okay!"

A moment later, she was out of sight.

Cahill hoped he would find Dulcie at the yacht club when he got back there, but she had gone on home. He tried to reach her by phone, but got no answer. Boyd Lucas had gone home, too, but Del Rio was still there, talking to a local Miami girl. Cahill sat at the bar by himself and had just ordered a brandy when Rachel McKenzie came up beside him.

"Well. I thought I had missed you this evening," her low, sexy voice came to him.

Cahill turned and saw her standing at his elbow. Her black hair was a dark frame around her moonlight-pale face, and she looked strikingly attractive. The dark Paris gown she wore clung to her small breasts and slim hips, making her look very feminine.

"Hi, Rachel. I decided to come back for a nightcap."

"I heard about your decision to race. I'm very excited about it."

Cahill smiled at her, and relaxed some inside. His trouble with young, seemingly volatile Dulcie settled into perspective with this rich, desirable woman openly flirting with him.

"I'll try to give you a good race," he told her.

"I'd like to hear about your strategy plans sometime," she smiled languidly. "When you can find the time."

"How about now?" Cahill said easily.

Rachel's dark eyebrows rose upward prettily. Everything she did, every pose she struck, was nice to look at. "Your place or mine?" she joked.

"Well, since you have a husband at home waiting for you, maybe it ought to be mine," he said deliberately.

Rachel lowered dark lashes for just a moment, then smiled. "I suppose you have transportation," she said.

It was just a short ride to Cahill's place. Cahill knew that Lucas was going to stop at a hotel to say hello to another throttleman before going back to Cahill's condo, so Cahill figured on beating him back, and he did. When he and Rachel got there, he thumb-tacked a note to Lucas and Del Rio on the outside door, to give him privacy until midnight. That would give him two hours with Rachel.

They had a drink when they first arrived, and Rachel asked Cahill some questions about the Miami race and how he intended to run it. They sat on the living room sofa and did not touch. It was all very genteel. Finally, though, Rachel put her glass down and turned to Cahill with a sultry look.

"Well, I can't stay out all night. And I don't think you brought me here to just talk racing. Did you?"

"No," Cahill said quietly. "I didn't." He was still aroused by Dulcie, even now. It thrust through what Rachel was doing to him, like a passion flower through thick, lush foliage.

Cahill pulled Rachel to him and kissed her, and suddenly she was a different woman. Her mouth hungrily explored his, her long fingers holding his face close to hers, her lips hot to the touch. Her body molded itself to him sinuously, and one of the insistent hands went to his trousers and caressed a growing bulge there.

"God!" he said, when she pulled away from him. He had never encountered such raw and open hunger in a woman.

"Rape me!" she said huskily to him, her nails raking along his arm and making the shallow scratches there. "Tear my clothes off, and force me open and violate me!"

Cahill took her into his bedroom and undressed her in

a frantic few moments. She had him in hand before he could get his trousers off. Then, when they were both unclothed and on the bed, there was a desperate, violent grabbing and straining and clawing, with Rachel tearing at his muscled flesh with her hands, raking him and pulling him to her. Their union was hot and brutal, and then, as climax neared, she cried out her passion into the darkness of the room.

"Oh, God! Oh, God!"

Then there was a frenzy of thrusting and reaching and agonizing cries from the depths of Rachel's throat that ripped through the room, with Cahill mauling her in one last surge of raw release.

"Oh, Jesus!" She lay there entwined with him, still richly full of him, feeling the throbbing hot inside her. "I knew—you'd be like this. I knew it would be—primitively exquisite."

It was a few minutes later that he lay beside her, disunited, trying to get his breath back. It seemed paradoxical that so elegant a woman, so cultured a female, should have been so uninhibited, so uncontrolled in bed. No woman he had ever been with had demanded so much of him, had urged him to such complete and willful ravaging. It seemed slightly masochistic to him, and he still felt a certain embarrassment about having been a part of it, for her and for him.

He looked over at her. "Are you all right? Did I—hurt you?"

"You were beautiful."

"I think I hurt you."

"Yes, you did. And you satisfied me. It all goes together, lover. Didn't you know that?"

"I think you're too complex for me, Rachel."

She smiled, and reached over and placed a very gentle, very soft kiss on his lips.

"Nonsense," she said. "You and I work very well together. We both have something inside us crying for release. Something dark and mysterious and maybe a little dangerous. I could glimpse it in your eyes the first time I saw you."

Cahill cast a narrow look toward her. "I don't know what the hell you're talking about," he said.

She smiled a wry smile. "All right, lover. If that's the way you want it."

But later, after Rachel was gone and Cahill was trying to find sleep alone in that bed, he lay awake mulling what she had said to him.

It was surprising how far down inside him she had been able to look.

It was further than he himself wanted to see.

Chapter Ten

Cahill was healing fast. His ribs no longer hurt when he moved, and he was walking well without his cane, with just a slight limp. Del Rio's therapy with the leg helped. Cahill might have some discomfort in the race, with the pounding he would take, but he could run it.

Tony Falco and Gus Beckering were sorry to hear that Cahill had changed his mind about the Miami-Bimini race. With almost anyone else driving the *Sonic Boom*, Falco figured he had the race won. And if he won at Miami, that was the season. The championship was his. The driver's and sponsor's trophies would for all practical purposes be reposing on his and Beckering's shelves. But if Cahill managed to win at Miami, he was right back in contention for the national title. Falco would still be ahead, 1725 points to 1664 for Cahill. But with the point system giving four hundred to a race winner and three hundred to second, Falco would then have to beat Cahill at Key West to retain his title. He did not want to be put in that position.

Dulcie was still angry and frustrated by the way Cahill had treated her on their reunion, but she was also having doubts about her reaction. Maybe, she thought, she had given him no reason to believe he should treat her any way other than he had. Maybe somehow it had been her fault, by giving Cahill a wrong impression about herself. But even if that was true, she figured it was up to Cahill to call her and apologize more seriously for the things he had said to her.

Cahill, though, was so distracted momentarily by Rachel McKenzie and by the impending race that he did not try to go to Dulcie, even though he felt bad about the way they had parted. With Rachel lavishing attention on him, and the press running after him to ask him about the race, he did not feel the need to go to Dulcie, nor the obligation. Also, he was beginning to have occasional flashbacks about the war again, with the race only a few days off, and he had begun to worry about his safety, and that of Lucas and Del Rio.

Rachel was like a child with a new toy. She insisted on driving Cahill around in her Lamborghetti, taking him out on her yacht, treating him to fancy meals at the finest restaurants. She even watched him and Lucas work on the *Sonic Boom* at the marina, getting in the way, asking them if they wanted coffee. But there was no fawning on the part of Rachel, no hero-worship. She was just having a new kind of fun, and Cahill was the playmate she needed to make it work.

There were a couple of more intimacies between them, as the race day drew near, and they were just as wild as on that first occasion. Rachel did absolutely nothing halfway. She maneuvered him into lovemaking on the deck of the yacht, within binocular range of two other boats, and the next evening she stripped down beside their car while it was parked in a dark corner at the marina, and seduced him in a rubber life raft sitting nearby. She never spoke of her husband; it was as if he did not exist. But it bothered Cahill that he was back there at their home somewhere, deserving fidelity, no matter what had happened between him and Rachel.

It was only two nights before the race that Rachel asked Cahill to take her to the yacht club with him, where they might talk boats and racing with other drivers and owners. Del Rio and Boyd Lucas had already arrived when Cahill and Rachel got there, and the bar was crowded with other racing people. Del Rio and Lucas spoke to them when they came in, but made no efforts to join them. They figured that Rachel preferred to keep Cahill to herself for the evening. Also, Lucas did not really like Rachel, or the fact that she was a married woman, and had let Cahill know his feelings.

"This is nice," Rachel told Cahill after a couple of drinks. "Don't forget, you said you'd introduce me to some drivers and owners. What about that other fellow, the national champion? Falco, isn't that his name? Is he here?"

"I haven't seen Falco here this evening," Cahill told her, giving her a curious look. "But you'll get to meet some other drivers. I'll wave them down as they go past."

"I'm really geared up for this race, Steve," Rachel admitted. She looked very sultry that evening, in a low-cut dress and high heels. Most of the men in the place had given her at least a second look. "I want you to win it."

Cahill cast an impassive look toward her. She had taken up a lot more of his time than he would have liked. But she was making life exciting for him. "I think what you'd like is to win it yourself, Rachel," he guessed.

"That would be fun, too." She smiled like a cover girl.

"You ought to get your husband to buy you a Class One boat and a driver."

She frowned briefly at the mention of Mac McKenzie, and at the way he had put his suggestion. "I already have a driver," she said, ignoring the jibe. "One I can root for, I mean."

Cahill grunted in his throat. "Don't expect too much. If it's winning you want, maybe you ought to get acquainted with Tony Falco. He's already a champion."

The crowd eddied around them. A driver came past, and Cahill called him over and introduced him to Rachel, and Rachel asked him some questions about his boat and his record. The fellow was a rather handsome Cuban-American. Rachel flirted with him as she spoke, and Cahill resented it. Just as the driver left them, Cahill looked up and saw Dulcie come into the place with Mary Ann and her new friend Ramos. When Cahill saw Dulcie, he felt a surprising jolt inside him, a lot of emotions suddenly surging through him. It made him angry, because he did not want to think she did anything to him on a deep level. But when he saw that lithe figure —fuller than Rachel's and more youthful—and the big, dark eyes, he could not help himself. Mary Ann and Ramos came right past Cahill's table, with Dulcie right behind them, and none of them saw Cahill until they were right beside him. Mary Ann spotted him first and greeted him buoyantly.

"Steve! We didn't expect to see you here!" Actually, Mary Ann had hoped that Dulcie would see him there that evening and that they would make up. Now she noticed Rachel for the first time. "Oh," she added.

Cahill rose from his chair, and his gaze caught Dulcie's. She held it for a moment, then glanced soberly toward Rachel.

"Nice to see you Mary Ann, Ramos," Cahill told them. "Dulcie."

Dulcie nodded, while Cahill clapped Ramos on the shoulder. "Phil Ramos is an owner, Rachel," Cahill said. "Ramos, girls, this is Rachel McKenzie."

Rachel was looking the two girls over with open contempt.

"Pleased to meet you, Rachel," Ramos said.

"The pleasure is mine," Rachel said in a sultry voice.

Mary Ann gave her a look. "We're old friends of Steve," she said rather forcefully. "Especially Dulcie here." Rachel met Dulcie's gaze and fixed on it. "We go clear back to Freeport, don't we, Steve?"

"That's right, Mary Ann," Cahill agreed, a little embarrassed by her proprietary interest. "Look, why don't you join us for a drink? Rachel has been wanting

136

to talk to an owner."

Rachel glanced toward Dulcie, then caught Cahill's eye.

"Don't mind if we do," Ramos replied.

They drew a couple of chairs up, and the threesome sat down with Rachel and Cahill. Dulcie had hoped they would get past without this sort of thing, but she did not want to appear rude by declining after Ramos had accepted for them. She ended up next to Rachel, and as Rachel asked Ramos questions about his boat, with Mary Ann giving Rachel acid looks, Dulcie could feel Cahill's eyes on her from time to time. Cahill was looking at Dulcie side by side with Rachel, and seeing the more sophisticated, elegant look of Rachel against the soft, youthfully stunning beauty of Dulcie. Cahill was surprised to see that Dulcie looked so innocent in comparison. There was an openness in her face that had long since gone from Rachel's, if it had ever been there.

"That one had Aeromarine engines, though, that were outdated at the time," Ramos was telling them. "You can't race in Class One without the very best equipment. Isn't that right, Steve?"

Cahill nodded. "I can't deny that."

"That's all just fascinating," Rachel purred.

"Engines and technical talk don't interest me," Mary Ann said bluntly. "I just like to watch them on the water, floating like birds out there."

Rachel smiled. "Isn't that sweet?" she said. She turned to Dulcie. "I guess you and Mary Ann go to all the races?"

Dulcie eyed her soberly. She was wearing her dark brown hair up behind her head, with ringlets beside her face, making her look particularly young and feminine. "I've been to one race," she said to Rachel. "In New York. That's where we met Steve."

"Oh, I thought girls like you followed the races all through the season," Rachel said nicely.

Dulcie colored slightly, and Cahill cleared his throat.

But Mary Ann replied first. "Girls like us? Jesus, what's that supposed to mean?"

Rachel just smiled, but Ramos came to her aid. "I think Miss McKenzie just meant girls who are acquainted with the drivers," he said quickly.

Rachel still said nothing. Cahill gave her a dark look.

"We're not exactly camp followers," Mary Ann said belligerently. "We just happen to like the races, that's all."

"Well, of course I didn't mean to suggest anything of the sort," Rachel protested, finally, but weakly. "Anyway, I'd be the very last to condemn a girl for following the circuit and taking her fun where she can find it."

Dulcie now turned and caught Rachel's gaze with a cold one. "I'll bet," she said deliberately.

Rachel stared narrowly at her, looking her over, wondering what there was between her and Cahill. "I mean," she went on, in a harder voice, "there are girls who make their very living this way, but I'm sure that neither of you sweet young things would even consider such a vocation."

Cahill sighed heavily. "Rachel. These are my friends."

But Dulcie was already rising from her chair, breathing shallowly. "I don't think we should use that term too broadly," she said, glaring at Cahill. "I happen to choose my friends very carefully. If you'll excuse me, I think I'll do my drinking at the bar."

Cahill rose quickly, and Ramos did, too.

"Oh, please stay!" Ramos said. "Miss McKenzie was just kidding around. Right, Miss McKenzie?"

"Did I say something wrong?" Rachel said, raising her dark eyebrows high.

Dulcie turned and left them without further comment, with them all looking after her. Mary Ann now rose, too, glowering at Rachel. "I think we'll join Dulcie at the bar. Okay, Phil?"

Ramos shrugged. "Sure, either way." He wore a

pained smile of embarrassment.

"It was nice of you to share your knowledge of boats with me, Phil," Rachel said. "Stop past the Lauderdale Yacht Club some day, and I'll let you tell me what's marketable about my boat. I want to get a value on it for tax purposes."

Mary Ann frowned toward Rachel so fiercely that Cahill could not help sighing inside at her frustration. "Why, I'll keep that in mind, Miss McKenzie," Ramos said, glancing toward Cahill for his reaction.

"Jesus!" Mary Ann grumbled as she turned and left.

When they were gone, and Cahill had taken his seat, he narrowed his eyes on the smiling Rachel. "What the hell were you doing there? Is that the way you get your kicks, Rachel?"

She held the smile. "You know how I get my kicks, lover boy. This was just low-grade entertainment."

"There was no need insulting them. I wouldn't have asked them over."

"You've made it with the little brunette, haven't you?" Rachel asked him with a slow smile. "I could see it in her face. She's got the heat for you."

Cahill scowled. He wished he could defend Dulcie, but he did not know how. "It's not like you think with her. She's not at all like Mary Ann."

"When did you make that decision? Before or after you'd laid her?" Rachel wondered.

Cahill glanced toward the bar where the three others sat. There was soft, sensual music being piped in overhead and a heavy odor of liquor in the place, with its nautical decor and paneled walls. "Come on, Rachel. Let's go somewhere else. I think it's suddenly a little crowded in here."

Rachel frowned. "You were going to introduce me to some more people. Racing drivers."

"Some other time," Cahill told her evenly.

She hesitated, then broke into a sexy smile. "Okay, Stevie. What do you want to do, take me out in back and feel me?'' She reached under the table and put her hand on his groin. "You're such an impetuous little boy!''

Cahill removed the hand, and rose from his chair. "No, not tonight, Rachel. I'm taking you home.''

Rachel rose, too. "The hell you are! The evening isn't over, by a whole lot.''

"I'm going back,'' Cahill said. "I've got to get some rest if I'm going to race.''

"Ah. Little Stevie has to get his rest, like a good boy. Well, maybe I can change your mind. In the car.'' She ran her narrow tongue lightly over her rouged lips, and smiled.

Cahill took her by the arm. "Maybe,'' he said.

On the way out, Dulcie turned and saw them go, but looked quickly away when Cahill caught her eye. Cahill thought she looked very pretty, sitting there sipping a drink.

As it turned out, Rachel's persuasive powers were sufficient with Cahill. As they drove toward her seaside home at Fort Lauderdale, where Cahill would let her out at a parking lot for her Lamborghetti, Rachel seduced him with her mouth as they roared along A-1-A, and Cahill was obliged to pull over at a seaside park and take her brutally on a narrow strip of sand at the roadside, with only Cahill's sports car giving them privacy.

He did not arrive back at his place until two A.M., long after Lucas and Del Rio had gone to bed.

It was the next day, the day before the race, that Tony Falco decided to make up with Eva. She had let him sleep with her after that night of their argument, but would have nothing to do with him otherwise. Falco, finally seeing he had pushed Eva too far, and not wanting her to leave him—her money and his driving were the only things that stood between him and poverty—

140

found Eva at their hotel suite that afternoon, on coming back from a business meeting with Beckering, Kralich and Wyatt, and showed a different face to her.

"Hey, look, baby," he said to her when he found her lying on a long white sofa in her underclothes that afternoon. "Let's cut out this bickering, what do you say?" He sat down on the sofa beside her and put a hand on her thigh.

Eva had been reading a magazine and now let it drop to the floor. Her short blonde hair was tousled and gave her a young look. Sun from sliding doors came in across her and made her tanned flesh look golden. She regarded Falco seriously. "This isn't bickering, Tony. Having a difference about a mother-in-law is bickering. This is well beyond that."

Falco sighed. "Listen. I get drunk once in a while, because of the pressures on me. That damned Gus is a bastard about this trophy this year. When I've got too much booze in me, Eva, I'm not myself, you know that. These girls are always around during race season. I don't mean to get involved with them, honest to God. I'm sorry about that little snatch from New York. It won't happen again. I'll keep my goddam nose to the grindstone, I promise."

"If I could believe that, Tony, I could forgive you. But I've heard that all before."

Falco was in a short-sleeved shirt, and it was open down the front, showing a tanned, hairy chest. He had unbuttoned it before he came over to her, for a purpose. Now he pushed the hand up her thigh to the soft place under the sheer panties and moved it there. "I'm telling you, honey. I'm going to be a goddam monk. There was nevery anybody but you, anyway—you know that. You still turn me on just like you used to. Christ, I had a stiff-on dream the other night, and guess who I was playing with. You, baby, if you can believe it. Who has one of those I-wish-I-had-you-in-bed things about his own wife, huh?"

Falco's hand was carefully massaging Eva now. "Did you really, Tony?" she said, unbelieving. "Did you dream about me?"

"I swear to God. Now, doesn't that show you who's really the apple of my goddam eye?"

Falco leaned down and kissed her, and she let it happen. He was pulling the cloth at her hips down, and she wriggled out of it. He kissed her breasts at the edge of her tiny bra and then moved down to her rib cage and stomach. He knelt on the floor beside her, and now gave her special attention.

"You'll always be the one, Eva, baby." In a low growl. A kiss down beyond the navel, with Eva catching her breath slightly. Another on the high inner thigh, as she raised one leg.

"You haven't been so—nice to me in a—long time, Tony."

He looked up at her. "Things are going to be different, baby."

He pulled her right leg toward him and then caressed a thigh with his mouth, moving up beside the warm place where her legs met.

"Oh, God," she murmured, closing her eyes.

Falco began making serious love to her.

"Oh—Jesus!"

She would give him one more chance.

It was later that same afternoon that Paige Lucas showed up in Miami. The *Sonic Boom*'s crew was getting ready to leave for the marina after a couple of hours at Cahill's condo apartment, when Lucas's sister arrived at Cahill's door. Cahill answered her knock and was surprised to see her there.

"Paige! What in the devil are you doing here?"

Paige, looking a little prettier than usual in a modified Hamill hairstyle, smiled wearily. "Hi, Steve. I had to see Boyd. Is he here?"

"Sure, come on in, Paige. It's a real pleasure to see you here." As she came in, he turned and called into another room. "Boyd! It's Paige!"

Lucas came in from a bedroom, looking brawny in a body shirt. He narrowed his eyes on Paige, not believing she could be there at Cahill's place. He had just written her a letter, saying they were all set for the race the following day. Danny Del Rio came out into the living room behind him, drying his dark hair with a towel.

"Paige, my God!" Lucas said. He came over and kissed her, and she smiled tiredly again.

"Hi, Boyd. Danny."

"Good to see you, Paige," Del Rio grinned, quickly combing his hair into place. Whereas Lucas was a bit taller than Cahill, Del Rio was shorter, with a stocky frame and hairy arms that now stuck out from the sleeves of a T-shirt that had a message printed on its front: *Disregard Previous T-Shirt*.

"You never came to a race," Lucas was saying. "Did you finally decide to watch your brother ride the open sea tomorrow?"

Paige looked from Lucas to Cahill, and Del Rio, then back to her brother. "I came to talk to you about the race, Boyd."

They all stared soberly at her. Her face was pallid, and waxed-looking. She looked very serious suddenly, and they all wondered why.

Lucas shrugged. "Sure, why not?" he said. "Come on and sit down, Paige. Did you fly down?"

She nodded. "You know how I hate flying, Boyd. But I wanted to get here this afternoon." She let Lucas guide her to a long sofa not far from the sliding glass doors that overlooked the ocean. She sat down there, heavily.

"Well, why don't we give Paige and Lucas some privacy, Danny?" Cahill said.

"Oh, no, I'd prefer you stay," Paige said. She looked very businesslike in her rimless glasses and seersucker suit over a plain cotton blouse. Her face told them that she meant what she said, so Cahill and Del Rio pulled up chairs. Lucas had joined her on the sofa.

"Is something troubling you, Paige?" Lucas wondered.

She sat staring past them for a moment, as if in a yoga trance. Finally, when she spoke, her voice had changed, and she did not sound like herself. "I don't want you to race tomorrow, Boyd," she said in the throaty voice.

"What?" Lucas said incredulously.

Del Rio and Cahill exchanged looks.

"I don't want any of you to race tomorrow," she added, looking at Cahill.

Cahill frowned, and Lucas touched his sister's arm. "What is it, Paige?"

She looked down, remembering. "I've had bad feelings about the races ever since that fellow died out in California recently. You remember who I'm talking about."

Lucas made a face. "Paige, we've been all through that."

"Wait, it's more than that," she said urgently. "For three nights in a row, I've had a dream. A dream about the races. About this race."

Del Rio raised his dark eyebrows slightly. "Don't let it bother you, Paige. I do the same thing, all the time."

Cahill sat there and studied her distraught face. He remembered his own recurring nightmares before the races.

Paige was holding Del Rio's gaze somberly. "It's more than dreaming about the race. For three nights in a row, I've dreamed that someone will die in the Miami race."

A silence fell over the room like a night fog, and it seemed to expand the small distance between all of them. Cahill felt a stricture inside him.

"These things happen," Lucas was telling her. "I've had that kind of thing myself. If you have fear inside you, it makes you dream, and sometimes the dreams aren't very pleasant. But they're not real life."

Paige eyed him. "I told you before Freeport. I had bad vibes then. And you crashed. Now it's worse than before, inside me. And more specific. In the first dream, I saw Steve driving, and he seemed to be in trouble."

Cahill's stricture inside him tightened. *I think there's a good chance you're going to kill yourself.* Ed Harris's face staring earnestly into his.

But Cahill was more concerned about Lucas and Del Rio.

"In the second dream," Paige went on, "a boat is out of control, and there is a lot of yelling and panic."

Lucas interrupted her. "Paige, don't do this. These things don't mean anything." But he recalled that she had always had a knack at sensing danger before anybody else.

"In last night's dream," Paige continued, ignoring him, "I saw a man in the water, maybe more than one man. And the smell of death hovered over the sea. Just before I woke, I saw your face, Boyd." There were tears in her eyes now. She removed the glasses, and held a small handkerchief to her nose. "I'm afraid that the man in the water is you, that you'll drown tomorrow, or be fatally injured somehow."

Lucas put his arm around her and drew her to him. Cahill got a glimpse inside his head of Josh Owens, blood on his pallid face. Del Rio blew out his cheeks and clasped his hands before him. "These dreams. They never come out like that in real life," he said quietly.

Paige looked at Cahill again. "You feel things; you have visions."

Cahill shook his head. "Mine are from the past, Paige. Not from the future."

"How do you feel about the race tomorrow?" she asked him, studying his handsome face.

Cahill cast a pensive look toward her. "About the same as always, Paige. Things happen to me out there, things I have to keep under control. So far, it's not getting any better. I keep hoping it will be."

"Then you're worried, too."

He hesitated. "Yes."

Paige turned to Lucas. "There, you see?"

Lucas sighed heavily. "Paige, I told you before. I can't live my life by dreams and feelings. Charlie Rossman couldn't get another throttleman now. Anyway, if Steve did have trouble again, I'd want to be there."

Del Rio nodded. "Me, too, Paige."

Suddenly Cahill wished he had never changed his mind about the race. He wished he had let Rossman find someone else to drive, so the responsibility would not be on his shoulders. He regarded Paige soberly.

"We're committed now, Paige. That's the way it is. But I promise you. I'll bring Boyd back safe from Bimini."

Paige's eyes were dry now, but her face was still sober and pallid. "Do you, Steve? Do you promise?"

Cahill nodded, his insides feeling like a vise had been screwed down on them. "You have my word," he said quietly.

Chapter Eleven

Paige Lucas did not try again to dissuade her brother from racing at Miami, but she could not be dredged up out of her deep pit of fear. She was put in the second bedroom for the night. Lucas slept on the sofa, and Del Rio moved in with Cahill temporarily.

That evening, Lucas stayed at the condominium to be near his sister, while Cahill and Del Rio went out for a couple of hours to relax. They avoided the yacht club bar at the marina, because they did not want to socialize. Rachel had called Cahill earlier, wanting to see him for a couple of drinks, but he told her he had business that evening. She had not liked the rebuff and had hung up with a petulance that Cahill would have expected only from a much younger woman.

Cahill and Del Rio went to a small, out-of-the-way bar on Collins Avenue, ordered scotch, and talked about race strategy. Tony Falco was allegedly going to race flat out to beat Cahill and tie a ribbon around the national championship trophy, and Del Rio was trying to guess at how to respond to that threat.

"You can't plan too much in advance," Cahill told him. "You have to let the race develop, and adjust as you go."

On the way back to Cahill's place, Del Rio noticed that Cahill seemed more tense than he had before the drinks. He had lapsed into silence, letting Del Rio do most of the talking as they drove along the ocean road in the darkness.

"You don't know what this means to me, Steve," Del

Rio told him. "Being in this race tomorrow with you, with a chance at the title. It's a lifelong dream with me."

Cahill, behind the wheel of his Jaguar, glanced at Del Rio.

"When I'm out there on the water, there isn't anything else," Del Rio went on. "Just the sky and the sea and the roar of the engines. It's like nothing else exists, like that's all there is. It's like the rest of it is just waiting. You know what I mean?"

Cahill nodded. "Sure, Danny."

"It's just as if beating those other boats is the whole thing, balled up into one pure, crystalline experience. It's work and love and—life."

Cahill said nothing.

"It was a little the same in the war. Only in a negative way." Del Rio glanced at Cahill. "I suppose it was like that with you, too."

Cahill grunted. "I guess."

"Losing Josh Owens and all," Del Rio said. He hesitated, not knowing whether to proceed.

Cahill felt the constriction inside him. "That was the worst of it," he said to himself. Green jungle flashed before him, and slashes of sunlight breaking through it. Josh's head in his hands and a hole in the back of it. Blood everywhere.

"You said something the other day about Josh getting it on a river bank. Just before the Hueys sat down there."

Cahill turned to him, distractedly. He was gripping the wheel hard. Up ahead loomed the condominium complex where he lived. He pulled into a driveway and then into a parking spot. He turned the engine off and sat staring through the windshield at a dark hedge between the parking lot and the building.

"I don't know how he got it," Cahill finally replied. "I can't remember. It's all a mess inside my head. I was wounded, and not with it. But I remember holding

Josh's head in my hands, there at the edge of the water.'' He wrinkled his nose. "And there was a smell. Of burning flesh.''

"I wondered about that, the other day," Del Rio said. "When you were talking about it at your place. I had heard a story about your rescue, and it was different from what you recall.''

Cahill turned slowly to him, grains of glistening perspiration beading up on his face. "You heard about us?''

"That's right. There was something about a boat.'' Cahill felt a lurching inside him. "I heard that Josh got it on a boat, a river launch. But you don't remember anything like that.''

Something grabbed hard at Cahill's insides and he cried out softly, and bent forward onto the wheel. He lay bent there, gasping out in sudden pain.

"What the hell, Steve! Are you okay?''

Cahill nodded, breathing hard. "I think so.''

"Jesus!" Del Rio said.

"There wasn't any—goddam boat," Cahill grated out.

Del Rio stared at his friend's face, and was very concerned about him. "Hell, it's whatever you say, Steve. You know how stories got fouled up in Nam.''

There was never any boat!''

A tension had sprung between them like a jungle animal, pressing against them in the closeness of the car. Del Rio watched Cahill slowly get control of himself. Slowly, very slowly, the tension eased.

"He died on the river bank," Cahill said more quietly. "He must have been shot on the river bank. There were Cong all around. I seem to recall going to get a flak jacket for Josh. From another soldier who was dead.'' Cahill got a split-second image of the dead soldier, and his uniform was different somehow. He definitely was not a Marine. "When I got back, Josh had been shot. Yes, I remember that much.''

Del Rio sat there. "It sounds like a tough time, Steve."

Cahill felt better. "Hell, let's forget it. Come on, Danny, we need some sleep tonight."

Cahill climbed out of the Porsche, and Del Rio followed. On the way into the building, they were both silent.

Del Rio figured they had said all that could be said about it. And maybe more than should have been.

The next day was windy and overcast. No rain was expected, but the seas were predicted at five to six feet.

That was bad luck.

There was a hurried meeting of the race committee and drivers, with some owners sitting in, and it was proposed by one owner that the race should be postponed. But that idea was heavily voted down. Too many arrangements had been made, too many owners were there from long distances expecting to race their boats. The Coast Guard was contacted, and they made no objection to the race proceeding. Small craft warnings were up, but conditions were not so bad as to be suicidal for a race. It was up to the committee, and the committee finally voted for the races to proceed, including the lesser class races.

At nine A.M. all the crews were down at the marina getting their boats into the water, and crowds were gathering on the docks. Rachel was there for a while, then disappeared inside the yacht club for a cup of coffee. She had come down without any breakfast. Cahill noted that she paid as much attention to Tony Falco and a couple of other drivers as she did to him, and that nettled him some. He looked around for Dulcie but did not find her.

Boyd Lucas seemed stoically grim to Cahill as they got the *Sonic Boom* into the water and ready to race. Del Rio kept saying the weather would not hurt them. It was the same for all the racers, he said, and he smiled a lot. Nobody mentioned Paige, who was huddling in her room at Cahill's place, hoping her worries were groundless, but not believing so.

Falco's throttleman Kralich came past the *Sonic Boom* at just after nine and told Cahill that after today's race, Cahill would be out of the running for the trophy. Lanky, stringy-haired Wyatt, Falco's navigator, was with him but kept his silence. Tony Falco came alone with Eva and did not speak to any of them. He was very tight about the weather. A few minutes later, Cahill saw Gus Beckering at the site where the *First Blood* was being put into the water, and he was discussing heatedly with Falco about something and glancing toward the *Sonic Boom* from time to time as he spoke.

By nine-thirty the marina was buzzing with activity. Most boats were in the water, and all the committee people, local officials, and press were there. Charlie Rossman arrived at about that time and found Cahill alone momentarily at the boat. Lucas and Del Rio had gone to speak with an official about the course markings on the way out to Bimini. Rossman was ebullient, despite the windy weather.

"I feel good about it, Steve. I think we're ready."

Cahill was leaning on a piling near the *Sonic Boom*. "We're as ready as we're going to get. The engines are running great, Charlie. We ought to get the most out of them."

Rossman narrowed his lined eyes on Cahill, his graying hair moving in a sea breeze. "Will we get the most out of you, Steve? Are you feeling up to it?"

Cahill regarded Rossman seriously. "I'm physically okay, Charlie. That's all I can tell you."

Rossman nodded. "Okay. I still think we're ready. Now, remember: This is a long course. If you get into any trouble, you've got some time to make it up, unless you're in the last stretch. Play it boldly but safely,

Steve. A trophy is only a trophy."

Cahill grinned. "Tell that to Gus Beckering."

Boyd Lucas came up then, and a race official was with him. "Hi, Charlie. Some morning, huh?"

"Hi, Boyd. Where's Danny?"

"He's on his way down here."

The race official had a notebook with him and was staring toward the *Sonic Boom*. He was a slim, rather young fellow with balding hair and a hawk nose. "This is what you call a Rossman Special, Mr. Rossman?"

Rossman nodded. "That's right."

"Did you find any faults in her, after her accident at Freeport?"

Rossman shook his head. "No, can't say that I did."

"The Freeport thing was my fault," Cahill told the fellow. "It had nothing to do with the boat."

"It was just bad luck," Lucas quickly put in.

The slim fellow held Cahill's gaze. "You ever raced in high seas before, Mr. Cahill?"

Cahill shrugged. "At New Orleans we had some crests out there."

"The last time we had wind for a race," the official told them, "there were three accidents. Two boats stuffed and one spun out. I've never seen anything like it. We sent five men to the hospital, and a sixth almost drowned."

Rossman scowled at the fellow. "What's the point, Mr.—?"

"Jones," the fellow put in. "The point is, we're telling all the drivers to respect the sea today. We're not out here to provide blood for the spectators."

The wind came off the ocean and whipped around them momentarily as a silence hung over them heavily.

It was Rossman who spoke first. "We're going to try to avoid offering them any of ours, Mr. Jones," he said sourly.

Jones nodded and grinned. "Good luck to you."

Jones walked on down the dock then, and Lucas eyed

Cahill to see what effect Jones's words had had on him. But Cahill's face was impassive. Del Rio came bouncing down the dock just at that moment. "Let's get on the water! They're lining up out there!"

Just moments later, with Rossman returning to the officials' table down near the grandstand, Cahill and his crew took the *Sonic Boom* out.

Cahill had never seen such a large crowd as had gathered at dockside to see the Class One race begin. The sleek boats lined up behind the pace boat as usual, with the crowds cheering behind the noise of the engines, and before Cahill was really ready for it to happen, the green flag started the race.

In a tremendous roar, the boats lurched through the Bay Harbor waters, out through the Bakers Haulover Cut, and into the open sea.

As soon as the front-runners were out in open water, the sea began slamming against their hulls. The crests were four feet near shore and higher as they sped outward toward Bimini. The race would be the longest of the season, and all the crews understood that it would now be the toughest and, probably, the most dangerous.

Cahill was wearing his safety belt harness this time out, and Boyd Lucas was greatly relieved. As the *Sonic Boom* forged ahead of the field, Lucas lost his fear and looked forward to beating Tony Falco to the finish. Danny Del Rio was high, exuberant. A lifetime dream was being fulfilled, win or lose. At the five-mile mark there were only three boats in contention for the lead: the *First Blood,* the *Sonic Boom,* and one called the *Crazy Cuban.* Falco was out ahead by a hundred yards or so, Cahill was running somewhere in between those two.

Cahill remained calm in those opening miles, giving curt orders through the intercom to Del Rio and Lucas, doing a good job of captaining the boat.

"Throttle steady, Boyd!"
"Oil pressure readout!"

"Distance to first marker!"

Lucas held the speed steady at just under full throttle, laying back on high seas, throttling up slightly on flatter water, trying not to stuff the boat into a brick-wall wave. Del Rio read off compass headings crisply, keeping Cahill advised of speed, distance covered, course corrections. He talked a lot more than Harris had, and his excited voice was pleasant to Lucas's ears. They needed Del Rio's exuberance. Cahill saw the second-place boat directly ahead of them as they reached the second marker, and the *First Blood* had gotten out in front now by a quarter-mile.

"Falco is driving like a maniac today," Lucas said loudly. *"Beckering must have put the fear of God into him."*

"We're not keeping up," Del Rio said. *"We're letting the* Crazy Cuban *pace us."*

"I'm going around it," Cahill said firmly. *"Give me some more throttle, Boyd!"*

Lucas glanced toward Cahill. Waves were smashing over the bow, and all of them were soaked in their orange suits and helmets. Face masks were wet-dripping, as were the controls of the boat. Water sloshed in the bolster. The bolster deck under their feet kept slamming upwards at them, pounding their feet, their legs, their bodies. Five-foot waves banged into the bow, and the boat rose through them, sometimes skimming, sometimes hitting them hard. Safety belts dug into flesh, muscles corded. Cahill's gloved hands gripped the wheel like steel vises, white-knuckled under the leather.

Lucas throttled ahead, and Cahill swung the *Sonic Boom* into a wide arcing turn, eating the second place boat's frothy wake for a long moment, and then pulling up alongside it. Cahill saw the three helmeted figures hunching over their controls, and they looked rather desperate to him. He guided the bucking *Sonic Boom* past them at almost full throttle and roared up into second place.

"Now we'll go after Falco!" Del Rio was saying loudly. *"Let's catch that sonofabitch!"*

At the wheel, Cahill felt just a slight unease inside him, as he pushed the boat ahead through the rough sea.

Onboard the *First Blood*, Falco turned and saw the *Sonic Boom* take second place, and his handsome face darkened under the face mask. *"Christ, he's gaining now! Come on Kralich, goddam it! Give me some speed! We've got to hold this lead!"*

Kralich, looking big and bulky at the controls, glared toward Falco. He did not like criticism. *"This frigging tub is almost flat-out now, on six-foot seas! You want to stuff it?"*

"I want to beat Cahill. I don't care how!" Falco said loudly. *"Run this thing wide open if you have to!"*

Lanky Hank Wyatt, tense at the controls, eyed Falco sideways. Beckering had gotten to him, all right. The boat jumped and bucked under them, and Wyatt could feel the beating in his feet, legs and back. A big wave came and they jammed into it, and Wyatt went forward toward the windshield, thrusting against his harness, jerked and slammed around. He hoped Falco's anxiety about Cahill did not cause them to stuff the *First Blood*, as Kralich had suggested. If they did, that might be the end of the race for them.

The *First Blood* leapt ahead and passed halfway point to Bimini. Skimming along the tops of the waves. The seas went down some, and Kralich, responding to Falco's orders, held the boat flat-out.

As they approached Bimini, Cahill came up on Falco very slowly. The sea rushed past and the sun burned down now out of a clearing sky, and minutes kept ticking past. Cahill had begun to think he might get through the race without trouble, but as he approached the flat, almost treeless aspect of Bimini, he began again to feel the stricture inside him, the tightening and nausea. He tried to put his mind on other things, tried to forget that he was in the race. But the queasiness increased as the *First Blood* roared into a shallow

155

harbor lined with white buildings only a few hundred yards ahead of him, and then he followed in.

There were sweep boats everywhere at the harbor, and markers for them to pass and make their turns around. Smaller crowds than at Miami were on docksides, waving and yelling toward them. Banners streamed on docks and boats. The two racing boats roared through all of that without stopping, made their turns, and headed back out into the open sea. Cahill managed a shorter turn than Falco and gained some yardage on him. Then they were both roaring back out into the ocean and heading back toward the mainland.

"Correct compass heading ten degrees, Steve!" Del Rio called out excitedly.

Cahill made the steering correction. He noted that they were heading back into the rougher seas they had just come through and that the sky was threatening toward Miami.

"Correction made," Cahill replied.

"We've made up some more ground," Lucas said loudly. *"By God, we're catching them!"*

Mile followed nautical mile, as they headed back. Bruises ached on their backs and legs, and the pounding was getting worse again. The sea was all around them and all over them. Spray was everywhere, and it no longer glistened in a temporary sun. Now the sky ahead was threatening again, and the water around them was a dull color. Cahill, his hands aching on the wheel, got a sudden flash of a muddy jungle river, and he was on it, in the *Sonic Boom*, racing along past the steaming river banks. But he was not wearing the racing uniform. He had a camouflage suit on and a military helmet, and so did the men beside him.

The boat slammed at his feet and legs, and his back crunched against the bolster back. Sweat popped out on him, and his face went ashen and straight-lined. He saw the *First Blood* ahead about two hundred yards; but it was not Falco's boat, it was a black skiff manned by black-suited enemy soldiers, just as at Freeport.

A big wave hit them, and they were all thrown forward. Lucas hit the windshield with his arm, bruising it badly. Cahill was almost jerked off his feet, despite the harness. It cut into his chest and almost pulled loose from its moorings. Del Rio, banging his hand into the dashboard, swore under his breath, in pain. Lucas throttled back slightly.

"Give it full speed!" Cahill yelled in a hoarse voice. Lucas turned and gave him a look. Del Rio heard the change in Cahill's voice, and also cast a dark look toward Cahill. Del Rio heard that kind of voice before, in a V.A. hospital, when another young soldier was having a nightmare about the war.

"We'll stuff it, Steve!" Lucas argued. *"These seas are rough!"*

"Full-out, goddam it, full-out!"

Lucas gave him more throttle than he wanted to, and the *Sonic Boom* jammed into wave after wave, throwing them about in their harnesses. Del Rio let go of the controls and hung onto a gunwale handle for dear life. Lucas propped one hand against the windshield, and Cahill wrestled the steering wheel, trying to keep the boat on an even keel. It skipped into the air, and flew level with the water for almost fifty yards and then slammed back onto its smooth belly just before hitting another high wave. They drew up to within eighty yards of Falco, and then fifty.

"We need more speed!" Cahill was saying, and he was really on the jungle river now. *"We've got to make that bend! They're cutting us up with lead!"*

Del Rio put a hand on him. *"Take it easy, Steve. There's no shooting here."*

But Cahill suddenly unsnapped his safety belt, violently. *"Damn it, I've got to get at that sixty millimeter!"* He started pushing past Del Rio and Lucas, toward the gunwale, forgetting the wheel completely.

The boat swerved, and Cahill fell against the others.

"Jesus Christ, Steve!" Lucas yelled, grabbing the wheel.

Del Rio took hold of Cahill forcefully and made Cahill look into his face, through their wet face masks. *"Steve, this isn't Nam!"*

Cahill focused on his friend, blankly.

"That's Tony Falco up ahead there. We've got to catch him and beat his ass! Remember?"

Cahill looked ahead, and saw the speeding boat, and it was the *First Blood* again. He looked down and saw that he was out of his harness.

"Uh. Yeah, Danny."

He moved back behind the wheel, snapping off his face mask as he had done at Freeport. Lucas gave the steering over to him and throttled out hard.

"You all right, Steve?" Lucas asked.

Cahill nodded, letting the sea spray hit his face. *"Yeah, I'm okay."* He righted the boat from a slight swerve, and it headed back into Falco's wake. They were close now, only thirty yards separating them. *"Give it more throttle, Boyd."* He found his harness, and snapped it back on.

"You know where you are?" Del Rio asked, eyeing Cahill.

Cahill nodded. *"I'm all right now, Danny, really."*

Now they drew up almost even with Falco. They could see the red racing stripe on the other boat and read the numbers printed on its side. Falco glanced and saw them, and then Kralich turned, too. Suddenly Falco wheeled the *First Blood* directly into Cahill's path and cut him off. Lucas throttled way down, without being told, and Cahill swerved to port to avoid a collision.

"That sonofabitch!" Boyd Lucas yelled.

"Now give it to them!" Cahill said grimly, getting under control again. *"Let them have it, Boyd!"*

The *Sonic Boom* lunged ahead at full throttle, cutting the waves like a loosed arrow. It came up on the other boat and pulled even, and then began pulling ahead.

Onboard the *First Blood*, Tony Falco was in a violent rage. *"He's passing us! Goddam it, he's passing us!"*

"He's cutting the waves better than we are," Kralich yelled. *"And he's driving crazy!"*

"He's going to stuff it for sure," Wyatt's voice came.

"To hell with that!" Falco yelled. *"Keep up with him, Kralich, or it's your frigging ass. I mean it!"*

Kralich growled something under his breath, and gave the boat more throttle. Out on their port, Cahill's boat was ten yards beyond them, but now they were keeping even. A light rain began dropping from the fierce-looking sky and partially occluded their vision. An enormous wave rose before them, and Falco steered to starboard. Kralich gunned down, but still the boat crashed into the gray wall of water like a freight train into a brick building. They were all thrown forward, banging onto the dashboard and gunwale despite the harnesses, and Wyatt felt his belt give at its mooring. They kept going. Cahill's sleek, white racer was now twenty yards ahead, with no sign of slowing for the seas. Falco could just barely see the boat, through the pelting rain.

"There's the goddam shoreline up there, isn't it?" Falco was yelling. *"We're almost in! We've got to catch that bastard!"*

Falco was right, the shore was now in sight through the rain. The seas were even rougher, though, and it was getting very dangerous. *"Throttle this sonofabitch full-out!"*

Kralich followed orders, and they pulled almost even with the *Sonic Boom*. Falco saw Boyd Lucas glance toward them. The *Sonic Boom* edged forward of them again, off to the port about twenty yards. It met a big crest, foam-capped, and Cahill angled the boat through it with deft handling. But when the wave got to the *First Blood,* it was even higher and thicker, and Falco failed to see it in time to do anything about it. The boat slammed hard into the wave, and there was a creaking of the hull and a loud snapping of windshield as it busted into pieces. Falco was thrown against the wheel, and Kralich banged an arm against the controls, yelling as he hit. Hank Wyatt was violently hurled forward, his harness pulled loose from its moorings, and he smashed into the jagged edge of the broken windshield. As he passed over it, his suit, life jacket and flesh were torn by the sharp edge, and then he plummeted over the gunwale into the sea.

Neither Falco nor Kralich missed him for a moment, but then Kralich glanced beside him and saw that Wyatt was not there. Wind, rain and spray from the sea were now all over them from the broken windshield, and Kralich could hardly see. He frowned toward the empty bolster beside him.

"Hey! Wyatt's overboard!"

Falco turned incredulously and stared at the empty space, still hurting in his chest from the impact with the wheel. *"Jesus frigging Christ!"*

"I'll throttle down, and you can make a turn around," Kralich said.

Falco hesitated only a moment, glancing to where the *Sonic Boom* was leaving them in its wake. *"No!"* he said feverishly.

"Huh?"

"I said, no. Keep on going. Hank has his life jacket. One of the trailing boats will pick him up, or a sweep boat."

Kralich turned and saw the bobbing dark figure in the water behind them, an arm extended into the dark rain, trying to catch their attention. He turned back to Falco. *"If you say so,"* he said doubtfully.

He gunned the big engines, and kept on the wake of the *Sonic Boom*.

But it was not Falco's day. Now, toward shore, with the seas lessening some but the rain still pounding down, Cahill ordered Lucas to keep the speed steady. He turned and saw Falco back there once and saw that

Falco was driving blind-crazy and gaining. Cahill thought he saw only two heads in the bolster and could not understand why. Then he was gunning for the finish, in good control of himself now, but still with the stricture inside him. The harbor loomed into view, and Falco was within a hundred yards behind them. Cahill could see the finish line inside the harbor, and Falco was roaring up fast, like a demon from hell.

"Put her flat-out!" he told Lucas.

The *Sonic Boom* roared into the harbor like a jet aircraft, barely touching the sea, making a wide, beautiful wake behind it. The finish line came into close view, and there were crowds of waving spectators everywhere. Falco was within twenty yards, but he was no longer gaining. The *Sonic Boom* finished well ahead of Falco's boat, exploding past the finish line like a guided missile, with ear-splitting thunder. The *First Blood* shot across the line moments later, with Falco already hunched dismally over the wheel.

It took only a few minutes for the *Sonic Boom* to coast over to the dock where everybody was waiting to congratulate the crew. When they pulled up there, Danny Del Rio already had his helmet off, waving it hysterically in the air. Cahill and Lucas pulled theirs off wearily, Cahill hardly believing yet that they had won.

"We did it!" Del Rio said loudly to the gray overcast above them. The rain had stopped. "By Jesus, we did it!"

Boyd Lucas grabbed Cahill's shoulders, and his eyes were slightly moist. "Nice driving, Steve. Nice goddam driving."

On the dock, Rachel waved at them unseen. Mary Ann was there, too, but Dulcie had not come. Paige Lucas had finally come down, expecting the worst, and was teary-eyed to find that her brother had survived the race. Charlie Rossman was there, ecstatic.

As Del Rio climbed dockside first, Cahill turned and saw the *First Blood* coming in to the dock, and now the temporary grin edged off his face. Hank Wyatt was definitely not aboard, and as Falco's boat was tied up, Cahill saw Falco gesturing toward the open sea, talking to a race official.

Cahill looked seaward, into that gloomy haze, and knew exactly what had happened.

Hank Wyatt had gone overboard.

He was still out there in that turbulent sea.

Chapter Twelve

Out on the open sea there was still wind and rain. Hank Wyatt bobbed about in the water, pummeled by the sea, trying to keep afloat. When he had gone overboard, he had lost most of his life jacket, broken his right arm in two places, wrenched his back badly, and suffered a deep cut across his chest and stomach. Now he had drifted off the race course in the rough sea, and was in serious trouble. Unable to swim because of his injuries, he kept going under and swallowing water as the waves crashed over him.

He had been stunned to see Falco drive on without picking him up. That kind of thing just was not done. It was the driver's first responsibility to take care of his crew and any other crew that was in trouble, before concerning himself with the race. Wyatt had yelled toward the boat in desperation as it sped on toward the mainland without him, but his words had been whisked away by the wind and rain.

Now the third-place boat came up fast, on course about fifty yards away. Wyatt, in severe pain and with panic building in him, waved frantically toward the racer with his good arm as it neared him. On its side he could see the name, *Crazy Cuban*. The three helmeted heads were plainly visible to him, but none were looking toward him. The crew did not even know of the accident and was intent on holding onto third over another boat that was coming up on them.

"*Help!*" Wyatt's urgent cry lifted above the sea. "*Help me!*"

The boat went on past, disappearing in the rainy haze.

Wyatt felt himself being pulled further off course. "Oh, Jesus!" he gasped out.

He tried to stroke out with his left arm—the right one just hung painfully at his side, causing him excruciating pain as each wave moved it—but he could make no headway against the water. His torso bled steadily into the sea, and that further weakened him. A big wave washed over him and he was underwater. He yelled in pain as he went under, and then he was trying to keep the sea out of his lungs. He was thrown about, turned over. He broke the surface again and was breathless, weak. He squinted through salt-smarting eyes and saw the fourth-place boat come past, but now he was a hundred yards off course, and the racer came nowhere near him. He waved weakly, and called out, but the racer sped on past, and dissolved into the mist.

"Oh, God! I'm going to die!"

The sea pushed him further off the race course. No sweep boat came looking, no racer turned aside. No one knew he was out there, and the rain prevented their seeing him.

Wyatt was weakening. His legs would not kick any longer, and his left arm was drained of all its strength. He went under again, as the rain stopped, and water was sucked into his lungs. He broke the surface coughing fitfully, a wild, panicked look on his bony face. His helmet was gone, he had torn it off immediately to be able to yell out, and his long face was pale and drawn, his stringy hair hanging across it, a piece of seaweed clinging to his head.

"I've got—to stay afloat. They'll send somebody out. I've got to—keep going."

A big wave dunked him, and he lost more strength. He came up coughing again, and now he was unable to keep his head above water. No matter what he did, it made no difference. He was a limp rag for the sea to play with. A six-foot crest loomed above him, and a look of terror crossed his features. Then he went under again, tumbling head over heels, down into the sea. He tried to hold his breath, but could not. He found himself inhaling water. He convulsed inside from lack of air, his body screaming for it. He took in more water, and his hands began grabbing spasmodically at the water around him. There were a few more minutes of flailing, and then everything went black for him, and it was over. He went spiralling into the gray depths.

On the surface, the sun broke out from cloud cover and made the sea glisten there where Wyatt had gone down.

The weather was clearing as the race went on.

Back on the dock, Paige Lucas felt a chill pass through her, and she looked seaward as the crowd around her cheered Steve Cahill and his crew. "It happened after all," she muttered to herself. "A man drowned out there."

Down at the boats, Cahill was on the dock and walking down to Tony Falco, who was still aboard the *First Blood*. A couple of officials were asking Falco questions, urgently. A Coast Guard officer was running away from them toward an official boat, to take it out.

"What happened, Falco?" Cahill asked him from the dock. "Where's Wyatt?"

Falco looked up at Cahill darkly. "We went overboard when we had our accident," he replied. "We didn't even know he was gone until it was too late to turn around. We figured the number three boat would pick him up. I didn't want two boats circling there for him, in that rain. We could have run over him."

Cahill narrowed his eyes on Falco. He did not believe him. "I think we'd better get back out there," he said.

"Wait, here comes the *Crazy Cuban,*" Falco told him. Art Kralich was standing on the dock, watching

Cahill's face and saying nothing. He turned now with Cahill, and saw the third boat come into the harbor. A fourth was not far behind.

But the *Crazy Cuban* did not have Wyatt aboard, nor did the next boat in. Falco rubbed a hand across his face. "I was sure they would pick him up," he muttered.

Another Coast Guard official ran up, breathless. "Wyatt must still be out there." He was glaring toward Falco and Kralich. "We've radioed the sweep boats to begin a search."

Falco was genuinely shocked. He had convinced himself, in the frenzy of the moment, that Wyatt would be immediately picked up by somebody else—somebody to whom point totals were not quite so important.

"Christ," he said, unbelieving. He grabbed at the controls. "Come on, Art, we're going back out there."

"Try not to get in the way of the other boats coming in," the Coast Guard man said sourly. "And take your orders from the sweep boats out there."

Cahill grunted. "I'm going, too," he said.

Within five minutes, both the racers were back out past the harbor. Other racers were now finishing, and their crews were wondering what was going on. The *Sonic Boom* and the *First Blood* joined the search for Wyatt all through that afternoon, and then had to give over the search to the Coast Guard.

By nightfall, it was clear that Wyatt had drowned. The victory banquet was called off, and many crews went home early.

The next day, Wyatt's bloated body washed ashore at Key Biscayne, and funeral arrangements were made.

The local race committee had a meeting within hours of the finding of Wyatt's body, with an official from the national committee present, and Falco and Kralich gave their story about the accident, lying glibly and giving the impression that they had not missed Wyatt until a time when it was not feasible to go after him themselves. The committee issued Falco a warning, but did not disqualify him for the last race at Key West.

Eva Falco was suspicious of Falco's explanation, too, and was cool toward him through the hearing and afterwards.

Cahill was very disturbed by Wyatt's death, and somehow he knew it went beyond the fact that another racer had been killed in the heat of a race. Rachel, in an evening meeting between them the day after the race, lavished praise and attention on him because he was a contender for the national title again, but she seemed so callous and uninterested in Wyatt's death that Cahill found himself beginning to dislike her. He called Dulcie to apologize for the way he had behaved toward her at the beach that night, but he was not able to reach her by phone.

Gus Beckering was very angry with Tony Falco, of course. He had not only lost to Cahill again, he had lost the best navigator Beckering had ever had. Beckering had flown down from New York just for the race, but now decided to stay on for a while. First of all, there was the funeral for Hank Wyatt, and then there was new strategy to be discussed. Now Cahill was right back in close second in the standings, and Falco had to beat him at Key West to retain his national title. Coming in second there would not do it. Falco had to win, and that made Beckering very nervous. Cahill had now demonstrated that he could beat Falco driving the *Sonic Boom,* so the national title—and Beckering's coveted trophy— were very much up for grabs.

The day of Wyatt's funeral was sunny and fairly cool. It was held at Dania, just outside Miami, because Wyatt had lived there at one time and had a couple of relatives there, a cousin and her husband. They were present, and about a dozen racing people, and a couple of race officials. Cahill, Lucas and Del Rio were all there, and Charlie Rossman, whose exuberance about the win was subdued by the death. Falco came with Art Kralich and got a couple of dark looks from other crew members. Gus Beckering was conspicuously absent. He did not want to associate himself with Wyatt's death or with Tony Falco. They all stood around the graveside silently, a breeze from the sea rippling over them, as the local Baptist minister said a few words over Wyatt.

"All go unto one place; all are of the dust, and all turn to dust again. But Christ Jesus has abolished death and has shed light upon life. He was offered once for all time to bear the sins of many, so that they might live again. Have mercy upon Hank Wyatt, Lord, and receive him into the kingdom of heaven. For the wages of sin is death, but the gift of God is everlasting life through Jesus Christ our Lord."

The sea breeze played about the somber figures. The cousin stood with her husband, and her eyes were watery. There were only a couple of other women there, racing people who had known Wyatt, wives of racers. The rest were men, standing there wondering if, some day, they might suffer the fate of Hank Wyatt, or a similar one.

"What has come of flesh is flesh, and what has come of spirit is spirit, and the spirit shall live eternal. Amen."

The casket was lowered into the ground, and the group began breaking up. Falco walked over to a nearby gate, where his car was parked, and Kralich was with him. Kralich was almost untouched by the tragedy; he had disliked Hank Wyatt. Falco stood at the gate, feeling guilty inside, wanting to explain away his actions on the race course to anyone who cared to ask. Nobody did, though, not even the cousin, until Steve Cahill walked over to Falco with Boyd Lucas. Danny Del Rio had gone on over to their car.

"Well. The big winner," Falco said sourly to Cahill.

Cahill eyed him narrowly. "What really happened out there, Falco? I know what you told the race committee. But I think there's more to it than that."

Kralich glowered toward him. "Go to hell, Cahill.

Boyd Lucas moved a step closer to Kralich. "You keep out of this, you bastard." He was still smarting from Kralich's knocking him down at Point Pleasant. He and Kralich had been having words ever since the first time they met. Lucas was as big as Kralich, but had never been an athlete. He had always worked with his hands and never went to college or became involved in sports. Kralich had had a couple of years of college, flunked out, and went right to the pros to play football.

Kralich frowned at Lucas. "Something bothering you, grease monkey?"

But Falco interrupted the exchange, by answering Cahill. "Are you accusing me of something, Cahill?"

Cahill shrugged. "I just don't see how you and Kralich could both miss seeing that Wyatt had been thrown overboard when you stuffed the *First Blood*. It doesn't wash, Falco."

"Well, I guess you know more than the experts, then," Falco told him harshly. He was not just trying to convince others that he had acted properly; he was trying to make himself believe it, to some extent, and Cahill was not allowing him that luxury.

"I know what it's like out there on the course," Cahill said. "I know what it would have been like if we had done the same thing. I think you didn't want to stop, Falco. I think you still had ideas of beating me, and that that was more important than going back for Wyatt."

"Why don't you go jerk your dingus, Cahill?" Kralich growled.

Cahill eyed Kralich narrowly. Lucas stepped toward Kralich, but Cahill put a hand on his arm. "Maybe it was you that wanted to leave Wyatt," he said levelly to Kralich.

"Why, you frigging sonofabitch!" Kralich barked out. He took a step toward Cahill, but Falco was already there, between them. His handsome face was dark with anger.

"You know what we told the committee. That's the truth, Cahill. If you don't want to believe it, that's your problem not mine. Just get off my back about it!"

Cahill held his stony gaze. "Maybe I will, maybe not. But I'll tell you one thing, Falco. You ever cut me off again, the way you did out there on the way in, and you'll have to answer to me for it."

The way he had said it made Falco hesitate to reply.

"I don't like the way you compete, Falco," Cahill went on. "I can't keep you off the course, because I don't make those decisions. But you stay to hell out of my way, by God. At Key West, and before we get there."

Falco gave him an acid look. "Believe me, hotshot, that will be my pleasure."

"You bad-mouth us around," Kralich grated out to Cahill, "and you won't have to find Tony. I'll find you, war hero."

"Over my dead body," Lucas growled.

With that, Falco stormed off toward his car, and Kralich turned and followed. Cahill just stood staring at them for a long moment, as they climbed into a rented sedan, and then he and Lucas moved off to where Del Rio waited at the Jaguar.

There was no doubt in Cahill's mind now. Falco had, in effect, killed Hank Wyatt, just to keep in the race.

The competition was getting deadly.

He could only guess at how it would be at Key West.

Chapter Thirteen

It was a period of grim determination for Gus Beckering and Tony Falco. It all boiled down to one race now, at Key West. Beckering was close-mouthed and angry, and even unshakable Falco was now tense. He began doing some heavy drinking again as he waited for Beckering to move him to Key West from Miami, and one evening he broke yet another promise to Eva and took a nineteen-year-old waitress to a beach motel and put her through his repertoire of bedside niceties. Art Kralich found Falco at the motel, quite by accident, just as Falco was finishing with the girl, and Falco turned her over to Kralich at Kralich's urging, despite her protestations. It was a thing Falco would not have done before Hank Wyatt's death. But Falco was different now. He had always been a fairly easygoing fellow, but now he was moody and angry with the world much of the time.

It was only a couple of days after the funeral for Hank Wyatt that Cahill and Rachel McKenzie had their last date together. Cahill was still somber about Wyatt's death, but Rachel was very blithe about it, and that bothered Cahill. He was beginning to see her shallowness now, just underneath the sophistication and poise.

They went to a small Chinese restaurant that evening, called Fu Manchu, just off Collins Boulevard, and Cahill was pensive through their meal there. He was not only thinking of Hank Wyatt, he was remembering how it had been out there on the race course for him. It had been the worst yet; he had been completely out of control for a while. Something was taking hold of him out there on the water and jerking him back to a place he never wanted to see again—the battleground of Asia. He had assured Del Rio and Lucas that he was all right after he had taken the controls again, in the episode, but he had been far from that. He had almost been sick on the way in, and only his tight grip on the wheel hid his trembling inside.

But even more importantly, he had already had a sweating nightmare since the race, and he had never before had one just after a race. It was almost like he was trying to kill himself out there, and because there was only one more race left in which to do it, that self-destructive urge inside him was intensifying with every day that passed. But why did he want to hurt himself, he wondered, and why did it have to be in the heat of the race, on the open water? He seemed to have no easy answers, and again he was wondering if he had been involved in some atrocity that was now bothering him, somewhere deep inside him. Maybe he had killed wantonly, in the heat of the fighting that took Josh's life, and now he was looking for the ultimate punishment. But what that would have to do with this season of racing, he did not know. He searched his head to try to recall what had happened just prior to Josh's fatal hit, but he could not. He was certain, now, that if he could remember that brief period, the mystery of what was happening would be revealed—maybe in time to save his life.

Cahill wanted to drop Rachel off after their late meal, but she was not through with the evening. Cahill reluctantly asked her up for a drink—Del Rio and Lucas had returned to Baltimore for the time being, with Paige —and when they had had one, Rachel undressed in Cahill's bedroom. Cahill came in and found her lying on his bed, staring at the ceiling.

"Well?" she said to him. "Are we or aren't we?"

Cahill obliged her, but it was not the same. They

coupled on the wide bed mechanically, without enthusiasm. Rachel seemed jaded to Cahill that evening, and he was sorry he had ever gotten involved with her. After a few times with her in his arms, she seemed to have lost interest, physically. It had begun with a wild, almost hysterical abandon with her, and had deteriorated quickly to apathy. Cahill did not mind, because he had lost interest in Rachel, too, for different reasons.

They lay beside each other when it was over, and Cahill held a thin Tampa cigar clenched between his teeth, staring at the darkness above him. The thin cigarillos were the only thing he ever smoked, and then only infrequently. Rachel glanced over at him, and let her eyes travel up and down his muscular frame. "What are you thinking about?"

Cahill took the thin cigar from his mouth. "The war," he said quietly. He was trying to remember, running all of it over in his head.

"Oh, God, Steve," she said cynically. "That stupid thing ended years ago. You ought to try to forget it."

Cahill looked over at her. Her slim nudity was bathed in a bluish light that came feebly through an open window, making her look like a Picasso painting.

"You think the war was stupid?" he said to her.

"Well, don't you?"

"It started out right," he said. "Then show biz took over."

"The whole thing was stupid and silly,"Rachel insisted. "The men who fought in it were dupes, for God's sake." Cahill gave her a narrow look. "I suppose you must feel like a damned fool for even going." She turned to him blandly.

"No," Cahill said. "I never felt like that."

She studied his face closely. "Well, I meant no offense, of course. You couldn't have know how it would be, I'm sure."

Cahill did not know why, but her callousness about

the war had made him suddenly very angry with her. Maybe it was because he did feel foolish about it all, after her comments.

"Rachel," he said tautly, "I think you ought to go."

She frowned at him. "What?"

"It's getting late, and I need some rest."

"Well, I'll be damned. No man ever kicked me out of his bed before. You're turned into a goddam bore, Steve!" She rose sulkily, casting a dark look toward him.

"You made that obvious in bed," he told her.

"Jesus!" she said.

She dressed without speaking to him, and when she was ready to go—she had already said she would take a cab home—Cahill rose and sat on the edge of the bed.

"Maybe we ought to cool it for a while, Rachel," he said to her evenly. "I mean, maybe we need a break from each other."

Rachel glared at him, looking regal now in her dark dress and high heels. "You sonofabitch! Do you think I want to come here again? You've always got your mind on the war, or something else, for Christ's sake. You're no goddam fun. My husband pays more attention to me. You're spaced out half the time. Who needs it? You just don't interest me anymore!"

"Whatever you say," he grunted out.

"You think I care about your press clippings, or that trophy you might win in Key West? That's all kid stuff to me, Stevie! I was attracted to you because I saw something dangerous inside you, something exciting. But you've closed all that in, you want to hide it. You're dull, sweetheart, and dull men are a dime a dozen."

"Sorry I disappointed you," he said sourly.

In the next moment, she stormed through the apartment and slammed the outside door loudly behind her.

An hour later, Cahill was asleep.

He dreamed about the war, though, and woke at midnight, sweating all over and cursing himself.

Propping himself with pillows, he lighted another cigarillo and sat in the darkness, the red glow from the cigarillo the only light in the room. He thought about Josh Owens, and how he, Cahill, had persuaded Josh to join the Marines. Cahill had believed that their country needed them, and he had never been one to miss a good fight. Josh had been doubtful if he had it in him to be a good Marine and had voiced that doubt to Cahill on several occasions. He had had trouble at boot camp, too, and Cahill had had to help him along. There had been one training sergeant who would have worked Josh until he croaked, if Cahill had not come between them. Cahill had taken the sergeant behind a barracks building one dark night and worked him over thoroughly, then threatened much more if he did not leave Josh alone. The sergeant said he intended to court-martial Cahill, but that was all bluster, and Josh made it through training after all. They had both become second lieutenants later, but Josh had taken a demotion to sergeant just to stay with Cahill. He figured he was not officer material, anyway.

"Why the hell don't you have a little confidence, Josh?" Cahill had asked him one night after they had finished basic training and were awaiting acceptance to officers' school. They were drinking beer in the Camp LeJeune exchange, sitting off in a corner by themselves. "You've got a lot on the ball, if you just knew it."

It was true. In school, Josh had always been one of the smartest kids. Learning came easy to him. But he had never had the aggressiveness of Cahill.

"You've got enough confidence for both of us," Josh had told him. "All I have to do is stick with you, Steve, and you'll see that I don't get into too much trouble." He grinned boyishly, a sandy-haired, slim young man with a disarming smile.

That had summed it up pretty well, too. They had gone to the same high school, where Cahill had acted as a kind of big brother to Josh, even though they were the same age. Then, in Vietnam, it had been Cahill who had made Josh a soldier and had forced him to learn how to survive.

Drinking the beer from a bottle, Cahill had shook his head soberly. "Damn it, Josh, you have to rely on yourself more. You have it in you to stand up to all of it. If we get over to Nam, I can't wet-nurse you. We'll probably end up in different units."

But Josh had worked it so that they were together to the end. And he had never lost his dependence on Cahill. He had expected Cahill to take care of him, to see him through the war just as he had seen him through everything else.

Lying there propped against the pillows in the dark, Cahill got a flash of Josh's head in his hands, and all the blood, and the vacant stare in Josh's face. But it could not be Josh's death that was bothering Cahill to the extent of giving him waking nightmares, he thought, lying there. He had had nothing to do with Josh's death, he had come upon it after the fact, he did not even know how it had happened.

Or do I know? he thought.

A cold sweat broke out over him, quite suddenly. He stubbed the thin cigar out, slowly, and rolled over onto his side. *To hell with it.* He closed his eyes and tried to put it all out of his head. After a long time he finally fell asleep again and did not wake until morning.

Cahill was back to his regular work for Charlie Rossman now, but it was different than before. The *Miami Herald* and other newspapers were after him regularly, for statements about preparations for the last race of the season at Key West, the one that would determine the national champion of Class One racing. In his own town, Cahill was big news. Tony Falco, who had stayed on at Miami under Beckering's orders before flying down to Key West, worked on the *First Blood* with Art Kralich, installing brand new engines and working the racer over. He kept away from the press as much as possible, because they always asked about Hank Wyatt and the accident, and when he was not working on the boat, he called around the circuit long-distance to find a navigator to replace Wyatt. He finally found a fellow named Jenkins, a tall kid who had been on several winning crews in production class races. Jenkins would meet them in Key West a few days before the race, to get a feeling for the *First Blood*.

Dulcie was still at loose ends. She had almost called Cahill, to congratulate him, after his big win at Miami. But she could not bring herself to do so after the way Cahill had spoken to her at the beach that night. She had no knowledge he had called her twice and missed finding either her or Mary Ann at their room. Still unemployed and becoming disillusioned with Miami, Dulcie began to wonder why she had come down there with Mary Ann.

When October arrived the weather cooled off some in Miami, and Boyd Lucas returned there to work on the *Sonic Boom* with Cahill in preparation for Key West. Danny Del Rio planned to meet them in Key West later. Cahill asked Rossman for some money to make minor modifications of the *Sonic Boom's* powerful engines, and Rossman okayed the expenditure. Cahill did not speak to Rossman about his increasing nightmares and tension, or to Lucas either, but Lucas could tell that Cahill was tight inside.

While Falco and Cahill were getting ready to have their respective boats transported down the length of the Florida Keys, a real break finally came between Eva and Tony Falco. One afternoon she overheard another driver telling the bartender at the yacht club about the nineteen-year-old waitress Falco had given over to Kralich—Kralich had talked about the night to a couple of people, despite his promise to Falco to keep his mouth shut—and suddenly Eva was furious. She had been lied to before by Falco, in his reform talks, but this time it just finally aroused her by sheer weight of cumulative effect. When Falco returned to their hotel suite early that evening, she was waiting for him with her bags packed at the door. Falco took one look at them as he came in and frowned. "Hey, what the hell is this?" he called to her.

Eva came in from a bedroom, stern-faced. She had gotten her anger under control, but she was more hardened, inside, than she had been earlier, or ever.

"Well, I see you found your way home," she said to him. She was dressed in a pretty, yellow dress that showed off her nice figure. "I'm glad you made it before I called a taxi. There are a couple of things I want to say to you."

Falco threw a newspaper onto a sofa, the same sofa where he had lied to her not so long ago, pledging reform. He came over to her, and she backed away from him a step. He made a sour face. "Eva, for God's sake. What do you think you're doing?"

"I should think that much would be obvious," she said. "I'm leaving you, Tony. I'm flying to Chicago on the nine-thirty flight."

Falco laughed lightly. "Come on, honey, what is this? Why are you leaving? What's the problem?"

"You're the problem, Tony," she said. "But we've been through that before. It seems you just can't help yourself. With the girls, that is. Well, I've finally had enough." Her voice had emotion in it, but it was controlled emotion.

"Hell, I told you, I'm through with that."

"Are you?" she said bitterly. "When, Tony, yesterday? Today? I wouldn't go back much further than that, if I were you."

Falco narrowed his dark eyes slightly. "What are you referring to?"

"I think you've already got that one figured out," she said. "The waitress that you and Kralich shared. God, Tony, how far have you slipped? You could at least show a little dignity about it. Dogs behave better, for Christ's sake.''

Falco's face had changed. He went and sat on the arm of the sofa, near her. "It was losing the race. I got drunk, Eva. I didn't know what the hell I was doing."

"Like you didn't know what you were doing out on that race course?" she said harshly. "When you left Hank Wyatt to drown?"

Falco held her gaze with a somber one. "I told the racing committee, the press, and you. I thought the next boat up would grab Hank out of the water."

"Why not?" Eva said. "He was only in third place, after all, and not a contender for the title. He didn't have so much to win by risking a man's life."

Falco glowered at her. "I was exonerated, Eva."

"What about the waitress? The way I hear it, Kralich raped her, with your blessing. Will she exonerate you, Tony? And if she does, will you expect me to?"

"What the hell do you want from me?" he said. "I'm trying, I really am, goddam it."

"Well, you're not trying hard enough, baby. Not for little Eva. From now on you can explain your weaknesses to somebody else. Because I won't be around."

Falco was sobered, finally. "Is this for good?"

Eva sighed. "I hope so," she said.

He came over to her, rising off the sofa. "Jesus, Eva. Let's talk this out, honey. We've had a lot of good times, haven't we? Is that all going for nothing, now? Don't you feel something for me?".

"Oh, yes," she said. "I still feel something for you, Tony. But that doesn't change anything. You're not the same man I married a few years ago. You're in love, all right, Tony, but it's not with me. It's with yourself and the image the public has of you. I hope that gives you happiness, eventually. But I don't think so."

Falco dropped his gaze to the floor. "Some time you picked, Eva. Just before the national championship race, and that goddam Cahill breathing down my neck.

I don't even have any cash of my own, right now."

"I opened an account for you at First Federal of Broward. It isn't a lot, but you can make it last for a year, I'd think, even with your extravagant tastes. After that, you'll be on your own. If you don't win that trophy for Gus Beckering, I'd guess you'll really be on your own. You might even have to go out and get yourself a job. But you'll make out, Tony. You always do."

Falco glared at her. "I'll never forgive you for this, Eva. Running out on me when I needed you the most. I'll never forget it."

Eva gave him a hard smile. "That's just the way I hope it works out," she said in a brittle, acid voice.

That same evening, Charlie Rossman got a surprise visit from Gus Beckering. Rossman had worked late at his plant, and Cahill and other employees were gone, so Beckering had the privacy he wanted. He drove up in a chauffered limousine, looking pallid and paunchy as he climbed out of the long car and waddled into the plant offices. He found Rossman in his shirtsleeves, going over some accounts.

"Well, well," Rossman said, as a night watchman led Beckering into Rossman's spartan plant office with its metal desk, metal filing cabinets, and fluorescent lighting. "It's been a long time, Gus. Did you come to congratulate me on my win here in Class One?"

Beckering grunted. "Congratulations, Rossman. Mind if I take a load off?"

Rossman offered Beckering a chair beside his desk, and Beckering slumped into it. He was breathing heavily from the walk into the building. "That Rossman Special of yours is a bastard," he said, in his grating voice. "You did a number on us with that one, Rossman."

Rossman leaned back in his swivel chair and grinned. "We kind of like it, too, Gus."

Beckering took a handkerchief and dabbed at his

flaccid face.

"You don't look too good," Rossman said. "Are you feeling okay nowadays?" He had never liked Beckering, but he hated seeing him look so unhealthy.

Beckering eyed Rossman sidewise, his face mottled red and his eyes rheumy. "I've got something, Rossman. The doc isn't too pleased about it."

"I'm sorry to hear that," Rossman said honestly.

Beckering shrugged. "You really found a driver in that Cahill."

"Yes, I did. Imagine, I had him here all the time, selling boats for me. Of course, that's still how he spends most of his time."

"The boys tell me he's got a screw loose up here," Beckering said, touching his head with a pudgy forefinger.

Rossman frowned. "That's pretty malicious talk, Gus."

"That's just what I hear. That he shouldn't be racing, because he's a danger out there. To himself, and to everybody else."

"He hasn't killed anybody yet," Rossman said meaningfully. "Incidentally, I'm sorry as hell about Hank Wyatt."

"That Cahill drives like a goddam madman," Beckering said harshly. "And that gets to other drivers. I was the first to tell Falco he should have turned around for Wyatt. That Cahill is driving him nuts."

"You're trying to blame Steve for the way Falco drives?" Rossman said incredulously.

"I'm not saying anything falls on his shoulders. It's just that Falco and other drivers are driving differently now, with Cahill in the races. Everybody is racing flat-out, and to hell with the consequences."

Rossman smiled. "I don't believe that, Gus."

Beckering cast a hard look at Rossman. "I want Cahill out of the Key West race, Rossman. I want the *Sonic Boom* out."

Rossman's face drew itself into straight lines. "What?"

"I'm prepared to buy the *Sonic Boom* at twice what it's worth on the open market. I've got a blank check in my pocket, Rossman. Say the word, and you've got yourself the biggest profit on a boat sale ever."

"You want the *Sonic Boom?*" Rossman said, his eyebrows raised.

"I want it under lock and key. I intend to win at Key West, with the *First Blood* and with Falco. With the *Sonic Boom* in or out. But I'll rest easier at nights with it out."

Rossman could not believe Beckering's nerve. "You think I'd sell my boat just before the last race for a few bucks?" He leaned forward onto the metallic desk. "With my crew ready to go?"

Beckering did not like the response. "All right, Rossman. I'll give you three times market. Put a generous retail price on the boat, and I'll write a check for three times that figure." He pulled a checkbook from a baggy tropical worsted suit jacket, opened it, and poised a pen over the top blank check. "Just say the word. A hundred fifty grand? Two hundred? What will it take?"

Rossman had to admit, deep down, that he was tempted. But he shook his head slowly. "Put your checkbook away, Gus. I'm going to race the *Sonic Boom* at Key West. Steve Cahill, Boyd Lucas, Danny Del Rio. They're counting on it. Besides, I'd like to see that national championship trophy sitting here in the office, just like you would."

"You've got years to win a trophy," Beckering said ominously. "I haven't."

Rossman held Beckering's hard gaze with a somber one. "I'm sorry about that, Gus. But I don't think the championship should depend on whether a man is sick or not. You have trophies on your shelf. Go home and polish them up. Maybe they'll look better to you.

Maybe it won't seem so important that you win this additional one."

Beckering rose grim-faced from his chair, leaning with both hands onto Rossman's desk. His face had clouded over darkly. "I won't play games with you, Rossman. This is too important to me. I've already talked to your two top retailers, the people who take eighty percent of your stuff.

Rossman frowned. "Huh?"

"I have certain connections who can make it pretty tough on them to get around to the shows. They've agreed to boycott your products at word from me."

Rossman grew red-faced. "Why, you—"

"Think about it, Rossman. You'd have to go out and dig up some more retail business immediately or go under. Eighty percent, Rossman. I checked the figures myself. You published sales figures recently, remember?"

Rossman rose heavy-shouldered from his chair. "You're sick more than in your body, Gus." It hissed out at Beckering like a jet of steam.

"Nevertheless. I tried to be reasonable. I don't want the *Sonic Boom*, do with it what you want. Just don't race it at Key West. If you haven't withdrawn it within forty-eight hours, I'll go to some people and set things in motion. I'm not bluffing, Rossman, I can do it with a couple of phone calls. You'll be scrambling to stay afloat if you make the wrong decision. You may just go under, like I said."

Rossman tried to control his voice, when he spoke. "Are you finished, goddam you?"

Beckering raised sparse eyebrows easily. "I think so."

"Then get the hell out of my office, and my plant!"

Beckering shrugged. "Forty-eight hours, Rossman. Forty-eight hours."

Then he lumbered out of the brightly lighted office.

The driver Phil Ramos had told Mary Ann Spencer that he was racing in Key West and had invited her to meet him down there at race time. But both Mary Ann and Dulcie were quickly running out of money, and neither had found a job in Miami. They were still at the inexpensive downtown hotel and were economizing by going to a nearby delicatessen to eat, but they could not last much longer without work.

Dulcie had been to a couple of employment agencies, and a clerk at one of them had advised her that if she wanted to go to Tampa, she would be sure of a job in a plant office there with some supervisory duties. Dulcie was thinking seriously of this, but she was still hoping, deep inside her somewhere, that Steve Cahill would show up at her door and apologize and make things right between them. Missing his calls, she had no idea he was trying to get in touch with her.

One night in early October, when Mary Ann wanted to go out to the Beach Yacht Club and Marina where a few area racing people were still hanging out, Dulcie agreed to go along in the hope that she and Cahill would meet there.

But Cahill was not there. Tony Falco was, and he was getting very drunk, trying to drown his troubles with Eva in booze. He made a pass at Mary Ann, and she rejected it, with Art Kralich grinning at her just a short distance down the bar. Falco made some insulting innuendos, and Mary Ann called him a couple of names, and Kralich grinned and grinned. Kralich came and asked Dulcie if he could buy her a drink, and Dulcie refused. Then Mary Ann innocently asked a heavy bartender if he had seen Steve Cahill.

"Hell, he hasn't been in here for a while. He's too busy humping that rich McKenzie broad. They go everywhere together. He can't keep his hands out of her lace panties." He laughed loudly, and Mary Ann gave him a hard look.

Dulcie, beside Mary Ann, heard every work of the exchange, and quite suddenly she was more angry with Cahill than she could ever remember being. "Goddam him," she murmured to herself.

Mary Ann looked over at her. They were both wearing low-cut, skin-tight dark dresses, and Dulcie's hair was blown out and long, almost at her shoulders.

"Hell, it doesn't matter, honey," Mary Ann said. "There's more than one honey badger in the woods."

Just at that moment, Art Kralich came up to Dulcie again, holding a beer. He looked very big, in a flowered sport shirt that hung out over his trousers. "Hey, honey," he said to Dulcie again. "You sure I can't buy you something?"

Dulcie turned, grim-faced, to him. "Why not?" she said loudly, so the bartender could hear her. "I'll take a double brandy, barkeep, and it's on this gentleman here."

Mary Ann gave Dulcie a look, but said nothing. Kralich was very pleasantly surprised. His big, square face lighted up as he sat down beside Dulcie, and they had a drink together. He talked about the Miami race loudly, because Hank Wyatt's death was still bothering him, but Dulcie did not listen. After two drinks together, Kralich asked if he could drive her home.

Mary Ann had gone off to sit with a driver she knew, and Dulcie felt very alone and still angry. The bartender was still within earshot when she turned to Kralich and said, "Sure, take me home. It's a nice night for a slow drive back."

Kralich was pleased as he had never been pleased about a woman. He knew that Dulcie had been Cahill's girl, and that Falco had been intimate with her in New York, and he had envied them both. Dulcie was the sexiest woman he had ever laid eyes on, and he wanted her badly.

Mary Ann protested weakly when Dulcie said she was leaving, but Dulcie paid no heed. She was hell-bent on showing Steve Cahill, and nothing could stop her. She would be seen leaving the place with Kralich, then she would have him drive her home, and leave him at the car. It would give her some small satisfaction, she figured.

Kralich did not talk a lot on the way to the hotel. Dulcie had been afraid, once she got outside the yacht club, that he would try to drive her somewhere else, but he did not. She found out why, when they arrived at the hotel. He parked his sedan on a side street, and she said goodnight to him.

"What do you mean, goodnight?" Kralich said gruffly to her.

Dulcie turned to him, in the car. "I mean I'm going up to the room and go to bed," she said to him.

Kralich grinned. "That don't mean you have to say goodnight," he said. "Let's go."

Dulcie shook her head. "Oh, no. I'm going alone. You asked to take me home, Art. That's what I offered to do with you, nothing else."

Dulcie started to get out, but a big fist closed on her left arm. She gasped, and winced under the pressure. "Hey!"

Kralich was grinning wickedly at her. "When I buy a girl drinks and give her a ride, I expect a little something in return." He reached beyond her with his other hand and locked the door beside her.

Dulcie felt a panic rise in her chest. She looked down the dark side street, and saw for the first time how alone they were. The windows were up, because he had been using the air-conditioner. Suddenly, the hand that had locked the door was on her thighs, pushing her nylon dress up.

She fought him hard, but he was a bull of a man. In just a moment he was massaging her between her thighs, forcing an opening for his hand there.

"*Stop!*" she yelled, beating at him with her other hand. "*Help!*"

The more she kicked and struggled, the more of her

was revealed to him. Her long thighs were bare now, and Kralich was working away between them, in the soft, warm place up there. There was a ripping of cloth, and she felt him trying to kiss her. She pulled away, turning her head, and he grabbed it with his other hand and held it while he planted his alcohol-odorous mouth on hers, bruising, hurting her.

When the kiss was over, Dulcie was breathing shallowly, disgust welling up in her. The hand between her legs was hurting her now, as he violated her with his strong fingers, pushing her backwards toward the passenger door, trying to get her on her back.

"Oh—Jesus!" she gasped out. "Oh—God!"

Kralich was fumbling with his clothing now, getting ready to mount her. There was not much space for him despite the size of the big car, but he was going to give it a try, right on the street there. He was inebriated and did not care. Dulcie had him worked up so much that he was going to have her, one way or another.

He had himself in hand now and was moving onto her. Her dress was up around her waist, her under-clothing torn off. She was exposed to him, and he was about to make a forced union, if she did not do something. She reached out and found him with her hand, and he looked surprised and pleased. But then she reached on down and grabbed at the part of him that was still enclosed in his trousers, and she squeezed hard.

Kralich's eyes went wide in sudden, raw pain, and a yell began in his throat and exploded into the close confines of the car. *"Ahhgh! Aaghuhh!"* He reached for her hand, but could not get it free of him. He finally tore it loose, and heaved onto the floor beside her, grabbing at himself and making noises in his throat.

Dulcie found the door lock, pulled up on it, and shoved on a handle. The car door fell open, and she toppled out of it, falling onto the pavement beside the car. She scrambled to her feet awkwardly, pulling her torn dress down, stumbling backwards a few paces,

· wild-eyed.

"*You goddam—bitch!*" the grating voice came from the car.

Dulcie did not stick around to trade insults with him. She turned and limped toward the front entrance of the hotel, around a nearby corner.

She was fed up with people like Art Kralich, Steve Cahill, Rachel McKenzie, and the others. She was fed up with Miami. She was tired of making herself available to men who risked their lives for gold trophies, brawled and drank for entertainment, and took what they wanted without asking.

She would leave for Tampa the very next morning.

What she found there could not be worse than this.

Chapter Fourteen

Steve Cahill knocked on the hotel room door and waited. There was a sound inside, of someone moving about. In a moment, the door opened, and Mary Ann stood there.

She was wearing only a sheer nightie, and her red hair was mussed slightly. He had gotten her out of bed. It was only eight A.M. Cahill looked her up and down, noting the dark places that showed voluptuously through the thin cloth, and grinned.

"Hi, Mary Ann."

"Oh, Steve. God, I'm not awake! Come on in."

Cahill came in and she closed the door behind him. He looked around the the room, with its one window, gray wallpaper, and littered floor. He was certain the litter had accumulated against Dulcie's wishes, because she was so neat. Then he got an empty feeling inside him, knowing without being told that Dulcie no longer occupied the room with Mary Ann.

"Is Dulcie around?" he asked, anyway.

Mary Ann gave him a look. "Now you ask. She left for Tampa yesterday."

"Tampa?" he said. She gestured to a chair, and he sat down.

Mary Ann went and sat down on a short, lumpy sofa, and the short nightie came up high on her thighs. She put one knee up without thinking about it and showed Cahill that she had no undies on under the nightie. "She found a job there. Says it's a real opportunity for her. Wants to be a manager there some day, or something. I tried to talk her out of it. You could have."

Cahill sighed heavily, trying not to look at the place between Mary Ann's thighs. "I called three times. I didn't even know for sure you were still here."

"Oh, Christ, I wish she had known that," Mary Ann grumbled. Her full breasts were outlined neatly by the sheer cloth, so that she looked almost nude to Cahill, even above the short hemline of the nightgown.

"Do you think it would have made any difference?" he said.

"Hell, yes. She likes you, Steve. A lot. But she thought you owed her a talk—I don't know. She might still be here if that goddam Kralich hadn't acted up the other night."

"Kralich? What do you mean?"

"He damn near raped her out on the street. She fought him off, but it shook her up."

"That sonofabitch!" Cahill growled.

"She wasn't hurt, Steve. But she was down on Miami when she left."

"Where's she staying there?" Cahill asked.

"She hasn't got a place yet. She's going to call me."

He nodded. "I'll be leaving for Key West soon, if things go right with the boat. Will you be heading down there?"

Mary Ann smiled craftily, and began moving the raised knee. Every time the knee moved to her right, it opened her thighs and revealed more of Mary Ann to Cahill for a brief moment. He felt himself responding to the stimulus and looked away.

"Phil Ramos has invited me," she said with the smile. "He thinks I'm special, I guess."

Cahill grinned. "You are, Mary Ann."

Suddenly she realized what she was doing and quickly put the leg down. "Christ, I didn't mean that, Steve. When I'm comfortable with somebody, I forget. I wasn't looking for anything."

Cahill rose, still grinning. "Hell, I know that, Mary Ann."

She stood, too. "I wouldn't seduce Dulcie's guy."

Cahill frowned slightly. "I don't think that's a proper description of our relationship," he said. "At least from Dulcie's point of view. I owe her an apology, Mary Ann, and I hope I can deliver one."

"What about that McKenzie dame? Are you two still a thing?"

Cahill shook his head. "We never were, really."

Mary Ann smiled, came to him, and threw her arms around his shoulders. "That's nice," she said. "I'll give you Dulcie's phone number just as soon as I get it."

Cahill had taken hold of Mary Ann when she embraced him, and now found his hands on ripe flesh behind her, where the short hemline pulled up to expose her ripe curves. He patted those curves, then stepped gingerly away from her.

"I think I'd better go while I still can," he said.

Mary Ann smiled a nice smile, and he did not even notice her crooked teeth. "You say the nicest things to a girl," she told him.

As for Eva Falco, circumstances brought her back to Miami at about the same time that Falco was leaving for Key West. She avoided her husband assiduously, though, during her return. She had talked to a lawyer in New York, by phone, and he was getting papers ready for a divorce. But that was not what brought Eva back to Miami. The bank account she had set up for Falco had not been opened quite properly, needing a signature on another document, and Falco had called her to say he could not withdraw money and to ask her forgiveness for his trespasses. She neither forgave him nor mentioned that she had talked to an attorney, but promised that she would make it right at the bank.

Actually, Eva could have done the whole thing by mail. But she had left without saying goodbye to several friends she had made around the circuit, and wanted to see one in particular to make amends for that omission. That one was Boyd Lucas.

Eva had been back in Miami only four hours when she met with Lucas at Cahill's condominium apartment. It was mid-afternoon, and Cahill and Lucas had been readying the *Sonic Boom* for its trip down the keys. Cahill had gone off to Dania, near Miami, to do some business for Rossman, so Lucas was there alone. When he saw Eva at the door, his square face broke into a big smile.

"Well, I'll be damned! Eva! I thought you were in Chicago." Falco had told everybody who would listen about his wife's "deserting" him, as he put it.

"I'm back just for the day, Boyd," Eva told him, with a warm, easy smile. Her blond hair looked breeze-blown and airy, and she looked prettier to Lucas than he had ever seen her. He figured it was because she had broken free of Falco. "I wanted to see you and tell you what had happened."

Lucas invited Eva in. She saw that they were alone, and was glad. They sat on a sofa together, and Lucas offered her a drink, but she declined.

"He just wouldn't quit, Boyd," she told Lucas. "I had no choice."

"Are you divorcing him?" Lucas asked.

She nodded. "I've already spoken with a lawyer."

"Then you're—free?" he said.

She nodded. "Yes."

Lucas felt a tightening in his insides. He had fallen in love with Eva, without even knowing it. Now that feeling was very close to him, with her sitting beside him and looking so lovely with the sunlight on her hair.

"I'm glad you came here, Eva," he said quietly. "I think you know that—well, that I think a lot of you."

"You've always been special to me, too, Boyd," she replied. "That's why I wanted to come and see you personally before—"

"Before what, Eva? What will you do, now?"

"I honestly don't know," she said. "My life has been so tied in with Tony's, and the racing circuit, that I'll be at loose ends for a while, I know."

They were quite close on the sofa. Lucas reached over on impulse and drew Eva to him and kissed her. Surprisingly to Lucas, she responded hungrily. When it was over, they were both wide-eyed with wonder at the sudden magic between them.

"Oh, God, Boyd," she whispered.

"I knew it," he said huskily. "I knew it all the time."

"I'm not—divorced yet," she reminded him.

"Does that matter? The piece of paper, I mean, that makes it legal? It's over now, isn't it?"

"Yes," she agreed. "It's over now."

Lucas reached and put a hand on her breast, and she did not pull away. "God, how I've wanted you, without even letting myself know it."

"I think it's been the same with me," she said.

Lucas was caressing the breast now. They kissed again, and it was electrical between them.

"Let it happen now, Eva," he breathed. "There's no reason why it shouldn't happen now."

Eva realized, now, that she had come to him for this. For affection, warmth, his arms around her. Lucas had always been good to her, been special with her. What was happening now was a natural result of the other. His hand went underneath her thin dress, at the low neckline, and fondled her there.

"No, wait," she said softly.

Lucas hesitated, frowning slightly.

"Let's do it right," she told him.

They moved to Lucas's bedroom, and undressed. Lucas was thrilled by Eva's animal beauty, unclothed. He figured Falco had to be some kind of crazy person, not to appreciate what he had had at home. That was the way it was with some men.

When they got onto the bed, they were both more than ready. There were a few moments of Lucas's grappling with her hot flesh, and then Eva gave herself to him, without restraint, without guilt. Lucas was a bigger man than Falco, and he awakened in Eva some primordial, animal hunger that had lain dormant through her marriage to Falco, and she responded anxiously to it. There was an urgent, very physical working between them, as if from deprivation, with low growling sounds building in Lucas's throat. At climax for them, Eva's eyes widened in further surprise as Lucas filled her with a completeness never known to her before, with great power and raw masculinity. Eva cried out over and over in those moments, announcing her pleasure to him in the privacy of the room. Then it was finally finished, with Lucas touching her damp flesh with his lips, placing caresses on her in gratitude for her generosity and her affection.

"Oh, God—Boyd."

He did not want to separate them. He lay with most of his weight supported by his big arms, his face close to hers, admiring her sculptured features, dewy with perspiration.

"I think—I'm in love, Eva."

"Oh, Boyd."

Several minutes later, he lay beside her on the wide bed, with a sea breeze moving a light curtain at the window.

"Will I see you in Key West?" he asked her.

"Tony will be in Key West," Eva said.

"Does that matter?"

"He'd be trouble for us."

"We've both had trouble before."

She hesitated. "Yes," she said. "But I have to be in New York next week."

"You could still make the race down there, if you wanted to."

Actually, the idea of seeing Cahill and Lucas possibly beat Falco out for the national title was an incentive for Eva that was difficult to ignore. "I'll give it some

194

thought," she told him. "If I can come, I'll call you there."

"We'll be at the Pier House," Lucas said. "We're already booked in."

"I hope I can make it, Boyd," she said.

It was later that same day that Lucas and Cahill were called in to have a talk with Charlie Rossman. Eva was on her way north, and Falco had not even known she was in town. Cahill thought that Rossman's request to see them together was a routine one, until he and Lucas got into Rossman's office and saw the somber look on Rossman's face. Rossman offered them chairs and they seated themselves before his desk. He looked very tired, and his grayish hair was rumpled and wild-looking.

"I'm glad I could get you two here together," he told them, slumping in his chair in almost exactly the same way as when Gus Beckering had confronted him there. "I wish Danny Del Rio could have been here."

Cahill frowned. "What is it, Charlie? Any trouble with the race committee in Key West?"

Rossman shook his beefy face. "No, nothing like that." His voice was hollow-sounding. Out in the plant, beyond glass windows in the office wall, an employee was using a whining drill on a new boat in construction, and Boyd Lucas was reminded of a recent visit to the dentist.

"Gus Beckering was in here the other day," Rossman went on.

"Oh, Christ," Lucas grumbled. "What did he want to do, sell the *First Blood?*"

Rossman held his gaze soberly. "No. He wanted to buy the *Sonic Boom*."

Cahill's frown deepened. "You're kidding."

"On the contrary. He offered me three times market for it. In all seriousness."

"That stupid jerk!" Lucas growled. "He thinks he can buy any goddam thing he wants." But Cahill was now studying Rossman's face closely. "Well, the sonofabitch can't buy the national title. He'll have to earn it."

"What did you say, Charlie?" Cahill asked quietly.

Rossman eyed Cahill with a weary look. "I told him I wouldn't sell the *Sonic Boom* to him."

"Good," Lucas said. "I hope you told the bastard off."

"But," Rossman added heavily, "I'm withdrawing the boat from the Key West race."

A new silence hung in the room that crackled with tension suddenly. Lucas rose slowly from his chair, and Cahill just sat there, staring grimly at Rossman.

"What?" Lucas said in disbelief.

Rossman sighed, and shook his head slowly. "Beckering threatened to put me out of business, if I didn't. I called my biggest customers yesterday and confirmed what he told me when he was here. He's put big pressure on them. If he gives them the word, they'll drop me like a hot potato. They have no choice. I have no choice. Not if I want to stay in business. I don't think I could recover from that."

"Why, that arrogant, ruthless bastard!" Lucas said loudly. "He can't just go around making threats like that! Can't we see the police? A lawyer? The goddam race authorities?"

Rossman shook his head again. "There's nobody that can do anything about it, Boyd, in time for it to make any difference. Anyway, I just don't feel like that kind of fight. Not just to win a trophy for my wall."

Cahill smashed a fist into his open hand, and Rossman saw the frustration in his face. "Ed Harris warned me about Beckering. He said Beckering wouldn't let us have the title. Not without some dirty back-alley fighting."

"I'm not up to that kind of thing," Rossman said apologetically. "Not at my age. Maybe twenty years ago it might have been different. But not now, I don't have it in me."

196

"Hell, let Steve and Danny and me handle it," Lucas said angrily. "We'll go to Beckering and give him some of what he's been dishing out. Maybe bust his frigging face. Give him something to think about."

Cahill turned to him. "He'd go right to the race committee," he said quietly. "Or to the national association. He has friends there, too. We'd never race a boat again."

Lucas was frustrated. "Well, why can't we go to the associates? Why can't we get the sonofabitch disqualified from the Key West race because of his threats to Charlie?"

"Maybe you could," Rossman said, "maybe not. But that wouldn't stop Beckering from putting me out of business."

Cahill and Lucas looked toward Rossman and saw the resolve in his heavy face.

"I'm sorry as hell, you two," Rossman went on. "I pushed you into these last races, Steve, I know. I thought it would be good for you, and I still do, despite the trouble you keep having out there on the water. Boyd, I know that you want to be on a championship crew more than you've ever wanted anything, and so does Danny. But I can't throw away what I've worked for my whole life, just to stand up for some questionable principle. Beckering has me by the short hairs, and there isn't a hell of a lot I can do about it."

Rossman heaved out another sigh. "I'm going to sell the *Sonic Boom*. I already have a potential buyer."

Lucas squinted his big face up. "Sell it! Oh, for Christ's sake, Charlie!"

"Beckering has made me sour on racing as a kind of pastime," Rossman admitted. "I doubt I'd be entering a boat next year, anyway, whether Beckering is in or out of it."

Lucas glowered at Rossman. "Goddam it, Charlie. Don't you know you've got the best goddam driver in the country, right here under your frigging roof?" He jerked a thumb at Cahill. "That you could dominate the race circuit for years and change it to something that's more to your liking? Hell, Beckering is on his last leg. He may not even be around next year. Or Falco, for that matter, with him and Eva busted up. You could change the whole scene in offshore racing, make it a more level-headed kind of competition."

Cahill saw Rossman's face, and glanced at Lucas. "Get off the soap box, Boyd. Charlie has made up his mind." He turned to Rossman, then. "Who are you going to sell the *Sonic Boom* to?"

Rossman met his gaze. "There's this retired industrialist over on the beach. Name's Ingram, he used to own a couple of auto parts factories in Ohio. He's always wanted to own a really fast racing boat."

"When will you be selling it to him?" Cahill asked.

Rossman narrowed his eyes on Cahill. "Probably very shortly."

Cahill nodded. "Well." He rose and stood beside Lucas. "I guess that's it, then, Charlie. Thanks for letting us know."

Lucas cast a hard look at Cahill. "You mean that's all of it? Just like that? After the whole frigging season, coming right to the wire with a real chance at the title? Jesus H. Christ!" He turned angrily and stormed from the office.

Cahill looked after him, and then spoke to Rossman. "He'll be all right, Charlie. I'll go talk with him."

"I really am sorry," Rossman said almost inaudibly.

Cahill, despite the impression he had given his boss, and in spite of his growing fear of getting out onto a race course, had not given up on the final race, the one that could earn him and his crew the national championship trophy.

When Cahill and Lucas had left Rossman's office that October afternoon, it was two weeks until the Key

West race, to be run the latter part of the month. To Rossman's surprise, Cahill helped facilitate the sale of the boat to Ingram, and the boat became the property of Ingram within a few days of that meeting in Rossman's office. Rossman had washed his hands of racing, for that year and the future.

But Cahill hadn't. Not yet.

He had gone to Ingram and evidenced an interest in the *Sonic Boom* himself.

He knew that if Rossman sold the boat to one or all of its crew, Beckering might still come down on Rossman, figuring the sale was merely an avoidance of his ultimatum, so that Rossman could still grab the trophy away from Beckering. But if somehow Cahill and the others of the crew could find a way to wangle ownership from Ingram, without Rossman's even knowing about the deal, Beckering could not accuse Rossman in any way. He would have to deal with the boat's crew if he wanted to keep them out of the Key West race.

Ingram had been pleased to meet Cahill. He followed racing closely, and had been impressed with Cahill's performances against Falco. Cahill had suggested the possibility, at first, that Ingram might want to sponsor the *Sonic Boom* in the last race, but Ingram was not interested. He did not want to risk so expensive a craft in a dangerous enterprise like the championship finale. So Cahill asked him pointblank if Ingram would re-sell the boat for a profit, and Ingram countered with a question: How much profit?

Cahill, of course, could not answer that without talking to Lucas and Del Rio. Cahill had saved some money, but he had no way of buying the boat on his own, and the banks would never have lent him a large sum on it. The very evening that the boat became Ingram's property, Cahill met Danny Del Rio at the Miami airport, having called him down to Florida in advance of Del Rio's plans, and Cahill, Del Rio and Lucas had a meeting at Cahill's place. Neither Lucas nor Del Rio knew what Cahill had in mind when they all sat down around his living room that evening. Del Rio now knew that Rossman had sold the *Sonic Boom,* though, and was very down about it.

"I talked to Ingram about the *Sonic Boom,*" Cahill told them as they sat somberly around the room facing each other.

Lucas frowned quizzically at Cahill, and Del Rio looked up in surprise. Del Rio looked rested and ready to race, but his rather swarthy face was set hard in depression. He and Lucas were dressed in sport shirts, and Cahill still wore a pastel dress shirt from the work day, with a tie pulled down at the collar. His blond-streaked hair looked windblown from a drive across town with Del Rio from the airport.

"What for?" Del Rio asked.

"About buying the *Sonic Boom,*" Cahill told them.

They both looked at him as if he must have had too much to drink at the airport lounge waiting for Del Rio to arrive.

"Did you come into a small fortune by chance, Steve?" Lucas said sourly.

"I'm not talking about me buying it," Cahill said. "I'm talking about us."

Del Rio raised his dark eyebrows, and Lucas grunted out a laugh. "I'd hate to show you my bank balance," Lucas said.

"I don't have much either, Steve," Del Rio said to him. But there was already an excitement in his voice that had not been there before.

Cahill leaned forward in a wing chair, like a boxer in a corner of the ring. "I'm not talking cash, either," he said seriously. "Listen to me, you two. You told me, both of you, how important this race season is to you. You, Boyd, have never had a crack at a national title before. You, Danny. You've dreamed about a chance like this. As for me—well, maybe I'm the one who should let it go. Things are still happening to me out

200

there, and it's not getting any better. But it's gotten to the point now at which I want to get to the bottom of it, no matter what it means, no matter what happens to me or what it does to me.''

Lucas felt a chill pass through him at the pause in Cahill's speech. He had conflicting emotions inside him that he hardly understood. He wanted the title badly; he wanted to beat Falco and Kralich and Beckering. But he was also scared for Cahill, whom he considered to be his best friend.

''But whether I race or not, you two deserve better than to be set loose like this, at the last minute. I think we ought to race at Key West, if just to knock Falco and Beckering off their pedestals. We could do it, you know, with a little luck.''

''You bet your ass we could!'' Del Rio said tightly.

Cahill sighed. ''Ingram bought the *Sonic Boom* for sixty grand. It was a good buy, and he knows it was a good buy. I have to hand it to Charlie for not selling it to Beckering, at least. That cost him a bundle.''

''What difference does it make?'' Lucas said heavily.

''Ingram will sell the boat to us, if we give him a profit,'' Cahill went on. ''He told me so. He didn't really want that much boat, anyway, he says.''

''How much profit?'' Del Rio asked.

''He wants us to make him an offer. I figure we can get it for seventy thousand even.''

''Christ, it might as well be a million,'' Lucas grumbled. He had already called Eva in New York, and she had given him a weak commitment to get to Key West. He worried now that her ardor might already have cooled.

''Not really,'' Cahill continued. ''I saw a couple of banks. One of them will go half on a loan, just to be associated with the race finale. They would want to be listed as co-sponsors in the Key West race.''

Lucas was now studying the floor, as if he had discovered an exotic insect there. ''Half, huh?''

"Maybe a few more bucks," Cahill said. "That means they'll probably go to forty if they have to. Which would leave thirty grand for us to raise. Of course, the bank would have to be paid off. If we won at Key West, there would be the prize money which would pretty well take care of it. If not, we could re-sell."

"Jesus," Del Rio was saying. "I do have some blue chip stocks I could peddle."

"How much would they give you?" Cahill asked.

"I own a hundred shares, and they're up to seventy dollars a share." Excitement was showing up in his face now. "My God, that's seven thousand."

"I have a little nest egg," Cahill said. "I've been building it for years. It amounts to just under fifteen thousand. I'd invest all of it."

Lucas cast a sober look toward Cahill, trying to understand him. If he were Cahill, he would have taken this opportunity to bow out. The whole race thing was getting very dangerous for Cahill. "Are you sure, Steve?" he said.

Cahill nodded. "There's a lot more at stake for me than money," he said simply.

Lucas blew out his cheeks and cracked his big knuckles. "Okay. I think I could come up with five. There are some people that owe me, and Paige and I have a small joint account."

"Would she go for it?" Cahill asked. "With her feelings about the races?"

Lucas grinned. "I'll sweet-talk her," he said. "But five would be an absolute maximum for me, Steve, and that would still leave us short."

Cahill reflected for a moment. "Yes, by about five grand, if we want to be safe."

"Well, that's it, then," Lucas said. "We can't swing it."

Cahill rose and began pacing the floor, thinking. Finally, he turned back to Lucas. "What about Eva Falco?" he said.

Lucas made a sour face. "Eva?"

"She's left Falco and says nothing would please her more than to see someone knock him off his perch. And she likes you, Boyd. Maybe if you asked her real nice, she'd come up with five. She has it to spend."

"Oh, Christ, I don't know," Lucas said darkly. "I'd feel like a bastard, asking."

"I'd ask her, if you wanted me to," Cahill suggested.

Lucas rubbed a hand across his square chin.

"I'm certain that if we get the last five, the boat is ours," Cahill told him.

Lucas looked up at Cahill. "I'll call her in New York."

"Can you do it tonight? Time is important."

Lucas sighed. "Sure, Steve. Tonight."

Lucas put a call in shortly thereafter, but Eva was not at her hotel suite there, and Lucas left his number for a call-back. So when Cahill and Del Rio left to go find Ingram and make sure he would sell at their price, Lucas stayed at Cahill's place to get Eva's call.

They found Ingram at home that evening, and he was already getting skittery about owning the *Sonic Boom* because some kids had found it sitting temporarily on his condo parking lot the night before, where Rossman had delivered it, and had begun vandalizing it before a watchman drove them off. There was spray paint on its sleek side, and a trim tab had been damaged. Cahill stuck to his offer despite the trouble, and Ingram reluctantly agreed to re-sell at the profit Cahill suggested. But Cahill would have to come up with the money within forty-eight hours, or the deal was off.

Del Rio and Cahill then drove out to the Beach Yacht Club for a quick drink, knowing now that everything depended on Lucas's convincing Eva she should invest five thousand dollars in an enterprise that might take Falco's title away from him.

Surprisingly, Tony Falco and Art Kralich were at the yacht club when Cahill and Del Rio got there. Cahill was glad that Lucas was not with them, because Lucas was spoiling for a fight with Kralich. Cahill himself was still angry about Kralich's assault on Dulcie, but since Mary Ann had reported that Kralich had not hurt Dulcie, he had decided to let it lie. He had called Mary Ann back, since his visit to her, to see if she knew Dulcie's location yet, in Tampa, but Mary Ann did not.

Falco saw Cahill and Del Rio at the bar and came over to them with a big grin. Kralich stayed where he was, down the bar a few stools, and just watched Falco's exchange with them.

"Well, well. If it isn't the two foremost ex-racers of Miami and—Baltimore, isn't it? Where's Lucas, drowning his troubles in booze?"

Cahill saw Del Rio's face, and put a hand on his shoulder. "I thought you had left for Key West, Falco."

"Not for a couple of days," Falco grinned, his handsome face looking boozed-up. "Beckering is all relaxed about the last race, now that the great Cahill is out of it. Of course, I'd have beaten you down there, anyway, you know. I'm unbeatable when the chips are down."

"Go to hell," Del Rio growled.

"Ah, a little bitterness. Well, I think I understand. Don't feel bad, my boy, there's always next year."

Kralich laughed so that they could hear him, then got off his stool and walked to the men's room, near the entrance.

Cahill was casual when he replied to Falco. "Don't concern yourself about us, Falco. I hear you've got troubles of your own. Incidentally, how's Eva getting along in New York?"

Falco's face lengthened. "You think I need a goddam woman tagging along with me, for Christ's sake? You don't know Tony Falco, mister."

"I just hate to see you completely dependent on Gus Beckering," Cahill said easily, not looking at Falco.

Falco scowled. "Tony Falco isn't completely

dependent on anybody, Cahill. Put that in your little notebook and underline it.'' He started away, toward a small group of racing people across the room. ''I'll try to get you a seat in the grandstands at Key West, Cahill, so you can see the race.''

''That sonofabitch,'' Del Rio said, when Falco was gone.

Cahill swigged the rest of a double scotch, then rose off his stool. ''Come on, Danny. This place has a foul odor suddenly. Let's get us some fresh air.''

''Amen,'' Del Rio said.

When they got outside, though, Art Kralich was there. He had stepped outside to flick a cigarette butt away and was just turning to come back in when they emerged from the bar.

''Leaving so soon?'' Kralich's hard voice came. ''Don't you feel part of the crowd here anymore, Cahill?''

Cahill and Del Rio stopped before Kralich, as he barred their way. Cahill eyed him ominously. ''I never was part of your crowd, Kralich.''

''Shit, who wants you?'' Kralich growled.

''You'e got a crummy mouth on you, Kralich,'' Del Rio said.

Kralich laughed gutturally. ''You can always try to change the shape of it, little spic.''

Del Rio's face became dark-hued. ''You sonofabitch!'' He moved toward Kralich, but Cahill put a hand on him again to stop him.

''Come on, Danny. We've got more important things to do.''

Cahill guided Del Rio past Kralich, and they headed toward Cahill's Jaguar. But they had gotten only a few steps when Kralich called after Cahill.

''Incidentally, Cahill. That Padgett girl is something else. She's got a lot to show, up under that little skirt. I had a hell of a time with her.''

Cahill stopped, heavily, but did not turn.

"Of course, it's obvious she's nothing but a cheap whore," Kralich's voice came, grating and low.

Del Rio turned first, and then Cahill, both grim-faced. "That does it!" Del Rio said in a low hiss.

"No, Danny," Cahill said. "It's my fight. It always has been."

Kralich heard the exchange clearly, and a big grin decorated his ugly, broken-nosed face. He assumed a boxing stance, eagerly. "You want to defend her frigging honor? Hell, come on, Cahill. This ought to be fun!"

"Let's get away from the door," Cahill said in a low voice. He turned to Del Rio. "And you keep out of it. You hear me?"

Del Rio nodded grudgingly. Cahill turned and walked over to some parked cars. Kralich was right behind him. When they got there, Cahill turned to face Kralich, and at that exact moment Kralich threw a ham of a fist into Cahill's face, catching him by surprise.

Cahill was lifted off his feet by the vicious blow and thrown to the ground onto his back. He hit there hard, dazed and bleeding, breathing shallowly. His eyes teared up and he could not see for a moment. He lay on his side, trying to get his head clear, Kralich standing over him. He grunted and struggled to his feet, and just as he rose, Kralich's foot came and struck him solidly in the hip and ribs. Cahill cried out a muffled cry and hit the ground again, feeling rockets of raw pain shoot up and down through his side. His nose was swelling rapidly across his face, and blood ran from it down onto his mouth and chin.

"You bastard!" Del Rio was saying to Kralich. "Fight fair!"

"Keep out of it, or I'll break you up!" Kralich warned him.

Del Rio remembered his promise to Cahill and stayed off at a short distance. Cahill lay there, getting himself together. He started to get up again, but thought better of it. He lay there letting his strength coil inside him, like a snake about to strike. Kralich came over him, and swung a booted foot at his head. He intended to hurt Cahill badly. The foot came, and Cahill grabbed it as it reached him. He deflected its force, and turned on Kralich's ankle, rolling with it. There was a loud cracking sound, and the ankle fractured under the leverage force. Kralich yelled loudly and hit the pavement.

Cahill got his breath back and scrambled to his feet again. He was still dizzy from the blow to his face, and his side dug pain into his insides when he moved. Now Kralich, despite his bad ankle, was also getting up. He hobbled to his feet, putting his weight on his good leg, his big face dark now with rage.

"You frigging war hero! I'm going to break you up good!"

Kralich lunged at Cahill then, looking like a Mack truck hurtling toward him. But now Cahill was finally ready. He stepped aside as Kralich came, slamming the heel of his hand down across Kralich's neck as he plunged past. The blow connected just about where Cahill wanted it to, and Kralich grunted and hit the pavement on his face, stunned and almost unconscious. Cahill had killed at least two men with that blow, but had purposely placed it off the vital spot that would have finished Kralich for good.

Kralich scrambled on the ground now like a beetle, trying to get his hands and feet under him. But he was out of it. He was making odd sounds in his throat, and his tongue was stuck out of his mouth. Del Rio's mouth had dropped open at the quick turn of events, and he now stared at Kralich in open disbelief.

Cahill walked over to Kralich and growled out a harsh message. "This is for Dulcie," he said in the strange, low voice. He kicked hard into Kralich's side, fracturing a rib audibly. Kralich yelled in new pain, struggling into a fetal position. Cahill stood over him, unsteady on his feet, blood on his lower face. He knew a dozen ways to end Kralich's life with just one more blow, and he was still tempted. He kicked the side of his foot into the side of Kralich's big face, carefully, and broke Kralich's jaw.

Kralich groaned loudly, but then fell into a state of dazed consciousness in which he was no longer with the real world.

"By Jesus!" Del Rio exclaimed under his breath.

"Go tell Falco that his navigator needs medical attention," Cahill said quietly, still breathing with difficulty.

Del Rio nodded blankly. "Sure, Steve. Sure, anything you say."

Just as Del Rio was going into the club, a car drove up nearby, and Boyd Lucas got out. He saw Cahill immediately, where Cahill was leaning against a Buick Electra, not far from Kralich's groaning figure. Lucas came over and stared at Cahill for a long moment and then at the downed Kralich.

"I'll be a sonofabitch. I think I just missed the best show of the season."

"I'm glad you weren't here," Cahill said, wiping at the blood on his face with a handkerchief. "What happened? I thought you were waiting for Eva's call?"

Lucas came up and touched Cahill's swollen face. "I was," he said. He looked down at Kralich, and grinned, then turned back to Cahill. "She says she'll not only go the five grand, but give us any additional we'll need to get the boat back and get it into the race at Key West."

Cahill just stared at Lucas for a moment, then his bloodied and swollen face broke into a tired smile. "Well, what do you know," he said with satisfaction. "It seems we've got us a title run after all."

Chapter Fifteen

Within twenty-four hours of Eva's call, the group owned the *Sonic Boom* in partnership. Cahill had partnership papers drawn up the next day by an attorney, and the *Sonic Boom* was re-entered in the Key West race, with Rossman listed as a sponsor, so he would get the trophy if there was a win there.

Charlie Rossman was surprised and pleased by the group's move. Cahill had wondered whether Rossman would take it all amiss, but Rossman could not have been happier. Cahill called Beckering and told him what had happened, and that Rossman had nothing to do with it, and that if Beckering wanted to make any further threats, he had better make them against Cahill. Beckering was subdued on the phone, figuring now that he would have to beat Cahill fairly, that Falco would have to finish first at Key West or lose the championship. He called Cahill a couple of choice names, but then hung up on him. There was no point in further talk about it. There was nothing he could threaten Cahill with that would make Cahill withdraw.

Just a week before the race, Cahill moved the *Sonic Boom* to Key West. The vandalism damage had been repaired, and the boat was ready to race. Cahill pulled the boat down the Keys himself, on a long trailer behind a hefty pick-up truck. Del Rio and Lucas took turns riding with Cahill in the truck and driving Cahill's Jaguar with a sign on the bumper that said, *Wide Load*. Del Rio and Lucas had never been on the Keys and were impressed with the multi-hued ocean surrounding them on the many long bridges—the Atlantic on one side of them and the Gulf of Mexico on the other. Great white herons stood dramatically in the shallow inlets, making snowy silhouettes against the turquoise and lavender of the water, and dark green mangrove forests crouched against a cobalt sky. They passed the old Caribbean Bar on Key Largo, where the film was made in the Forties with Edward G. Robinson and Humphrey Bogart, and Lucas wanted to stop for a beer, but Cahill wanted to put some miles behind them. At Marathon, on Vaca Key, they stopped at the Seven Mile Grill and had deep-fried shrimp and Lucas got his beer. By sunset they were at Key West, at the furthermost point in the Keys. The island city looked amber-hued in the fading sun as they drove down to the local marina on Roosevelt Boulevard, parked the *Sonic Boom* behind the marina's wire fence, and then drove on downtown to check in at the Pier House Motel on the Gulf. After cleaning up in their room with a balcony overlooking the water, they strolled down to Sloppy Joe's Bar, where Hemingway used to do his drinking. There were a lot of young people in there, some looking pretty rough, with beards and ragged shirts on. One middle-aged fellow at the bar looked like a latter-day Robinson Crusoe, with three iguanas decorating his bony shoulders, on harnesses. It was not much like Miami.

They found a table in a back corner, where a ceiling fan moved the heavy air over them. A waitress brought them all beers, and Del Rio downed half of his in one gulp.

"There are a lot of Cubans here, I see," he said happily, wiping at his mouth with the back of his hand.

"They've been here for a hundred years," Cahill said.

"I saw a sign in a store window back there," Lucas said. "It said, 'English Spoken Here.' Are they putting us on?"

Cahill grinned. He had felt more relaxed, driving

down the Keys, than he had in a long time. Maybe it would be different here, because of the slow, backwater mood of the town. Maybe he could finally run a race without going a little crazy out there.

"We don't have to worry over what language to speak to the natives," he said to Lucas. "It's the sea here that poses us a problem."

"What problem?" Del Rio asked.

But Lucas answered for Cahill. "The water is shallow down here, and there's no surf. We're inside a big barrier reef. You don't have to fight high seas generally, in a race here, but you have to keep your boat afloat."

"That's right," Cahill agreed. "You have to watch your markers closer here than at Miami or New York. If you get far off-course near shore, you could go aground on a sand bar. Also out at Sand Key, where we turn to head south."

"Is the *First Blood* any more shallow-drafted than us?" Del Rio wondered.

"We're about the same. You'd have to race a skiff in these waters to be safe. We just have to stay in the channels and on course, that's all. And we should get the most out of our engines here. This is a fast course, because the seas will probably be like glass. We'll be racing flat-out most of the time, and the team that can sustain that kind of run will win."

"I'm not afraid of that kind of race," Lucas said. "I think the *Sonic Boom* can hold her own in an ears-back, laid-out run."

Cahill was looking at a nearby wall that held memorabilia from the Hemingway days. "I just wonder if we're through with Gus Beckering," he said pensively.

Del Rio frowned at him. "Through? Why wouldn't we be? What can he do now that we own the boat?"

"I don't know," Cahill said. "But he may think of something. I get the idea that he doesn't have Falco's confidence that Falco will beat us in a fair race."

Lucas grunted out a small laugh. "I hear Kralich is walking around with a cast on one leg, to his knee, and his ribs taped. He looks like you did when you came out of the hospital at New York."

"But he says he's ready to race," Del Rio reminded them.

"I didn't want to put him out of the race," Cahill said. "I didn't want Beckering to have any excuses if we happen to beat him."

"What can we do about Beckering?" Lucas wondered. "You never know what's in his head. How can we defend against that?"

"We can't," Cahill said. "But we can be watchful."

"We ought to take the boat out a couple of times here, too," Lucas suggested. "To get a feeling for these shallows. It could make a difference in the race."

"I thought we'd put her in the water tomorrow morning," Cahill said. "To see if there are any kinks to be worked out of her."

"I'll arrange it before we hit the sack tonight," Del Rio said.

The following day they took the *Sonic Boom* out, and it was different with the boat now. There was more excitement in the thing, because the boat belonged to them. Del Rio compared it to owning a race horse; it was not like an inanimate object to him. He treated it like a woman, and his behavior affected that of Cahill and Lucas. It was like having a big side bet on the race, owning the craft they would ride in it.

The boat performed well, as usual. They took it out to Sand Key and then to the Marquesas, a group of islands beyond Key West that could be reached only by boat. Out beyond them yet lay the Dry Tortugas and Fort Jefferson, where Dr. Mudd was imprisoned after Lincoln's assassination. The threesome had never seen such beautiful waters. The colors were all soft ones, aquamarine and turquoise and sky blue. Dolphins jumped in the sun-glinting water, and there were fishing

212

boats out for tarpon. Two shrimp boats were heading out to their trawling grounds, with booms lowered like the limbs of a crustacean.

"She's ready," Del Rio said confidently, on their return to the marina. "She's really ready."

A couple of other racers had arrived now, and excitement was building. At the bar at the Sportsman's Inn, a short walk from the marina, the race committee chairman came in with the national trophies, and they looked impressive. A couple of people congratulated Cahill on getting control of his boat, and wished him luck. The local newspaper, the *Key West Citizen,* ran a big column about the races coming up, and townspeople began coming over to the marina to study the big racing boats. It was understood that this was not just another national race, as it had been at Miami. The driver of the two contenders who beat his adversary here would be the Class One national champion. The race was big in the sports world. There would be wire service reporters there, and a couple of big-city newspapers would be represented. A Miami TV camera crew would arrive shortly.

It was all very colorful.

Cahill seemed to be getting along fine. Tony Falco had not arrived yet, and things seemed relaxed to him. Except for missing Dulcie more and more with each day that passed, he was feeling good. He had heard definitely now that Mary Ann was coming down to Key West with the owner, Ramos, and expected to get Dulcie's phone number from her when she arrived.

But then Cahill took the boat out again with his crew, and things were different from the first cruise. The boat was not at top speed when it happened, and there was no unusual excitement. But very suddenly, with the boat cruising along nicely and no pressures on Cahill at all, he got a wrenching in his stomach that made him gasp aloud in pain. Neither Lucas nor Del Rio noticed, because of the roar of the engines. The pain shot through him again, with nausea, and hot flashes of memory burned into his skull like sulphuric acid. The *Sonic Boom* was not a racer, momentarily, but a Navy patrol boat on a hot jungle river. The boat was gray in color, with camouflage markings. It had a canopy over a wheel house and guns were mounted fore, aft, and amidships. Fatigue-clad sailors wearing helmets manned the controls and the guns, hunched over them, faces grim and flushed.

The nausea welled up. "Boyd. Throttle down."

They were not wearing head gear, so Lucas had difficulty hearing Cahill. He turned, though, and saw Cahill's ashen face and slowed the boat immediately. Now Cahill was pushing himself to the gunwale of the boat, unsteadily. Del Rio turned, too, and surprise etched itself into his face. Cahill was being sick over the gunwale, heaving and heaving.

Lucas cut the engines, and the *Sonic Boom* coasted quietly to a rolling halt in the calm sea. Cahill hung over the edge, and color slowly returned to his face. He wiped his mouth and turned to his silent comrades.

"It must have been something I ate. Maybe this Cuban food doesn't agree with me."

"Jesus, Steve!" Del Rio muttered.

"It isn't the food," Lucas said somberly. "You got it again, didn't you? The nerves."

Cahill slumped against the bolster, his blondish hair blowing in a sea breeze. "Yeah," he said.

"Christ," Lucas said.

"What the hell am I doing out here, Boyd?" Cahill murmured, feeling his stomach unwind some. "What am I trying to prove?"

Del Rio leaned toward him, past Lucas. "Listen, Steve. For the first six months after I got back, I couldn't eat anything but cream of wheat and poached eggs, for Christ's sake. I jumped out of my shoes when somebody slammed a door behind me. I saw Cong hiding in bedroom shadows at night."

"That was the first six months," Cahill said.

"I told you, some guys were triggered by things they didn't even understand. Years later, like this. But it all passes, for most of them."

Cahill glanced toward him. "And the rest?"

Some ended up in loony bins, Del Rio recalled dismally. *Others quietly committed suicide.* He swallowed hard. "Don't worry about them, buddy. You aren't one of them."

Cahill held Del Rio's gaze, and Del Rio finally averted his to the deck of the bolster.

"Okay, let's take her in," Cahill said quietly. "I think I've had my look at the sea for today."

The day after that incident at sea, Tony Falco arrived in town, and he had a surprise companion with him: Rachel McKenzie.

Cahill was having a drink that evening with Del Rio at the oldest bar in town, Captain Tony's Saloon. It was a rather dark, low-ceilinged place that gave the appearance of an English pub if you did not look at the clippings and photographs on the walls and the flotsam of seashore decor behind a small stage at the rear. You half-expected to see men with peg legs at the tables, wearing double-breasted blue uniforms with brass buttons on them. Cahill and Del Rio were sitting at a table near the rear of the place when Falco came in with Rachel on his arm. She saw Cahill immediately.

Cahill could not believe that Rachel had come down to Key West for the final race, or that she was with Tony Falco. His opinion of her had dropped considerably since their last meeting, but now it plummeted even further. He groaned inwardly as Falco and Rachel headed for his and Del Rio's table.

Falco was not grinning this time. He was very tense again, since he had heard of Cahill's entry into the race with the *Sonic Boom*. "I didn't think I'd be seeing you again, Cahill," he said acidly as he and Rachel stopped at the table. "I guess life is just full of unpleasant surprises."

"Oh, Tony," Rachel smiled nicely, holding his arm in a very proprietary way, showing off to Cahill. "Hi, Steve. Danny, isn't it?"

Del Rio nodded unenthusiastically. "Good to see you again, Rachel."

"You didn't offer to bring me down to the race," Rachel said sweetly to Cahill. "So I came with Tony. We've been having a ball on the way down."

"I'll bet," Cahill grunted.

"I hear you own the *Sonic Boom* now," Falco said. He was wearing a brightly flowered sport shirt out over expensive-looking slacks, and his dark hair was slicked back. He looked too sober, Cahill thought.

"The three of us do," Cahill replied. He thought it just as well not to mention Eva's involvement.

"I didn't know you had the means to invest in such an enterprise," Rachel said with a pleasant smile. "I'm happy for you, Steve. Do you mind if we have a drink with you, before we go to the Casa Marina for dinner?"

Cahill winced inwardly. He wanted to tell Rachel and Falco to go drink by themselves, but he had never learned to be rude to others.

"Suit yourself," he said.

Rachel sat down beside Cahill, and Falco seated himself between Cahill and Del Rio. "I saw your boat at the marina," Falco said to Cahill, ignoring Del Rio completely. "It was still dripping sea water. I guess you've had it out already."

"We wanted to get the feel for the shallows," Cahill told him.

"You get off course here, you'll pay the bill," Falco grinned rather harshly.

"We've heard that," Cahill said.

"Tony and I have a lot of interests in common," Rachel broke in. "I hope you won't take offense, Steve, but we seem to be more in tune than you and I were.''

A small silence settled over the table.

''I think that's nice, Rachel,'' Cahill said. ''And understandable.''

Falco's dark eyes narrowed slightly on Cahill.

''Tony likes some excitement in his life, like me,'' Rachel said deliberately. ''He's a different man, now that he has freed himself of marital strings.''

Del Rio grunted out a small laugh. ''I didn't know it was Tony that did the freeing up.''

Falco turned a hard, arrogant look on Del Rio. ''So you're still part of the crew, heh, Del Rio? It must make you pretty smug, riding in on another man's point total.''

Del Rio's face fell into straight, sober lines.

''I mean, it should be Ed Harris out there on race day, I suppose. But then, that's the way the world works, isn't it? We all profit occasionally from the other men's efforts. More power to you, I say.''

Cahill felt the new tension electrifying the air. ''Danny is making it all happen, Falco. We wouldn't have won at Miami without him. He's given us the new blood we needed to make a real run at the title.''

''All this race talk is getting boring,'' Rachel complained.

Nobody paid any attention to her. A waitress came and took Rachel's and Falco's orders and left. Falco turned back to Cahill. ''Do you think you'll survive it, Cahill? Your run for the title?''

Cahill held Falco's hard look. ''I think so.''

''It's being said around that it won't make any difference about your getting back into the race,'' Falco persisted. ''That you're a loser, Cahill. That you get in trouble out there, in your head, and that it's getting worse. That's just what I hear, of course, it could all be bullshit.''

''It is bullshit,'' Del Rio said darkly.

''How you men talk!'' Rachel said, arching her eyebrows.

"It's funny the things you hear around the circuit," Cahill said evenly. "They're saying this new man of yours, Jenkins, has a lot of guts to take Hank Wyatt's place. Most men would rather be tied into a barrel and thrown over Niagara than to get into that tub with you, they say. But I don't listen to that stuff, myself. I have my own opinion."

Falco's face had sagged into hard lines suddenly. "Buying that Rossman boat doesn't make you national champ, Cahill. Neither does your frigging war record. You're going to have to beat me in, mister. And you know what? I'm going to jam that boat of yours up your frigging ass!"

"Listen, you bastard—" Del Rio growled, rising from his chair.

"Gentlemen, please!" Rachel said with a half-scared smile.

"We'll see whose ass is sucking Kevlar," Cahill said in a hard, low voice, "when this race is finished, Falco."

Several nearby customers had turned to hear this exchange. Now Falco, oblivious of them or the waitress who had just come up with their drinks, rose quickly from the chair he was sitting on, bumped into the waitress, and she dumped her tray of drinks all over the floor. The stuff went crashing, as Rachel rose to get out of the way.

"Well, I'll be damned!" the waitress muttered.

"I'm going to bury you out there, Cahill!" Falco said loudly, but his face did not reflect confidence in that prediction. "I'm going to run your ass off the goddam course!" Without even turning to Rachel then, he stormed off and out of the saloon.

Several customers nearby grinned and applauded. Rachel, unflustered, gave Cahill a knowing look. "You see what I mean about Tony's being exciting?" she said easily. Then she, too, left the place, after laying a bill on the table for the waitress.

"Jesus Christ!" Del Rio said under his breath.

"Who is that creep?" the waitress wondered, picking up two glasses with Del Rio's help.

"Just a crazy race driver, honey," Del Rio told her. "Don't pay him any mind."

That night later, Mary Ann showed up at the Pier House with Phil Ramos, and she got in contact with Cahill and gave him a number where Cahill could reach Dulcie in Tampa. Mary Ann was obviously letting Ramos pay her way at Key West, just for her sharing his bed with him, and Cahill knew it could just as well be someone other than Ramos, if the offer had been made. Mary Ann was down to prostituting herself in exchange for a good time, and Cahill was sorry to see that. He was glad he had not succumbed to her charms at Miami, in that brief meeting, and that Dulcie was no longer living with her.

Cahill was beginning to realize that he had pegged Dulcie wrong. Every day that passed, he missed her, and wished he had made more of an effort to see her before she left Miami. Now, with her phone number in hand, he called her that same evening, from their motel room. This time he got lucky. After three rings, her voice came on the other end, sounding soft and sultry.

"It's me, Dulcie, Steve."

A long silence on the other end. "Well. I guess I didn't expect to hear from you again."

"I tried to get in touch with you," he said lamely. "In Miami. But you were never at your room."

"I was trying to find a job," she said. "I have one, finally. Here in Tampa."

"Do you like it?"

"It beats serving drinks to alcoholic ad executives," she said. "Mary Ann tells me you own the *Sonic Boom* now."

"We've all got a piece of it. Even Eva Falco. She left her husband, you know."

"Jesus, good for her," Dulcie said. "Tony is a real bastard."

Cahill hesitated. "Dulcie, I wanted to apologize for the things I said that night at the beach. I don't know what gets into me. I haven't been myself all through the racing season."

"It's all right," her voice came. "I gave you some wrong impressions. How is Rachel?"

Cahill sighed heavily. "That was another silliness of mine," he said quietly. "Rachel is seeing Falco now. I think maybe they were made for each other."

Dulcie laughed in a subdued way.

"Listen, Dulcie, I—miss you," he said.

She made no reply.

"I was hoping you would hate your job there," he admitted. "So I could talk you into coming down here for the last race."

"Well," she said. "It isn't exactly what they promised me. It's a glorified clerk's job. But it's the only thing I have, Steve."

You have me, he wanted to say. But it sounded sophomoric and unbelievable to him, despite his sudden, deep feelings for Dulcie.

"You could—share a room with me, here at one of the motels. I checked, and there's some still available."

Another long silence. Then she said, "I don't think that would be wise of me, Steve."

He wanted to beg her, but he could not. He wanted to explain that it was different now, that he could not think less of her, no matter what she acceded to with him. But it was all too complex for him to put into words.

"You have to do what you think is right for you," he said. His voice made him sound lonely, to her. "I understand that, Dulcie."

"I can't do what Mary Ann is doing," Dulcie told him. "I'm trying hard to like myself again. Some days, that seems like an impossible task. I don't want to make

220

it any harder on myself than it already is."

His voice was now heavy. "Sure, Dulcie. It's all right, really."

"I hope you beat Tony by a mile."

"I'll be out there trying," he told her.

When Cahill hung up, a few minutes later, he felt a depression well in on him that was completely disproportionate to anything he would have expected.

Somehow, he had gotten attached to Dulcie. He had not even known when it had happened. But it was a fact of his life now, like the growing fear he had of this last race. He had the burgeoning feeling that he had aborted something that was good for him in his relationship with Dulcie and missed an opportunity to escape from some relentless pursuit of misery he had gotten himself involved in by buying the *Sonic Boom*. He had had a good out from the race, nobody could have blamed him for not coming to Key West. But now here he was, alone, for all practical purposes—since he could not really share his growing fears with Lucas or Del Rio, and he did not have Dulcie to comfort him—and heading into something that seemed suddenly as dangerous as the jungles of Vietnam had in those earlier, darker days.

Across town that evening at the Casa Marina Hotel, Gus Beckering had just arrived from the local airport and had called a conference with Falco, Kralich and the new navigator Jenkins. Disgruntled and out of sorts, Beckering discussed race strategy with them for an hour, then sent Jenkins out for some liquor, so he could have some time with Falco and Kralich alone. Kralich was still limping on a cast, had a taped rib, and sported a lightly wired jaw that made him mumble when he talked. He now hated Cahill more than he ever had Boyd Lucas. Beckering reprimanded him for brawling with Cahill and questioned him about his readiness to race. But Kralich was not impaired by his several injuries, to any extent. He threatened, in fact, to bust Cahill's skull with the cast.

"You'd better try to find him asleep," Falco offered sourly.

Now with Jenkins gone, though, Beckering wanted to talk about the re-entry of the *Sonic Boom* into the Key West race.

"That goddam Rossman got me into this," Beckering grumbled, sprawled on a short sofa in the hotel suite. An open window nearby looked over palm-dotted grounds, a swimming pool and bar, and the ocean. "He got Cahill all worked up about the goddam national title. He probably knew Ingram would re-sell to Cahill. I ought to bring the bastard down despite his pulling his boat out. Now we've got a real competition on our hands."

"I don't think Rossman has the guts to cross you," Kralich offered. "I think Cahill went behind his back to buy the boat. Cahill's your man, not Rossman. It's always been Cahill," he mumbled through the cast.

Beckering looked from him to Tony Falco. Falco sat in an overstuffed chair, looking glum. He had already had a couple of drinks at a local bar. "It didn't matter about that missed race, you said," Beckering grated out at him. He looked like a moth-eaten bear, slumped on the sofa there. "It didn't matter about your goof at Point Pleasant, you told me. You could beat Cahill when you had to. Well, you didn't beat him at Miami, by Jesus, and I'm not sure you can beat him here!"

Falco was more subdued than usual, and more tense. "This will be a flat-out race, if the weather holds. I don't think there's a driver on the circuit that can beat me in the *First Blood* running an open-throttle race. That's what I'm best at."

"I'm beginning to think what you're best at is boozing and balling," Beckering grumbled. "You sure got more practice at it than you do at racing."

222

"I'll be sober for this one," Falco said grimly. "I want to beat Cahill's ass."

"You wanted to at Miami," Beckering reminded him. "Kralich wanted to bust his head, and now he's limping around on a cast and mumbling through a wire. I told you before. You're taking this frigging Cahill too goddam lightly."

"That's all past now," Falco said. "I intend to beat him here. I'll use everything I know and I'll beat him."

Beckering shook his head. "You don't seem to get the idea. I didn't want the *Sonic Boom* in the race here when I was in Miami, and I still don't want it in the race."

Falco eyed him narrowly.

"Why should we take the chance that Cahill might beat you?" Beckering said urgently. "If we don't have to?"

"Cahill won't sell you the boat, for Christ's sake," Falco said moodily. "He isn't a Rossman."

"I'm not talking buying the boat," Beckering growled. "I'm talking keeping the boat out of the race. Any way we can."

"Now you're on track," Kralich mumbled through the wire, rubbing his leg above the cast.

Falco gave him a look, then turned back to Beckering. "What do you want me to do?" he said sourly. "Get a contract out on Cahill?"

Beckering was taut-faced. "You don't listen very well, Tony," he said in his gravelly voice. "The boat is still the key. Cahill has to have a racer under him to win that title. A damned good one. He can't do it without the *Sonic Boom*. So let's get rid of it."

Falco furrowed his dark brow. "Get rid of it? Steal it?"

"Sometimes I wonder what the hell you use for brains, Tony," Beckering growled. "I think I can see why Eva gave you the heave-ho. She expected more of a man than she got."

Falco's face reddened. "Don't push your luck with me, old man. I'm the only thing you've got to win that trophy with."

"You threatening to quit?" Beckering laughed in his throat. "There isn't another owner on the circuit that would take a chance on you after Hank Wyatt's death at Miami."

Falco just glared at Beckering, while Kralich got a slow grin on his big face. He took a lot from Falco, and Beckering was the only one who could really put Falco down. "Gus knows what he's talking about, Tony. You better cool it, man."

Falco gave Kralich a brittle look. "My God, now I'm getting advice from the Neanderthal!"

Kralich glared at Falco suddenly. "What the hell does that mean?"

But Beckering interrupted the exchange. "Art here knows more than you give him credit for. He knows you don't play games if you want to win. That right, Art?"

Kralich turned reluctantly from Falco. "You bet your ass," he said harshly, through the wire.

Beckering grinned with dark satisfaction. "You two together could put the *Sonic Boom* out of commission for good." He looked from Kralich to Falco.

Falco frowned. "Jesus Christ, Gus. You're talking sabotage."

Beckering shrugged his heavy shoulders. He wore a dark dressing gown that hid most of his flabbiness, but his face was flaccid now, with loose-hanging flesh that was red-splotched. He was losing weight with every week that passed, and he looked terrible.

"There are a lot of vandals around, nowadays. The *Sonic Boom* sustained some damage in the short time Ingram owned it, and that was in the papers. What if some smart-asses down here had read that, and thought it would be funny to hit it again? To take it out of the race?"

"Oh, Christ," Falco muttered.

"Or maybe some local can't stand having the races here, and wants to make a point by taking a boat out. Some of these islanders don't like all this hoopla, you know. They've done crazy things before. One of them might just decide to set the *Sonic Boom* on fire."

Falco looked at him quickly. "Arson? Not a chance, Gus. Fires have a way of getting out of control. Count me out. No way."

Kralich just sat there, looking thoughtful, making no objection.

"Is that an unequivocal no?" Beckering said caustically.

"I'm telling you, Gus. I can beat Cahill." He rose and stood facing Beckering. "I have to beat him, goddam it. It's a thing with me, now. If I burned his boat out from under him, I'd have lost my last chance to prove myself against him. I can't give that up."

Beckering was disappointed. He had thought he could count on Falco because the driver had come to dislike Cahill so much. "What the hell am I going to do with you, Tony? You want the frigging world. But you don't know how to go about getting it. You don't have the moxie, the drive."

Falco turned and walked to the door of the suite. "Just let me tie a can on Cahill's tail my way," he said. "Come on, Art, I want you to take me down to the boat."

Kralich rose sullenly. "Just watch your mouth, Tony. I mean it."

Falco opened the door and left. When Kralich got there, he glanced back at Beckering for a moment. "What you were talking about. You and me, maybe we'll discuss it again some time, Gus."

Beckering figured he could count on Kralich. "You know where to find me, Art," he said with a harsh grin.

Chapter Sixteen

It was only a few days until the races.

Cahill was spending his time finishing engine modifications begun in Miami, with Lucas and Del Rio assisting him. In the daytime he thought of Dulcie, and at night he had cold-sweat nightmares, and now they were fixed on one scene. There was the river patrol boat, moving fast downstream, engines roaring behind it, and both he and Josh Owens were aboard and under fire from the banks of the river. He could not see more than that, but he knew now that it was unlikely his torment stemmed from any atrocity against the Cong. It had something to do with Josh, he was sure. But the river scene would always end before he could learn what it was all about, and he would wake up gasping out his raw fear into the darkness.

At least, though, he now understood why his involvement in racing the *Sonic Boom,* and before that the *Now It Ain't,* had been triggering these terror-filled moments in his head. Whatever had happened back there in Vietnam to cause his present troubles, had happened while he was on a speeding boat, under enemy fire. So whenever he raced a power boat, or got close to race day, he was automatically punching a response button inside him somewhere that evoked the frightening and still-mysterious ride down that jungle river. Also, Cahill now knew, something had happened on that terror-filled ride that he had tried to forget, had occluded completely from consciousness until his entry into this race season. He was on the verge of remembering, too; it was just a matter of time. He wondered whether, when he did, he would be able to handle it. It was as if his subconscious were trying to hide the river incident from him forever, but failing that because of the race season, was intent on re-playing the incident so that it came out in an acceptable version to him. He wondered what that version might be, and whether it would leave him alive when it was played out.

"It's going to happen in this last race," he said to himself one dark night, lying there with dampness on his brow and in the palms of his hands. "I know it. How the hell can I win with this going on?"

Cahill felt as if he were betraying Lucas and Del Rio by not insisting they get themselves another driver. Not only was he leading them into a dangerous situation, but his motives were different from theirs. They only wanted to win a race. But he had this new compulsion to confront what was inside him, and he was now certain that the finale race would force that confrontation. So his motivation did not depend on winning the race, as theirs did, and as they had the right to expect that it did.

Cahill tried to avoid Falco and Rachel, but it seemed he was unable to do so. In Sloppy Joe's Bar one evening, Rachel came in with Falco on her arm and sat at the table just next to Cahill and Del Rio. Falco did not seem to mind much. He enjoyed flaunting Rachel before Cahill. To Falco, it was as if he had stolen Rachel from Cahill. He did not understand that Cahill had voluntarily broken with Rachel. Rachel, for her part, no longer wanted Cahill, but enjoyed displaying herself with another man when Cahill was around.

Rachel spoke to Cahill when they sat down, but Cahill and Falco did not speak. Rachel, looking very sexy in a split-bodice dress that showed her small, firm breasts when she turned a certain way, sang with the music, talked rather loudly, and attracted a lot of attention. After she and Falco had been there for just a short time, Mary Ann came in with owner Phil Ramos, and they and another driver joined Rachel and Falco at their table. Ramos and Mary Ann spoke back and forth with Cahill and Del Rio, despite Cahill's lack of interest.

The music was live, from a three-piece ensemble, and when they began a carioca, and Mary Ann and Ramos got up to dance to it, Rachel got up by herself and began dancing alone, sinuously and suggestively. The dress showed her off nicely to the nearby male customers, and they gave her encouragement. Mary Ann and Ramos came and sat back down, watching Rachel. She snaked around the tables, moving gracefully, with Mary Ann regarding her darkly. A drunk from the bar came and danced with her for a few minutes. He put his hands on Rachel's breasts and hips, and she made no complaint. Cahill looked over at Falco and saw a grim look on his handsome Italian face. Rachel finally dismissed the drunk and returned to sit down at the table.

"Oh, God, that was fun!" she smiled breathlessly.

"Especially that last part, huh?" Mary Ann said.

"You looked beautiful," Ramos told her, making Mary Ann scowl slightly.

Falco rose. "I'm going over to Tony's. Anybody else coming?"

"We're having fun here!" Rachel protested.

"You can stay if you want," Falco said. "But I'm going."

At their table, Cahill and Del Rio were enjoying the exchange. Rachel glanced toward Cahill, as if hoping for an invitation to join him, but he gave her none. "Oh, hell," she finally said. She and Falco moved off, and out into the night street.

"That's some dame, eh?" Ramos said to Cahill.

"Yeah, some dame," Cahill said.

Del Rio sat and grinned. The other man who had come with Ramos and Mary Ann to the table, a fellow called George, returned from the bar with a drink and smiled suggestively at Mary Ann, putting a hand on her back, and Ramos did not mind. Cahill was surprised, because he thought Ramos was enamored of Mary Ann.

"Did you get in touch with Dulcie, Steve?" Mary Ann asked Cahill, ignoring the driver named George.

Cahill nodded. "We had a nice little talk."

"Will she come down for the race?"

"I guess not, Mary Ann."

Mary Ann was wearing a T-shirt with nothing under it, and the fellow George could not take his eyes off it. He leaned over and said something into Ramos's ear, and Ramos shrugged and nodded.

"Hey, why don't we have a little party at our room?" Ramos said after a couple of minutes, speaking to Mary Ann. "You like parties, don't you, honey? Plenty of booze and music?"

Mary Ann smiled. "Why not?"

"George here will come up with us, and maybe a couple other drivers," Ramos went on.

Mary Ann nodded. "Okay, but it'll be a little crowded, with four couples."

"Oh, we won't invite any other girls," Ramos said casually. "Who needs them, huh? You won't mind having to hug and kiss four drunks for a couple of hours, will you, honey?"

Mary Ann's face had changed quickly. She searched Ramos's eyes now, looking for confirmation of what she had already guessed.

"You want to come, Cahill?" Ramos asked. "Del Rio?"

Cahill held his gaze. "You mean, there would be just us men and Mary Ann?" he said slowly.

Ramos grinned a wide grin. "Mary Ann wouldn't mind that. She doesn't have to do anything she doesn't want to, up there. She knows that. Don't you, honey?"

Mary Ann caught Cahill's somber gaze for just an instant and then averted hers to the floor, flushing slightly. She wanted to tell Ramos to go to hell, but that would end it for her at Key West. She would be just drifting back up to Miami then, with no man, no Dulcie. "Yeah. Right," she said softly.

Cahill frowned.

"Maybe we can get Mary Ann to do a little dance for us, like that Rachel did," George grinned. "I'll bet you could outdo her, baby." He looked hungrily at Mary Ann's full T-shirt.

"We'll make a night of it," Ramos said. "What do you say, fellows? You want to join the fun?"

Cahill was still eyeing Mary Ann. He had not thought that she had come so far down. "I think I'll pass," he said. "It doesn't sound like my kind of thing."

Ramos shrugged. "How about you, Del Rio? Mary Ann can be a lot of fun, when she gets a couple of drinks in her. You can take my word for it." He grabbed Mary Ann's arm and squeezed it, and Mary Ann smiled uncertainly, still avoiding their looks.

Del Rio glanced toward Cahill. It was an invitation that was hard to pass up, but when he saw Cahill's sober face, he quickly declined. "No. I guess not."

"Suit yourself," Ramos grinned. He rose. "Well, let's round up my other two buddies." George and Mary Ann got up, too, and George put a hand on Mary Ann in a proprietary way.

"You don't have to go," Cahill said suddenly to her.

Everybody looked toward him in surprise.

"Hey. You may be a contender, pal," Ramos said, his grin gone. "But don't butt into our fun, okay?"

Mary Ann ignored Ramos's reaction to Cahill's comment. "The hell I don't," she said solemnly.

A moment later, she was moving off with them. Cahill looked glumly after them, and for a moment he wished he had never become involved with the racing circuit.

The next day, Eva Falco showed up in Key West.
She checked in at the Pier House Motel in midafter-

noon. Within an hour, Boyd Lucas had moved his things into her room. He was so glad to see her that, for the rest of that day, he found he could not even think about the race, which was now only four days off.

Cahill thought of calling Dulcie again, but could not bring himself to do so. She had been quite clear in her response to his invitation to come to Key West. Also, Cahill was having more and more trouble inside him. He had awakened both Lucas and Del Rio in the middle of the previous night, coming awake yelling nonsensical gibberish into the blackness. He was glad that Lucas would be sleeping in Eva's room. Now it would be only him and Del Rio, and Del Rio knew exactly what Cahill was going through.

Falco learned of Eva's coming that same day, when he met her by accident at the beach. He was with Rachel, and Rachel and Eva got a look at each other for the first time. Falco mistakenly thought Eva had come down to make up with him, and was more embarrassed by Rachel's presence than he need have been.

"Boyd Lucas!" he said incredulously, when Eva told him why she had come. "You came to be with Lucas?"

"Boyd and I always got along well," Eva told him airily. "I don't see why you should be so surprised, Tony. Incidentally, your taste in women seems to have improved. But I would think you could still find them your own age."

Rachel had not heard that remark. She had met Eva briefly, then excused herself to return to swimming. When Eva was gone, Falco found himself in a black mood. It did not sit well with him that she had flown all the way to Key West just to be with another man, even though divorce proceedings were pending, and even though he himself was well occupied with Rachel. It particularly displeased him that the man should be Boyd Lucas, a member of Cahill's crew.

Falco's mood prevailed throughout that day and continued at a party that Rachel took him to that evening.

Rachel, it turned out, had some rich friends in Key West, a retired couple in their fifties who had made it big in the wholesale coal business in Virginia. They lived in a three-level house on a canal on the Atlantic side of the island and went north to an equally luxurious home in North Carolina for the summer months. The party was one of those in Key West that slowly progressed from inside to a large poolside patio outside, as the evening waned.

Rachel drank rather heavily through the evening, and by the time it was half-gone, she was dancing to stereo music again, as she had at the bar. Again, she wore a very revealing dress, with a low-cut neckline, low back, and splits up the sides. She looked particularly sultry that evening, and glamorous, and most of the men there, including the younger ones, were giving her the eye.

None of this set well with Falco, who was accustomed to his women keeping well in the background and hanging on him. But Rachel was not that type. In fact, she was already tiring of Falco. There were a couple of other drivers at the party, and she was paying as much attention to them as to Falco, particularly one named O'Brien. As the evening progressed, Rachel became quite inebriated, and Falco was morose. He came to her where she was entertaining O'Brien and another man at poolside, in late evening, and suggested they leave.

"Go back to the hotel? Whatever for?" Rachel asked him.

Their hostess, a plump, graying woman came past with cocktails, and Rachel grabbed one. "I'm having a wonderful time!"

"Don't be a wet blanket, Tony," the driver O'Brien said, also inebriated. "The night is young, and Rachel's a gas."

Falco took Rachel's arm. "Come on, I know a nice quiet bar where the drunks leave you alone." He gave O'Brien a look.

But Rachel pulled free of him with a slight frown. "Tony! I told you, I'm enjoying myself. Just relax and have some fun, you really are a drag tonight."

Before Falco could respond, Rachel had turned back to the men. "Hey, nobody's gone into the pool yet!" she said.

"By God, you're right!" the driver O'Brien responded. "Well, we'll have to fix that pronto!"

O'Brien began undressing, tearing off a shirt. Rachel giggled, and spilled part of her drink. O'Brien was taking his shoes off, and his trousers. A couple of other guests had come to watch. In a moment, he stood in boxer shorts and socks. "I now initiate this pool for all who care to follow!" He jumped crazily into the chlorined water, making a big splash, and emerged a moment later, his head dripping.

When Falco turned back to Rachel, she was already pulling her dress off over her head, to quick applause from the growing crowd around her. As the dress came off, it became clear to everyone who did not already know that Rachel wore no bra. She bounced a bit as the cloth cleared her breasts, and there was a low whistle from the gathering.

"That's the way, honey!"

O'Brien emerged from the pool, staring openly. "Hey! This party is livening up!"

Falco scowled. "Rachel."

But she did not hear him. "I'll be damned if I'm going to get my undies wet," she said, kicking off her high-heeled shoes. She stood in just a pair of scant panties, and now she pulled them down over her hips. Kicking them also aside, she stood at poolside absolutely nude. The hostess raised her eyebrows slightly, but made no comment.

"Jesus," a man near Falco muttered.

A moment later, Rachel had dived into the pool expertly, her lithe, naked body splitting the water like an Olympic athlete's. There was more applause.

"Goddam it, Rachel," Falco said to himself.

"Come on, Tony," O'Brien said giddily. "Get your feet wet with your woman." He laughed a hard laugh.

Falco ignored him, trying to decide what to do. O'Brien shrugged, then pulled his boxer shorts off. A couple of women gasped, and the same men who had applauded Rachel now gave O'Brien a hand, also.

"Then I'll join her," O'Brien said with a grin. His nude hulk splashed once again into the pool near Rachel, where she was bobbing with just her head above water.

A couple of people glanced darkly toward Falco, as O'Brien closed the distance between him and Rachel, in the water. Then O'Brien was splashing water at Rachel, and they were grappling there, wet and naked. More on-lookers turned and studied Falco's saturnine face. Rachel's giggling laughter filled the background, as O'Brien handled her bare flesh. Suddenly the half-drunk O'Brien lost control, and grabbed Rachel un-abashedly and kissed her hungrily on the mouth. Their heads started going under in the embrace, and Rachel broke free, and then glanced toward Falco, whose face was set in hard lines.

"Well, I think I'll get back into my things," she said to the husky fellow in the water with her.

"Here's a towel, honey," the hostess said quickly, hurrying to the pool's edge as Rachel came to the ladder.

But the fellow O'Brien was right behind Rachel. As she climbed the ladder to the patio, he grabbed her buttocks and assisted her, a big grin on his square face. Rachel now looked slightly embarrassed as she came to receive the towel. Falco walked over to her and they ex-changed brittle looks.

"You goddam whore," Falco said clearly and dis-tinctly.

Suddenly, absolute quiet descended on the gathering. O'Brien was clambering from the pool. "Hey. You

234

can't talk to the lady like that!"

"I don't see any ladies in the vicinity," Falco growled.

Rachel, who had wrapped the towel around her nakedness, now dropped part of it and slapped Falco hard across the face. The slap resounded across the patio area.

"You can insult me, damn you, but not my friends," she said.

Without even thinking, Falco hauled off and returned the slap, catching Rachel squarely on her left cheek. She gasped and fell backward a step, her cheek blazing under the impact.

"Hey, you creep!" O'Brien cried out, still naked.

He came at Falco, and Falco threw a fist at him, and it grazed O'Brien's jaw. But O'Brien was a tough youngster. He absorbed the blow, then landed a hard right to Falco's head. Falco stumbled backwards two steps, lost his balance, and fell into the pool.

O'Brien laughed at the result, his anger quickly gone. But nobody at poolside joined him. Somebody proffered him a towel, and he tied it around his waist as a dripping Falco climbed from the pool, his clothes hanging wet on him, his shoes squishing water. The host, a silver-haired, dignified-looking fellow, came over to Falco.

"I have some things upstairs you can change into."

Falco eyed him darkly. "Go to hell," he said. He turned and hurled a vitriolic look at the fellow O'Brien, who already looked a little sorry he had hit Falco.

"Your racing career is finished, punk," he said to the towel-draped driver. "You won't be able to buy a place in next year's races."

The young driver swallowed hard, knowing Falco would make good on the threat. Sobering up fast, he tried to apologize. "Look, Tony, I just didn't want you insulting—"

But Falco had already turned from him. "As for you,

damn you," he told Rachel, "you can pack up and fly back home, as far as I'm concerned. Just keep away from me and my crew."

Rachel's dark eyebrows raised slightly. Her cheek was bright red from his slap, but she would not reveal any pain to him. "After tonight, my love, I wouldn't touch you or your crew with a ten-foot marlin pole," she replied sweetly.

Some woman tittered in the background. Fuming, Falco turned and strode through the spacious house alone, knocking over a liquor cart as he went, the bottles crashing to a tiled floor behind him. Then they heard the front door slam hard, and he was gone.

Chapter Seventeen

The same night that Falco went back to the hotel room alone, angry and frustrated, Eva spent the night with Boyd Lucas. It was a long, sensual night of sweet exploring, fiery climax, and pledges of love. Eva had finally found a man she could respect and like, and she was glad that Lucas had come into her life at a time when she so needed love and understanding.

Cahill had let himself get down. His tension about the race was different from anything he had previously experienced, it constricted his insides day and night, and made him testy with Lucas and Del Rio. He felt alone, despite their presence, and he knew that what he needed was Dulcie. But he had ruined it with her, through his own stupidity.

The one bright light in Cahill's life, in those last days before the final race, was the beautiful thing that was happening between Lucas and Eva Falco. He had been surprised to see Eva show up at Key West, because of Falco's presence there, but he was glad she had had the guts to defy Falco on his own turf. As for Falco, he was known to be bitter about Eva and Lucas, and Cahill hoped he would not cause them any trouble.

The day after Falco's blow-up at the pool party, at a local Cuban restaurant called the Fishermen's Cafe, down near the shrimp docks, the confrontation that Cahill had expected finally occurred. It was just three days until the big races, and everybody was talking about them. The newspapers were carrying daily reports on arrivals of boats and drivers, and guessing who the winners might be in the various classes. The big race, though, was the Class One open, and the betting was mostly on whether Cahill could beat Falco for the national championship.

Cahill, Lucas and Eva had gone to the restaurant for a late lunch, and when they got there, Falco and the new navigator Jenkins were just finishing their meals. Falco saw the threesome come in, and they spotted Falco immediately. They ignored Falco and went and seated themselves at a booth at the other end of the place. But Cahill could see the deep anger working in Falco's face, as he and Jenkins prepared to leave.

There were Spanish-speaking locals in booths around Cahill's party, and rough-looking shrimp fishermen at the long counter where they hunched over long platters of picadillo or jewfish with black beans and yellow rice. Advertisements in both Spanish and English hung on the walls, and a blackboard behind the counter announced the menu for the day. Cahill, Lucas and Eva ordered, and Cahill was beginning to think Falco might leave without coming over. But then Falco was up and he and Jenkins were moving toward them.

"Oh, shit," Cahill muttered.

Eva and Lucas looked up just in time to see Falco walk up. He was wearing a gaily patterned sport shirt that belied his dark mood. The young Jenkins, looking gangly and bucolic, stood at a small distance behind Falco, having little idea what was going on.

"Well, well," Falco said in a hard voice. "The pretender to the throne, and two of his followers."

Cahill sighed heavily, and nodded. "Falco. Jenkins."

"How's everything, Cahill?" Jenkins asked innocently.

Cahill ignored the rhetoric as Falco turned to Lucas and Eva. "Having a good time, Eva?"

Eva held his hard gaze. "As a matter of fact, yes," she responded. "Where's your sweet little Rachel? Sleeping in from a hard night?"

Falco did not reply. Instead, he turned a metallic gaze on Lucas. "You're bedding my wife, aren't you, Lucas?"

A couple of heads turned, in the next booth, and Cahill's gut tightened even more than it already was.

"Oh, for God's sake, Tony!" Eva said hotly.

Lucas's face reddened, and Jenkins, suddenly embarrassed, turned away.

"That's none of your goddamn business, Falco," Lucas said in a low, tough voice. He glanced around him, in embarrassment.

"Not my business?" Falco growled. He was still chafing from the treatment he had received at the hands of Rachel. "You're prodding my wife, and it's none of my business?"

Lucas rose to his feet, looking big and dangerous. "You sonofabitch! Step out on the street, and I'll break you in half!"

Now half the restaurant was looking toward them. Cahill rose quickly, and stepped between Lucas and Falco. "What Boyd meant to say was, haul your ass out of here now, or Jenkins here will be driving for you Saturday." The words had come out softly, but they made Falco's eyes narrow slightly and the hair bristle on the back of his neck.

He held Cahill's gaze for a long moment, then turned back to Lucas and Eva. "Hell, you can have her, and good riddance. She was never much good in bed, anyway. But then, you probably won't know the difference, grease monkey."

Lucas was so infuriated that he started to take a swing at Falco as he left, but Cahill caught his big arm and held it until Falco was out of range. "Let him go," he said urgently.

In the next moment Falco and Jenkins were gone, but people were still staring at Cahill, Lucas and Eva. "I feel like killing that bastard," Lucas said in a tight voice.

Cahill looked down at Eva. "You want to have your lunch some place else?"

Eva shook her pretty blond head. "No," she said, glancing at the men nearby who were grinning toward her. "We placed our order here. This will be fine."

Cahill sat back down. "We won't have any more trouble from Falco now," he said. "He'll be too busy running the race in his head."

"I ought to bust him up good," Lucas said.

"Sit down, honey," Eva said quietly to her new lover. "It doesn't matter what comes out of Tony's ugly mouth. We have each other. All Tony has are a shaky national title and Gus Beckering."

Lucas turned to her, and clasped her hand with his big one. Her strength through Falco's onslaught had made it easier for him. "After Saturday," he said grimly, "it will be only Beckering."

Cahill, though, found it difficult to share Lucas's grim optimism about the big race. Falco was angry and determined, now. And there was no better driver in the country—maybe in the world—than Falco in a flat-out, high-speed, no-tricks-or-fancy-strategy race. He was the coolest driver on the circuit under the pressure of high velocity. In a boat, he was not afraid. He was master of the situation. Just the opposite from Cahill, who was finding himself going to pieces more and more as the races climaxed.

That afternoon after the confrontation between Eva and Falco, Cahill went down to the marina and worked on the boat with Danny Del Rio, replacing an engine part with a modified one of his own design. It was a hot day, and they kept in the shade of a building canopy, not talking much, just getting their work done, content that they were spending their pre-race time in an effort to improve their race performance. It was a fly-buzzing afternoon, with almost no breeze off the Gulf, and a flat, hazy sea. Boats anchored on the bight did not move on the water, they sat there as if bolted to a sheet of hot metal. No gulls or pelicans were in sight, they had all gone off to find shade in which to roost through the heat of the day.

"This reminds me of Nam," Del Rio said, as they worked in the shallow shade at a work bench. He figured it was better to talk about something when it bothered you, rather than turning your back on it.

Cahill staring into a carburetor before him on a long work bench, turned and glanced at Del Rio. "Yeah?" he said darkly.

"The heat. Remember the heat? How it pressed on you like a weight?"

"I remember," Cahill said.

"Some guys couldn't take it. A private in our outfit went bananas one afternoon, ran off screaming into the jungle with the sweat running off him. Said he couldn't breathe. We never saw him again."

Cahill stopped his work for a moment. "Josh hated the heat," he said slowly. His guts began tightening up. "He kept talking about iced beer and cold showers. Christ."

"Josh was—a pretty good friend of yours. Wasn't he?"

"We were like brothers. I was the big brother, always having to pull Josh out of scrapes and jams. One night in Saigon he had an argument with a whore in a cathouse, and I had to pull a gun to get out of there with him." He shook his head. "He was always getting into something, and expecting me to get him out of it. That's the way it was."

"And you didn't mind?" Del Rio said.

Cahill looked over at him. "What was to mind? Josh was Josh, and you took him for what he was."

"Sure, I understand," Del Rio said.

Cahill was now wiping his hands with a cloth. "I appreciate what you're trying to do, Danny. But it doesn't work, I've tried it. In my head."

"Hey. I didn't mean anything."

"Sure," Cahill smiled. "But it's going to go the way it wants to." He looked at Del Rio somberly. "Keep an eye on me Saturday, Danny. You recognize the symptoms faster than Boyd. Don't let me do anything foolish out there."

"Hell," Del Rio told him. "You're going to be all right, I know it. When we get out there—"

Cahill was looking beyond him now, though, to where a taxi had pulled up in the marina compound. Del Rio turned, and saw Dulcie Padgett stepping from the vehicle.

"Well, I'll be damned." He grinned, and observed Cahill's face. Cahill looked as if he were seeing a mirage on the hazy sea.

Dulcie turned and just stared toward Cahill for a moment, as the taxi pulled away. She was wearing a wispy lemon-hued dress, a matching, wide-brimmed hat, and high heels. She looked like a *Vogue* or *Mademoiselle* cover. She was the most beautiful thing Cahill had ever seen.

She came over to them, moving easily, looking as cool as a spring zephyr. "Hi, Steve. Danny. I thought I might find you at the marina."

"Hey, Dulcie!" Del Rio exclaimed. "You look like a million bucks!"

"It's—good to see you again, Dulcie," Cahill told her quietly.

"How are things going?" she asked. "Are you ready for the big race?"

Cahill shrugged. "As ready as we're going to get, I suspect. Good weather is predicted here, as usual, and the boat is in top shape again."

"We're going to give Falco a run for his money," Del Rio promised her.

"I thought—you weren't coming down here," Cahill said.

Dulcie averted her dark eyes for a moment. "I didn't like what I was doing there in Tampa. I quit, the day after you called. I haven't decided what I'm doing next, but it won't be in Florida. While I'm thinking about it, I figured I might as well come down and watch a good race. Is Mary Ann here?"

Cahill nodded soberly. "She's here, Dulcie. I don't think Phil Ramos is treating her very well."

There was a brief silence among them. Then Del Rio broke it. "Hey, I'm going to go install this in the boat," he said, grabbing the carburetor. "Excuse me, Dulcie."

Dulcie smiled as he turned and left, and then she and Cahill were alone. Cahill wanted to reach out and grab her to him, to smother her with kisses. But he was not sure he had the right.

"Did you get a room?"

"Yes. I thought I ought to."

"I'm so damned glad you came."

"Me, too."

"Eva Falco is here. She and Boyd are really hitting it off," Cahill told her.

"Hey, that's great. Eva is a nice lady. How is Tony taking that?"

"Not so well. Rachel and he aren't talking, I hear. I suppose he's pretty mad at the world right now."

"That might make him a tougher competitor."

It surprised him how Dulcie saw into the heart of things so readily, without being centrally involved. "That's occurred to me," he admitted.

"You're looking a little—tired, Steve."

"Really? I guess all this is wearing on me some. What I need is some relaxation."

Dulcie lowered her dark lashes.

"Can I drive you to your place? Where are you staying?"

"At the Pier House."

"That's great. So are we."

Dulcie smiled uncertainly. "Oh, good, Steve." She

had purposely booked at the Pier House because she knew that was where he and his crew were staying. She wondered why she could not just tell him that. "I'd love to ride back there with you."

"We could have a couple of drinks."

"Okay, but I'll have to see Mary Ann."

"That can be arranged," he grinned. He was feeling better already.

A short time later, Cahill left Dulcie at the motel, after making a date with her for the evening. Dulcie located Mary Ann's room, which Mary Ann shared with Ramos, and Mary Ann was there alone. When she answered the door, Dulcie stared at her in surprise. Mary Ann had a swollen lip and a cut on it, from the night before.

"My God. Dulcie!" she said when she opened the door. A crooked grin crawled onto her pretty face.

Dulcie smiled hesitantly, seeing Mary Ann's mouth. "Hi, honey. What in the world happened to you?"

Mary Ann closed the door behind her, and sighed heavily. She was wearing a sheer nylon blouse, no bra, and a pair of tight-fitting slacks with high heels. Her red hair was tousled and uncombed. On a bed across the room was a suitcase which Mary Ann was packing.

"Phil had a little party for a few of his friends last night," she said darkly. She acted as if she did not want to talk about it.

Dulcie touched Mary Ann's face. "Did that bastard Phil do that to you?"

Mary Ann shook her head sidewise. "God, you look pretty, honey."

Dulcie took her by the shoulders, as they stood facing each other in the center of the sun-streaked room. "What happened?" she said firmly.

Mary Ann sighed. "Phil said he was asking a couple of his men friends. But six showed up. I was the only girl."

Dulcie's face changed.

"Phil wanted me to show them a good time. I balked, but it didn't do me a lot of good. They stripped me down, and they laid me. One after the other, the drunken bastards. They didn't even give me any privacy. They stood around and watched and made jokes.

"Oh, God!" Dulcie murmured, her eyes moist.

"Phil left for more drinks, and the last two got rough with me. They held me down when I back-talked them, and one hit me. It was like I was nothing. Christ, it even hurts to walk."

"Jesus, Mary Ann!" Dulcie brought Mary Ann to her, and embraced her gently. "Jesus."

"I'll be all right. Honest."

"Didn't you go to the police?" Dulcie asked her.

"What, a girl like me?" Mary Ann grinned wryly. She planted a kiss on Dulcie's cheek, and walked to the bed, where she threw a couple of blouses into the suitcase. "I told Phil not to show up here until I was gone, or I'd jump off the balcony and give him real trouble. I think he believed me."

"Does Steve know about this?" Dulcie said.

"He just knows I came up here. Don't tell him what happened, Dulcie, he might try to do something noble, for Christ's sake." She glanced at Dulcie. "Are you two a thing again?"

Dulcie shrugged. "I'm just here to be near him. I don't think Steve takes us seriously. But he seems to need me now. After the race, we'll go our own ways. Why don't you stick around, now that I'm here?"

Mary Ann turned to her. "No, honey, not here. I've already got a plane ticket back to New York. I'm going to go beg for my job back at the Two Friends. It may have been boring, but it beat this by a country mile."

Dulcie smiled. "I'd like to say I'll see you there, but I don't think so."

"You were never right for a job like that. Me, I've got nothing on the ball. I always depended on my body to get along, and look what that got me. But it's all I've got. You're different, kid. You've got a head on your shoulders. You could be anything you want. I know, I'm not so dumb about people. And you can get any guy you really want, too," she added meaningfully.

Dulcie smiled wearily. "I don't want a guy who doesn't want me, Mary Ann. It has to be a mutual thing, or it will never work. Steve is a mixed-up guy. I don't know what he wants. And I doubt that he does, at this point."

"If I had a chance with a guy like that, I'd do anything to nail him," Mary Ann said pensively, looking past Dulcie as if trying to see her future in the foliage beyond the sunny window.

There was a long silence between them, and Dulcie recalled that day at the Two Friends, when they had decided to go to the Freeport boat races. That seemed like a thousand years ago.

"We'll always be friends, Mary Ann," she said suddenly and impulsively. "And we'll keep in touch. If you are ever in need, I want you to call me, and I'll come. Are you listening?"

Now Mary Ann's eyes watered up. "I love you, honey," she said. "I really do."

A couple of moments later, Mary Ann was packed, and Dulcie accompanied her to the ocean. They engaged in only small talk at the airport, and then suddenly Mary Ann was waving goodbye to Dulcie from the ramp of a small jet. Standing there waving back, Dulcie wondered if she would ever see Mary Ann again.

That evening, Cahill came to Dulcie's room and picked her up there, and they walked to a small restaurant in the quaint old harbor section of town, under old-fashioned street lamps and *cocos plumosa* palms, with their lacy fronds. They had a shrimp dinner at the restaurant, with Cahill just staring at beautiful

Dulcie most of the way through the meal, content not to speak but just be near her.

After the meal they took a short walk through the small downtown area, looking in shop windows and enjoying the softly lighted look of the place. Down side streets were residential sections hard upon the commercial, where yellow light showed from behind louvered doors and windows, and tropical foliage crouched darkly against aging frame structures. Dulcie enjoyed the feel of it, and the smell of the ocean that came to her everywhere.

"This place is not conducive to a race," she told Cahill. They were heading back to the parking lot at the motel, to take a ride in Cahill's Jaguar. "It's too relaxed."

"Wait until Saturday," he told her. "I hear the locals come down to the docks in mobs. They like anything that takes place on the water."

They drove across the island, to the beaches on the Atlantic, along Duval Street. The longest street in the world, Ripley had named it, because it ran from the Gulf of Mexico to the Atlantic Ocean. A Ripleyesque joke. Long-haired young men lounged in front of bars, awaiting their connections of various sorts. Out on the beach road, there were no lights, and a sea breeze blew through the car windows. Cahill could see a blinking light out on the gulf stream, in the darkness. That was Sand Key, where a turn-around would occur in the race. They found a secluded place along the walk that fronted the water and parked. They were both reminded of that other beach, at Miami, when Dulcie had gotten angry with Cahill. But neither mentioned it.

"It's very balmy tonight," Dulcie said, when they were parked. "It cooled off nicely when the sun set."

"It does that here," he said. "I've been here when you couldn't go out in the afternoon, because of the heat. But the nights were always pleasant."

Dulcie turned and studied his handsome profile, with

its square jaw and aquiline nose. He was not as pretty as Falco, but he was somehow more masculine. He emanated quiet strength, despite the trouble she knew he was having, inside him.

"Your bad dreams," she said. "Are you still having them?"

Cahill looked over at her, and his face had fallen into straight lines. "Yes. I still have them."

"Maybe you should see a doctor. After the races are over."

"I won't have them after the races are over," he told her.

Dulcie regarded him curiously. "What's it all about, Steve?"

"I don't really know. Not yet."

"You think you will, then?"

"Yes. Before or during the race. That's the way I feel."

"Is it serious?" she said.

He stared through the windshield. "I think I'm trying to kill myself."

Dulcie felt a sinking inside her, and her face felt suddenly flushed. She looked over at him, and saw that he was breathing shallowly.

"In—the races?"

"Yes, in the races."

"Then Saturday is your last chance of the season," she heard herself saying hollowly. Her voice sounded as if it were coming from the far end of a long tunnel.

"That's right," he said.

"Oh, Steve!"

He turned and touched her arm with his hand. "I wish I hadn't told you. Christ, what a thing to unload onto your shoulders."

Dulcie held his somber gaze. "I knew something was wrong. Inside you. I mean, before I began hearing people talk."

"Do they talk?" he said.

"Some."

"I guess I can't blame them."

"For God's sake, Steve," she said with sudden urgency. "If you have this feeling that you're trying to—well, that you have some kind of death wish—if you can identify it to that extent, surely you can get some control over it."

Cahill shook his head. "It doesn't seem to work that way. The last half of the season, it's gotten worse in every race. It won't end until I know what's behind it. Or until—oh, hell, Dulcie. Let's not ruin our evening."

She sat there for a long moment, quiet. Then she opened her door and climbed out of the car, standing and looking out toward the blackness of the sea, her arms crossed across her breasts. Cahill got out, too, and came around to her. She looked up at him, put her arm through his, and guided him away from the vehicle, off toward a remote cabana which canopied a picnic bench. They walked slowly, silently in the sand until they got there. Then she stopped him, and looked up into his eyes.

"Please don't race Saturday, Steve."

He frowned down at her. "Are you serious?"

She nodded desperately and, seeing the desperation, he knew how wrong he had been about her, before. Not just wrong, but dead wrong. "You don't need this. You're not a Tony Falco, who lives and dies grabbing for gold trophies. There's more to you than that."

Cahill touched her face gently. He wanted her so much that it made him ache inside with frustration. "It's not the trophy, Dulcie. Charlie Rossman put his finger on it. I have to confront this thing, to beat it. There's no running from it. It's now or later, and it might as well be now."

"Jesus. I knew you'd say that."

"I shouldn't have said all this to you. I didn't mean to."

"I'm glad you did. I'm glad you shared it with me." She turned from him, and looked up and down the deserted beach. They were very alone, behind the cabana. She reached down to the hem of the pale yellow dress she wore and pulled it up over her head in one long, slow movement.

Cahill swallowed hard. Dulcie had nothing on suddenly, except for one piece of scanty underwear on her svelte hips, and her shoes. She kicked the shoes off and turned to him.

"You wanted me on that other beach," she said throatily. "Maybe it will be better now. Maybe we both need it more."

"Oh, Jesus, Dulcie," he muttered.

He grabbed her to him, and she felt the strong arms enclose her in a vise-like grip. His hands went to her breasts, her hips, her thighs, as they kissed hungrily under a starry sky.

"I've thought about you day and night," she admitted huskily, despite her best resolves. "Ever since your call. I wanted you, Steve. I wanted you so damned much."

She helped him unbutton his shirt, and then it was gone, lying in the sand at their feet. Her hands ran over the firm musculature of him, and her breath came shallowly as she unfastened his trousers. "Don't talk, baby," he whispered. "Don't talk."

In moments they were on the sand, with Dulcie's dress spread under them. Near them the light surf washed up onto the hard beach, and a gull cried off over the water. A car passed on the beach road, but they were protected by the picnic table and the cabana. His mouth was on her breasts, his hand firmly moving between her long thighs. For some reason she was much more desirable to him than before, more captivating than Rachel, sexier than Mary Ann, the most sensual woman imaginable in his wildest fantasies. She made a soft, hungry sound as he plunged into her, her thighs hugging him to her moving hips, her mouth exploring his urgently.

"Oh, God, yes," she whispered hoarsely, not realizing how she was speaking. "Yes, now. *Now,*

now!"

Her cries were raised above the sound of the sea near them, and a sliver of moon revealed diamond-like dampness on their faces and bodies as it ended, their flesh tightly entwined, the hot currents of passion still tingling between them.

They dressed in silence, huddled under the canopy of the cabana. No one had come, their privacy had not been disturbed. As Cahill was buckling the belt at his waist, a motor boat went roaring past out on the water in the darkness, with its running lights showing. They both stared out at it for a long moment until it had disappeared into the night. Then Dulcie turned to him, fitting a high-heeled shoe to a slender, elegant foot.

"Did that help?" she asked him.

Cahill grinned at her. "You'll never know how much."

That reply pleased Dulcie. She knew, now, that she was in love with Steve Cahill, and that he was in trouble. She had made the trouble easier for him, if for just a little while. She would not look beyond that. No matter what happened in the race or afterwards, she would have this night.

"I enjoyed it some, myself," she said to him.

She was smiling. "No kidding?" he said. "I would never have known." She broadened the smile, and he wanted her all over again.

"Maybe you'd like to come to my room the rest of the night," she suggested. "That is, if you don't think Danny will mind."

Cahill grunted. "Danny is a big boy now. He's not afraid of the dark."

A few moments later they drove off toward the motel, across the island. For the moment, Cahill had no feelings of desperation, no visions of death. He was full of the scent, the sight, the feel of Dulcie.

On that new-moon night, there was nothing more he could ask.

Chapter Eighteen

It was Thursday morning.

Forty-eight hours until race time.

Tensions were mounting.

Cahill had left Dulcie's bed early, just after dawn, to meet Lucas and Del Rio at the marina, to discuss race strategy. The positions of a couple of markers were to be changed, which would vary the shape of the course slightly, and Lucas had the last-minute data on that. He also wanted to discuss open-throttle racing with Cahill.

Tony Falco was so tight about the race now that he lost all interest in the affair proceeding between Eva and Lucas. Rachel was keeping away from him, and he did not mind that, either. He was gradually closing in on himself, narrowing his thinking onto one subject, bending all his efforts toward one goal: beating Cahill on Saturday.

Gus Beckering, though, had lost some of his confidence in Falco through the last few races, and still had no intention of leaving the championship issue in Falco's questionable hands. When Art Kralich came to see him that Thursday morning, therefore, without Falco's knowledge, Beckering received his throttleman cordially. He took Kralich down to the long portico facing the sea, at the Casa Marina where they were staying, and they found two wicker chairs that looked out over the manicured grounds, the pool, and the ocean. Beckering ordered a coffee with milk, but Kralich had already had his breakfast. The wire was off his jaw now, but he still could not chew much or talk well, and that kept his anger flaming for Cahill. The cast on his leg was a bit cumbersome, but did not slow him down much. Somehow he looked more dangerous walking stiff-legged than he had previously. After Beckering had sipped at his coffee for a couple of minutes, he turned to the ex-football lineman beside him and studied his thick face. Kralich had not announced his reason for coming, but Beckering knew pretty pretty well what it was.

"Well, Art. I don't see you very often without Tony. Is the *First Blood* ready to fly?"

"She's ready," Kralich said. "If Tony's ready."

Beckering furrowed his brow and pursed his lips, making his lined, sagging face bunch up into an ungainly mask. "Do you doubt that he is?" he wondered.

"I don't know. He's got woman trouble by the barrelful, and I think he's letting that goddam Cahill get to him. I never seen him so frigging tense. You can't talk to him. You know how he can get. But he's worse, now."

Beckering stared out past the greenery where chameleons jumped from frond to leaf, past the palm trees to the turquoise sea. He sipped at the coffee.

"He could blow the whole works," Kralich went on, watching Beckering's face. "Cheat you out of that trophy that you had won, till Cahill got in our way."

Beckering eyed Kralich sideways.

"I know how much you want that trophy this year," Kralich added significantly.

"And you want to do something to help me get it?" Beckering suggested.

Kralich shrugged. "Anything you say, Gus. I want Cahill's ass reamed, and I don't care how." He hesitated. "Something like you mentioned the other night, maybe."

"A dock fire?" Beckering said quietly.

"Why not? I can pull it off. I sure as hell don't need

Tony."

"Could you make it look like an accident?"

"Hell, yes. Set a couple of gasoline cans around. Tip one over, right beside the *Sonic Boom*. Drop a match on it. Who could tell how it happened?"

"You'd have to be completely alone."

"I didn't intend to do it in front of a crowd," Kralich said. "It would be a three A.M. kind of thing, when everybody is off asleep. There's no real guard at the marina. The cops are supposed to check out the boats a couple times a night, but they're pretty casual about it."

Beckering felt something in his insides unwind slightly. He would rather have had Falco committed to this kind of tactics, but he would settle for Kralich.

"If anything went wrong," he said deliberately, "I'd deny we ever had this little talk."

Kralich gave him a sour look. "Sure, Gus."

"In fact, I'd take it amiss if you mentioned my name in connection with it."

"Hell, don't worry. What would be the point?"

Beckering studied Kralich's square face. "And you'd do this just to get even with Cahill?" he said slowly.

Kralich met Beckering's hard gaze, then averted his own. "Well. It did occur to me that you have more to gain in this than me, Gus. And I would be taking all the chances."

Beckering's face settled into harder lines. "Go on."

"Well, I was thinking. It would be nice to have a letter of recommendation from you. For next season. I mean, if you weren't entering a boat next year for some reason—"

"I get the idea, Art," Beckering said evenly. "In case I kick off, you want to jump on some other bandwagon."

Kralich looked embarrassed. "I didn't mean to put it that way, Gus."

Beckering laughed a gutteral laugh. "Anything else?"

"Well, just that, and—maybe a bonus for this year's

effort. You know, a little special something for helping you rid yourself of Cahill. Not payable, of course, if I don't keep him out of the race."

"And such a bonus would amount to what?" Beckering said nicely.

Kralich dropped his gaze to the floor of the portico. "I was thinking maybe five grand."

"Well," Beckering said smoothly. "I see you've learned something from Tony. Greed."

Kralich glanced up at him.

"But I'm not complaining," Beckering added. "I can afford what you suggest. And the letter would be no problem. I wouldn't even have to lie, you are a good throttleman." He leaned toward Kralich. "But you get neither if you fail. Do you understand that completely?"

"Sure," Kralich nodded. He held his mouth partially closed when he spoke, because his jaw was still painfully healing. "But nothing's going to go wrong. Cahill won't have a boat to race Saturday. Take my word for it."

Beckering let a wry grin decorate his flaccid face. "How I wish I could," he said wistfully, with a ragged sigh.

"When should I do it?" Kralich asked him. "Tonight or tomorrow night?"

The half-grin was gone when Beckering replied. "Why wait?" he said. "Do it tonight, by all means."

Kralich rose grimly. "I'll get right on it," he said.

Early that evening, Cahill and Dulcie had dinner at a local Cuban restaurant, and then stopped past Captain Tony's Saloon, where Lucas and Eva had gone to have a drink with Del Rio and a couple of other drivers. When Cahill and Dulcie arrived there, Del Rio had left with the other drivers, but Eva and Boyd Lucas were sipping drinks at a rear table. Cahill and Dulcie joined them, ordering light beers. Lucas was rather sober, despite the

255

good time he was having with Eva. Paige had called him from Baltimore, and was not feeling well. She had caught a virus and could not make it, and she missed Lucas's usual brotherly care. Also, she had bad feelings about Cahill in this last race.

"Falco was in here just before you arrived," Lucas told Cahill and Dulcie when they had sat down. He had decided not to mention Paige's call to anyone. "He didn't speak to us at all. Seemed moody."

"He gets that way when he doesn't have a girl on his arm," Eva said sourly. She knew that Falco and Dulcie had been intimate at Freeport, but never held it against Dulcie. She knew that Dulcie despised Falco as much as she herself did. "I guess that McKenzie woman must have ditched him. I haven't seen them around together."

"I don't know what his problem is," Lucas said quietly. "But he's spending a lot of time down at the boat. I think he's worried about Steve."

Dulcie and Eva both glanced at Cahill, and he was staring into his beer. "Then that makes the feeling mutual," he admitted.

Dulcie studied his serious face. "Don't you think you can beat him?"

"Hell, of course he does," Lucas put in quickly.

Cahill looked up at her. "I think we were lucky at Miami, Boyd. Damned lucky. You can't keep beating a driver like Falco with luck."

"You're going to be all right, Steve," Lucas said, understanding Cahill's meaning.

"That's what I've told him," Dulcie said.

"I hope to hell you beat him," Eva said darkly. "I hope you beat him good."

"Just don't expect too much," Cahill said. "No matter what else he is, your husband happens to be damned near unbeatable in the cockpit of a racing boat."

"He's bad for racing," Eva said. "He and Beckering

—and that creep Kralich. They need to be brought down. It would be particularly sweet if you were the one to do it, you and Boyd and Danny."

"Hell," said Cahill, looking suddenly tense. "What got us onto this? There must be something better to jaw about."

"I hear Castro is talking about releasing a mass of malcontents onto the U.S. as immigrants," Dulcie quickly broke in. "Most of them would probably come here to Key West before being taken north for processing. There's some concern here about proper facilities."

Cahill turned to Dulcie with a smile and leaned over and kissed her on the cheek.

"I heard about that," Eva said, also smiling.

Dulcie, looking very pretty with her hair down, put her arm affectionately on Cahill's shoulder. "Film clip at eleven," she said seriously.

Lucas laughed. "It's nice to have you here, Dulcie. Steve was really down before you— Well, I know he appreciates your coming down."

"For Christ's sake, Boyd," Cahill said.

"I'll keep my big mouth shut now," Lucas said to him.

Eva started to change the subject again, but she stopped short. Cahill looked over to see why, and saw Rachel walk up to their table. She had the driver O'Brien on her arm, the fellow who had swum nude with her at the party.

"Hello, all!" Rachel said sweetly, but with a touch of hardness just under the surface. "Thank God I missed Tony here. I seem to run into him wherever I go. Oh, sorry, Eva. No offense intended."

Eva held Rachel's pleasant look with a more sober one. "None taken," she said.

"I see you're not growing any wallflowers," Rachel smiled, eyeing Lucas. "That's good, I'd hate to see you sulking around after a—well, a person like Tony."

"I've never sulked around after any man," Eva said evenly. "Let alone Tony."

"That's good, my dear." Rachel turned to Dulcie, ignoring Cahill for the moment. "My, look who else showed up for the big race. You look so—different now. Did somebody buy you some clothes and a couturier, sweetheart?"

Dulcie saw the quick anger in Cahill's face, and laid a hand on his thigh, under the table. "I bought the clothes myself, Rachel," she said easily. "And unlike some women, I've never felt the need to have a hairdresser dictate style to me."

"Well, isn't that quaint," Rachel said nicely. "Oh, I don't think any of you have met Jeff O'Brien. He's just entered one of the production class races. He doesn't have much experience, but you've never seen such enthusiasm!"

"I can imagine," Eva said under her breath.

"Glad to meet you all," O'Brien said, grinning. "I hear you're some driver, Cahill."

Cahill looked up at him and said nothing.

"Say, why don't you join us?" Lucas said uncomfortably, not knowing what else to do.

Rachel hesitated, but O'Brien did not. "Well, that's real nice of you-all," he grinned. He pulled up a couple of chairs, and Cahill groaned inwardly. Rachel and he sat down, and Rachel turned to Cahill, while O'Brien caught a waiter's eye.

"I've missed you, Steve," she said to him slowly and deliberately, as if Dulcie were not there.

Cahill eyed Rachel darkly. He was glad he had broken with her as quickly as he had. She was nothing but trouble. She seemed to get her kicks in life by making other people squirm.

"Steve has been very busy," Lucas put in loudly, "making our boat right. We've got her in top shape now."

"I was hoping you'd call me at my room," Rachel

went on, ignoring Lucas.

"I know how hard you've both worked," Eva now said. "But I think it will all be worth it, Saturday."

"I think about you in bed at night," Rachel told Cahill.

A silence fell over the table. O'Brien frowned slightly. "Hey. What's going on here?" he said.

Cahill cast a hard look at Rachel. "Let it go, Rachel," he told her quietly.

Subtle expressions played across Rachel's chiseled face, and then gave way to a rather hard one. "You were better than Tony," she went on. "That's what I think about in bed. How good it was between us. You remember, don't you, Steve?" Her black eyes darted to Dulcie and then back to Cahill.

"Christ!" O'Brien muttered.

Eva was shaking her blond head, and Lucas looked like he might explode with anger at any moment. Dulcie, looking very cool, snapped her fingers at the waiter who had just taken Rachel's and O'Brien's order. "Waiter!" she called curtly. "Cancel that order for the lady and gentleman."

The waiter looked puzzled. "Are you sure?" He glanced at Rachel.

"We're sure," Dulcie told him.

As he left shaking his head, Dulcie fixed Rachel with a level stare. "Now if you don't mind," she said, "I don't think Steve wants to talk any more with you."

Rachel's face grew suddenly hard lines. "Maybe Steve would like to tell me that," she said.

Cahill caught Rachel's eyes. "Let the game-playing be over, Rachel. Or go play it somewhere else."

Rachel's sculpted face crimsoned slightly. "On the other hand," she said icily, "you did tend to fade rather quickly. You never could seem to keep your mind on it. Maybe it's because of all of that mix-up inside your head."

Cahill's face was suddenly veined and dark. He was

259

holding a glass in his right hand, and his grip on it abruptly shattered it over the table. Beer ran onto the table top, and a cut from his fist showed crmson blood dripping from it.

"Oh, God!" Eva murmured.

Dulcie rose, and spoke directly to O'Brien. "Get her out of here. Now. While she can still walk out."

O'Brien swallowed hard, and rose, too. Rachel was glaring intensely at Dulcie.

"Are you threatening me, you damned street walker?"

Dulcie started around the table, and O'Brien quickly pulled Rachel to her feet. "Uh, we might as well move along, honey."

Rachel threw his arm off her, but as Dulcie approached, she moved backwards one step. "You goddam camp follower! You think I have to drink with the likes of you? Any of you?" She backed up two more steps, to keep out of Dulcie's reach. "I buy and sell losers like you! Look at you, all sitting there waiting around for some goddam boat race like it was some momentous event, for Christ's sake! Who cares about it, or about any of you! You make me laugh!"

Rachel began laughing then, as O'Brien pulled her toward the door to the street, and that hard laughter was still audible after she was no longer visible to them. Dulcie came back and took her seat again, ignoring all the eyes on them.

"Jesus H. Christ!" Lucas growled.

"She's absolutely outrageous," Eva offered.

Dulcie touched Cahill's arm, and he was trembling inside. She was suddenly frightened for him. He was in a very emotional state, from a relatively minor event. She took a handkerchief from her purse, and cleaned the small cut on Cahill's hand.

"Let's forget Rachel," Dulcie said softly. She was all churned up inside, herself. "She's not worth our anger."

260

"That's the God-awful truth," Eva agreed. "It's just too bad she and Tony broke up, the way I see it."

Cahill looked over at Eva, and a weak grin crept onto his square face. He was quieting down inside some.

"They were made for each other," Eva added.

They were all relaxing now. Cahill rose from his chair, and looked down at Dulcie. "You want to take a walk? I need some fresh air, I think."

Dulcie nodded, rising. "Me, too."

As they left, many faces of other patrons turned toward them, full of concern or interest. Cahill was glad to get out of there.

He wished it were all over.

Later that night, Danny Del Rio, coming in from an evening with a couple of other racing people, could not sleep. For no good reason, therefore, he got in Cahill's Jaguar and drove over to the yacht club marina, at well past midnight. He had been very relaxed about the race, but tonight it had seemed to creep up on him, all of it.

When he got to the docks, he went and looked over the *Sonic Boom*, where it hulked in the black water at a slip. Its sleek white hull looked built for speed, its outdrives resembling some kind of rocket engine's superstructure, with the flanking, streamlined trim tabs. A boat like this, in a race like this, could establish a new speed record for offshore racing.

Del Rio checked the boat's lines, and they were secure. He walked down to the far end of the dock, and found a pleasure boat owner there, recovering from a party aboard. The fellow started asking Del Rio questions about racing, and Del Rio felt like talking. He went aboard, sat with the owner, and accepted a drink.

Almost an hour later, while Del Rio was still out there on the dock, Art Kralich drove into the marina grounds and parked his rental car as close to the dock as he could get it.

There appeared to be nobody about. He got out of the car and looked around carefully. There was nobody in sight. He hobbled onto the dock on his cast and went down to the *Sonic Boom*.

"Hmmph," he grunted, showing the craft his contempt for it.

He looked down the long dock, and saw nothing. Del Rio and the owner were on the Chris Craft and hidden from view. Kralich turned and went back to the car and opened its trunk.

There were two cans of gasoline sitting there. He took both of them from the trunk and closed it. A sharp odor from the cans assailed his nostrils. It was a good smell to him. A symbolic smell. It meant the finish for Steve Cahill.

Kralich picked up the cans easily in his big hands and carried them down the dock, setting them down just beside the *Sonic Boom*. He looked around a last time, and then glanced at a watch on his hairy wrist. It was almost three A.M. The middle of the night. If it would ever be safe, it would be now.

He unscrewed a cap on the first of the two cans, and began dumping the gasoline onto the wooden dock. It splashed onto thick planks, a piling, a coil of line. He did a good, thorough job. But he did not pour all the gas from the can. He screwed the cap back on, and set the can right at the edge of the dock, beside the boat. In a moment the second can was open, and now Kralich poured gasoline onto the deck of the *Sonic Boom,* tied close to the dock. The smelly stuff ran onto the aft deck, the engine cover, the canvas over the bolster. Then more on the dock itself. Finally, he laid the can on its side on the dock, right beside the boat, and allowed the rest of the fuel to spill from its mouth.

The stench assailed him. He stepped back away from his handiwork. The fire would jump immediately from the dock to the boat, and begin consuming it. Nobody could possibly get to it in time. It was about fifteen seconds back to the car, another thirty to get in and start it. He would drive out of the area in less than one minute from the start of the fire. That should put him out of trouble. There would be nothing to connect him or Beckering with the arson. The fire would probably not even be considered arson.

Everything was going just fine.

Kralich pulled a small book of matches from his pocket. On the cover it said, *Billie's Restaurant.* He opened the folding cover and pulled off a match. A little short of breath, he struck the match to light it.

It did not light.

Swearing under his breath, Kralich tried again, but with the same result. He threw the dud match violently from him, and jerked a second one off the book, sweat popping on his brow, his breathing suddenly audible in his ears. He put the match to the book.

Down the dock, the yacht owner stepped off his boat and looked toward Kralich. Del Rio came off behind him, his drink finished. He was going to return to the motel for some sleep. He thought he might be able to find it, now.

"Hey," the owner said, squinting down the dock. "Isn't that somebody down at your boat?"

Kralich looked up and saw them, and sudden tension jumped into his chest and throat.

"What the hell," Del Rio said slowly. "Hey, you! What do you want down there?" He had not recognized Kralich.

Kralich struck the second match, and lit it. He started to throw it onto the gasoline, and it flickered out before he could. *"Sonofabitch!"* he growled under his breath.

Now Del Rio had smelled the gasoline, and he started toward the *Sonic Boom,* at a fast walk. *"Hey!"*

Kralich saw him coming, and could not wait. He had to get to the car. Frustrated but scared of discovery, he began running on the cast, sticking the matches in a shirt pocket. In just moments he was at the car, and climbing inside it, his big face flushed. Del Rio was running now, too. He stopped at the *Sonic Boom*, and saw the gasoline and the cans.

"Jesus in heaven!" he muttered.

He ran on toward the car. But Kralich had started the engine now, and the car was pulling away, digging up dirt with its tires, patching out on the gravel. Del Rio got a glimpse of a square face inside the dark Buick, then the car roared away and out of sight, onto the boulevard beyond.

"Sonofabitch!" Del Rio grumbled. He stood there getting his breath back, thinking of how it might have been if he had not come off that yacht just when he did.

He went back and looked at the spilled fuel again. The yacht owner had come down, and was staring incredulously. "By God. You guys play for keeps, don't you?"

"Somebody else does," Del Rio said. "Watch this for a few minutes, will you? I've got to make a call at the pay phone at the end of the dock."

"You've got it," the other man told him.

At the phone, Del Rio called Cahill and got him at their room. Cahill had not gone to Dulcie's room that night, because the race was too close and he knew he would not be good company for her.

"Steve, this is Danny. I'm down at the marina."

"Huh? You know what time it is, Danny, for God's sake?"

"Listen, Steve. Somebody tried to burn the boat."

A long silence. "Burn—?"

"There's no damage, but we'll have to wash the gas off her. I got here just in time; the bastard was running off. I think it was Kralich."

"Kralich!" Steve Cahill spat in a low, guttural tone.

"I *think* so, Steve. I'm not sure. The guy limped, and he was big. I saw a silhouette of his face in the car, and it could have been Kralich. But I couldn't swear to it."

"I'll be right down there. Don't leave the boat under

264

any circumstances.''

"I'll be here," Del Rio told him.

It took Cahill only twenty minutes to get there, but by that time the yacht owner and Del Rio were already washing the *Sonic Boom* off with a neutralizing agent. Cahill pitched in and helped, and there was not much talk. It was four-thirty when they finally finished. The yacht owner went off to bed, and Cahill and Del Rio stood wearily beside their boat. The odor of gasoline was gone from the boat and the dock. There was no need to call the fire department. Cahill went and put a replacement canopy over the bolster, and then stepped back onto the dock beside Del Rio.

"I'm going to go pay Gus Beckering a visit," he said.

"Now?" Del Rio asked soberly.

"Now."

"Then I'm going along."

Cahill held Del Rio's somber gaze for a moment. "Okay. Let's go."

It was a short drive to the Casa Marina Hotel across town. The lobby was deserted at just past five A.M., with dawn still to make its appearance in the eastern sky. Cahill pounded on Beckering's door loudly, but there was no need. Beckering opened up immediately, wide awake, dressed in an expensive but tent-like dressing robe. Lights burned brightly in the room, and over at a draperied window stood Art Kralich, looking sullen and scared.

"Well, well, it seems no one can sleep tonight," Beckering said evenly to Cahill, seeing the wild look in his eyes.

Cahill did not wait to be invited in. He pushed past Beckering, with Del Rio right behind him. "I knew I'd find you here, you stinking bastard!" he said to Kralich. "This time I'm going to break you up but good!"

Del Rio rushed to interpose himself between them, though, as Beckering sighed and closed the door to the corridor.

"Don't, Steve," Del Rio urged breathlessly. "He's already trying to heal a busted jaw and leg. There wouldn't be any satisfaction in it."

"What the hell is this crazy man doing here, anyway?" Kralich bluffed it out. He had just told Beckering about his failure, and Beckering was furious with him. Kralich now wondered if he would defend him.

Del Rio ignored Kralich. "Please, Steve."

Cahill felt his pulse pounding in his head. He came closer to Kralich, pushing Del Rio along with him, and Kralich stepped backwards slightly. *"You know goddam well what I'm doing here, you frigging snake! You tried to burn the* Sonic Boom!"

"I don't know what you're talking about," Kralich grated out.

Cahill came and smelled Kralich, grabbing at his arm. Kralich pulled violently away. "You washed up, didn't you? You knew we'd be here. You know what the penalty for arson is in this state, you stupid jerk?"

"You're crazy, Cahill. You sound like a crazy man," Kralich said darkly.

Now Beckering came over to them, looking pallid and tired. The pouches under his sunken eyes were especially deep at that moment, despite his otherwise well-groomed look.

"You think Kralich tried to fire the *Sonic Boom*?" he said in his gravelly voice, full of calm and assurance.

"I don't think," Cahill growled. "I have two witnesses, including Danny here."

Beckering raised his thin eyebrows. "Well, I don't know what Danny saw," he said carefully. "But I don't see how it could have been Art here."

"I saw a man limping away from the boat," Del Rio said. "So did another guy. It looked like Kralich to me."

"Did you get a good look at his face?" Beckering said. "This man who limped away from the boat?"

266

Del Rio glanced at Cahill. "No, not really. But the guy was the size of Kralich."

When Beckering spoke again, it was with more arrogance. "Ah, the same size. And he had a limp. Well, you have my deepest sympathy for your trouble tonight, gentlemen. But I assure you, it was not Art at the marina tonight. He's been with me for the past couple of hours, discussing race strategy. Neither of us could sleep, it seems. I presume this incident occurred within that period?"

Del Rio gave Cahill a weary look. But Cahill closed the distance between himself and Beckering, and spoke very quietly to Beckering now, close to his face.

"You know goddam well when it happened, Beckering. Kralich could not have been here more than an hour. You didn't decide to back him until this very moment, did you?"

Beckering's mouth twitched under Cahill's proximity, and for the first time he really understood what Falco had to deal with, in beating Cahill. Or trying to.

"Art came up here to my room at about three, or maybe a little before. He was concerned about Tony's race strategy. We've been discussing race rules and the altered course. More than that I can't tell you, since you're a competitor. But I could give much more detail to the police, if it were required," he added slowly and significantly.

Kralich allowed a slight grin to move the corner of his mouth. But when he caught Beckering's eye, and saw the hard glint to it, the grin melted.

"You're a frigging liar, Beckering," Cahill said in a low voice. "You put him up to this, didn't you? Kralich would never have thought of it on his own. You failed to keep the *Sonic Boom* out of the race by threatening Charlie Rossman, so you decided on a more direct method. Why don't you just admit your guilt, Beckering, like a man?"

Beckering had tiny diamonds of perspiration glinting

on his upper lip now. "If you have no evidence to support these false charges, Cahill, I suggest this conversation is over. I've had a sleepless night, and I need some rest."

Cahill moved even closer to Beckering, so that his presence was menacing to the older man. "I'm not going to the police this time, Beckering, because I've got other things on my mind right now. Like a race Saturday. But if you send that ape to cause me any more trouble, you bastard, I can guarantee he won't be limping around on any cast. He won't be ambulatory at all. Neither will you."

Kralich started to protest such abuse, but thought better of it. Tangling once with Cahill was more than enough. Beckering just stood there, meeting Cahill's brittle look, saying nothing and hoping Cahill would now leave.

"Come on, Steve," Del Rio said quietly. "Let's go get some breakfast somewhere."

Cahill pointed a finger at Beckering's face. "Don't forget, Beckering."

Beckering managed a slight smile. "You've made your feelings quite clear, Cahill. I can assure you that the only trouble you'll have from me and my crew is on the race course Saturday. We intend to prevail there. But my fervent hope is that the best crew will win, of course."

"It will, Beckering," Del Rio said sourly. "It will."

When they were gone, a couple of minutes later, Beckering finally turned to Kralich with a deadly look.

"You absolute moron! I should have known you couldn't handle it without Falco!"

Kralich frowned defensively. "Now, wait a goddam minute, Gus. I was careful as hell. It was blind luck that put Del Rio there at that exact time."

Beckering's flabby face was purplish with fury, and he was breathing hard now. He made a conscious effort to control his frustration and anger. "Five thousand dollars! A bonus, for God's sake! You just ruined my last chance to grab this trophy without sweating out this goddam Cahill! Now I *have* to depend on Tony." He swallowed back his rage. "I'll give you a bonus! I'll let you race Saturday, in spite of this crap you pulled off tonight! But after that you're finished, for as long as I'm around. Whether we win or lose."

"Gus, look—"

"Now get to hell out of my sight," Beckering wheezed, in the low, gravelly voice. "Get out of here and don't let me see your ugly face till race time!"

Kralich figured it was pointless to protest further to a dying man. So he limped across the room grimly, and left without another word.

Now it would be up to Falco.

Chapter Nineteen

Rachel McKenzie flew out of Key West later that morning, and nobody saw her off, not even the friends who had hosted the party. She had spent part of the night with O'Brien, but had left him in the midst of hurled insults, because he could not perform for her over and over in a three-hour period. Rachel had called her husband then, in the middle of the night, about the time that Kralich had arrived at the marina with the gasoline, and she had sweet-talked him in a practiced way, saying how she missed him. Now she would go home licking imaginary wounds, as she had done so often before, and there would be another period when she sat in her spacious living room with Mac, watching him read the financial page and catching up on Fort Lauderdale gossip. Soon there would be friends from up north arriving at Palm Beach, opening up their luxurious homes there, and Rachel would find further distraction for a while. Her interlude with power boat racers would be behind her, merely another small chapter in an already too lengthy odyssey for Rachel. In six months she would begin to forget all the names of those she had met and been intimate with, except for Cahill and Falco, and it would all blur together. That was the way it was with Rachel and always would be.

But at Key West, tension was mounting quickly. It was only twenty-four hours before the races, and all the drivers and owners had arrived for the open and production events. But most locals were talking about one race only—the Class One open that featured the duel between Falco and Cahill. The fast race, the big one with the super-boats and super-drivers. Cuban-Americans discussed it hotly in Spanish, and old-time Bahamian "conchs" gathered in knots in the area of the shrimp docks and made wagers for more than they could afford.

When Dulcie called Cahill at his and Del Rio's room, she got no reply. Cahill had not been able to go back to sleep after returning from Gus Beckering's. He had lain wide-eyed on his bed, staring at the ceiling as the sun filtered weakly into the room, letting the new day make its impression on him. Then, finding little rest, he had gone off to find Del Rio. Lucas was sleeping with Eva Falco, so Cahill did not want to disturb him. He walked down to Shorty's Restaurant on Duval. Del Rio had left, but Cahill stayed and had a leisurely meal, trying to get Gus Beckering and Art Kralich out of his mind. He was very tired, but that did not bother him. He had had no nightmare on that previous night, because of the diversion, and he figured that was good. He would be gearing mentally for the race now, and he knew that it was dangerous to gear too high, particularly for him.

The fact was, Cahill had the persistent feeling that he had become swept up in a maelstrom that was carrying him along against his will, trying to suck him into its deep vortex, and that he had very little control over what happened to him. As that feeling grew and pervaded him at every level, he began to wonder whether his fight for survival through it meant anything, whether he would be able to influence events at all. Not even Dulcie's presence in Key West could help him now, in these last hours. Whatever help she could give had been given. Now, increasingly, there were only the boat and the race course and running the race itself a hundred times in his head, fantasizing the competition, trying to visualize how to make it turn out right, keeping from the top of his head the growing anxiety, the flashes of death scenes, the jungle river.

Dulcie was surprised that she did not find Cahill at his room. She had accepted the fact that he wanted to be alone to rest that night and the next, but she had just assumed he would be having breakfast with her that morning. A small anxiety settled in on her again as she dressed, the fear that she was losing Cahill to his inner self, and that she would not be able to retrieve him when the race was over. Or, worse yet, that he would somehow not survive the race—that the dark thing inside him would succeed in killing Cahill.

When she was dressed, Dulcie stopped past Eva's room. Eva and Lucas had had an early breakfast and Eva had returned to the room alone, planning to join the men at the boat later. Eva was happy to see Dulcie at her door.

"Dulcie! What a nice surprise!" She looked past Dulcie, wondering if Cahill was with her. "Come on in."

"Are you alone?" Dulcie asked.

"Yes, Boyd went down to the marina."

Dulcie looked around the room as Eva closed the door behind her. There was a patio door to a balcony, and a glimpse of emerald water beyond. The bed was still unmade, and one of Lucas's large-size shirts hung on a chair. Dulcie suddenly wished she had the same secure feeling about Cahill that Eva did toward Boyd Lucas.

"Can I get you a cup of coffee?" Eva asked.

"Oh, no, Eva. I was just wondering whether you had seen Steve this morning." She was a little embarrassed to ask, because she knew that Eva figured she ought to know where Cahill was.

"Why, not yet, Dulcie." Eva looked pretty in a white blouse and gaily printed skirt. "Boyd and I figured he was with you."

"I haven't seen him since last evening," Dulcie said. "We're not fighting or anything. It's just that Steve has the race on his mind now."

"Danny called Boyd early this morning," Eva said. "He had just left Steve. Did you know about the boat?"

Dulcie frowned. "No, what?"

"Art Kralich tried to set fire to it."

Dulcie's mouth dropped slightly open. A hot memory burned through the front of her head, in which Kralich's muscular hand was between her legs, violating her, tearing her clothing, mauling and bruising.

"Oh, Jesus. Did he—?"

"No, Danny was there and ran him off. But they're still cleaning up this morning. The *Sonic Boom* will be all right."

"Thank God," Dulcie said, and immediately felt a quick counter-emotion. *Maybe he would be better off if it had burned. Maybe he should never race again, tomorrow or ever.*

"I wish I had been with him," she added.

"I think it's best you missed it," Eva guessed. "Danny had to prevent Steve's attacking Kralich, at Gus Beckering's room over at the Casa Marina. Danny thinks he could have killed him."

Dulcie trembled suddenly, letting a shiver shake through her. Eva came and put a hand on her arm. "You're worried about him, aren't you?"

Dulcie hesitated, then nodded. "Very much. Maybe it wouldn't be so bad, maybe I could last through it better, if I was sure of him, if I knew that he—"

"Don't judge him by how he acts in the next day or so," Eva told her. "He thinks a lot of you, Dulcie. I can see it in his eyes when he looks at you."

"If I felt closer to him, if he let me come closer, maybe I could help," Dulcie said. "Selfishly, I worry that if he gets through this without me, that if he doesn't need me in the next twenty-four hours, that will be the end of it again between us. That he'll regard me as just a diversion to take his mind off things, and we'll drift off in separate directions again. I don't want that, Eva, but I don't know what to do about it.''

Eva looked into Dulcie's lovely, youthful face. Her hair was down, long and dark, and her eyes looked particularly big and vulnerable that morning. Wearing a light blouse and shorts, showing off long, tanned thighs, she was the kind of girl that any man would take two looks at, on the street. Eva could not imagine Cahill losing interest in so attractive and sensitive a girl. But she had to admit that she had seen less logical things happen between men and women, not the least of which was her marriage to the narcissistic Tony Falco.

"Just keep yourself available until this is past, Dulcie," Eva counseled her. "After the race, you'll know."

Dulcie smiled uncertainly. "That's what I'm afraid of," she replied in a subdued voice. "God, how I wish the past couple of days could have gone on forever."

Eva touched her cheek. "Have some faith in him, Dulcie. And—in yourself."

Dulcie caught Eva's soft look, and realized that she had found a friend in this disillusioned wife of the man who had violated Dulcie so insensitively, those many nights ago. "Thanks, Eva. I'll try to do that. I really will."

When she left Eva's room a few minutes later, she felt a little better. She had been going to go find Cahill, but now decided against it. It was up to him to come to her when he was ready. The thought crossed her mind that she might never see him alive again, except in the cockpit of a racing boat, from a distance.

It could happen that way.

She decided not to think about it.

Cahill did not seek Dulcie out the rest of that day. He

wanted to, very much, but he knew that he was not in a mood that would be conducive to their relationship. Cahill was becoming so tight inside as the day progressed that he disliked anyone seeing him that way, even Lucas and Del Rio. He became outwardly tense, and was quick to take offense. Lucas, making sure the *Sonic Boom* was ready to race, finally gave up trying to get along with Cahill in the cleaning up process and went downtown to have a couple of beers and relax by himself. Danny Del Rio stuck with Cahill, but did not speak much to him. Somebody had to keep an eye on Cahill, he figured, as this day and night passed, and it might as well be him.

Cahill soon understood that he was being baby-sat, of course, and that caused a blow-up between him and Del Rio about mid-afternoon. Cahill left the marina, too, and drove clear across the island to have a drink by himself, hoping to keep away from the racing crowd. But he was unsuccessful. Just before he left the place, in early evening, Tony Falco showed up at the motel bar. Falco did not see Cahill at first, but then suddenly he was at Cahill's elbow.

"Well. It looks like you got the same idea as me," Falco said in a congenial voice.

Cahill, sitting on a barstool, turned and gave Falco a hard look. "It looks like it," he said.

Falco sat down beside Cahill, without being asked, and ordered a martini. The bartender went away and got it, brought it to Falco. Falco picked the full glass up and studied it. "I heard about Kralich, and what he tried."

Cahill glowered at him for a moment. "I'll bet you did," he said darkly.

Falco swigged part of the drink. "It was a stupid trick," he went on.

Cahill looked at him. "You should have told him that."

"I did," Falco said evenly. "When Beckering hinted

275

that he would approve of some kind of sabotage of the *Sonic Boom*. I told him I wanted nothing to do with it. I had no idea that Kralich would try something on his own.''

Cahill studied Falco's open face, and believed him. ''Okay. You didn't know about it.''

''I just wanted to say I'm sorry it happened,'' Falco said evenly.

Cahill stared toward him for a moment.

''I've been doing some thinking the past couple of days. About what happened at Miami, and about Eva's leaving me. Maybe we all get what we deserve, I don't know.''

Cahill stared into an almost-empty beer glass.

''I should have turned around for Wyatt,'' Falco said almost inaudibly. There was a long silence between them. Cahill swigged the rest of the beer. ''You would have. Even if it meant losing the race, wouldn't you?''

Cahill shrugged. ''I think so.'' A shocking flash of memory exploded into his head, of Josh Owens's sweating, hysterical face. Josh was yelling something at Cahill, but Cahill could not hear what it was.

''That's the way it is with people like you,'' Falco said without bitterness. ''You always do the right thing. It's automatic with you, like shaking hands after a tennis match. You don't have to think about it.''

Cahill's stomach was quickly constricting into knots. ''That's not true, Falco,'' he said quietly, but not knowing why he said it.

''Hell, you don't have to deny it, I know. You're a frigging war hero, aren't you? I found a way to keep out of the war. That's the way it's always been with me. Let the other guy take the beating. Look out for number one.''

Cahill closed his eyes against sudden intestinal pain, and saw the river boat, plunging along through the muddy delta river. Machine guns were clattering out their grim messages in his ears, and there were mortar and rocket explosions everywhere. He gritted his teeth, squinting his eyes tightly shut, breathing shallowly. But Falco did not notice.

That's the way it is with people like you. You always do the right thing. It's automatic with you.

"But I know now that I let Wyatt down. It was the craziness of the moment. Wanting to win too much. I was turning into a Beckering."

Cahill felt the ugliness lessening. He opened his eyes, and got his breathing under control. Falco glanced over at him, and saw the sweat beaded up on his brow.

"Are you okay?"

Cahill nodded.

"You sure? You look terrible."

"I'm all right," Cahill told him.

Falco stared at him for a moment, then spoke again. "I know what you think of me. I just want you to know that I wasn't involved in that stupid stunt of Kralich's. Also, that I intend to go for the trophy fair and square. I don't want to beat you any other way. I never felt that way about any other driver. But I want to beat your ass good, and I don't want any question about it after I've done it."

Cahill glanced over at him.

"I don't know whether that means you brought out the best in me, or the worst. It's like some goddam fever I've caught. Christ, I couldn't even sleep last night. Maybe I caught whatever's bugging you. I don't know. But I'm giving you fair warning, Cahill. If you intend to come in ahead of me tomorrow, you're going to have to be humping that Rossman boat. You're going to have to hump it good."

Cahill nodded. "That part I already knew," he said, his voice a little hoarse from what he had been through. "If it makes it any easier for you, Falco, I'll let you in on a little secret. Despite the fact that I've disliked you almost from the moment I met you, and despite the fact that I think that reform speech you just delivered is

277

more bullshit than truth, I respect your driving. I guess if I were a betting man, my money would be on the *First Blood* tomorrow."

Falco held Cahill's look with a sour one. "If that's supposed to make me like you, forget it."

Cahill returned the look. "If you ever got to liking me, Falco, I'd wonder what kind of a sonofabitch I'd become."

Falco hesitated, then grinned a hard grin. "Okay, Cahill. See you at the races." He rose and laid some money on the bar. "You'd better be ready to cut water."

"We'll try to make it interesting for you," Cahill told him.

That evening, Cahill avoided everyone, including Dulcie. He called her in early evening, though, and explained that he had to be alone. He was apologetic, she thought, but not affectionate. Dulcie was very unhappy after he hung up. She wanted to help him, but he would not let her. She had the awful feeling that even if Cahill survived his ordeal, it would be over for them, that whatever had happened in the war had probably exorcised something in him, the part that would have allowed him to give of himself freely and accept what she had to offer him.

Lucas and Del Rio also worried about Cahill, but elected not to intrude on his privacy. Lucas slept with Eva that night again, but he had had another call from Paige in early evening, when he was alone in the room, that had sobered him again. Paige did not know about Eva, so she unabashedly admitted how much she missed Lucas, how very lonely she was in Baltimore without him, and how things would not be right there until the races were over and he returned to their home. Again, Lucas did not mention the call to Eva or anyone else, but he thought about Paige a lot that evening.

By the time Del Rio got back to his and Cahill's room that tense night, Cahill was already asleep, but tossing fitfully. At midnight, and then again later, Cahill woke Del Rio with choked cries into the blackness. Del Rio was scared and began wondering if Cahill would really be able to race the next morning.

Cahill's yells into the darkness were the result of just one nightmare scene that repeated itself several times that night, mostly in the first hours of sleep. Cahill was aboard the gray Navy river launch, with the camouflage on its sides and canopy, and bullets were flying around him and Josh Owens and the small crew. Firing of guns fractured the hot delta air as the boat plunged along, and shells exploded in the muddy water around them. Josh was going a little crazy with fear, as the fatigue-suited and helmeted sailors at the guns rattled out their fury at the Cong attackers on the banks.

"I can't take it!" Josh was yelling above the fire. *"We've got to get off here, Steve! We're all going to be killed!"*

Cahill could feel, in his sleep, the twisting anger and frustration inside him, because of Josh. Josh had never been a hero-type, had always depended on Cahill to pull him out of scrapes. But he had never gone completely to pieces quite like this before, showing the Cong and the Navy what appeared to be raw cowardice.

"Get down, goddam it, Josh! I'm telling you, goddam it, get down and shut up!"

It was part of that speech that came out garbled, twice, in the darkness of the motel room that night. The second time, Cahill could not seem to come out of the fantasy, and kept yelling into the black room. *"If you won't use a goddam rifle, Josh, keep out of the goddam way!"*

"Steve! Steve, can you hear me? It's Danny."

Finally, Cahill had wakened and looked around, stunned that he was not in the jungle firelight, on that muddy river. He focused on Del Rio for a moment as if Del Rio might be one of the Cong who were trying to kill him. Then he realized where he was and apologized to Del Rio darkly, lying there sweating onto his pillow.

The nightmares dissolved away as dawn approached on that Saturday morning. But Del Rio had been shaken by the experience. They went out for breakfast at seven, and Boyd Lucas joined them at a small restaurant not far from the motel. Eva had told Lucas that she would come down to the marina docks with Dulcie later.

Cahill was quiet at breakfast, embarrassed by what had happened through the night, and very tense about the race. His tension, too, spread to Lucas and Del Rio. Just a look from Del Rio to Lucas told Lucas that Cahill had had a bad night, and Lucas took the cue and did not try to engage Cahill in conversation.

The streets were now crowding with cars and pedestrians in downtown Key West. The race would be watched from Mallory Dock, behind the old town square, on the Gulf, and from White Street Pier, on the other side of the island, where the boats could be seen on their way to and from Sand Key. The press had now gathered in large numbers—from Miami, Atlanta, New York and Chicago. They sought out drivers in these early hours, and tried to cover them for a quick interview. Cahill managed to avoid that trouble by driving the threesome to the marina by back streets and by ducking around the crowds at the marina.

The *Sonic Boom* was all right. They suited up quickly at the marina, boarded the boat in their orange race suits, and revved her engines up. They sounded good. The work on them had paid off.

It was a perfect morning. The temperature was in the seventies, and the humidity was relatively low. As had been predicted, the sea was like a plate of glass, the racers mirrored photographically on its flat surface. All around the *Sonic Boom*, on land and in the water, there was frenzied activity. Boats were being lowered into the water at the last moment by trailer and crane. Officials moving from boat to boat, class to class, checking identification. There had been an inspection party on the previous evening, which Cahill had attended briefly after his call to Dulcie. Now the officials were making sure the boats were preparing by class, answering questions about rules, getting sweep boats and check boats out onto the surface. Newsmen kept getting in the way, slowing things down, getting their last-minute stories.

Dulcie and Eva showed up at shortly after nine, and their passes allowed them to join the small throng at the marina docks. The *First Blood* was docked near the *Sonic Boom,* and Falco had just arrived and was aboard with Kralich and Jenkins. Falco's eye caught Eva's as she went past and they exchanged long looks for a moment, but she did not greet him. She and Dulcie moved on down to the *Sonic Boom,* where Cahill was checking out the controls with Lucas and Del Rio, with the boat's engines off.

"Hi, everybody," Eva called out. "Are you cleared to race?"

Lucas looked up and grinned. He looked mammoth in the race suit. "Hi, honey. We're all set."

"Hey, there they are," Del Rio grinned.

Cahill was holding Dulcie's sober gaze, feeling awkward and embarrassed, as if he had just met her, and they had never been intimate.

"You look ready," Dulcie said.

"Like hell," Cahill grinned slightly. He felt awful. Besides the fatigue from lack of sleep, there was a growing nausea in the pit of his stomach.

"The best of luck to you, Steve," Dulcie said. "Whether you win or not."

Cahill cast a sober look at her. He nodded. "Right."

Eva was talking to Lucas and Del Rio, giving them a pep talk. Now, though, the big moment had arrived. An official was moving Class One boats off toward a starting position out in the channel near Mallory Dock. The open race boats of classes one and two would race together, with separate trophies for each class. Then, after they were gone, the larger, production classes would start off: sport, modified, and regular production boats. Boats from that separate race would be coming in all morning, long after the excitement of the big Class One race was past.

"Well, it looks like we've got to move out," Cahill said to Dulcie. "I'll see you when it's over, Dulcie."

Dulcie nodded, her eyes tearing slightly when she saw the distraught look in Cahill's face as he donned the orange helmet. Lucas had started the port engine, and now the starboard one roared into life. They were beyond being able to talk back and forth, now. The two women retreated from the dock's edge as Del Rio and Lucas donned their helmets and all three men strapped in. An official waved them off, and Cahill slipped the racer into gear and it moved slowly away from the dock. A young local came running down to the dock's edge at the last moment, yelling at the boat.

"Give them hell, Cahill! Beat Falco good! We're all pulling for you!"

Cahill did not hear. He was heading toward the more open water of the big channel, watching the buoy markers. "Keep the throttle way back, Boyd, it's just a few hundred yards. What's the oil pressure, Danny?"

"Right on the button, Steve," Del Rio's excited voice came over the intercom. "She's ready to move. I can feel it!"

"Ten knots at low throttle," Lucas was reading out. "Here comes the *First Blood*, right behind us."

Cahill and Del Rio turned, and saw Falco coming up on their port, slowly. Kralich and Jenkins had donned the helmets, but Falco was holding his under his arm, steering with one hand, looking like Cortez about ready to conquer the Aztecs.

"Goddam showboat!" Del Rio cursed.

"Talk about ready," Cahill muttered.

At the starting line, there were almost twenty boats gathering in the open category race. The pace boat was already in position and ready to move out. A dozen helicopters fluttered overhead, some official and some private. Coast Guard boats idled at the perimeter of the racers, keeping order. The racers lined up one by one, in all their glory—white, yellow, red, black, green, two and three tones of color on some. Even their idling engines, plus the noise from the helicopters, made a cacophony of sound that vibrated the otherwise calm morning air. Up ahead of the starting line, at Mallory Dock, heavy throngs of wildly waving and cheering spectators had gathered, rooting for their favorite boats and drivers. Some would bring chairs, even lunches, and sit all morning, watching the boats come in from Sand Key on their first round of a three-circuit trip.

Almost before Cahill was aware that it was time, the yellow flag was up on the pace boat and it was moving forward, and the lined-up racers inched ahead at its stern. Cahill felt a lurching in his gut and thought he might be sick over the side of the boat. But he felt a little better as the green flag went up and then swooped down.

The boats roared away, the three orange-suited figures in each one seeming to strain forward with the movement of their craft. Great wakes of white foam churned up behind them, making waves that would pound at the docks nearby long after the racers were gone. Bows lifted out of the water on such an angle that it appeared their crafts might sink at their sterns. Then they were skipping along the flat channel past Mallory Dock and the yelling crowds, and out into the open sea.

Cahill had advised Lucas to open the throttle gradually, so that when they passed their first markers to head for Sand Key, the *Sonic Boom* was running in about the middle of the pack. The *First Blood* was up at the fore, in second place, and moving smoothly and well. The markers were rounded and the race made its turn toward the abandoned lighthouse at Sand Key. Cahill's nausea was under control for the moment, and things were going smoothly. Del Rio sneaked a glance at

283

Cahill and was satisfied with what he saw. If the race went like this, they would have a chance.

But Falco was not so easy to catch. His lead widened as the boats came back from Sand Key to a marker at Stock Island and headed in past Mallory for the first complete circuit of the three-circuit race. Falco was now out and ahead of everybody, and was putting a bigger and bigger lead between himself and the next boats. Cahill moved steadily up through the pack on the second circuit, taking his time, not panicking. But he was almost flat-out. The *Sonic Boom* fairly flew over the water, just touching its surface. Other boats faded in its wake, and now there were none between Falco and Cahill.

Near the end of the second circuit, Cahill felt the nausea gradually returning. Del Rio and Lucas, who figured he was doing well, did not notice. Cahill gritted his teeth, and spoke through the intercom. *"Flat-out, Boyd! Flat-out!"*

The *Sonic Boom* chased the *First Blood* into the dock and harbor area that second time in. The two boats roared past the cheering crowds only a hundred yards apart, washing big waves up against the concrete dock. Falco gained ten yards on the turn-around, and then they were skipping back out toward the open sea for a last run at Sand Key.

Now, with Cahill on his stern and coming up, Falco was worried. He had been cutting corners at the markers, almost grazing check boats, and now as they approached a marker to turn them on a Sand Key course, there was a different situation from previously. The check boat at the turn had momentarily left its position to give aid to a stalled Class Two racer, and there was only a buoy marker to show the channel and course. Instead of heading around the starboard side of it, as they had done previously, Falco now steered to the port, cutting a corner. He wanted to gain a couple of seconds on Cahill.

"Hey!" Jenkins's voice came to him, through their intercom system. *"To the right, Tony!"*

Kralich looked toward Falco, studying Falco's eyes behind the face mask. Falco had hardly spoken to Kralich since the incident at the marina docks, and Kralich resented Falco's setting himself above Kralich.

"We're going the short way," Falco growled. *"Who'll know the difference?"* All his resolutions about fair play were forgotten in the excitement of the moment. He was in a panic about Cahill, and reason no longer ruled. He wanted to win, to beat Cahill any way he could, to be cheered at the winner's circle when it was over, as the new champion.

"Damn it," Jenkins's voice came, *"we're on the very edge of the channel, and it's low tide! The water here will be very shallow for the First—"*

But he did not get to finish. The boat lurched and bucked, slowing with every split-second, churning up brown sand in its wake. Falco had steered too far off course and was digging up bottom with his props. He had not allowed for the tricky shallows that surrounded this particularly narrow course.

"Christ, we're on bottom!" Kralich's tough voice came.

The boat was slowed to half-speed, kicking up dirty water behind it. *"Shit!"* Falco swore, jerking the wheel around to starboard, trying to un-mire them.

"Get it hard to starboard!" Jenkins was yelling. *"Thirty degrees should do it! Cut it hard!"*

Falco, wrestling the wheel, saw the *Sonic Boom* go sailing past, making the *First Blood* look like it was standing still. *"Oh, Christ!"* he moaned.

"You crazy jerk!" Kralich said angrily. *"You just gave Cahill the lead on a silver platter!"*

The *Sonic Boom* flew past, with Cahill and his crew surprised at their good fortune. Falco had managed again to get himself into trouble, grabbing for an unfair edge. Their boat skipped out in front with a roar now,

Lucas holding the throttle wide open on this flat sea, getting the most out of Falco's mistake, making the lead as wide as he could. Finally, Cahill looked back and saw Falco on course. But he was suddenly a long way behind.

"We've got him, by God!" Lucas yelled. "That son will never catch us, now!"

"He cut his own goddam throat!" Del Rio cried out.

But behind the wheel, Cahill was going dizzy and sick. The real world was beginning to swim before his vision, and blur with what was forming in his head.

This is it, he thought, sweat forming on his face behind the mask. *This is when it will try to kill me. I'm going to know, now. I'm going to find out what the hell it's all about.*

The boat blurred in his vision, and suddenly he was on the camouflaged Navy launch. He was not holding onto the wheel, but a gun mounting. The acrid odor of gunsmoke was thick in his nostrils, and the clattering and explosions of gunfire. One sailor lay dead at Cahill's feet, a stitching of holes across his bloody chest, and another lay in a twisted, awkward position across the deck, in a pool of viscous, crimson liquid. There was a sailor manning the wheel, under a canopy that had caught fire, and two others on guns—one on the bow, and one at the stern. Cahill's sixty millimeter was mounted on the side of the launch, at midships, and the sailor at Cahill's feet had died manning it. Now Cahill was picking off short blasts into the jungle at the river bank, where black-suited Cong were out in the open, firing off automatic weapons, mostly AK-47's. They were also firing mortars and rockets at the racing launch, which were exploding loudly on all sides, in the water. One had gone off onboard, killing the sailor in the pool of blood and setting the canopy afire. But it had not hurt the hull enough to stop them.

Cahill remembered now. The launch had picked up the wounded Steve Cahill and Josh Owens at the river bank. Shortly afterwards, this attack had come from the jungle. Josh, wounded and hysterically afraid, was crouched at the gunwale, eyes wide, mouth ajar.

"*Pick up his rifle, Josh!*" Cahill now shouted into the intercom.

Del Rio and Lucas quickly glanced toward him. Cahill was trembling all over.

"*I can't take it!*" Josh was yelling back at Cahill, in his head. "*We've got to get off here, Steve! We're all going to be killed!*"

"*Keep down, and arm yourself, goddam it!*" Cahill yelled back, disgust heavy in his voice. "*The rifle there near you, pick it up and use it!*"

"*Are you okay, Steve?*" Del Rio's scared voice, from another world.

But Cahill did not hear. There was the roaring of the river launch and the gunfire from the jungle and the exploding mortars. The launch neared a skiff on the river with Cong aboard, firing weapons toward it. The launch veered at the skiff and rammed it, breaking it in half, with Cahill firing the machine gun at its occupants. They fell into the muddy river, cut up by hot lead.

But then the sailor at the bow gun was hit in the side, and went plummeting into the water, dying as he hit. The boat kept going. Cahill whirled toward Josh, desperately. "*Josh, forget the rifle! We need you on the big gun! Now!*"

But Josh was crawling to Cahill, his face white. "*You said it was over! That we were as good as home! But we're going to die in this stinking place!*"

Cahill was getting heavy fire from the river bank and had crouched down away from the gun for a moment. At that moment, with Cahill trying hard to keep from getting killed, himself, Josh arrived at his side, grabbing at Cahill's clothing.

"*I can't take it, Steve! There's been too much, I can't take it any more! Jesus Christ, I can't take it!*"

Suddenly Cahill was very angry. All of Josh's weaknesses seemed to shout at him, filling him with open disgust. He was momentarily tired of protecting Josh, of fighting his fights, of pandering to Josh's cowardice. He shoved Josh away from him.

"Get off me, goddam it! Get off me once and for all! Be a man once in your whole frigging life!"

Josh stared at him numbly, terror etched on his narrow face. Bullets whined around them, and Cahill was scared himself. He kicked out at Josh's thigh, savagely. *"I'm telling you, get away from me! Go man that gun and act your frigging age! You make me sick, for Christ's sake!"*

Josh had winced under the kick and now crouched there trembling with terror. But Cahill's words had finally had their effect on him. Stiff-jointed with horror, he rose to his knees and then his feet. Bullets flew around him.

"Okay, Steve." Hollowly, desperately. *"Okay."*

Josh started for the big gun, Cahill watching. He took just two steps away from Cahill, his doubtful island of safety, and suddenly his head whiplashed back and forth and Cahill clearly saw a piece of his skull blown away at the back of his head by a flying chunk of hot lead. Josh was thrown in a tight circle, then he hit the deck hard on his back, eyes wide, his jaw working.

Cahill's face changed, and he swallowed hard. *"Josh? Josh!"*

A flash of Josh's sticky head cradled in Cahill's hands. Aboard the *Sonic Boom*, he yelled into the intercom, as sudden knowledge flooded into his skull. *"I killed him!"* he shouted. *"I might as well have pulled the trigger on the gun!"*

Boyd Lucas just stared, but Del Rio understood. Now Cahill was gripping the wheel hard, and breathing shallowly. Josh had not died on the river bank, as he had told himself later. He had carried Josh off when the boat made it through the firefight, still in a daze, and his own mind had begun hiding from him what had really happened.

Cahill saw a big course marker ahead of him now, and it was not a marker to him, but another Cong skiff. He was at the wheel of the Navy launch, and he had to ram the skiff, which was loaded with explosives, to avenge Josh's death. But that was not all of it, he understood somewhere deep inside him. There was a penalty to pay for what he had done.

"Steve, you're headed right for the marker!" Lucas's big voice boomed out in the intercom. *"What are you trying to do, kill us?"*

"I've got to ram them!" Cahill said in a low, hoarse voice. *"I've got to make it right!"*

Lucas turned to Cahill as the big iron buoy loomed up on the boat. He grabbed the wheel and tried to wrest it from Cahill's grip. Cahill fought him, though, and threw a fist at Lucas. Lucas's face mask was splintered, and he fell on the dashboard. The boat flew past the buoy, almost grazing it, before Cahill could get control of the boat back. Then Cahill was unbuckling, and turning to leave the bolster.

"I've got to get Josh!" he said in a croaking voice. *"Maybe he isn't—"*

But now Del Rio grabbed at Cahill, as Lucas took the wheel and steered the *Sonic Boom* back onto course, at a lower speed. On their starboard, the *First Blood* crept past them, coming up at a faster speed. Falco turned and saw what was happening. A big grin broadened his face under his mask. Cahill was in trouble. Falco thought he had blown the race by running the *First Blood* into the shallows, but now Cahill had given him the lead back. The *First Blood* moved on past as Del Rio caught Cahill and prevented him from leaving the cockpit of the boat.

"Steve, for Christ's sake, Josh is dead! He's been dead for a long time!"

Cahill was not listening. He tried to break free of Del Rio, and Del Rio, in desperation, slugged him alongside the head, cracking the Kevlar helmet and jarring Cahill inside it. Cahill focused slowly on Del Rio.

"*That all happened a long time ago, goddam it! Josh is long dead, and there's nothing you can do to bring him back, not even by giving up your own life!*"

Cahill stared at Del Rio blankly. Lucas, behind the wheel, had the boat on course and moving again. But Falco was almost two hundred yards ahead now, as they approached the Sand Key markers.

"*I can't run this frigging boat myself!*" he complained loudly. "*Falco is beating us!*"

Del Rio ignored him and stared hard into Cahill's sweaty face, behind the helmet mask. "*It wasn't your fault. You had every right to do just exactly what you did. I know, I had the same kind of thing happen. Josh had no right to expect a savior. What he was finally caught up with him. You didn't kill Josh, the Cong did. With his help. If he had been a fighter, he would have survived. You don't have to do this to yourself. Do you hear me?*"

Cahill hesitated, then nodded. "*I hear you, Danny.*" Something was slowly draining out of him, a tension that had been living inside him for years, and which he had been covering up.

"*Do you believe me?*"

Another hesitation, then an uncertain nod.

"*Then let's get back at the controls. We've got a race to win!*"

Cahill turned, and saw the *First Blood* up ahead of them, heading for Stock Island over two hundred yards ahead. He grabbed the wheel away from Lucas. "*Get on the throttle, Boyd,*" he said hoarsely. "*And give it as much as you can find in her. Rip her apart if you have to, but catch that sonofabitch!*"

Lucas and Del Rio were back at their own controls. Lucas stuck a thumb in the air, with a grin, and opened the throttle wide. The boat lurched forward, skimming the water, hitting ninety knots. At that speed, the slightest spin-out or stuffing of the boat would have killed them all. But the sea was like glass. They closed the distance on the *First Blood* to a hundred yards, slowly but surely. The extra work they had done on the engine was showing, and so was their determination to beat Falco. The boats made the Stock Island turn and were heading in to the Mallory harbor and the finish, only a few minutes away now.

Cahill's gut was quieting, and he felt really whole, inside, for the first time since the war. *"Lean on it, Boyd!"* he said in a low, easy voice. *"She's taking all we can give her. I think she'll top ninety! If she can, we might make it!"*

The boat was flying, pounding at the flat sea with its hull. It was only fifty yards behind Falco now, as they made a big wide turn to head into the harbor. Suddenly, though, a private small boat came roaring into the race course, driven by some hyped-up kids.

"Look out!" Del Rio warned.

But Cahill had already made a quick maneuver that set the boat right on its side, zooming around the interfering boat in a flashing instant, saving a collision that would have ended the race for them, and losing only a second or two. Their wake almost capsized the smaller boat, but it survived the near-miss. Cahill, as cool as Lucas had ever seen him, wheeled the *Sonic Boom* right back onto course with such expertise that it was beautiful to watch. They had lost only a couple of seconds and ten or fifteen yards. None of them even spoke of the incident. They all were crouched forward on their harnesses, watching the harbor loom up on them.

Falco was now only fifty yards ahead again. Thirty. Twenty. They were coming into the harbor's mouth in the channel, and crowds were jamming the docks to see this wild, unprecedented finish for the national title. But Cahill did not see them. He guided the *Sonic Boom* out of the *First Blood's* wake, and the Falco boat was now only a boat-length ahead. The Mallory docks flashed past at ninety knots. The boats were even, but Falco had a foot or two on them. The finish line hove onto them, and they roared across it, with the checkered flag swooping down, the *Sonic Boom* eight inches in front of the *First Blood* as the flag dropped.

They were not even sure they had won, until Del Rio turned and saw their numbers hoisted on a pole at the shrimp docks, near the finish line.

"We did it!" Del Rio yelled. *"We beat him, by Jesus!"*

Lucas jerked his helmet off, his big face stricken with the shock of winning. "It's ours," he said numbly, as he slowed the *Sonic Boom*. "We're goddam national champs."

They looked at Cahill at the same moment, and he wore a sure grin underneath the helmet. He pulled it off as the boat slowed even more, and he guided it toward the marina docks, where more people were jam-packed together, waving at the winning boat. The *First Blood* had dropped back now, and glancing toward it, Cahill saw Falco leaning heavily on the dashboard, limp and defeated. Kralich slammed a fist into the windshield, and Cahill allowed his grin to widen slightly.

Del Rio's helmet was thrown off, and Del Rio grabbed Cahill with new affection and embraced him warmly. Lucas slapped a hand onto Cahill's shoulder.

"Christ, Steve," Lucas said hoarsely. "Christ."

Cahill nodded. "I know, Boyd." His voice broke slightly, as he turned to Del Rio. "Danny, I owe you."

"Like hell," Del Rio said.

Cahill guided the world's fastest boat into the marina docks, where his new, avid public awaited him.

Chapter Twenty

"We want Cahill, we want Cahill, we want Cahill!"

The marina dock crowd was chanting in unison as dock hands helped tie up the *Sonic Boom*. Del Rio stepped off the boat, and a cheer went up. Lucas jumped onto the dock, and another cheer arose. Then Cahill came ashore, his flaxen hair blowing slightly in a new sea breeze, and the crowd present roared its approval and admiration. The mayor was there to shake Cahill's hand, and reporters were everywhere. People elbowed and shoved each other to get closer to Cahill—to the new national champion. Down the dock, the *First Blood* was tying up, and nobody was there but a couple of dock employees. The king was dead. The public had crowned another one.

"What was the turning point, Steve?"

"We hear you had some trouble out there."

"Did you hit another boat?"

"How does it feel to be the national champ?"

Cahill regretted that they were not paying more attention to Lucas and Del Rio, but that was the way it always was. The driver was their hero, and always would be. He looked around for Dulcie but did not see her. Eva had now broken through the crowd and was hugging Boyd Lucas tightly, as a photographer took their picture. Out on the marina parking lot, Cahill got just a glimpse of Gus Beckering, ashen-faced in the back seat of a chauffeur-driven limousine. The car now pulled slowly away, as Beckering glowered toward

Cahill, and then it was out of sight.

The mayor was dragging Cahill to an elevated platform on the dock. Cahill accompanied him reluctantly. When they got there, there was a lot more cheering and yelling. The mayor made a short speech, telling the crowd how great Cahill was, and presented him with the local race trophy. Then a representative of the American Power Boat Association came up and awarded Cahill the national championship driver's trophy for Class One offshore racing. It was a big, gold cup that shone in the sun and dazzled the eye. Cahill held it aloft, and the crowd went wild.

"This trophy really belongs to Boyd Lucas," Cahill told them, "and Danny Del Rio and Ed Harris and Charlie Rossman. Without all of them, I'd never have made it even part way."

The mayor then got Lucas and Del Rio up on the stand, and there was more yelling and picture-taking. Just as they were coming down to the dock level, Tony Falco walked past, trying to avoid the newsmen. He cast a hard look toward Cahill, and their eyes locked soberly for a brief moment. Then Falco was shouldering his way past the crowd.

"What happened out there, Tony?"

It was a lone reporter, wanting a story from the loser's view. "You had quite a lead at one point. What happened to it?"

"No comment," Falco said brusquely, pushing his way into the open.

That would be the last look Cahill would ever have of Tony Falco. Cahill looked after him somberly for a moment, then he and his crew were on their way to the parking area with Eva, who was holding onto Lucas as if she might never let go.

"Where's Dulcie?" Cahill asked her, when they were fairly well free of the crowd.

"She went back to her room," Eva said. "I thought she was coming back here for the finish. Maybe she got held up in traffic.''

Eva, Cahill's crew and a couple of other drivers insisted on going over to the Sportsmen's Inn, across the boulevard, for a couple of drinks in celebration of the big win, and Cahill agreed even though he had little interest in socializing at that moment. His big win had been inside himself. He was still coming down from that, and it was a very private thing with him. Emotions were still swimming through his head, but the one he had kept deeply hidden all that time—ugly, self-destructive guilt—was dissipated now. Del Rio was right, Josh's death was not a cross Cahill had to bear. It was the war, and split-second circumstances, that had caught Josh in their maw. And something else. Josh's weaknesses themselves. Cahill had undertaken an impossible task in promising Josh he would survive Asia, and no God in heaven would hold him to it. It was a kind of weakness on his part, as a matter of fact, not unrelated to Josh's own flaws, that had grabbed at Cahill's guts and refused to let go. Now it was time to quit flailing himself for a thing for which he had minimal responsibility. It was time to be a whole man again.

At the motel there were a couple of kids and a young woman who asked for Cahill's autograph. He obliged them in embarrassment. Inside, the small group sat around a big table—Cahill, Lucas, Del Rio, Eva, the two drivers who had joined them, and a girlfriend of one of the drivers—and toasted Cahill and his crew. The two trophies sat in the middle of the table, the national one looming over the individual race trophy. They drank champagne, and there was a lot of laughing and joking, and some talk of next season, when Cahill would be hands-down favorite to repeat as champion.

"There will be endorsements of products, T-shirts, the whole commercial explosion," one of the drivers was saying loudly. "You're going to be rich, Steve!"

"You'll be offered jobs," Del Rio said happily.

"Positions!"

Eva caught his gaze seriously. "Will you stay on with Charlie Rossman?" she asked.

Cahill thought a moment, then nodded. "Probably. If he wants me."

"He doesn't deserve you," Lucas offered.

Cahill shrugged. "Charlie's all right, Boyd."

"I thought you didn't like selling much," Del Rio suggested.

"I'm going to talk to Charlie about designing," Cahill said. "He thinks I might have some talent for it. We'll see."

They were still discussing that topic, sipping the celebration champagne, when a bartender came over to their table, a sober look on his face. Cahill looked up at him curiously, and they all stopped talking.

"Sorry to interrupt, but I suppose you all knew Gus Beckering."

They all just stared at him. "*Knew* him?" Lucas said. "What the hell does that mean?"

"I just heard. He committed suicide in his room at the Casa Marina. Less than fifteen minutes ago."

A heavy silence hung over the table for a moment.

"Jesus H. Christ!" Lucas muttered.

"Are you sure?" Del Rio said.

"I got a friend at the front desk there. They just found the body. He cut his wrists. There's blood everywhere, it's a real mess. He must have gotten up after he did it, and—"

"That's enough," Cahill said harshly.

The bartender looked at him. "Sure. I just thought you'd want to know." He stood there for another moment, then turned and left.

They sat around the table, nobody saying a word. The champagne fizzed in their glasses. Cahill glanced at the national trophy, and it had no luster for him. He rose from the table.

"I'm going back to the motel," he announced.

"Sure, Steve," Del Rio said. "Want me to come along?"

"No, I'd just as soon be alone," Cahill told him.

Just a couple of minutes after Cahill left, Lucas and Eva got up, excused themselves, and walked out into the motel parking lot.

"He was riddled with disease, anyway," Lucas said, leaning against the building wall under the shade of a canopy.

"Does that matter?" Eva said.

"No. I guess not."

Eva studied his thick face. "My divorce will be final pretty soon, Boyd. But I'll have to be in New York when it happens. Would you like to join me there? We could take in a couple of plays. Enjoy ourselves." Lucas had hinted at a permanent relationship, even marriage, when her divorce was final. "Then when I get that paper in hand, we'll be free to—well, do whatever we want."

Lucas looked over at her. "I can't do it, Eva."

Eva frowned slightly. "What? Go to New York?"

Lucas shook his head. "Marry you. Live with you, whatever. It wouldn't work out. Not at this time." His voice was barely audible.

Eva looked quickly away, her cheeks burning suddenly. "I see."

"It's Paige," he said to her. "She isn't well lately. The races haven't helped, I'm sure. I have to call her when I get back to the motel. She'll be waiting to hear from me."

Eva looked over at him. "But what does that have to do with us?"

Lucas sighed heavily. "I'm her life, Eva. Her whole goddam life. I kind of forgot that, here with you. I can't just abandon her."

"I wouldn't mind Paige being with us."

"I know. But she'd mind. She'd give me over to you. And her life would be over."

Eva thought about that. "Well," she said. "When

did you decide all this?''

"I've been wrestling with it for a couple of nights now. I was so taken with you, Eva, that I didn't think. You know how much I love you.''

Eva's eyes watered up, and she looked away.

"I thought we could go on seeing each other,'' he went on lamely. "And maybe I could find a way to work things out. Find Paige a man, or get her involved in a job. Maybe in six months, or a year, things will be different.''

Eva nodded, not looking at him. "Sure, Boyd,'' she said.

"Will you go on seeing me?'' he asked tentatively. "Baltimore and New York aren't that far apart. I've even got a cousin there.''

Eva finally looked at him, and her eyes were slightly red. "We'll see, Boyd. We'll see.''

Across town at the Pier House, Dulcie had been waiting in her room. Waiting for Cahill to call her and tell him he had won. She had heard the news from the motel desk and was very happy for Cahill. But she was worried whether he would even remember her in the post-race excitement, and that if he did he would not really care that she was still there in Key West. Things never seemed to work out on the race circuit. Friendships were temporary, associations tentative. Love affairs hot but fragile. When she did not hear from Cahill, she was certain that he no longer needed her. He was a different man now, she understood, from the one who had gone out there to win the national title. He had stood up to his inner torment and obviously conquered it. Ironically, she had helped him become the kind of man who no longer needed her love.

When an hour passed beyond the finish of the Class One race, and then an hour-and-a-half, Dulcie lost hope that Cahill would contact her. She wanted very much to go to him, but she could not. She had brought him to a point at which she could do no more for whatever relationship they had between them. The next move was his, it had to be.

At ten after two, having eaten no lunch, nor made a move from her room, Dulcie began packing to catch the next plane out of Key West. She was about half-finished when she heard the knock on her door, and her heart jumped in her chest. When she opened the door, Cahill was there.

Dulcie, looking lovely in a beige dress and heels, studied Cahill's face, and it was somber. Her insides felt as if a weight had attached itself in there, trying to drag her to the floor.

"Hi," Cahill said quietly. "Can I come in?"

Dulcie nodded. "Sure, Steve."

He came into the room slowly. He had changed into a sport shirt and light slacks, and looked exquisitely handsome to her.

"Congratulations on your big win," she said.

Cahill turned to her, from studying her luggage on a nearby bed, the bed where they had made love a couple of nights ago. "Thanks," he said. "It's over, Dulcie. It's finally over for me."

"I figured as much," she said. "I'm very happy for you, Steve."

He nodded. "Gus Beckering killed himself right after the race. In his hotel room."

"Oh, God!" she murmured.

"I would have been here sooner, but I went over there to see if there was anything I could do." He turned from her and walked over to an open patio door and stared out at the sand and water. "How can it get to be that important, Dulcie? I know he was sick, but there must have been something left for him."

"It's so damned awful," she said, knowing how he must feel, wanting to go to him.

"Wait till the papers get hold of it," he said. "Jesus, it will be a three-ring circus."

"Was Tony over there?" she asked.

Cahill grunted acidly. "He wouldn't even come up to Beckering's room, him or Kralich. He took off for the airport as soon as he heard."

"Tony never was much for facing up to things," she offered.

Cahill turned back to her. "This was it for me, Dulcie. I doubt I'll ever race for a trophy again."

"I think I understand."

"It was a one-time thing for me. It and you came along when I needed you, and I'm very grateful for that."

Dulcie's throat was dry.

"Now I'm going to design boats, if Charlie Rossman will let me. I don't want to stay around here for another minute. I'm driving north this afternoon."

"It's all right, Steve. I see how it is."

He frowned slightly. "I don't think you do." He glanced at the open suitcase again. "Just what did you have in mind here?"

Dulcie followed his look, and shrugged. "I'm leaving, too."

"Oh. Going back to Tampa, maybe? Or following Mary Ann back to New York, to serve drinks in a bar again?"

She gave him a look. "No, nothing like that. I have some ideas."

He came over to her. "Well, I hope they include frying my eggs in the mornings. And keeping me away from bars, and siding with me when Charlie Rossman doesn't like my boat designs."

Dulcie's face had softened through his short speech, and there was a sudden thickness in her throat that she had to swallow back. She smiled uncertainly. "You don't need me now," she said.

"I don't want any of this living-together crap, either," he went on, as if she had not spoken. "Commitment, that's what I expect. You think you can give it to me? I'm talking ring, certificate, vows, the real thing."

Dulcie kept a straight face. "You expect a hell of a lot from a girl."

Cahill nodded firmly. "That's right."

She reached up and touched his lips with hers, softly and sensually. "God, I love you, Steve Cahill."

"That's the luckiest part of all," he said.

Twenty minutes later they were packed up and their luggage was loaded into the back of Cahill's Jaguar. Cahill made a quick call to Del Rio, told him he was leaving with Dulcie, and asked him and Lucas to bring the *Sonic Boom* on up to Miami. Cahill had the notion that Charlie Rossman might just be interested in the boat again, at least as a partner in ownership, if they were to give him half a chance.

As they passed the marina on their way out of town, Cahill slowed the Jaguar momentarily, and they took a long last look in that direction. The production races had finished, and a smaller crowd was still hanging around, talking with drivers and owners, and there was still a lot of excitement crackling in the air. Cahill felt a warm emotion inside him for that scene that would never be lost to him completely. A moment later the marina was behind them, and they were driving on out of town and heading up the Keys. As they crossed the first bridge out of town, with the turquoise water all around them and black-and-white gulls crying overhead, Dulcie suddenly turned to Cahill.

"My God, the trophy! The big trophy—you forgot it!"

Cahill turned to her and shrugged. "I have the feeling it will catch up to us, one way or another."

Driving north over that sun-dazzled highway, with Dulcie snuggled tight against him, Cahill recalled that in ancient Greece, the athlete who won the chariot races was crowned with a wreath of olive twigs, proffered lavish gifts and virgin maidens for his enjoyment, and given a great feast lasting for days. There would be a stately parade, wherein his path would be strewn with rose petals, and later a proud statue of him would be erected.

Ruminating about that, though, Cahill thought this was better. His gift had been an intangible but priceless one, and he had never been much enamored of parades and statues, anyway. He had Dulcie instead. And with just a little luck, she might find inside her the magic requisite to investing them with a certain disregard for the truth—the hard verity that no champion reigns forever, and no race is finally won.

If so, that would be enough for Cahill.

There was little more he could ask from it all.

THE GLORY TRAP
Dan Sherman & Robin Williamson

PRICE: $2.25   T51646
CATEGORY: Novel

"SOPHISTICATED AND DIVERTING!"
— *The New York Times*

He was a discredited and marked agent. She was a young British woman on the run. Together they fled into the vast European underground, living in shadows under the unrelenting threat of death! Explosive espionage suspense!

"ROUSINGLY GOOD ADVENTURE!"
— *King Features Syndicate*

DAN SHERMAN IS A FIRST-RATE STORYTELLER!"
— Morris West, author of *Proteus*

ACTS OF MERCY
By Bill Pronzini & Barry N. Malzberg

PRICE: $2.25   T51617   CATEGORY: Novel

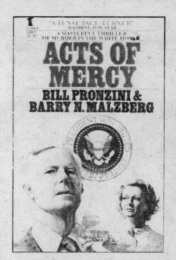

"TENSION THROUGHOUT!"
The New York Times

Capitol Hill reels with shock, the nation rattles with terror, when murder invades the White House and creeps into the highest echelons of power!

"BREAKNECK PACE!" . . . . Booklist
"DEFT TOUCHES!" . . . . New York Post
"EERIE!" . . . . Buffalo Evening News
"BIZARRE!" . . . . Milwaukee Journal
"SHOCKING!" . . . . Hartford Courant
"SENSATIONAL!" . . . . Charlotte Observer